La Última y Nos Vamos

"No, *cabrón*," Rubio said good naturedly. "You must have the penultimate drink."

In Mexico you never take the last drink, unless, of course, you are about to be shot. If I had sat down to drink it with him, we both might have had the last one. As it was, I was still on my feet when the young man came back into the cafe, pistol in hand. He paused in the entrance, took deliberate but hurried aim, and fired.

The first bullet hit the iron chair and it rang like a bell. The second was high into the wall behind me. The third burned my right leg. The fourth shot was mine. I had sighted and squeezed off one round while he was hurrying his second and third. Mine took him high in the chest and knocked him down.

The Golden Ear

Austin L. Olsen

Principal Characters

· ✈

- Tell Cooper: World War I pilot, owner of a budding airline
- Willard Riley: U.S. vice consul and mogul
- Rodolfo Hernández: military officer who befriends and rescues Tell
- Guillermo "Memo" Gómez: Tell's chauffer, airplane mechanic
- Antonia Canela or "Toña": military officer and Tell's first love
- Jorge Rubio, the "Toad": Army officer, Riley's goon
- Juan "Johnny" Ávalos: Toña's friend and Riley's business partner
- Helen Anderson: journalist, Tell's wife
- Tell "Dos" Cooper II: son of Tell and Helen, World War II pilot
- Guillermo Andrés Canela: Toña's son, World War II pilot
- Elena or *Elenita*: Tell and Helen's daughter
- Carmencita: Riley's wife
- Jorge Rubio Montejo: Rubio's son
- Sofia: Riley and Carmencita's daughter

· · · · · · · · · · · · · · · · · · ✈

For the historical context of the novel, turn to page 366 for a brief listing of pivotal events in Mexico, including key historical figures, spanning from 1907 through the Mexican Revolution and to the beginning of the novel in 1920.

Chapter 1

· · · · · · · · · · · · · · · · · · ✈

Tell Cooper, Puebla, Mexico, 1920.

I first met Willard Riley in the oldest city built for Europeans on the American continent, Puebla de Zaragoza, commonly called Puebla by its inhabitants. A consulate had been set up in an old town house to process claims by American citizens against the revolutionary government. One of the major problems was to decide which claims should be sent to which government. The rains had not yet begun with the clock-like afternoon showers, so Riley had placed a table out in the cool garden and was receiving petitions there.

He was a delicately built, small-boned man. His hair was flaming red and his eyes as blue as those of a Siamese cat. I thought him to be older than I, but he was only twenty-three, two years my junior. His English was Bostonian.

My West Texas accent had the edge taken off it by two years in Eastern schools as well as two years in France during the Great War. Although I am not quite six feet tall, I towered over Riley. He did not care for the contrast, for he sat down immediately and motioned for me to stand before him, on the other side of the table.

"What is your claim?"

His voice was high and reedy. I thought again of a cat. A thin, nervous, unworldly cat. It is inconceivable to me now how I could have been so blind.

"Tell Cooper," I said, holding out my hand.

"Please state the nature of your claim," he said, ignoring my hand. "We are extremely busy."

I glanced around me at the small garden. A man was trimming the bougainvillea climbing the far wall, and a woman slowly swept the blood-red flowers from the flagstone path.

"I can see that. Are you the consul?"

"Yes," he said, looking past me. "Over here, Colonel Green."

A robust man, some twenty years older than I and who might have been on his way to a formal garden party were it not for his large white Stetson and his high-heeled cowboy boots, he moved over to the table, took a thin black cigar from his mouth and smiled at me before he spoke to Riley.

"What did you do with James, Will, shoot him?"

"James is in Mexico City with the ambassador." He glanced at me and added, "I am the acting consul."

"So is James," the colonel said gravely, then repeated, "So is James," and then burst out in hearty laughter.

I joined in for his laughter was infectious.

"I am Colonel Francis Green, young man." He switched the cigar to his left hand and held his right out to me.

"Former Captain Tell Cooper, *Lafayette Escadrille* and, later, the 103rd pursuit squadron," I said, taking his hand and losing it in mine. I was meant to be a much larger man for I have the hands and feet of a giant.

"Fighter pilot?"

"Yes, sir."

"What are you claiming, captain?" Riley asked.

"Nothing. I came to the consul for help in locating a Colonel Hernández. I would like to sell him a few airplanes."

"Airplanes," Riley said. "What airplanes?"

"Pleased to meet you," I said to Riley.

"My pleasure," he said, shrugging my sarcasm off. "What airplanes?"

"I represent the American manufacturers of de Havilland Scouts. They carry two forward-firing Marlin machine guns and the observer's cockpit carries a Browning .30-caliber."

"You must tell me the name of your intended client and your price," Riley said sternly.

"You don't waste much time in pleasantries, do you Will?" Colonel Green said.

"No. sir. I believe in getting right down to business." He turned to me. "Well, captain?"

"Well, mister acting consul," I said, letting my West Texas accent loose, "as I said, his name is Hernández and the price depends on how many you want to buy."

"I do not care for your levity," Riley snapped.

"None intended," I lied. "But the cost does depend on the numbers. We have quotes for ten."

"Ten." Riley nodded to himself and then held his hand out to me. "I am Willard Riley and I have many contacts both here and in Mexico City."

2

I accepted the handshake, although I wondered at both his temerity and transparent greed. I was certain that he would be looking for a finder's fee.

"Then you can put me into touch with Colonel Hernández?"

"Obregón's man?"

"Why, yes," I said, surprised.

"Of course I can." He hoisted a watch from its pocket by winding its chain around a long, thin forefinger, flipped the face open and said, "Gentlemen, it is about lunch time. Would you join me?"

"Sorry," Colonel Green said. "I just popped in to find out if the train is running. I must get back to Mexico. If not today, tomorrow."

"It had better be today," Riley said. "Carranza is gathering engines and cars from everywhere to transport his government and army to Veracruz."

"I have heard that," Colonel Green said. "I shall take today's train." He nodded pleasantly, touched his Stetson and left, walking briskly.

Riley stood up quickly, waved goodbye at the colonel's back, smoothed his trousers, straightened his coat and then beckoned me to precede him. It was one of the few times in our long association that I was awarded that privilege.

Outside, in the full glare of the overhead sun, I lifted both hands high to the rim of my Panamanian straw hat and tilted the brightness from my eyes.

"It is quiet," I said as we walked. "Mexicans are usually a clamorous people, whether in joy or anger."

"Perhaps you should fire a shot or two in the air to arouse them."

I stopped in my tracks and narrowed my eyes at the little man. "You are an observant man. My Colt is the double-action, swing-out-cylinder, six-inch barrel—a large revolver. I paid five dollars for a holster to conceal it."

Riley shrugged and said too nonchalantly, "I, too, carry a pistol."

I glanced at his tight-fitting coat skeptically.

"Here," he said, patting a flat coat pocket.

"Of course," I said. "You have one of those pretty little Brownings. Twenty-five caliber. Fits in the palm of your hand. A friend of mine was shot with one years ago in Del Rio, Texas."

"What happened?"

"Nothing much," I said, laying on the Texas accent. "He never even knew he was shot till he found the hole in his shirt the next morning."

I paused, grinning. waiting for his laugh. It never came.

"Shall we take a cab?" he asked.

My face flushed with embarrassment and anger. To hell with the man. I could do without him. Just then there was a clatter of iron on cobblestone and a troop of cavalry followed by supply wagons and an ambulance swept by. The last vehicle was driven by a grim-faced man who earlier that day had taken me proudly in his own hansom cab to the consulate. It was the same cab, but the word *ambulancia* had been crudely lettered in red paint on the side facing us.

"There goes my cab," I said.

"Mine too," Riley said and then grinned at me. "Come on. We can walk a few blocks."

"All right," I said and stepped out. I soon realized that the little man was trotting alongside me, trying desperately to keep up without breaking into a run. His lips were drawn back over clenched teeth. He would not look up at me. I slowed down, but he kept up the pace, grimly. My anger spent, I called out to him.

"I'd kind of like to stop in at the Pearl Hotel."

"Of course. We must all be careful," he said.

We slowed down and then stopped. I cocked my head into a question mark.

"There are so many diseases," he said. "By all means, wash up and then meet me at the *Tres Gaviotas* restaurant. It is three blocks east of your hotel on the same street." I nodded, turned the corner and walked slowly in the direction of my hotel. I stopped at a newsstand and bought a day-old copy of the *Herald*, a Mexico City English-language newspaper.

The lead story, based more on conjecture than fact, referred to the Agua Prieta declaration of April 20, 1920, a few months earlier, implying that General Álvaro Obregón was leading an army from the northern state of Sonora to Mexico City to confront Venustiano Carranza. There was also an item about two generals who, in a shoot-out over a bar bill, had killed an unfortunate bystander, an Englishman. As the dead man had only one bullet hole in him, the unscathed duelists played dice to see who paid the bill and who got credit for the kill. It was a time and place where life—any life at all—had little value.

I glanced up from my paper just in time to avoid the eye-level iron bar holding rigid the canvas canopy at the entrance to a restaurant. There was a primitive painting of three seagulls on a weathered board swinging above an open door. I assumed that the owner must be from Veracruz, the state with the ocean nearest to the high, inland city of

Puebla. It would be the cafe Riley had suggested.

It was cool and dark inside. I waited a few seconds for my eyes to adjust, then saw a large square room with a dozen glass-topped rattan tables, each with an uneven number of cast-iron chairs. Half of the tables were occupied. There was a small bar at the far end with the usual brass foot rail over a water trough. A long rectangle of faded green paint showed the one-time presence of a mirror as well as the scars from the bullets that must have shattered it.

I picked a corner table and sat with my back against the wall, facing the entrance. A waiter smiled at me and took one step before I wagged a finger negatively. He nodded and turned away. I read the entire newspaper before I looked up and nodded. The waiter wandered over to the table. I flipped my watch out and found that I had been in the bar for half an hour. Mexican waiters do not intrude. If you want them, you must make a signal of some kind.

"Have you seen a red-headed man come in?" I asked, looking for Riley.

"Glass or bottle, señor?" The waiter, his eyes almost closed, smiled as if watching a favorite dream.

While I pondered that non sequitur, the door to the water closet opened—in those days the bathroom was called simply *el water*—and Riley peeked out. He swept the room with his bright blue eyes, then stepped out and came straight to the table. He sat to my left. I suspected that it was because of the revolver under my right arm.

"Do you want the bottle or a glass of red wine?" the waiter asked.

"Wine?" Riley asked.

"*¡Pelirrojo!*" I said. I had solved the mystery. The waiter had been listening with only half a mind at most and had caught only the word "*rojo*," or red, and finished the sentence for himself.

"He certainly is," the waiter said, admiring Riley's hair. The glaze had left his eyes.

I began to interpret, but Riley interrupted. His Spanish was good enough for him to understand the waiter. I grew up speaking border Spanish and was sent for three summers in a row to school in Mexico to learn grammar. I felt that my Spanish was as good as many Mexicans and better than some.

"I drink very little," Riley said. "But I will join you in something Mexican, perhaps a mescal and a cold beer."

"I drink very little myself," I said, grinning, "so I will have the same."

Riley ordered the drinks, insisting on dark beer from a brewery in Veracruz.

"Outside of your accent," I said, "you speak pretty fair Spanish."

"One day I shall lose the accent and one day my vocabulary will be better than yours."

Riley understood constructive criticism and would react to it for his benefit, but he could never accept it without anger.

The waiter shuffled back with a tray loaded with a bottle of mescal, with a worm floating listlessly in the transparent liquid; a plate of quartered limes; a tiny clay *cazuela* full of coarse salt; two oversized shot glasses and two mugs of dark, almost black, cold beer.

I motioned the waiter away and filled the two shot glasses. The worm fell to the glass nearer Riley. He quickly reached across it and took the other.

I licked the flat spot between my thumb and trigger finger and shook some salt on to it. The salt stuck. I said "*salud*," sucked on a lime, threw the shot of mescal down and then touched my tongue to the salt, both sides, top and bottom. It keeps the taste buds active.

Riley left his mescal untouched, but sipped at the beer.

"Hernández comes here sometimes. I could introduce you."

"Could?"

"Yes, could. Look, Captain Cooper, I can help you."

"Then help me to meet Hernández."

"But we could do a lot better than you alone."

"We?"

"Yes, *we*. I can help you get two, maybe three times the price for those airplanes that you are asking."

"*We* is a lot of people," I said, citing an old Mexican saying.

"No," he said, deadly serious. "We is just you and me."

"How do you double the price when you don't even know what it is?"

He ignored my question. "How much commission do you get? Eight percent? I will get us twenty; ten apiece."

"Slow down. My people pay me eight. It is fair and they have my word on it."

"But they will not pay the difference. The buyer will."

"Why?"

"Because," he said, speaking slowly and enunciating carefully as if dealing with a child, "we will pay the purchasing agent a commission from our commission."

"I guess I understand. We will pay some patriot a bribe so that we can make even more money."

"There you have it in a nutshell."

I shook my head slowly, negatively.

Riley's eyes bored into mine. "This is the real world you are in now. No more knights battling in the air, waving at an enemy with a jammed machine gun as you graciously allow him to fly away to fight another day. In the real world you must have money to have power, and power is everything."

"And honor?"

"Brutus was an honorable man. So were they all honorable men. But when Caesar tried to take away some of their power, they killed him."

"I will admit to an occasional lapse from my Daddy's teaching, but I have a code and, by and large, I stick to it."

Riley stared at me as unblinking as a lizard. Finally he shook his head as if in pain and then smiled and surprised me by breaking out in genuine laughter.

"All right. I will introduce you to Hernández. You two will get along famously. He has the same disease as you."

He lifted his untouched shot glass to me in salute, threw the shot down and chased it with a long gurgle of beer. He ignored the lime and salt and held his glass out for a refill. I filled it for him and he drank it as quickly as the first. I wondered how such a small man could drink so much and so quickly without getting drunk.

"I will mention just one more matter concerning the two of us," he said, "and then we will talk of other things, of ships and snails and sealing wax and cabbages and kings, but first I shall offer you the opportunity to become incredibly rich. No!" he held a hand up to fend off my objection. "Let me finish. I am the son of an indigent Irish politician. A charming, alcoholic ward-heeler. But I will not be an Irish clown. I will be a power in this country. But I need money, now. You have a background of wealth. I can hear it in your voice, even when you put on that phony hillbilly accent. You have the sweet aroma of affluence about you. I absolutely must have ten thousand dollars. Now! It will mean millions one day."

I found myself caught up in his total earnestness. I believed him. The prospect of wealth was pleasing to me and he was right. I had been on the fringes of, but never one of, the very rich. Several of the pilots of the *Escadrille* were rich men's sons. I could borrow such a sum, I thought, easily. But then I would no longer be one of the old *Escadrille.*

"No," I said reluctantly. "I have no money. No property. However, I can fly any kind of airplane. I speak Spanish fluently and am rated a good, cool shot. My balance sheet, sir." I nodded my head in a short bow.

"You have another asset on that simplified balance and because of it I shall one day make you rich in spite of yourself. I shall pay you by the pound for your integrity."

"I hope the job includes room and board," I said, grinning.

"Of course," Riley smiled back. "And now, would you tell me how you reconcile that schoolboy's code of honor with the fighter pilot's predilection for sneaking up behind his foe and shooting him in the back?"

Although we both roared with laughter, that question led us into a long and serious philosophical discussion; we might have been two college sophomores debating and drinking beer in a fraternity house.

He quoted Nietzsche and I, Spinoza. We criticized the decadent new art movement, praised the stories of O. Henry and Stephen Crane and then, as the mescal heated our blood, we talked about women.

I remember, vaguely, a bordello full of luscious brown-skinned girls that made my thighs ache. I remember a madam extolling the prophylactic properties of something called a Doughboy Kit. She claimed that it would prevent its user from contracting any kind of venereal disease. Riley did not believe her, but when one of the girls opened her housecoat and pushed two large, firm breasts into his face, he groaned, grabbed the kit with one hand and the girl with the other and trotted upstairs, pulling the giggling whore after him.

I can bring back only one other scene from that night now. I see a lanky, homely young man trying to sober up by eating tacos filled with more fiery peppers than meat, and washing them down with mugs of dark beer, pausing only to recite poetry to the amusement of girls who were not only illiterate in their own language, but understood not one word of English.

The line that young Tell Cooper recited over and over was: "I could not love you half so much, loved I not honor more."

8

Chapter 2

· · · · · · · · · · · · · · · · · · ✈

Riley was as good as his word. Two days later a messenger brought a note to my hotel.

> *If you were as ill as I, you needed the extra day to recover. You have an appointment to lunch with Colonel Rodolfo Hernández at one o'clock today at the Tres Gaviotas restaurant.*
> *Regards,*
> *Will Riley*

Years later when one of his sycophants would brag about how well he knew W. Willard Riley—or if he were daring, Will Riley—I would smile inwardly and remember how two young men who should have been inimical had taken a strange liking to each other. Many people call me Tell, as did Riley, but I am the only one to ever call him Willy. Only a few close associates, two of his mistresses, a half a dozen generals and a few presidents called him Will without the deferential title of respect *Don* in front of his name. His poor alcoholic wife, Carmencita, called him Señor Riley.

On the back of the note I scribbled *Thanks, Willy. I owe you a dinner*, and sent it back.

There were two other tables at the Tres Gaviotas with just one man seated at each, but I knew instinctively that Hernández was at the third. In spite of facial smallpox scars, he was a handsome man, a Mexican version of my own father. His black hair was streaked with gray, but his shaggy moustache was still jet black. He rose as soon as he saw that I was approaching his table. His teeth flashed white in a wide smile.

"Señor Cooper?" he asked.

"Tell Cooper Carter, at your orders," I said, adding my mother's maiden name as required by Mexican custom.

"Rodolfo Hernández Ochoa, your servant." His voice was as deep and resonant as that of a professional baritone.

We shook hands and I accepted the indicated chair, even as I glanced behind me to note the occupied table at my back.

"Do not worry," he said gravely, but his brown eyes sparkled, "I will guard your back."

"These are perilous times," I said, smiling.

"True, as you must know. Were you not a captain in the Great War?"

"I was. You are a colonel, no?"

"I was with my General Obregón in Sonora."

"I flew with Didier Masson in the *Escadrille Americaine* in France. He was also with General Obregón. Did you know him?"

"I saw his airplane, from the ground, many times. He painted one of those Indian crosses on the side of his machine so that we could recognize it."

"He showed me a picture of it, an old Curtis with a swastika painted on it. He said it was Greek."

"Whatever it was, he needed no identification. It was the only airplane in the sky. He was our air arm. All one of him."

We laughed together and then he motioned toward a large bottle of amber liquid. "I have had the good luck to find a bottle of mescal from Jalisco," he said. "Some people are beginning to call it tequila after the village where it is distilled. Would you care to try it?"

I did and agreed. It was excellent, with a bite, but no greasy aftertaste. We talked about the different kinds of mescal, ranging from the Oaxacan type, cured with a raw chicken breast, to the northern *sotol* distilled in the high Sonora desert, which, we both agreed, tasted somewhat like coal oil. The colonel did not think it quite as tasty.

After the third lime-drink-salt ritual, the colonel opened the formal, business part of our luncheon.

"I understand that you have some magnificent airplanes for sale?"

"Magnificent, no. Good, yes."

"Merely good?" I assume he smiled, for his moustache twitched. Otherwise he was impassive.

"Yes. The front-firing machine guns tend to jam and, although to a lesser extent, so does the engine."

"What does the aviator do?"

"If it is the machine guns they can usually be cleared in the air. If it is the engine he must look for a flat place to land. Sometimes he can fix it himself. Other times he may have to bring a mechanic and parts in. At times a new engine might even be needed."

"Then one should not merely buy a simple airplane?"

"No. That is why we propose ten machines, a truckload of parts, another truck, complete with machine shop, and an airplane mechanic."

"And the price?"

"We can deliver everything to you at the port of Veracruz for ninety thousand in gold."

"No. Not—"

"It is a good price, colonel."

"I believe you, young man. What I was going to say is do not deliver to Veracruz. Not until we discover the intentions of General Carranza."

"Excellent. We will need time, anyway, to deliver."

"And we, as well, need time to raise the payment in gold." Gold could mean real gold or, usually, U.S. dollars, paper or gold.

"How about your commission?" he asked.

"It is included."

"And the airplanes are in good condition?"

"Good. Actually, they are better than new. They have been reworked several times to remove problems not apparent at first."

"Who will acquaint our pilots with this airplane?"

"I will. At no extra cost. I, and a mechanic as well, will be at your disposal for three months after delivery."

"Excellent organization. My General Obregón will like that. He has always understood the advantages of air reconnaissance. I myself prefer the horse, even against the motor car. Although," he added ruefully, "I would certainly rather ride a train back to Sonora than a horse."

"It would be a long ride on a horse," I agreed, "but still the machines are noisy and smelly. And you cannot scratch their ears or feed them apples."

"It is true. You are a horseman?"

"My father was a cattle buyer from El Paso, Texas. I helped him drive cattle back from Mexico when I was small."

"Cooper. Ward T. Cooper! He is your father?"

"Was," I forced myself to say. His death was still an ache in the dark of my mind.

"Was?"

"He was killed while I was in France. He was trailing a few cows up from Chihuahua when Pancho Villa's men killed him."

"Villa? But your father was on our side. Why should they kill him?"

"When did General Villa need a reason to shoot a man?"

"I am sorry. Your father was a fine man and I am proud that he was my friend. Knowing him, I trust his son. It would be an honor if you would allow me to call you Tell," he added, switching to the intimate *tú* form, an honor not often awarded to one neither family nor lifetime friend.

"It is my honor, *coronel*—"

"No. Unless we are dealing as military men, call me Rodolfo."

"*Don* Rodolfo," I said. He smiled his agreement. He, as the older, merited the title, roughly equivalent to "esteemed," before his first name. Otherwise, with both of us using the *tú* personal pronoun, one to the other, we might have been friends of a like age.

"I have some people that have been loaned to me to help me deal with procurement for the Obregonistas. I will send one of them to work out the details with you."

We shook hands on the deal, had one more drink to seal it, and then ordered thin strips of beef, Tampico style, black beans with *epazote* served in small clay pots and, as a treat for *Don* Rodolfo, there were white wheat tortillas, northern style, as large as the tray the waiter brought them on. It was all I could do to finish a half of one. He shook his head sadly, commented on the weakness of the youth of today, paid the bill and then walked me back to my hotel. I embraced him as I would have my father and said goodbye. My eyes were wet.

In the hotel foyer, still blinking away tears, I turned suddenly and blindly up the stairs and almost trampled a girl so breathtakingly beautiful that I could do no more than stutter as I held her in one arm to keep her from falling.

She looked up at me, not in anger, but unsmiling. Her hair, so black that it reflected light, framed a finely boned face with high cheekbones and obsidian eyes. Her skin was the golden brown that Mexicans call cinnamon.

Her color lightened slightly as blood rushed to her face. Her black eyes flashed. I released her so clumsily that she almost fell again. I jerked my hand to help her, but her eyes flashed *no*!

She caught her balance and stepped around me, as graceful as a jaguar, and was out of the hotel door before I could get my wits back. I bolted through the lobby and out the door in time to see her get into a carriage with an older man. Her father, I thought hopefully. I trotted after the carriage.

After ten blocks, the tequila and beans were fighting for priority in abandoning ship, but I ran grimly on and might have lasted another block, but I ran into a cordon of soldiers. The carriage drove on through, but I was stopped.

Up ahead, at the telegraph office, a group of agitated men danced around the entrance, yelling conflicting instructions to the operator and calling out different versions of incoming messages.

"What is happening?" I asked an onlooker, a portly gentleman with a benevolent look about him.

"President Carranza has left Mexico on a dozen trains with his whole government and all of his soldiers, and they are on their way here to shoot all of the Obregonistas, the Hillistas, the Villistas and all of the *gringos* too."

I thanked him politely and edged away. Once out of the crowd, I turned about and walked briskly away; it was no place for an American *gringo* associated with Obregón. The first landmark I recognized was the consulate. I rapped on the closed door, but there was no answer. I tried to open it. The door was locked. The bell rope had disappeared. I drew my revolver and rapped loudly on the door.

"The consulate is closed," a voice shouted from within.

I glanced over my shoulder and saw a crowd moving down the street toward the consulate—to lynch all of the gringos, I thought. I hammered on the door again and yelled, "Please tell Señor Riley that General Cooper is here to help defend the consulate!"

I was wondering how badly I would be cut if I clambered over the brick wall guarding the consulate—shards of glass were set into the top of the wall—when I heard Riley's high-pitched voice.

"Is that you, Tell?"

"Yes, Will. Open the door. A mob is at my heels."

The huge wooden door swung open. Riley stuck his head out. He looked like a redheaded woodpecker. "Likely Obregonistas out to ransack the homes of the Carrancistas."

"Let me in before they ransack me," I said.

He stepped aside. I darted in and then turned to help him run a long iron bolt from post to post.

"When were you promoted, General Cooper?"

"It's just a brevet rank," I said. "Are you still the consul?"

"I am. James is still in Mexico and there will be no train today."

"I heard that Carranza is bringing an army here to kill everybody, including me."

"Never trust a rumor, Tell. However, Carranza did leave. He has commandeered all of the locomotives and cars that he could get his hands on, loaded up most of his people, including the Secretary of the Treasury as well as the entire treasury, and is off to set up a new government in Veracruz."

13

"He means to fight his way through the state of Puebla to Veracruz?"

"He was given safe passage through Puebla by General Sánchez."

"Well then," I said, relieved, "there will be no fighting."

"Carranza has already been attacked," Riley shook his head at my naiveté. "He has abandoned the train and is somewhere in the mountains to the north."

"But you said he was granted safe passage."

"Tell, when will you learn that the world is not as you wish it to be? I have seen a copy of a telegram sent to Carranza. I quote: 'President and my father, though everyone else betrays you, I shall not. If but one man remains loyal to you, I am that man.' That touching document was signed by General Guadalupe Sánchez."

"That is the same general that issued the safe conduct?"

"Yes."

"But then," I asked, puzzled. "Who attacked the train?"

"General Guadalupe Sánchez, who else?" He grinned crookedly. "By this time tomorrow there will not be one admitted Carrancista in Puebla. Better stay off the streets."

"But I am not a Carrancista."

"Good. You are learning."

"Actually," I said smugly, "I am practically an adviser to General Obregón's air arm."

"You sold the airplanes!"

"Yes," I said proudly.

"Who signed the contract?"

"Colonel Hernández himself gave me his word."

"Tell, Tell," he said sadly. "There is no hope for you. You had better come along with me. I have a carriage. I will see you to your hotel safely."

It did not turn out that way. Just one short block from the sanctuary of the hotel a squad of soldiers commanded by a drunken officer stopped the carriage.

"Who are you *cabrones* for?" A tall, thin second lieutenant pointed a revolver at the head of our horse.

Riley answered angrily. "I, sir, am the consul here for the United States of America!"

"*Chinga tu madre, cabrón*!" the officer retorted, suggesting that Riley go to hell by using the obscene "screw-your-mother" phrase, and adding the versatile expletive that can mean bully, lowlife, idiot, ace, pal—but often denotes the harsher "bastard."

Riley reached inside his coat too quickly to pull out his diplomatic passport. The officer swung the pistol barrel and pointed it at Riley's head. The click of the hammer being cocked made my heart skip a beat.

"We are for the great Republic of Mexico," I said quickly.

He swung the muzzle to cover me. He moved closer, extending his arm, blinked as if trying to focus his eyes on me and said, "Are you *cabrones* for Obregón, Villa, González, or that *cabrón*, Carranza?"

"The first three," I said and jammed my right hand down over the firing pin hole of his revolver. He pulled the trigger. I felt relief, no pain at all, only the warm, wet blood trickling down from where the firing pin had imbedded its point in the fleshy skin between my thumb and forefinger. I tightened my fingers around the cylinder and upper grips holding his fingers captive. I drew my revolver quickly and touched its barrel to his nose.

"I am an officer attached to the staff of my General Obregón," I said loudly in my best parade-ground voice. "Who is this animal?"

"That animal," a young soldier answered, "is Lieutenant Solís. I told him not to stop the carriage, but when he gets full of *aguardiente*, he don't listen."

Not one soldier cocked his rifle or even pointed it vaguely in our direction. I wondered if they might cheer if I shot the lieutenant. That unfortunate was rapidly losing color from his face and his eyes bulged and tried to cross as he peered unhappily into my pistol barrel.

"Let go of that pistol!" I shouted.

"I can't," he wailed. "That big paw of yours is breaking all of my fingers."

I slipped my pistol back under my right arm, turned the barrel of the other pistol well away from Riley and myself, and with my left hand re-cocked the pistol, withdrawing the nail-like firing pin from my hand. I released the hammer again, easing it back down in place and handed the big revolver to Riley. He sat hunched back against the cushions, staring at me wide-eyed. It was a side of me that he had not suspected. Not many did.

The young soldier brought his rifle up smartly in salute and asked, "General, could you return the pistol? Lieutenant Solís will get in a lot of trouble with no pistol. He is a *cabrón*, but not a bad *cabrón*. He has not been an officer long enough. Only today."

I tried to keep a straight face, but I could not. His unwitting humor, or so I thought at the time, and the release of nervous tension, defeated me and I laughed too loudly. The young soldier, looking much relieved, joined in and then, man by man, the whole squad was roaring with laughter. Lieutenant Solís, leaning against the carriage to stay on his feet, smiled up at me hopefully.

"What is your name, soldier?" I turned to the soldier who was speaking.

"Corporal Guillermo Gómez León, at your orders." He came to attention again.

"You will need to talk to your commanding officer. I will need a written apology."

"Yes, sir."

"Also, I am in need of an orderly. More of an aide really. Would you like the post?"

"Yes, sir."

"Good enough, sergeant." I took the pistol from Riley's lap where he had let it fall, reversed the muzzle and handed it to him, butt first.

"Corporal Gómez, sir. I am a corporal."

"Have your orders written for Sergeant Gómez. It is an important post."

"Yes, sir."

"Ask for Captain Cooper at the Hotel Perla," I said in dismissal and motioned the driver to proceed.

"Yes, General Cooper," Gómez yelled, snapping to attention.

As soon as the wheel made a half a turn, Solís, his support vanished, fell flat on his back in the street. Riley lay back against the cushions, his head lolling loosely from side to side, eyes half closed. I drew out my small silver flask, poured a few drops onto my wound, bound it with a handkerchief from Riley's sleeve and then held the flask to his lips. He came to, sputtering and coughing.

"What happened?" he asked.

"You fainted."

"I did not," he shrilled angrily.

"It's all right. You were shocked and scared. So was I."

"You might have been. I was not."

"Sure," I said. "But in any case we have gone through this little flask of brandy and I need a drink. Stop off at the hotel. The driver will wait."

I was wrong. The driver would not, for any amount of money, continue to drive his precious cab across a town filled with bellicose citizens and drunken soldiers. Riley rejected my offer of a shared room and it was only after a shouting match with the harried hotel clerk that he agreed to bunk with me.

Typically, he never thanked me. Nor did he mention the affair with the drunken officer.

The bar was crowded with refugees from the street, but I persuaded a waiter to bring two chairs and a serving table from the restaurant and set it up in the lobby between two huge clay flowerpots.

We both had one stiff brandy and then tacitly agreed to drink beer and talk. Mostly we talked. That is, he talked. He had an excellent grasp of the Mexican Revolution and seemed to know not only its history but its direction as well.

While I had been east to school and then in France, Francisco Madero, backed by men from the North, had swept the old dictator, Porfirio Díaz, out of office. Madero, who trusted everyone, including members of the spirit world, then placed his trust in a conniving and, when sober, able general, Victoriano Huerta. Through a palace coup, Huerta forced both Madero and his vice president to resign, and then had him and his vice president arrested and quickly shot while "attempting to escape."

The next in line for the presidency, the Minister of Foreign Relations, accepted the presidency long enough to appoint Huerta as his successor before leaving the Presidential Palace at a fast trot.

Huerta was finally forced out by an outraged coalition of revolutionaries including Carranza, Villa, Obregón and others, including Emiliano Zapata, who had never stopped fighting anyone who claimed to be president of Mexico. He fought the usurpers, but trusted no one. And rightfully so, for it was the revolutionary president, Venustiano Carranza, who shamefully finagled the assassination of the small dark man from Morelos. It was Carranza, too, who sent Obregón to defeat Villa and then pensioned the ex-bandit off on an hacienda in Chihuahua.

Now, it appeared to be Obregón, that shrewd one-armed man from Sonora, who held the Mexican reins in his strong left hand.

"Could he, a one-armed man," I posed the question to Riley, "hold the reins and crack a whip at the same time?"

"He wears spurs. The kind with long sharp rowels."

"You are a horseman?" I was surprised.

"No, but I know what spurs are for. And, if anyone can ride the Mexican horse, it will be Obregón. If anyone can stabilize this country, the way it was under Díaz, it will be Obregón. And if that happens, we can get rich, Tell. Very rich."

"If I get my commission on the airplanes, I will be rich."

"Peanuts. Now, if I could just get my hands on twenty thousand dollars . . ."

He sat silent for a minute, drank deeply from the large mug of beer and then said, "If you know of a way to beg, borrow or steal ten thousand dollars, get it for me and I will see to it that you will be a millionaire before your thirtieth birthday."

I laughed and then was immediately sorry, for a naked look of hurt mixed with anger flared in his blue eyes, and he drew away from me.

"I'm sorry, Will. It is just that I can't imagine Tell Cooper as a millionaire. The only time I ever even knew wealthy men was when I flew in the Lafayette Squadron. A few of the pilots were rich—sons of very rich men. One of them, Penn, helped me to join the squadron."

"How long would it take you to get the money from him?"

"Who?" I asked, startled.

"The one who got you in the squadron."

"Penn Melton?"

"Yes," he said impatiently. "That one. How long?"

"It is not a question of time."

"But it is, you fool. If it is to be done, it must—"

"Then better it were done quickly," I finished his sentence with the line from Macbeth. He did not smile.

"Goddamn it, Tell. Do not joke." He reached out and grasped my hand. Mine was twice the size of his, but his grip hurt.

"Sorry, Will. I know that this scheme means a lot to you, but I do not borrow from my friends."

I expected an angry recrimination, but he merely shook his head as if to frighten off a mosquito and said, "Could you get the money? Would you not loan it to one of them if they asked you?"

"Of course, if I had the money, but—"

"Would you do it for me?" he interrupted, his jaw out-thrust, a challenge in his voice.

"I believe I would," I said, "but the fact remains that I do not have the money. However," I added quickly before he could retort, "you can count on me for five thousand dollars—if the sale of the airplanes goes through."

He stared at me, a look of obvious frustration mingled with pity on his face.

"Maybe," I said hopefully, "you could make me a half of a millionaire. A four-bit millionaire." I saw the beginnings of a smile on

18

his thin lips and added, "It's more my style. Tell Cooper, four-bit millionaire."

He tried to keep the smile from turning into a grin and then the grin from laughter, but could not and soon we were both roaring with laughter.

"I hope that I do not need the five thousand," Riley said, "for I would not like to put our friendship to such a stringent test."

He held up his beer and we clinked glasses on the thought. It seemed like a logical toast at the time, but I wonder now if there was ever another so direfully prophetic?

Chapter 3

· · · · · · · · · · · · · · · · · ✈

Carranza is dead. I have heard a half a dozen accounts of his death. The one I like best is that he was shot from his horse, a saber in one hand and a pistol in the other. That one must have come from someone who still admires that wily white-bearded patriarch. Another has him shot while trying to escape. And, of course, there was the report of a firing squad. I hope that however it happened, it was quick and unexpected. In any case, as Riley predicted, there are freshly painted signs all over the city proclaiming the virtues of Obregón. On many of the signs they merely painted out Carranza and substituted Obregón. Almost all of the slogans are the same now that General Zapata is dead. His simple and compelling "Land and Liberty" is now a part of every politician's vocabulary.

Rodolfo Hernández is no longer an ex-colonel—if indeed he ever was an ex—but an active one. I know because Sergeant Gómez reported for duty with orders signed by my drunken adversary, Lieutenant Juan Solís Lagos. The order was countersigned by Colonel Hernández. The orders were written on the back of another document in which Lieutenant Solís begged to be pardoned for his indiscretion. When I read a postscript added to his apology stating that the order for the airplanes was confirmed and again countersigned by Colonel Rodolfo Hernández Ochoa, I forgave him instantly.

I was to contact a Captain Jorge Rubio Contreras to work out the details.

I have a mouth large enough to push my ears back when I grin, and Gómez responded with a polite smile of his own. He offered me congratulations which were necessarily vague, for even had he been tempted to read the documents, he could not, for like most of his contemporaries in the army, he was illiterate. I sent him off with the note from Hernández and a post-script from mine asking for an appointment to see Captain Rubio.

Within the hour the sergeant was back with an oral message.

"Captain Rubio will meet you at the New York Cafe at ten fourteen this morning."

"Ten fourteen? Not ten thirteen or fifteen?"

"No, sir. He said ten fourteen."

20

Gómez assumed the stony expression traditional to enlisted men when confronted with the absurdities of officers.

"Was he joking?"

"I think not, my major."

I smiled. Just yesterday I had been a general.

"I am only an ex-captain, sergeant."

"I do not know what a captain-sergeant is, but you had better be a major when you meet Captain Rubio."

"But I have neither uniform nor insignia."

"Neither does Captain Rubio." Gómez allowed himself a small smile. "He is wearing a red shirt and a purple tie."

And when he finally showed up at the cafe, that is what he wore. And much more, all gaudy. His foot-high black sombrero was crisscrossed with silver thread. And although he had enormous shoulders and torso, they were set on spindly legs encased in skintight black *charro* pants that buckled under the instep of high-heeled red boots. His belt buckle, barely visible under a bulging stomach, was gold and silver. His head was large, his face flat, as if his sculptor had pushed the flat of his hand against brown clay. His eyes were mud-colored and protruding. I thought of a fairy-tale frog acting as court jester. All he needed was a flute.

"You are the Mister Cooper?"

I had expected the voice of a bullfrog, not the high-pitched croak of a tree frog.

"And you would be the Señor Rubio," I said, just as curtly.

We shook hands warily. Had we been dogs we would have been circling each other cautiously, teeth bared, wondering whether to bite or run.

"I am Captain Jorge Rubio Contreras," he said, trying to crush my hand. My hand was not only larger but stronger, so he dropped it.

"I am Major Tell Cooper Carter."

"Major? You are a salesman, no?"

He was getting right down to business. No small talk before the crass commercialism. Not a word about being two hours late.

"Yes, I sell airplanes. What do you sell?"

"Sell? I sell nothing. I buy. Maybe I buy some of your airplanes."

"And maybe not," I said. I dropped two silver pesos on the table. "For my coffee," I said. "I drank a lot of coffee waiting for you."

"You got here early. You gringos always arrive early."

"No. You got here much too late. I'll deal directly with Colonel

Hernández."

He laid a hand on his pistol butt. It was a Colt semi-automatic, fully cocked, without a holster, stuffed in between his belly and belt on his right side. I was standing and he sitting. I was reasonably sure that I could draw and shoot before his muzzle could clear the table top. I did not want to shoot him but it would not do to let him know that. I reached into my vest pocket and brought out a roll of cotton. I had bought it that morning to apply iodine to an ugly scratch. From it I made two smaller rolls and stuffed one of them into my left ear.

"Why the *chingada* are you putting cotton in your ear?" He laced the question with a crude swear word.

"I cannot stand loud noises," I said. I tamped the other roll in my right ear. I could still hear, but the sounds were muted.

"You are one loco gringo," he said, but he moved his gun hand a couple of fingers away from the gold-inlaid grips.

I had heard many times in my youth along the border of a Mexican standoff, but I had never been in one before. I waited for him to make a move, but he did not. I wondered how long I would have to wait before he cracked. I had visions of the waiters stacking up the fancy iron chairs and turning off the lamps with the two of us still frozen in our stupid little tableau.

Then I heard for the first time that husky voice that would never cease to enchant me.

"Am I too early, Jorge? I thought you would have finished by now."

I turned my head warily, keeping an eye on Rubio and then forgot him. My mouth fell open. It was the same lovely girl, smiling at me now, eyes flashing in the slash of bright sunlight from the door.

"We did finish, Toña," Rubio said. He took his hand altogether away from the pistol.

"You are W. Tell Cooper?" She turned to me.

"W. Tell Cooper," I repeated idiotically.

"Good. I suppose that I shall have to introduce myself." The black eyes flashed at Rubio, but with no humor in them. "I am Lieutenant Antonia Canela Sánchez." She held her hand out to me. Mine engulfed hers.

"I am Captain Tell Cooper Carter, at your feet," I said, stumbling over the simple Spanish phrase.

"You said you were a major," Rubio said.

"Yes," I agreed with him. I even liked him at that moment.

"Could I have my hand back?"

I heard the words as an echo and turned an ear toward the sound. She repeated the phrase, loudly, as if talking to a deaf person. Which, I suddenly realized, I was. I dropped her hand and then reached up and removed the cotton from my ears.

"I forgot the cotton," I said feeling the blood in my cheeks.

"I see you did," she said. "And, now what is your rank, captain or major?"

"I guess I am a major. I think I was promoted this morning."

"Congratulations," she said dryly and turned to Rubio. "Am I to be working with Major Cooper?"

"The major does not want to do business with us. We do not have sufficient rank."

"*We* is a lot of people," I said. "I would be delighted to discuss the details with you, Lieutenant Canela."

"Shall we sit down?" she asked.

"Of course," I held a chair for her. She frowned and sat at another.

"Major Cooper," she said. "I am a soldier, just like you."

"Not like me," I muttered in English as I sat down. "Not by a long shot."

"What did he say, Jorge?"

"I do not know," Rubio said importantly. "He speaks a low-class American English."

"I beg your pardon," I said to her. "The words just popped out."

I told her what I had said and waited apprehensively for her reaction. She laughed huskily and shook her head at me as if admonishing a mischievous boy. She was not taking me seriously, but then, neither was she angry. A girl once told me that if I had been just a touch more ugly I would have been handsome. Being ugly is a disadvantage with girls. Men do not seem to mind. Maybe, I thought, if she got to know me as a friend, she might not mind either. In any case, I told myself, a cat can look at a king, or in this case, a queen. I sat back in my chair and looked.

"First of all," Rubio said, "we must rewrite the contract."

After a long silence I realized that I was expected to say something, so I asked, "Why?"

"It is too vague and does not take into account all of the additional expenses."

"There are no additional expenses," I said.

"Your commission?"

"It is already included."

"Import duties?"

"But the airplanes are for the government."

"Exactly." He smiled for the first time and I noted that his predilection for gold was not limited to his apparel. "The government pays duties just like any one else. The duties are high. However," he gestured magnanimously, "we will allow you commission on the total cost. Toña will have a new contract for you tomorrow."

"That will not be necessary," I said, "but I will do whatever Colonel Hernández desires."

Rubio frowned. He took out one cigar, bit the end from it and spat it on the floor.

"Would you care for a little coffee, Lieutenant Canela?" I asked.

"Please." She smiled at me, and I grinned back foolishly.

"Lieutenant Canela," Rubio said, "is not officially an officer. But I made her one anyway. Lieutenant! Haw! When I took her out of that miserable hut that was her *jacal* in that miserable pueblo in Tabasco, she was a fifteen-year-old brat named María Luisa Vidales. Now she is eighteen and Lieutenant Antonia Canela."

"When I joined the Revolution I became a new person. So I took a new name too." Her eyes flashed. "I learned to read and write and fight. I can shoot a rifle or machine gun as well as any man and better than you, Jorge."

"You are still a little wildcat, Toña." He leered at me. "Maybe I take you back in my bed, eh? I don't care if your tits are too small for my hands. I got big hands, like the gringo major, eh, Toña?"

His words stunned me. I do not know why I did not smash that leer into his golden smile. I think that I was in the state induced by heavy artillery fire—what they called shell shock in the Great War. In any case, any move by me would have been superfluous.

She tossed her black hair, swept a hand under it and I saw a flash of silver. The thin blade in her hand flickered like a snake's tongue. Except for his eyes, Rubio was frozen in his chair. Her wrist flicked and he was left with an inch of cigar stub in his mouth. Another flick and most of his cravat, a billowing piece of purple silk, floated down onto the floor. There was no trace of blood, but the cutting edge must have been no more than the thickness of a cigarette paper from his throat.

"You shame me, Jorge. Not because I have sex with a man. I do what I do. I am only ashamed that I did live with you. Apologize to Major Cooper for your coarse manners."

24

"Apologize to a gringo—"

The flat of the blade tapped his cheek.

"All right! I apologize." He would not look at me.

"Is that sufficient?" Her voice was controlled, but looking into those intense black eyes, I would have done whatever she asked. Even if it meant apologizing to Rubio. Not even a hundred pounds of woman, but what intense energy! She might burn a man to a cinder, but had she asked, I would have given her the match.

"Yes," I said softly. "It is sufficient."

"Good." She tossed her head again and the knife disappeared somewhere behind her lovely brown neck. "When shall we meet again?"

"This afternoon," I suggested.

"No. I must draw up the contract, make copies and show them to Colonel Hernández—"

"No," Rubio interrupted, then added in what he obviously meant to be a conciliatory tone, "do not bother Colonel Hernández. I will authorize the new contract."

"Yes, Captain Rubio." She stood up. "I will have it on your desk tomorrow morning." She nodded at me, saluted Rubio, who waved a hand in dismissal, did an about face and marched out. I watched her leave, smiling, my anger gone.

"You find the girl amusing." Rubio matched my smile with a smirk.

He looked even more like a toad. I wondered why he did not grow a moustache. He was not a priest nor a bullfighter, so he had no excuse. My own was a shaggy, rust-colored affair, but it did hide the worst of the scar that ran from just under my right eye to the corner of my lip. Without it I looked as if I were constantly and sardonically amused. With it I merely seemed quizzical. Perhaps, I thought, Rubio believes I am as I perceive him. I resolved to settle our differences.

"Who understands women?" I said. "Would you accept something stronger than coffee so early in the morning?"

"It is now afternoon," he said.

"Right. I drank too much last night and I am a bit *crudo*. If I express myself badly, blame it on that and my poor Spanish."

"Of course, hombre. You speak good enough, but what an accent!" He laughed loudly. I forced a smile. My accent was north central Mexico while his was as exaggeratedly coastal as that of a Cuban comedian.

We drank a double shot of that vile hangover remedy, Fernet Branca, and chased it with mineral water from the nearby town of

Tehuacán. I listened while he talked.

"Since I was a young man I followed the Revolution. No one helped me. No one. One morning I saddled *Don* Joaquin's best horse, a fine black gelding with a white foot. When he mounted, he called for his *carabina*. I gave it to him, muzzle first. And it went off. Sad, eh?"

Rubio reached across the table to pound me on the shoulder to make sure that I understood the subtlety of his story. I laughed perfunctorily.

"We were of the same size, so I took his boots, spurs and hat and rode away to join the Red Shirts. Of course, they were not called that then."

"I have heard of them," I said, mimicking his accent, chopping off word endings and eliminating S's and D's entirely. "They were called *bandidos*, no?"

"Yes, of course." He took it as a compliment. "Like Villa. Now there is a real man. Of course," he added hastily, "he never should have opposed my General Obregón. But Villa is *muy macho*."

"Sure. A real he-man." I wondered as I had many times before if Villa himself had sent the men who killed my father.

We switched to whiskey, which means Scotch in Mexico, and toasted the Revolution, his native state of Tabasco and General Obregón.

When we drank to the general he looked angrily across the room at two men drinking coffee at another table. There were no other customers in the cafe.

"You over there. You do not drink to my General Obregón?"

"Of course we do," the younger of the two said. They lifted demitasses of coffee in response.

"No! Not with coffee. Give those two whiskey," Rubio yelled. A waiter sprinted to their table with a bottle and glasses.

"I can buy my own whiskey," the older man spoke in a clear cultured Spanish.

"You do not like my whiskey?" Rubio spoke, softly for him. He turned in his chair so that they could see the butt of his pistol and tapped it significantly.

"I am unarmed," the older man said.

"Do you drink to my General Obregón, you *hijo de la chingada*, or not?"

Blood drained from the old man's face. The insult to his mother— "son of a bitch"—was the absolute challenge. The younger took him by

26

the shoulder and gripped so tightly that his knuckles were white. "Of course we will drink to the general," the young man said, then turned, his voice unnaturally high, and spoke to the older man. "Please, *papá.*"

The son lifted a glass and drank quickly. Then so did the older. The old man stood up heavily, then bowed slightly, turned and left. The younger shot a glance of sheer hatred at us and followed after his father.

Rubio roared with laughter. He might have been the boy that put the tack on the new teacher's chair.

My grin might have been painted on. It had been fixed in place for so long that it hurt. I knew that I must either leave or fight, so I stood up.

"No, *cabrón*," Rubio said good naturedly. "You must have the penultimate drink."

In Mexico you never take the last drink, unless, of course, you are about to be shot. If I had sat down to drink it with him, we both might have had the last one. As it was, I was still on my feet when the young man came back into the cafe, pistol in hand. He paused in the entrance, took deliberate but hurried aim, and fired.

The first bullet hit the iron chair and it rang like a bell. The second was high into the wall behind me. The third burned my right leg. The fourth shot was mine. I had sighted and squeezed off one round while he was hurrying his second and third. Mine took him high in the chest and knocked him down.

The next shot was an explosion almost in my ear. I jumped and twisted to see Rubio, pistol still in his hand, but also still in the waistband of his pants. He had apparently shot himself in the groin.

"Get me a doctor," he screamed. "That *hijo de la chingada* has shot my balls off."

Chapter 4

A local newspaper ran a story with enough of the facts so that I recognized the incident. An eyewitness had reported a gunfight in the New York Cafe between a Mexican youth of good family and a barbarous Texan over the affections of a beautiful Indian girl. The Texan had lost one of his unnamed *extremities,* but was recovering. The Mexican boy was in a local hospital fighting for his life.

No mention was made of Rubio, who had come within an inch of shooting off one of his own *extremities* but was lucky enough to have lost only some superfluous fat from the inside of his right thigh. My own wound was also superficial, but anyone who has had a hunk of lead thrust violently into his flesh is liable to die of blood poisoning, so I did not feel safe until the angry red crust turned into a hard brown scab. It was then that I found a note from Lieutenant Canela slipped under my hotel room door. I was to meet her, health permitting, at the temporary offices of the procurement department.

When I called Sergeant Guillermo Gómez, whom I had taken to calling Memo, which is the nickname for all Guillermos, to arrange transportation for me, he had a big surprise.

"I have found a motor car."

"But a motor car would have to belong to a general or a minister," I objected.

"No. We have bought one and for only seven hundred pesos."

"Where did we get the money?"

"We signed a promissory note."

"I didn't know *we* could sign our name."

"I can draw my *rúbrica,*" he said indignantly, referring to a mark made instead of a signature.

"Of course you can. After we look at this car, I will begin to teach you to read and write."

"Read. Could such a thing be?"

"Of course. But not free. You will have to repay the time we steal from Colonel Hernández."

"I will repay. Double, triple, quad—"

I held up a hand to stop him while he still had some of his life left.

"When can the car be delivered?"

"It cannot be delivered for it does not want to run. However," he added triumphantly, "any man who can make flying machines obey, will not have even a little bit of trouble with a stubborn motor car!"

"I am not a mechanic. I am an aviator. A pilot who knows just a little about internal combustion engines."

"There you have it, major. Not another officer in Puebla can even pronounce such complicated words. And," he wheedled, "it is such a lovely motor car."

Memo was right. It was, or had been, a lovely car. So had the hacienda where it was stored. Hardly a building had four walls. None had roofs. The red roof tiles littered the floors inside crumbling adobe walls.

One old building had been cleaned up and a rough shelter built over the motor car. There was a cot and boxes piled one on top of another to form a rude chest of drawers. A table with three wooden legs and a wobbly pillar of broken bricks in place of the fourth stood in a corner. It held a basin, a clay water pitcher, a cased set of razors, one for each day of the week, a bottle of Armagnac and a small silver bell.

Amused, I picked up the bell. It rang, startling me. I dropped it hastily and turned away just in time to look into the smiling face of a young man dressed as casually as someone off to play golf or tennis. His hair was dark, as was his skin; his eyes were brown.

"Tell Cooper Carter," I said." At your orders."

"Juan Ávalos de la Vega, your servant."

We shook hands.

"I seem to have bought your automobile," I said.

"I fervently hope so."

"Sergeant Gómez tells me that we have signed a note for it."

"True. Unfortunately, I cannot exchange the note for food nor lodging."

"Would three hundred dollars in gold be acceptable?"

"Does a man from Alvarado swear?" Even the tiny children in that picturesque little fishing village use the most awful profanity as they play in the streets.

Memo handed me the purse. I counted out the coins, bright yellow eagles. Ávalos signed a bill of sale, Memo drew his curlicue as witness, and the car was ours.

"A drink to the sale?" Ávalos indicated the bottle.

"Thank you," I said. "It has been two years since I last tasted

Armagnac."

He smiled. Of course, his teeth were white and even. He was a handsome man. "It is not exactly Armagnac," he said, speaking faultless French.

"What is it then?" I asked, speaking fluent, but terrible soldier's French.

"It is Armagnac on the outside," he shrugged in the fatalistic Mexican manner, "but it is *aguardiente* from Puebla on the inside."

I did not know whether or not he jested until I drank. Then I knew it was a local firewater for my eyes watered and I could not suppress a cough. I turned away quickly and beat on the hood of the car.

"How shall I get it out to see if it runs?" I said, when I could speak.

"Start it up here. It is your garage."

"But you live here."

"Not one day more. I am moving to the city." He snapped the razor case shut, extracted a few shirts, stockings and a scarf from the makeshift bureau, folded them carefully and then dropped them into a burlap sack. "Voila!"

He glanced at my rented carriage and then said, in English, "If you allow me to send the luggage with your vehicle, I will help you start your automobile. Could you then give me a lift into town?"

"*Mais oui*," I said.

"*Merci*," Ávalos said.

"Mer, sí," Memo parroted and then in Spanish said, "English sounds a lot like Spanish."

"Except," Ávalos said, "that English was French."

"Mer, sí," Memo said enthusiastically. "Maybe my Major Cooper could teach me to write in English. I already know some words. Goddamn. Son of the bitch. I learned them from Nacho, the bellboy at the hotel, the one who speaks all of the English."

I exercised a great deal of self control and did not laugh, nor did Ávalos. Of course, he was a well-educated gentleman. However, I think that he would have been one had he been raised on a dirt farm. Had it not been for his one perceived yet damning aberration, he might have been a vital force in bringing Mexico out of the chaos of those times.

The car was a Renault limousine. There was a glass partition, miraculously intact, between the driver and passengers. They could, however, communicate with the front seat by twisting a knob, which would in turn move another knob, attached near the steering wheel, which pointed to a dial on which was embossed, in English: *Club*,

30

Home, *Office,* and a blank space.

I smiled when I saw the blank.

"I, too, always wondered what that space meant," Ávalos said, speaking English. "But the chauffeur would never tell."

"Mister Ávalos," I said, "you speak better English than I do."

"You flatter me, but do not call me Mister Ávalos. He, God rest his soul, was my father. I am Juan or Johnny."

"All right," I said. I held out my hand and switched to Spanish. "Call me Tell and use *tú*, if you will?"

He nodded yes and we spoke *tú* to each other from then on, in good times and bad. Often it takes a lifetime to reach that stage of intimacy with a stranger, but young men in troubled times live by different rules.

I unbuckled the motor cover and raised both sides while Memo propped them up with sticks. I followed the wires from the magneto to the spark plugs. They were all connected and intact. However, when Memo cranked the starter, the engine did not even cough. One of the wrenches from my airplane kit fit the spark plugs, so I pulled them and cleaned each one. I used an American dime to space them. Memo cranked away. Nothing. I suddenly realized that the plug had been completely dry. Not a trace of gasoline. A thin iron rod fastened to a metal bulb protruded well above the hood, indicating an almost full tank. I tapped it. It did not move. It was frozen with rust. I used pliers to pull it up free, then worked it up and down until it slid easily and released it. The red button on top of the wire dropped out of sight. The tank was empty.

Memo trotted to the carriage and brought back the five-gallon can of gas and then, while I filled the tank, went back for the lubricating oil.

I saved a pint or so of the gasoline and dropped a little into the throat of the carburetor. Memo spun the crank. The engine caught, backfired, and rapped his wrist. Luckily it was not fractured. Black smoke puffed out of the exhaust. I adjusted the throttle and the spark and mixture and then started toward the front of the car, but Johnny Ávalos waved me back. He was a natural athlete and had caught the rhythm of the crank by watching Memo. I got in behind the wheel. He spun it easily and the engine caught. I adjusted spark and mixture until it sounded right and then set the throttle to run slowly until it warmed up.

The springs were all intact. The steering gear looked solid. There was still oil in the crankcase, but we added more. Except for two cracked windows and a few bullet holes in the side, the body was in good shape. The tires worried me, but Johnny pointed to a pile of bricks off to one side and mimed that the wheels—not the tires—had rested on them.

I signaled Memo to sit up front with me and Johnny behind in the passenger compartment. I closed my eyes, mentally following the system of clutches and gears, then put it into gear and released the clutch. I felt the rear of the car strike the table and send it cartwheeling. The brake worked well. Both Memo and I banged the back of our heads on the plate glass partition.

"Does it go forward?" Memo asked, hanging onto the protruding lip of the dashboard with both hands.

"Observe and learn," I said, "for you will soon be driving this car."

He shook his head in complete disbelief. I tried again, hit on the right gear and we shot out from the makeshift garage into the bright sunshine, onto the rough wagon road, jolting and swaying. Memo crossed himself and shut his eyes.

When we reached the relative smooth roadway, I found the high gear and added throttle until we were racing along at twenty miles an hour, leaving the buggy far behind.

We were soon in Puebla. Up ahead prudent drivers pulled their wagons and buggies off the road and talked soothingly to their horses. I slowed down just as the clicker by the wheel began to move from space to space until it stopped on the blank. I looked back at Johnny. He held thumb and finger up in the "wait a second" sign. I interpreted that to mean he wanted me to stop so I did. This time it was Johnny that hit the glass, but not with his head. He merely flattened his nose. It hardly bled.

I got out to meet him. He held a handkerchief over his nose.

"I meant to tell you that it has good brakes," he said, then added. "I am to report to my new office and I had better change shirts, but we seem to have outrun my luggage."

I smiled. His luggage was still a gunnysack.

"We'll have coffee at my hotel," I said. "The carriage must come there to collect the fee. Besides, you can use my room to change and clean up."

He nodded and got back in. I drove slowly and carefully to the hotel. Memo had recovered enough courage to watch me operate the controls. When we reached the entrance I saw that Johnny was braced against the back seat, his hands against the partition, while Memo did the same with the dash board. I eased the car to a perfect stop.

"Sit at the controls and practice, Memo," I said. "After you learn to drive, maybe I will teach you to fly."

"In this?"

I left him there, patting the controls as if the automobile was a nervous horse.

Johnny and I sat outside on the sidewalk under a red-and-white striped canvas shade and sipped demitasses of sweet, thick coffee.

To the west, the slope of the towering snow-topped volcano with the tongue-twisting name of Popocatépetl glinted white as the sun, at its zenith, lit up the whole mountain.

"I read that one of Hernán Cortés's captains climbed up to the rim and then lowered himself down into the mouth of the volcano to get a supply of niter—or was it saltpeter?"

"Niter," Johnny said. "I climbed the mountain once. It is not a difficult climb, merely a long, cold one."

"How high is it?"

"Around sixteen thousand feet."

"I have never flown that high, but others have, of course, and one day soon airplanes will be able to reach over thirty thousand feet."

"You are an aviator?"

"Yes. I flew in the war in France."

"But you are so young."

"I am twenty-five, about your age."

"I am thirty-five," he laughed.

I would never have believed him to be the older. Nor did our other friends until some twenty years later, when he began to lose his hair and I did not.

"You shot down airplanes?"

I nodded yes.

"Is it permitted to ask how many?"

"It is not only permitted, but encouraged. I had eight confirmed."

"And unconfirmed?"

"Those we do not discuss," I said, smiling to take the sting out of the words. "And as for you, is it permitted to ask what is it that you do at your new office?"

"You may ask, but it is not encouraged. I am in charge of breaking up the *latifundios*—the huge amounts of lands pertaining to the old haciendas—and redistributing the land to the deserving."

"You are an army officer?"

"I am supposed to act like a major."

"Me too," I said happily.

I told him about my dealings in Puebla and mentioned my only other young friend there, Willard Riley.

"I know him. He is a most intelligent young man, but a very cold one. He has nothing of the romantic, gregarious Irish about him."

"He seems like that at first," I said earnestly. "But I think that it's just his shyness. He's a very shy man."

"Perhaps. But he is, above all, ambitious."

"True," I agreed, thinking of the million-dollar offer. "He is sure that he'll be a millionaire some day. And, the truth of it is, I believe him."

Johnny held up a hand, but whether in agreement or not, I did not know, for just then the buggy clattered up to the hotel entrance. The driver dropped the weighted reins to the street to hold his horses and walked over to our table. He had the old burlap sack in one hand.

Johnny accepted it graciously and borrowed a peso from me to tip the man with. I paid the driver and called for the bill for our coffee. Johnny insisted on paying. He tried to sign the bill but the waiter would not accept his signature, so he was forced to change one of his bright golden pieces for a pocketful of silver.

I loaned him my room key and went out to the car. When Johnny came back down, I was in the car explaining the functions of the spark and mixture controls to Memo. Johnny jumped in the back and flipped the address switch to *office*.

I touched my forehead with one finger and got behind the wheel. Before Memo, who was holding his sore wrist with his good hand, could reach for the crank, Johnny slipped out, danced to the front, bent down and spun the crank. The engine, still warm, caught on the first try. Johnny bowed as an actor receiving applause might, then hustled back to his seat to once again assume the posture of a bored aristocrat. Even Memo, who I knew had been prepared to dislike him, smiled.

As we drove, Johnny pointed one way or the other, and Memo sitting beside me, like a human extension of the clicker by the steering wheel, pointed with either his left or right hand.

Suddenly Memo yelled, "Whoa!" and braced himself against the dash board.

I stopped the car smoothly as I asked, "Whoa?"

"He pulled back on the reins," Memo said, nodding at Johnny in the back seat.

We had stopped in front of what looked like a small hotel. Something tugged at my memory. I pulled a folded paper from my pocket.

"Procurement Bureau? Shared offices?"

"What?" Johnny asked.

"She works for the Procurement Bureau?"

"She?"

"Lieutenant Toña— Antonia Canela."

"A female warrior?"

"My God! Yes," I said.

"No taste for them myself, but come on along. She will likely be in the east wing."

"I thought this was your new office."

"So it is."

"You have not worked here before?"

"Never. Not one day. Not here or anywhere else until this very day."

"How do you know about the east wing, then?"

"Elementary, my dear doctor. It is the one section that was built as a separate unit."

"Another elementary question. How do you know that?"

"The result of keen observation. I watched my father watch the architect watch the builder. This was our house."

"And the hacienda? That too?"

"Yes, that too."

"What will happen to them now?"

"This place," he waved at the house, "has already been through the hands of several governments. Now, unless there is another radical change, it will be the center for this area's land redistribution officer."

"You?"

"Me."

"And the hacienda?"

"It will be split up into small units and given to the most deserving."

He walked me through a large door, down a long hall and into what might have been a library once, but was now without books. He pointed to a door at the far end. We shook hands and agreed to lunch the following week.

The door at the far end was open. Lieutenant Canela, her back to me, was speaking angrily to a sergeant, standing at attention, but twisting his hands nervously at his sides.

"How can I sign for machine guns I have never seen?" Her voice was angry.

"Captain Rubio has seen them," the sergeant said defensively. "He says they are magnificent."

"Then why does he not sign for them?"

"I don't know," the sergeant said miserably.

"Where are they?"

"At the station. They came from Mexico."

"The capital?"

"Yes, from the city."

"Why were they addressed to the United States Embassy then?"

He shook his head sadly and, still at attention, managed a despondent shrug.

"But they are ours?"

"Yes. General Huerta confiscated them years ago, before he ran away." He screwed up his face and then added, "I heard the name. They are Gad . . . Glat—"

"Gatlings," I said, helpfully.

She whirled. "Major Cooper! What do you know about this?"

"Nothing. But I could take you to the American consulate. I have a friend there."

"Yes, I know. Let's go. We can talk about the airplanes on the way."

"Of course, señorita." I gestured, "Your carriage awaits." I got a blank look, then reached for the portfolio she carried and got another such look. I jerked my hand back, sighed, and then I took my proper position as her superior officer, to the right, and we marched out together. I resisted the urge to whistle a Souza march.

"A motor car! Not even all the generals have motor cars."

"Maybe I'll be promoted."

"You are rich!" It was an accusation.

"No, I am not and, unless I sell some airplanes soon, I will be both poor and hungry."

Memo was waiting, the crank in his left hand. His right wrist was by now visibly swollen. He leaned back warily and poked the crank at the car's radiator. I took the crank away from him and motioned with my head at the lieutenant. He ran toward the back door, but I shook my head quickly and motioned to the front. He blinked, looked again at the girl and then, grinning at me, held the door opposite the steering wheel open.

She said nothing, but turned her eyes on him. He stepped back quickly. He reached for the door, but she slammed it shut after her—before he could touch the handle. Again, the start of the still-warm engine was easy. I drove too fast and swerved several times so that her firm but surprisingly soft breasts pushed against my right arm. She did not shriek or even gasp, just tightened her lips and clenched one strong brown hand on the dash.

"Would you like to learn to drive?" I asked hopefully.

"No!"

I was shocked. I would have bet that the fiery revolutionary would have been eager to learn.

"No, not the car. But I would like to learn to fly."

"You mean to pilot an airplane?"

"I could hardly fly without one, could I?" She smiled.

"Maybe I could teach you in one of the DH-4s when they get here."

"Why not?"

I shrugged. Why not indeed? She was strong enough and unafraid. If she also had the coordination and depth perception, she would be a good pilot.

We left the car, its motor running, in front of the consulate. I told Memo that if I was not back in two fingers of sun time, he was to switch the engine off. Five fingers held vertically at arm's length against the sun measures about fifteen minutes, depending on the length of the arm and the thickness of the fingers.

The door to the patio was open, but the garden was empty. I heard a buzzing of voices from the interior and led the beautiful soldier in with me.

"Open it up for Christ's sake, James," one of the men said loudly.

James, a bluff, fleshy young man—the real consul, I assumed—held a small box wrapped like a present with a green ribbon and bow. He held a sheet of paper in the other hand.

"It must be a joke," James said. "Willard must be playing a joke on us."

"Willard Riley," I said, "does not play jokes."

James looked at me blankly.

"Major Tell Cooper, a friend of Riley," I said and plucked the paper from his hand.

The message had been printed in block letters. It would have been written by a child or someone nearly illiterate. I translated it into English as I read.

> *We have the gringo consul. If you want to see him*
> *again, you will pay us ten thousand dollars in gold.*
> *You have one week to get the money. We will send*

more instructions. You have seven days from today.
Or we will send you another larger piece of Willard
Riley.

The note was signed: *The True Revolutionaries.*

"They meant to get you," I said to James.

He paled and shook his head negatively. I dropped the message on his desk and then caught the box from his hand just as he let it fall.

I untied the ribbon, unwrapped the box and lifted its top off. The top fell from my nerveless fingers and fluttered down onto the floor. Inside the box itself, which was small in the palm of my large hand, was a slice of ear. It was glued by dirt and dried blood to the box. A slice that size taken from my ear would scarcely have been noticed, but it would have been a third of Riley's tiny ear.

"How soon can you raise the money?" I asked James.

"How soon?" James said, staring blankly at the ear and then, handkerchief to mouth, ran from the room.

"It is a small piece of ear," Toña Canela said. "Is your friend a small man?"

"Yes," I answered, "but only in size."

Chapter 5

By the time Lieutenant Canela summoned me to read the new contract, three days had gone by and Willard Riley was four days closer to losing another slice of flesh. Bureaucracy moves faster than a man paddling a canoe with a fly swatter, but not much. All of the forms had been filled out and James had taken them to the embassy in Mexico City. No one doubted that the money would arrive. But, would it get there before the dismembered body of Will Riley?

When I walked into the procurement office, only Canela and Rubio were there. Rubio grimaced when he rose from his desk.

"My wound hurts like hell. You just got a scratch, hombre. I got a bad one. I have to tell you that you made a good shot. He knocked me off balance with his first bullet, or I would have got him for sure."

I looked at the fat man in amazement. It was a wonder that he had not claimed to have shot the young man.

"I read that the man will survive," I said.

"And a lucky thing for you, major," Canela said as she shook hands with me.

"Yes," I agreed. "I did not want to shoot him, let alone kill him. I had no quarrel with the man."

"But you still shot him," Rubio said, not quite suppressing a smile.

"Yes."

"You did not know he was the godson of *El Turco?*"

"Who is *El Turco?*"

He smirked openly and would have dug an elbow into Canela, but she made a fist so he pulled the elbow back.

"That is what some people call General Plutarco Elías Calles. Next to my General González, he is the biggest man in the state—maybe the country. And you shot his godson!"

"I understand," I said. "And you fired a shot at that same godson and missed only because you were off balance."

"It was just a warning shot," he said hastily.

"You should aim higher when you fire warning shots or one day you will turn yourself into a soprano."

"Watch yourself, gringo!" Blood darkened his cheeks. It occurred to me that he was angrier at my reference to his abnormally high voice than the self-inflicted wound.

I waited until his color was back to its ordinary light brown and then tossed a flattened lead slug onto his desk top. It finally rattled still.

"What is that?" He eyed me suspiciously.

"It is yours. From your pistol. I thought you might want it. A souvenir."

"Where did you get it?"

"A policeman found it embedded in the floor, beneath your chair."

He made a motion toward his pistol. I reached with my right hand for the cotton roll.

"Stop it!" Canela shouted. "Or I call the guards."

I put the cotton back, but I kept my jacket open for a quick draw and my eyes on his right hand. He watched my left.

She gave us each a copy of the contract. It had grown from eighty thousand to one hundred thousand.

"Twenty thousand dollars for import duties!" I was shocked.

"It is necessary," Rubio said. "Besides it has nothing to do with you. Also, if you look, you will see it is initialed by my General González."

"My commission is eight percent of eighty thousand dollars. I want no more."

"As you wish." Rubio did not try to hide his glee.

"I do have a request."

"What?" Rubio asked, suspicion flaring in his eyes.

"I would like my commission at once if possible. I have an urgent need of cash."

"Me too. Also Toña. Everybody needs cash." His lip curled. He wanted me to beg.

"Is it for the consul Riley?" Toña asked.

"I would rather not say," I said stiffly.

"I think that we could arrange an advance," she said.

"No!" Rubio shouted, glowering at her.

"Would you accept a smaller commission if it were paid today?" she said, ignoring Rubio.

"Yes."

"Five thousand?" Rubio said quickly.

"Six," Toña said. "The general would not approve of usury."

"Of what?"

"Of cheating a friend out of a fair commission." She stared him down.

"Okay," he said, "but you sign all the papers, Toña."

40

"Are you speaking to me, Captain Rubio?" she said.

He glanced involuntarily at the roll of black hair at the base of her neck.

"Okay, Lieutenant Canela. Don't be so touchy. You take care of everything. I have better things to do than listen to some gringo explain in bad Spanish why he needs his *pinche* commission before he delivers his *pinche* merchandise."

I could have pointed out that my "damned" commission was an insignificant amount compared to the total, which would have to be put into an escrow account in the United States before the airplanes would even be shipped to Veracruz. I did not, because the lieutenant raised her eyebrows at me, smiled slightly and shook her head gently.

I did take a kind of petty revenge.

"I am sorry I speak with such an accent," I said, burlesquing his own coastal Spanish. "I will try to do better."

"You had better," Toña warned me angrily in the same accent. My God, I thought, it is also her very own accent. But when she spoke, I found it charming.

"Yes," Rubio said, mollified. "Work on your accent. Already it sounds better."

He teetered on his high-heels over to a hat rack, retrieved his gold and silver sombrero, sat it squarely on his head, and then, still keeping an eye on my gun hand, sidled out the doorway. The tall crown caught and the hat was tipped over one eye. He caught it quickly with his left hand and backed hastily out of sight. A toad of a man wearing a huge golden crown. I laughed out loud and said, "*El Rey Sapo!*" Toña tried valiantly not to laugh but it was no use. I had chanced on a perfect description of Rubio: the Toad King.

When she caught her breath, she shook her head at me in mock reprimand, but there was no anger in her eyes. She called her secretary, an army corporal. He objected to everything she requested until she suggested that he might prefer duty at one of the more remote posts in the territory of Quintana Roo. He shook his head furiously in negation and then bobbed it up and down in complete agreement. It was still bobbing up and down when he sat down in front of his old typewriter and began banging away.

"It is not fast enough for a Browning or a Maxim," I said, "therefore it must be a Gatling."

She made a megaphone with her hands and yelled into it in the corporal's direction. "It is a Remington, but he cannot type as fast with two hands as I can with two fingers."

The clatter increased and the rhythm steadied. She nodded to herself and then fished a pack of chocolate-colored cigarettes from her desk. I refused one. She stuck one carelessly in the corner of her mouth and looked up at me through long, black lashes.

"Light?"

I seldom smoked, but, out of habit, carried matches. I shook one out of a small nickel safe and lit it with a flick of my nail. Before the flare died down and I could move to her cigarette, she moved to the light. I could feel her body heat and smell new exotic odors. My heart beat so loudly that I thought she might hear it. She drew in smoke, paused to exhale and then looked straight into my eyes.

"Now, what about those *pinche* machine guns?"

"Enough of romance," I said.

"What?"

"About the 'damned' machine guns. I'll make a deal. A favor for a favor."

"What's the favor?"

"Company for dinner."

"Done. I'll send Captain Rubio. He likes to eat with you. 'Never a dull moment,' he says."

I held up my hands in surrender. "Please. What I had in mind was a witty, intelligent and fascinating female. Namely, one Lieutenant Antonia Canela."

"And you will tell me all about the Gatling guns?"

"Yes. And you may tell me about your adventures in the Revolution."

The restaurant in my hotel turned out to be not only one of Puebla's best, but her favorite as well, so we met there. I would gladly have called for her, but she said no in a way that left no room for negotiation. I had been at our special table for a half an hour before she arrived, precisely on time. She wore a simple cotton dress patterned in a light green and gold that enhanced her dark skin. It was cut in such a fashion that as she strode to the table each thigh was outlined in breathtaking clarity. I stood up, hypnotized. She held her hand out to me, smiling.

I had acquired the pleasant French custom of kissing a lady's hand. While the Lieutenant Canela had been too formidable for that, this bewitching creature in the light summer dress was not. I lifted her hand to my lips and, like a moth to a flame, would have let her warm skin consume my lips, but she withdrew her hand.

I straightened up, wondering what my punishment might be, but she was smiling.

"Do you always kiss hands?"

"Only when the urge is overpowering. You are beautiful. And your dress is lovely, but it is you who adorns it."

"Did you learn how to talk like that with the girls in France?"

"No," I said truthfully, wondering where I had found the courage and the speech. "I usually just stutter."

I moved toward her chair, but she waved me back and said, "Sit down, major."

I sat, lifted an arm in a prearranged signal and our waiter, the oldest and by far the best, trotted to our table. The cork was popped, the champagne pronounced acceptable and our glasses filled.

She held a glass up at the light to watch the bubbles rise. "What is it?"

"Champagne. Moët Chandon."

"It is French from France?"

"Yes."

"It is likely very expensive. Mexicans should consume what their own country produces."

"Like machine guns?" I asked, smiling.

"Agreed. Some things we must import. But one day we will make them here. We already make all kinds of *vino*."

While *vino* does mean wine, the word is also used to mean alcoholic drinks in general, which is what she meant. I doubt if even the famous family of the martyred President Madero would pretend that their vineyards produced more than an adequate table wine.

"Try it," I said, lifting my glass to her. "To a long and pleasant association."

"Sure." She drank it down as if it were a glass of beer.

The bubbles got into her nose and she sneezed. She laughed in delight. "It is very good. More!" She held her empty glass out for me to fill. The waiter took it from her. "One of these days we will make champagne here too. But only after we have given all of the people land, liberty and plenty of tortillas and beans—and meat too!"

I drank to that. After the waiter had filled my glass and hers again, she said, "Now tell me about the machine guns."

"Do you remember an American ambassador who was named O'Shaughnessy?"

"The one that helped Huerta kill Madero?"

"No. That was Lane. This one came in later. He was a Huerta man too, but all he did was get Huerta's permission to bring in some machine guns, quietly, for the embassy. Well, they brought in a couple of tons of guns and ammunition in boxes labeled *stationery.* But the boxes carried the name of the commanding officer of the Springfield Armory. Someone smelled a rat and they were held up in customs in Veracruz. Then the Americans occupied Veracruz and confiscated them. Later on, after that was settled, the Marines went off to another war and the old Gatlings were forgotten."

"Then why do we have to pay ten thousand dollars for some old machine guns?"

"Why indeed?"

She held her glass up for more champagne. An angry light was flashing in her obsidian eyes. I almost felt sorry for Rubio.

"I am glad I did not sign for those old guns. Could we send them back?"

"Sure. But you could also confiscate them as contraband and give them to one of Obregón's units that is short of automatic weapons. They are old but reliable and better than nothing."

"You know a lot about machine guns."

"No, not much. Of course, I have fired thousands of rounds from airplanes, but that is quite different. The guns are fixed to the airplane so you really aim the airplane itself, watch the red tracers and correct your aim. It is like trying to squirt a running dog with a stream of water from a garden hose."

"You have done that? Not the dog," she laughed, "the airplane. You have shot down another airplane?"

"Yes."

"You point the airplane and pull the trigger," she said, understanding, "but where is the machine gun?"

"At the end of the war we had two. They fire through the propeller; that is, there is a device that keeps the gun from firing when the propeller is exactly opposite the barrel."

I took out my pocket notebook and a pencil and sketched the propeller and gun.

"Of course. I see how it works."

I added a rough outline of a Fokker and penciled in a ring sight over the German cross.

"To fly and turn and shoot too. How could you do such a thing?"

44

"I was lucky enough to learn that before *I* might have been fired at and killed." I was startled to realize how true my words were.

"What is it like being up as high as a volcano, among the white clouds, the warm sun shining on you?"

"The enemy came at us out of the blinding sun, and sometimes we would hide in those white clouds. And we drank cognac before each flight so that the castor oil fumes from the engine would not make us vomit."

Her jaw dropped. Her almond-shaped eyes nearly stretched into circles.

"Then there are no soft clouds and sunshine?"

"Yes, there are." I remembered the exultation of outwitting death and, when the danger was done, of how vividly blue the sky was and bright green the fields were. "Yes, there were moments . . ." I let my voice trail off. It was too poignant. I did not want to conjure up any of the laughing faces that I would never again see this side of the grave.

"But that was then and this is now." I shook off the depression. "I will teach you to fly and you can decide for yourself. And now, your turn. Tell me about the cavalry charges, jumping your horse over the cannon, being surrounded by cheering revolutionaries."

"There was some of that, but mostly it was carrying beans and *chiles* and *masa* for tortillas in my *rebozo*, and even stealing food for Jorge when there was none. That is all I did until one day a boy my age, from my own *pueblo*, dropped dead, his rifle still loaded. I picked it up and followed the riders. There were others like me, on foot, but armed."

"Other women?"

"No. Not that day. A fierce man on a roan gelding came straight at me, to run me down, I thought. I emptied my rifle at the horse. Like you, I was lucky. I missed the horse, but I killed the rider. Someone caught the horse and brought it to me. From that day on I was a mounted soldier."

"And Rubio, what did he do for the *frijoles* you brought to him?"

"I was just sixteen then. He was my *Juan,* my protector. He was a good brave fighter; skinny then, like the rest of us. He was promoted and one day he told me I was a lieutenant. Then," she laughed, "I learned to read and write and I left his bed."

"And him?"

"Almost. I was on my way to join Emiliano Zapata. There was a man! He never turned his back on his people. Never!"

"I would have liked to have known him," I said sadly.

"I, too, wanted to meet him. But before I could see him, Carranza sent that animal Guajardo to murder him."

"How?"

"He took all of his men and pretended to desert. To prove himself, he captured a town full of Carrancista soldiers. The ones that lived, he had them shot."

"And all the time he was a Carrancista himself?"

"Yes. No. What he was and is, is a Guajardista." She laughed, but there was little humor in it. "Do you know the name of the general who led the attack on the Carranza train?"

"Was it Sánchez, the one who called him *father*?"

"No, but that one is cut from the same cloth. The general who sent Carranza to die in the Puebla mountains was Jesús María Guajardo."

"The same?"

"The very one." Her eyes were angry, even as she looked at me. I changed the subject quickly.

"What about the plan to redistribute the land?"

"It is not redistribution. Like Zapata said, it was stolen from the farmers to begin with. We are only taking it away from the rich *hacendados* who stole it and giving it back to the villages."

"But some of the land was never taken that way. In Chihuahua and Sonora—"

"Who cares? I am talking about Puebla, Veracruz and Morelos. The sugar land that made rich men richer. It was like gold. The haciendas ate up other people's land and sucked up other people's water to make sweet, white gold. They ship it out for yellow gold and then use it to live in France or Spain, or even your country."

"But the other land. The land that was never communal—"

"It belongs to those who work it." Her voice grew louder. "To those who fertilized it with their own blood."

"Easy," I said softly. "I am not an enemy. I would like to understand."

"Sorry." She smiled an apology. "I wish I could stop making speeches to my friends."

"I'll drink to that, *amiga*," I said, hoping that she included me as a friend.

She lifted her glass to me and looked into my eyes. The anger was gone, but there was a depth to them that seemed to draw me in with or without my consent. I had seen a fly trap on the eastern coast and wondered if the fly thought that he could also crawl back out of the dcpths.

"Major Cooper!"

"What?" I blinked my eyes back into focus and saw her peering at me anxiously.

"Are you all right?"

"Yes. Are we about through with military matters?"

"Yes, I suppose that we are."

"Then," I said, taking a deep breath, "would you stop calling me Major Cooper? Please call me Tell?"

"No," she said, grinning crookedly, "you are much older than I. So, I shall call you *Don* Tell."

But, as we got into the meal, she forgot to use the deferential *Don* and soon we were chattering away like old friends and calling each other Tell and Toña.

I had ordered the dinner hours before. I had prepared the steaks myself, in the French peppered style. The gazpacho was cold and very Spanish. The salad dressing cost Memo an hour of his time, which he spent locating the Roquefort cheese. Dessert was strawberries and cream.

Toña ate with such gusto and natural enjoyment that when she laced her pepper steak with a Mexican hot sauce from the table, so did I. Finally sated, we leaned back in our chairs and watched lazily while large brandy snifters were heated over candles until the golden liquid began to vaporize, throwing shimmering shadows against the glass bowls and emitting a sweet, strong fragrance.

"You have a *novia*?" Toña asked.

"No. No girlfriend. Not here. Not in the States."

"France?"

"No, not France."

She reached across the table to trace the scar from my eye to my mouth with a finger tip.

"You are attractive, Tell. Your face is strong with a story to tell."

"Yours too. Pity about the scar."

"I have no scar," she said indignantly.

"I know, that's the pity."

She laughed, was silent for a long minute and then said, "I have scars where you cannot see them."

"Do they have stories to tell?" I asked.

"Yes. Each has its story."

"I love to read."

47

She sipped at the cognac, but peered at me, her nose hidden behind the oversized brim of the glass. Then, as if she had made a decision, she sat her glass down and said, "You may take me home now, Tell."

"An honor. I will take the long way."

"Do you know where I live?"

"No, but if you show me, I'll take the long way."

"As you wish, but I thought you might be in a hurry to see my scars."

I gulped, flushed red and, had I been standing, would have tripped over something.

"Come on Tell." She laughed. "Let's go now. You must count the money and then sign a receipt."

"Receipt?"

"Yes. Come on." She stood up.

I wrote my room number on the bill, signed it, dropped a handful of silver coins on the table and left, half-trotting behind Toña.

The clerk saw us approach and opened the hotel safe. He plunked a canvas bag onto the counter. It was sealed.

"Open it," she ordered.

The clerk twisted the seal off and poured the golden coins out onto the wooden counter top.

"Okay," I said using the American slang that had already become an international word.

"Okay, no, you *cabrón*. Count it!"

Both the clerk and I winced at her language, but I did manage a sheepish grin. I counted out one hundred and twenty fifty-dollar gold pieces.

I signed her receipt, got a new one from the hotel clerk and had the gold returned to the safe.

I had discovered that Nacho—the hotel bellboy who spoke all the English—could also drive. I had him bring my car to the hotel entrance. The moon was full, which was fortunate, because the gas lamps mounted on the fenders would not work. Memo, who had worked hours on them, before giving up in disgust, had said, "They do not want to light." In Mexico inanimate objects often have a will of their own.

"You have your own room?" I asked as we drove away.

"No. I am in a barracks with fifty men."

I opened my mouth to register an angry objection but luckily caught myself in time. I peeked from the corners of my eyes and her lips were quivering with suppressed laughter.

48

"Only fifty," I said. "Maybe they don't know you are from Tabasco."

She whooped with laughter and then turned on me, beating me with clenched hands on my shoulder and chest. I pulled over, caught her wrists in my hands and, when she bared her teeth at me, met her mouth with mine. The laughter stopped. Suddenly we were gasping for breath, tearing at each other's clothes. Some second sight, sixth sense or, most likely, just my earthly but extraordinary peripheral vision made me stop and look around me. Noses of all sizes and shapes were pressed up against the glass windows.

"Tell," Toña moaned. "Do not stop. Come back."

"We have an audience," I said in a shaky voice.

"*Pelados*," she called the rude onlookers.

I had not turned the magneto off, had not even thought of it, luckily, so I clutched the big car into gear and at full throttle went careening down the street. I did not slow down until there were no more lighted windows. Then I drove the car off the road into a ditch, switched off the magneto and sprang at that small, fragile girl. She came back at me spitting and scratching. I felt blood run down one cheek and I drew back quickly, both bewildered and afraid.

"What is it? I thought—"

"You thought that you could take a woman the way you break a stubborn horse, just jump on and spur?"

"No. But I was still full of hot blood and much passion, and I thought that you also were."

"Well, now you know. I am not!"

"Of course," I said, hurt. "I will take you home immediately. I am terribly sorry, Lieutenant Canela. I thought that you liked me."

"Tell," she said casually, "like you is one thing. Coupling with you in front of half the *pelados* in Puebla watching is another."

"All right," I said stiffly.

"Oh, come on, *Don* Tell," she said, dabbing at the scratches with what must have been a scented handkerchief. "Take me to my little house and I will show you my scars."

I drove on, numbly, until she tapped me on the shoulder and said, "Here."

I pulled on the brake, switched off the magneto and was out of my door, around the huge front end of the automobile, opening her door before she could twist the door handle.

"Watch out for the pothole," I whispered.

She shook her head at me and laughed loudly. I looked at the other darkened dwellings fearfully. She stepped out, avoiding the hole easily, took me by the hand and led me toward a small, square adobe dwelling. It would have been one level above a *jacal*, a country structure made from mud and sticks.

"Do you have a key?" I said softly.

"What for?" she asked in her normal voice. "What would a thief steal from me?"

I suppose that my voice betrayed me for I meant to speak as normally as she had. "Your bed, clothes, pots and pans. Who knows?"

"Look, Tell," she placed her arms akimbo, hands on ample hips, "if I was Toño, the macho second lieutenant from Tabasco, and I invited you to my quarters for a drink, would you sneak up whispering and looking around like a coyote trying to spot the dogs?"

"No," I said miserably. Then I surprised myself by booming out, "No, buddy. Let's have a drink from your bottle in your quarters."

"I do not drink," she said mischievously, "but come on in anyway."

She left the door open and by the light of a whisper of moon, she found a candle stub and, snapping a match like a cowboy across one taut cotton-clad buttock, ignited the match and then the candle. She kicked the door shut with a foot and came into my arms. I engulfed her.

"Something hard is poking me," she said.

I hoped that it was too dark for her to see the red infuse my face. Not even the French girls were so frank. I stammered something, I knew not what, and she laughed at me.

"Do not be so pretentious. I think it is your pistol. If you remove it, I will lay my knife down beside it and we can fight fair."

I whipped off my jacket and slipped the holster and pistol off.

"Boots too," she said.

I sat down on the bed and tugged at them. They would not come off. She turned, straddled my leg and pulled. I had no recourse but to push, with the flat of my hand, her exquisite bottom. After she pulled the other boot off I left my hand there. The full buttock just fit my hand.

She straightened up, not moving away from me, flipped her dress up over her head and somehow the knife flew out and embedded itself in the table, quivering alongside my revolver. Some other white undergarments flew up and floated down, and when she turned, her body, golden brown in the candlelight, was nude except for stockings reaching up to full, firm thighs and held there by white garters.

"Now, you help me."

50

I could scarcely breathe as I rolled and slipped the first stocking from that incredibly smooth skin. And when I managed to take a breath and slowly roll the other down, my erection was both obvious and painful. She pulled my head over to her bare stomach, pressed it to her and then let her hand slide down the side of my face slowly, past my tie and shirt and touched the tip of that burning, iron-hard flesh. I groaned audibly and said hoarsely, "I have too many clothes on."

"Yes," she said, and stood back.

My clothes came off quickly too, all but the tight trousers. I had to unbutton the fly all the way to get out of them and I was hoping that she would not laugh at me, for I was still young enough to want to be thought a man of the world, full of savoir faire and such nonsense.

I tried to get up off the narrow bed, but she pushed me back down gently, then, kneeling above me, reached downward and with sure, firm fingers, guided my burning member into her. I took her cupcake-shaped breasts in my hands, letting the raisin-colored tips slide up and down against my palms, but then she was moving so furiously that I had no control left at all. I climaxed and so did she, and as we dug our fingers in each others flesh, all I wanted was to fuse my being with that of the wild, lovely Toña Canela.

But as we lay there on her bed smoking in languid relaxation, she a dark brown cigarette and I a lighter, milder cigar, I wondered if I would be able to accept the bright new world that she envisioned or if I might persuade her to share the more mundane one that I lived in. How our lives, subsequently so strangely intertwined, might have changed, had I—or she—been more tolerant of the other's beliefs and illusions, I will never know.

51

Chapter 6

· · · · · · · · · · · · · · · · · · · ✈

I plunked the heavy bag of gold—now containing five thousand dollars—onto the top of James's desk.

"The ransom money will not be here in time," he said, ignoring the canvas bag. "How can I explain that to the bandits?"

"Revolutionaries," I said. "Successful bandits, like these, are either presently or about to become revolutionaries. However," I added in a matter-of-fact voice, knowing that James was on the edge of panic and needed an authority figure, "they will be reasonable. You can send them five thousand when the new instructions get here and then ask them to wait a week for the rest."

"Two weeks," he said glumly, then looked up at me, blinking and said, "What five thousand?"

"A loan from a concerned citizen," I said. "I want a receipt."

"A receipt." He opened the bag quickly, nodding his head reassuringly as he talked. "Of course. A loan from concerned citizens." He dumped the golden coins on his desk and began to stack them.

"Miss Ramírez," he called out, arranging the coins in rows of ten, five to a stack. "See if you can locate Colonel Green on a telephone."

"You will have your money back in three weeks," he said, but it sounded more like a question than a statement. He wrote a receipt on embassy stationery, dated it, signed it and gave it to me. While I watched, he wrote another for his file. I signed that one.

"Count on your money back within the month," James said.

I merely nodded and walked out, whistling. After all, I was young, had a thousand dollars to spare and a wondrous girl.

Memo opened the door for me, closed it after me and then ran around to the other side to get in beside me.

"Maybe you should ride in the back," I said.

"No. That would not be right. You are a major and I a mere sergeant."

"We could change hats," I suggested.

He screwed up his mouth so tightly and crookedly that he looked like a badger about to chortle. "Girls too? I got one twice the size of yours, but I'll trade even."

"Sergeant!"

"Major, calm yourself. I'll throw in my cousin Alicia—as *pilón*. She is ugly, but what a beautiful cook!"

"No, not even with your cousin to boot." I knew that it was no use to pull rank. He had my number. "How do you know that I even have a girl?"

"From Nacho, the bellboy. He knows everything. Is it true that she paid ten thousand dollars in gold for you?"

"She got me for six," I said, strangling with laughter.

"Oh," he said sadly. "Only six thousand. Oh, well, I like that new blonde, anyway. The sexy *gringa* with blue eyes."

Why is it that the wild, erotic dream girls are always a different color or race or nationality?

Memo opened the door for me with his usual flourish. This time when I got out, I kept a hand on it so that he could not close it.

"It is time that you learn to drive," I said.

"Tomorrow?"

"Now."

"You mean today, after lunch?"

I pointed. He slunk into the driver's seat, being careful not to touch the controls.

"You have watched me drive long enough. You know how to start the engine, engage the gears and put on the brake and steer. In short, everything you need. The engine is running. You have fuel for an hour. Go!"

He looked up at me, still badger-faced, but with the sad begging eyes of a hound. He opened his mouth, but before he could speak, I pointed toward the white-tipped volcano and yelled angrily, "Go! Now! Or report to Major Rubio for duty."

He paled, crossed himself, yanked off the brake and, gears grinding, careened down the street. I turned my back in case he was watching through the rearview mirror, then took two nonchalant steps before I could hide behind the enthralled hotel doorman and watch the big, black car lurch down the street, scattering pedestrians like quail.

I sat at a sidewalk table and called for coffee. Four coffees and two cigars later I heard the discordant sound of an engine sputtering a protest at too rich a mixture and an advanced spark. I left a silver peso on the table and went out into the street. My black limousine grew in size and color as I watched. Part of a clothesline was wrapped around a front fender. Its clothes fluttered like signal flags from a battleship. The fender itself was peeled back so far that I could see the tire.

Behind him, but closing rapidly was a horseman and a half a dozen runners. I waved both arms in a stop signal and then leaped to one side. The car slid to a stop a few feet past where I had been standing. The driver's door was flung open and Memo danced out, laughing and shouting.

"I did it, major! I did it. I drive pretty good, eh?"

"You sure do. Why don't you turn around and say hello to your admirers?"

Memo turned, cried out in surprise, "*puta madre!*" and ran for his life. General Obregón once said that there was not one general who could withstand a cannon shot of fifty thousand pesos. I took five pesos out of my purse and prepared to meet the charge.

I gave three pesos to the rider on the theory that a mounted soldier is worth more, a peso apiece to the two speediest of the men on foot, and a handful of change to be split up among four curious urchins.

There was no sign of Memo in the lobby, so I called for Nacho. I said nothing, but made the shrug that in Mexico means, "Well, what is going on?" or, in this case, "Where the hell is my driver?"

"He is hiding in the closet behind the trunks," Nacho said and held out his hand. I shook it and said, "Leave him there until sundown. Then wake me up and let him out. Then, maybe a tip."

"Sure thing, Major Cooper, sir." He saluted and I almost returned it. He had some excuse. At least he was wearing his bellboy cap.

My siesta was over long before sundown. The rap on the door came at four o'clock and was followed by a note slipped under my door. James wanted to see me at the consulate as soon as possible.

"Nacho," I called. "Is that you?"

"Yes, my major."

"Turn Memo loose and ready my automobile."

"Yes, sir."

An hour later I was at the consulate. A shoeshine boy had brought in the message. He claimed to have received it from Doc Jones, the local gringo drunk. James had questioned him but he would neither deny nor confirm and kept asking for a refill.

"At least we have the new instructions," James said. He kept looking at me strangely, as if he were apologizing for something.

"Good," I said. "Pay them off. Get Will back and then find the bastards that kidnapped him and shoot them."

"Someone has to deliver the ransom at midnight to the old Ávalos

Hacienda."

"I know where that is," I said before I could stop myself. When James's eyes lit up, I knew what an idiot I was.

"Great. You have a motor car! You can drive out, making sure that you are not followed by bandits, deliver the ransom and return."

"I like the *return* part," I said.

"Aw, Tell. All they want is the money."

"Exactly. It is common knowledge that I was paid six thousand dollars in gold a few days ago."

"I know. You donated five . . ." He stopped and blinked at me. "You got six?"

"I kept something to live on," I said defensively.

"Of course," James said. "We all gave what we could. I, myself, gave four hundred dollars."

"Good. You can come along with me to pay the ransom."

"The note said *one* man, remember? Besides, the consul must be at the consulate so as to be, ah, . . . available to ah, . . . negotiate."

"All right, James." I did not point out to him that negotiations were over. "I'll be over at eleven to pick up the money."

"I will wait up for you myself," James said, beaming at the admiring throng made up of one secretary, the cleaning woman and myself.

"James," I said, remembering something Will Riley had told me. "You hunt ducks?"

"Yes. That is, I did before the ducks got guns too."

He laughed loudly and was joined by both the secretary and the maid, neither of whom spoke English.

"Lend me a twelve-gauge double?"

"All I have is a new Browning that Colonel Green loaned me."

"Not the semi-automatic?"

"Yes. Five shots as fast as you can pull the trigger."

"Good. Have it and a handful of double-aught buck here for me at eleven."

"Buckshot for a duck gun?"

"You said it, James. These ducks shoot back."

Memo, a first-rate scavenger, had located a carbide lamp, the kind market hunters use at night to shine up the eyes of a deer or even an alligator. The animals react as if hypnotized. Memo had bolted the light onto the intact front fender. It hissed and popped, but it threw a beam nearly a hundred feet ahead.

I passed the pile of stones that had been the gatehouse and parked in front of the lean-to that had once housed the car. The light cut like a sword through the darkness. The moon was changing from old to new and its silvery edge gave no more light than did the stars. The deep black shadows around the crumbling walls could have held a dozen or a hundred armed men.

I left the motor running. My revolver was on the seat beside me, the shotgun on the floor. I opened the door wide and got out slowly, raising my hands as high as my head. I glanced up at the sky. The Big Dipper had pivoted enough to pour coffee onto the North Star. It was midnight.

Hands still high in the air, I pirouetted like a Parisian mannequin before I walked around the car and opened the other door. I took out the two canvas bags slowly and walked into the light. My feet, large as they are, made deep tracks in the sandy soil. I sat the bags down and then lifted my arms high as if to say: "I have done my part, now you do yours."

I turned my back on the canvas bags and walked, again slowly, back to the car. Every sound was magnified. The crickets sounded like an orchestra of discordant violins. My back muscles tensed. There was a smell of wood smoke. I forced myself not to spring back into the car.

I eased in behind the wheel, engaged the gears and made a slow turn. Just as I passed the ruins of the gatehouse, but before I reached the road to Puebla, a group of men on horses blocked my way. I reached for the shotgun but stopped when I saw that they were uniformed.

They had an officer with them, my recent antagonist, Lieutenant Solís. I slipped the revolver inside its holster under my right arm, got out of the car and moved into the light.

"General Cooper?" Solís asked.

"I am only a major now."

"I wish to God that I was a private again, or at the most, a corporal," Solís said and swung down from his horse.

"You do remember me?" I asked, half hoping that he would not.

"Some. You pointed a gun right at my nose. I might have stayed cross-eyed."

"I think not."

"On the other hand, you did not shoot me."

"True," I said, hopefully.

"Therefore, I shall merely arrest you, confiscate the ransom money and take you back to my General González."

"No *ley fuga?*"

56

"Never will you be shot while running away. Unless, of course, you really run away."

"Fair enough. But I no longer have the gold."

"Of course you do. You had it when you left the consulate. We almost caught you there. But that *pinche* motor car runs too fast."

"I delivered the ransom. Just ten minutes ago."

"Who did you give it to?"

"No one. I left it according to instructions."

He took his pistol out, reluctantly, I thought. "You will tell me where it is or I will shoot you."

"You said no *ley fuga*."

"I did. However this will not be the law of escape, but the one of suicide."

"You will suicide me?"

"No. If you do not tell me, you will already have committed suicide."

He cocked his pistol. "I left it back there," I said. "Just past the old gatehouse. Maybe a hundred yards." I did not think he meant to shoot me, but I did not want to test him.

"Out in the open?"

"Yes."

"Did you see the riders leave?"

"No. I saw nothing. I heard nothing."

"No horse. No wagon. Ten thousand dollars in gold. A man on foot would not get very far."

"Not far," I agreed.

"All right. I will ride in the car with you." He thought for a minute and added, "So will Private Bolaños. He has a pistol and has been told to shoot you if you resist. Even if it means shooting me too."

"You are a courageous man," I said.

"No. I am just more scared of General González than of being shot by Bolaños."

I drove back slowly, telling Solís that it was so that I would not outrun the horses again, but in reality, allowing whoever was there time to collect the ransom and get away.

When we drove back past the shed, there were no canvas bags. I got out and pointed out my tracks up to the lighted area to prove that I had been there. But the gold was not there.

"Juan!" Solís bawled. "Get over here." He turned to me. "Juan is a Mayo Indian from Sonora and one great tracker."

Juan trotted up, handed his rifle to Solís and began to sniff around the ground like a hound on a trail. He motioned to Solís and me to move back and crouched down on his hands and knees. He lifted up and walked slowly up to the center, turned and called back: "It has been swept. With a broom, I think. The tracks have been swept away."

"Well, find the *pinche* tracks!" Solís yelled. "Not even a ghost can ride a horse loaded with gold and not leave tracks."

"A ghost," Juan said and crossed himself.

There were rattles and creaking as all the other riders shifted weight to cross themselves.

Solís threw the rifle back to Juan and shouted, "Get the lanterns. Make a big circle and find—"

Suddenly there was an instant, intense and soundless darkness. Moans of terror and supplications to the Virgin of Guadalupe filled the air. Horses caught the nervousness of their riders and pitched and kicked. Solís, frustrated, said, "*puta madre,*" softly, almost reverently, damning the unexpected occurrence. It was the carbide, of course—or rather the lack of it. The pieces of white mineral had finally burnt away in the water, and the change from that unnaturally bright light to a moonless dark night had been terrifying.

"Light the *pinche* lanterns!" Solís yelled.

"Who has the damned lanterns?" someone else shouted.

"Pedro has one in his saddlebag."

"Pedro!" I heard Solís yell again. "A lantern!"

"I cannot, my lieutenant."

"Why not?"

"Bolaños was holding my horse."

"So?"

"He went with you in the machine, while I was peeing. If I had a light, I could find my horse."

"Will someone—everybody—go through the saddlebags and find a lantern!"

"Lieutenant," the hoarse voice belonging to the soldier named Pedro called out. "I know where a lantern is."

"Well, *pendejo*, where?" Solís said, using a favored synonym for an idiot.

"In your saddlebag. Remember when you put one in the left—"

"Look in all of the *pinche* saddlebags," Solís interrupted angrily.

Horses neighed and grew even more nervous as strange hands fumbled in other men's saddlebags. One man was bitten and cursed a

58

horse named Lobo, and the man was cursed in turn by Lobo's owner. Finally a coal oil lantern was found, lit and brought triumphantly to Solís.

He held the lantern high in the air and called out to the Indian. "All right, Juan, find the tracks."

That is when it began to rain. Torrentially. The lantern's cracked glass hood was leaking. Solís cried out, cursed and then flung the lantern against an adobe wall. It exploded and we were again in the dark. I could understand his frustration, for the rain would wash out any trail in a few minutes.

"Pedro," Solís said in a normal voice, "find the lantern in my saddlebag. It has a bottle of *aguardiente* in the right one. Light one and bring me the other." He reflected for a long second and added, "Light the lantern."

We waited inside the car until another lantern was lit. Bolaños tried to get back inside, but Solís would not let him in.

"You get the lantern and lead off. We will follow you in the motor car."

And we did. Between pulls on the *aguardiente*, which tasted a lot like Johnny Ávalos's Armagnac, we talked about the ransom.

"My General González will be very angry that I missed you—and the gold."

"But you got to me as quickly as you could."

"True," he said, a note of hope in his voice. "It was the fault of that *pinche* Captain Rubio. He should have told me earlier."

"Jorge Rubio?"

"Yes. Jorge Rubio."

How, I wondered, had Rubio known?

We drove back to the city, changing gears to match the walk or trot of the horsemen. The general's house was easily as big as the one that held the procurement offices. There was a light in a downstairs window, but not one elsewhere. Two soldiers protected by a roofed-in patio challenged us. They recognized Solís and scurried back to their dry corner.

"What should I do?" he asked.

"Come to my hotel in the morning. We will have breakfast and then I will come back here with you and explain that I was instructed by my ambassador to pay the ransom and do absolutely nothing that might endanger the life of vice consul Willard Riley. That is why I left the consulate early."

"Early! You will tell the general that you left early?"

"Why not? You did not shoot me. Neither will the general shoot me—or you."

"I will do it." He stuck his head out the window and bellowed, "Pedro!"

"Yes, my lieutenant." Pedro's normal voice was as loud as the lieutenant's bellow.

Solís shrieked, then said angrily, "Do not sneak up on a man like that, Pedro. Now, take a lantern and guide the major back to his hotel."

He found the handle and twisted it open. He turned to me and said enviously, "What an invention is a motor car! You don't have to unsaddle it now and walk it cool nor give it a rubdown. No hay or oats and water. It does not eat too much gasoline and bloat or blow its stomach up so that the cinch slips later on. It does not kick or bite. *Puta madre!* I would like to be in the motor car cavalry."

"That is the future," I said. "In the great war the machine guns and barbed wire did away with cavalry charges."

"Same here. I was with Villa at Celaya. Obregón sat behind barbed wire with machine guns and fed us lead. Then he let his cavalry loose. He is one smart general. I left my little black mare, Lolita, screaming in that *pinche* barbed wire."

"But if you were with Villa . . ." I let my words trail off. He knew what I left unsaid.

"They did not shoot me because I was just a plain soldier. Not even a corporal."

"So you volunteered to be an *Obregonista.*"

"Like you, major, I decided not to commit suicide."

"And now you are with González."

"I came to Puebla to see a girl. Rubio heard I was a soldier and volunteered me. Then some *cabrón* found out that I could read and write so they made me a lieutenant. I would rather be a plain soldier again."

"Did you get leave from Obregón to come to Puebla?"

"Who knows?"

"Maybe you are still Obregón's soldier."

He shrugged. I supposed that it did not make any real difference. González controlled Puebla and, even if he were an Obregón ally, if he decided to shoot a man who might have been with Obregón, who would protest?

The downpour had obscured my celestial clock, but the earthly one in the hotel lobby chimed three just as I entered. I reached past the dozing night clerk, speared my key ring from its nail and trotted up the stairs, yawning, my eyelids heavy with sleep. I pushed my key into the lock and twisted. It turned, but did not unlock the door. I shook the door, jiggled the knob and cursed the key, the door and the hotel.

Then the door swung open and I was looking into the tiny muzzle of a diminutive automatic pistol.

I took an involuntary step backward and lifted my hands to my shoulders.

"Tell! God, am I glad to see you. Come in quickly, out of the light."

I could not yet see the face that went with the pistol, but I knew the voice well.

"Hello, Willy," I said. "When did they let you go?" I stepped quickly into the dark room and shut the door behind me.

Chapter 7

· · · · · · · · · · · · · · · · · ✈

The electrical plant was not yet working, but the night light, a gas jet, was lit. The curtains were drawn. I turned the gas up to see Riley. His eyes, outlined by dark circles of fatigue, seemed even more deep-set than before. Although his face was waxen, there were red splotches of color on his angular cheek bones. And there was the ear. The right one looked as if it had been cropped by a careless veterinarian working on a boxer dog.

I let my eyes linger on the ear. He covered it quickly with his cupped right hand.

"How are you?" I asked, inanely.

"I have been beaten, starved, threatened with constant death and my ear has been hacked off with a machete."

"A machete!"

"It felt like a machete. Maybe it was a Bowie knife or one of those long cane knifes they all carry."

"They?"

"You know. The revolutionaries. Or bandits. I do not know." His voice cracked and his mouth kept moving after he had spoken, but no sound came out.

"Sit down, Willy. You're safe here."

The bedsprings creaked as he took his hand away from his ear long enough to hand me his little pistol. Out of habit I released the magazine and snapped the action back to eject the round in the chamber. There was none.

"They gave you the pistol back," I said, "but they did not charge it for you."

"What? Oh, the pistol. Yes, they gave it back. I suppose they did. I cannot remember."

I found my last bottle of cognac under the night table and brought it out. I poured him a half a water glass of the dark brown liquid. He took it in his left hand and drank it down like so much water.

He moaned and then swung his feet up on the bed and propped his back against the headboard. He held his glass out for more cognac and then began to talk in his normal voice, but speaking unnaturally slow as if mulling over each word.

"I was walking home a week ago, I think, when masked men with guns like yours accosted me. They forced me into a carriage, blindfolded me and took me for a long ride."

"How long?"

"An hour. Perhaps two."

"And when they released you?"

"They moved me. Several times. Then I was taken out and blindfolded again. They pushed me out of a carriage, still blindfolded, and clattered away. When I yanked off the dirty handkerchief from my eyes, I was alone, standing in front of the Tres Gaviotas. I was afraid to go in, so I walked here."

"How did you get into my room?"

"I picked the lock," he said, smiling proudly. "It was easy."

"A regular Jimmy Valentine."

"I did not learn to pick a lock from short stories."

"No?"

"No, indeed. Had it not been for my mother I might have been nothing more than a petty thief. Our neighbors mostly were and I learned from them. My father was a thief too, but he called it politics."

"Your father was a politician?"

His eyes were closed, but he answered me. "He was almost an alderman once. What he did was run errands, deliver bribes and get the vote out. He really was a just a petty thief." His eyes snapped open and blazed with passion. "I will never be a petty thief!"

"Of course not," I said soothingly for he was at the edge of hysteria. "I had better run over to James's house and report you safe."

"No. Let them wait. I have had a rotten time, Tell, and I must sleep, but I will not be able to sleep unless you stay here with me. I must have rest before I meet James and the others."

"What others?"

"You will see. There will be others."

His eyes closed. Within seconds his head fell to one side, his mouth opened slightly and he slept. When I eased him down and gently stretched him out on the bed, he murmured, "Mind the ear."

I rolled up in the other blanket on the floor knowing that I would not be able to sleep. The next thing I knew, the sun was shining through the cracks in the window drapes and someone was hammering on the door.

I was on my feet in an instant, pistol in hand. Riley sat up in bed and clapped his hand over his ear.

"¿*Quién vive?*" I challenged the person outside the door.

"Lieutenant Solís."

"Who?" Riley whispered in alarm.

"It's all right," I said softly and then spoke again to Solís. "Give me a minute."

"Of course, hombre." I heard a low chuckle. "If your lady friend is shy, I could wait for you in the restaurant."

"You have good ears," I said to Solís and then spoke again to Riley, whispering this time. "He is a González man, but harmless, I think, when sober."

"Is he the drunken officer that pointed a pistol at me?" Riley said loudly, indignantly.

"The same."

"And he is a González man?"

"Yes, but—"

"It is all right," he said assertively. "I know the general. What does the lieutenant want?"

"He's in trouble concerning your kidnapping," I said. "I thought to help him."

Riley laughed. "You are unique. Sure. Can we have breakfast first?"

"Thank you, Mister Riley," Solís said through the door, in Spanish, but pronouncing the English word without accent. "I will wait for you downstairs in the restaurant."

Riley was clean shaven. I discovered why when I tried to shave with my safety razor. The blade was dull and full of red hair. I took the blade out, honed it and re-lathered. While I shaved, he rummaged through my clothes. My socks reached his knees. So did my cut-off summer underwear. He doubled the cuffs of both shirt and trousers several times and then pinned them in place. We left the stud out of the shirt collar and cinched up the tie. I threw his bloody coat and trousers into a waste basket.

Solís stood up when we reached his table. He saluted me and shook hands formally with Riley. He placed a chair for Riley and would have helped me to my chair, but I sat down too quickly.

Riley ordered coffee and toast.

"*¡Hombre!*" Solís exclaimed. "Did they feed you so well that you are not hungry?"

"No. Only a few dry tortillas and water. I am hungry all right, but I think my stomach has shrunk."

"Allow me," Solís said and ordered a rancher's breakfast. It varies

64

from area to area, but is invariably a huge meal. This one started with slices of mango and papaya followed by a large plate of dried, shredded beef cooked with chile and egg, a pot of black beans flavored with epazote and an endless supply of thick white-corn tortillas. There were four different kinds of salsa, each hotter than the other, and the coffee cups were refilled constantly.

I ate ravenously. I had missed two meals the day before. Then I thought of Riley. My God! A week of dried tortillas and water. I spooned the mixture of beef, egg and chile from my plate onto his and motioned to the waiter to serve him more beans. The waiter shrugged helplessly as Riley's bowl was still full. Then I realized that Riley had more food on his plate than either I or Solís.

"What's the matter?" I asked. "Too much chile?"

"No. Not at all. It is very good. Delicious." He filled his mouth and chewed grimly. He had that tenacious look that I later came to know too well. He chewed and swallowed, not speaking a word, until he finished all of the food on his plate. But by then he was sweating and pale. Too pale. Suddenly, he jumped to his feet, and with one hand holding his napkin to his mouth and the other clapped over the bandage on his ear, he ran toward the men's toilet.

"It is nothing," Solís said. "I have seen it happen many times. A man goes without food for too long and then eats too much too quickly and . . ." He made a graphic gesture that not only conveyed his meaning perfectly but stopped me from finishing my own breakfast.

"I suppose so," I said. I could not remember such a case from my own experience, but then I had fought in a different kind of war. We were, of course, killed just as dead and sometimes horribly, but we lived in warm, dry quarters, slept between clean sheets, ate fine French food, and the bar was never closed.

"Have you often gone hungry?" I asked.

"I was born hungry. Only when I fill myself with *aguardiente* does my stomach relax and say, 'Okay, Juan, you are now drunk. You do not need to eat.' "

"*Aguardiente* always makes me hungry."

"Me too. But if I do not give in right away the urge leaves me. It is a matter of will power."

Riley came back to the table as if nothing had occurred and sat down. He finished his coffee.

"How are you?" I asked.

"My ear is bleeding."

"Come on, I'll take you to a doctor."

The waiter brought me the bill, but Solís took it from me, glanced at it casually, wrote in a tip for more than the entire bill and signed it with a flourish.

The waiter rolled his eyes, despair written on his face.

"Do you always sign bills here, Lieutenant Solís?" I asked.

"I sign everywhere. One thing about my General González, he lets us sign for all our bills. Of course," he added sadly, "we don't get paid."

I caught the waiter's eye and nodded at the bill. He understood immediately that I would pay and thanked Solís profusely. "Hey," Solís said on the way out, "I like this place. Good service. Some cafes, the waiters don't even say thanks. Sometimes they even curse!"

I believed him.

Memo was waiting with the car. His eyes bugged out when he saw Riley, and, although he glanced quickly at the bandaged ear, he did not stare. "Today I drive," he said. It was not quite a question, but neither was it a statement.

"Yes," I said. "You are the driver."

Before I got in, I told Memo to take Riley to the nearest surgeon, Doctor Calderón.

"But the Colonel Rubio says for the three of you to meet him at his office."

"Colonel Rubio!" I said.

"The three of us?" Solís said.

"Yes, sirs. He is now the Colonel Rubio, and General González told him to talk to you, lieutenant. Also, he knew where the Mister Riley was, and he said to bring him as well."

"The colonel can go to hell," I said. "Take Señor Riley to the doctor."

"Never mind," Riley said matter-of-factly. "González has spies everywhere. He even had a man on Carranza's own staff." A note of admiration crept into his voice. "And that is when they were like brothers."

"To see Rubio, then?"

"Yes," Riley said as he got into the car.

I led the way into the procurement office, but neither Rubio nor Toña was there. Her secretary, who was back typing at his regular speed of about a word a minute, ignored me. Solís put the corporal's tie into the ink roller and wound his nose down into the half circle of the typewriter's printing typebars. Thus the corporal became cooperative and told us politely, if in a muffled voice, where to find Rubio.

We found a beautiful old mahogany door with a freshly painted legend on it: *Coronel Jorge Rubio C.* The title was in gold, his name in purple.

A sergeant seated at a desk by the door cocked an eyebrow at Solís and then stood up. "Pardon me, my lieutenant," he said, "but you bear a strong resemblance to an old military *compañero* of mine from the North."

"*¡Flaco!*" They embraced. Solís turned to me and said, "This *cabrón* and me, we hit the wire together in Celaya. If he could read, he would be a general, for he is one *chingón* of a soldier."

Flaco, so called because he was skinny, might have blushed at the compliment—"a heck of a soldier"—but his gaunt face was the color and texture of an old saddle, so there was no way of telling.

"Major Rubio wants to see me—I mean us," Solís said.

"The major is a colonel now. A few minutes ago that civilian major—Ávalos—he came trotting in to see my boss, Rubio, and then they are hugging each other and everybody falls out to hear that we have a new boss, Major Rubio, and he's a colonel besides."

"Tell the colonel that Willard Riley, vice consul of the United States of America, is waiting to see him," Riley, obviously tired of waiting, spoke sharply.

"Of course, my esteemed vice consul," Flaco said. He rapped on the door three times, listened, then opened the door and went in. He came back out immediately, shut the door, knocked again three times and waited. There was an answering rap of three from the inside. Flaco hesitated, then cracked the door open, sighed in relief and opened it all the way, motioning to us to precede him.

The room was immense. Rubio sat at the far end behind a table that looked large enough to have once belonged to the original inhabitants. He was grinning, puffing on a cigar, papers scattered all over the table.

"Cooper, you *cabrón*. Don't you ever make appointments? I am a busy man."

"Sorry. If the bandits would have informed me that they were going to release the hostage to me last night, I might have made an appointment to see the new, important colonel."

I thought that sarcasm dripped from each word, but either Rubio was too thick-skinned or he chose to ignore it. He laughed, and so did Riley, but—I was sure—at him, not with him.

Solís, not taking any chances, did not even smile, but saluted. Rubio waved away his salute and glared at him.

"I would like to explain why we did not inform General González of the ransom payment," I said, and would have continued, but Rubio let his temper show and his voice rose.

"No need to explain anything. If Lieutenant Solís had been sober, the escort would have arrived in time to take you safely out to the Ávalos Hacienda. But you went alone. Bandits might have stolen the ransom. And then who knows what might have happened to the . . . ah, vice consul. Maybe he would have lost the other ear too." Rubio laughed loudly and lifted out of his chair as if to touch the bandaged ear.

Riley flung Rubio's offending hand away.

"Maybe the Señor Riley should let his hair grow," Rubio said, then sat back down, grinning at his own wit.

The only other one to smile was Riley. It was the kind of smile that Fierro, Villa's favorite killer, must have had on his swarthy face when he lined up prisoners, three deep, to shoot them, for economy's sake, with one bullet.

"I'll do just that, *Jorgito,*" Riley said, addressing him as if he were a small child by adding the "ito" suffix that indicates small size or young age. "Perhaps you would be wise to braid yours. It is long enough."

"*¡Hijo de la chingada!*" Rubio's face was bloodless. His hand was on his pistol, twitching. My own hand was under my coat and he had an eye on it. He shouted another obscenity: "*¡Chinga tu madre!*"

"Call General González," Riley's voice rang with authority. "And tell him that you have insulted both the United States of America and Willard Riley!"

Rubio sneered, but to my utter astonishment, removed his hand from the pistol butt and with a pained reluctance, grinned. "Just a little, joke, eh Willard?"

He saved a little face by using Riley's first name, but it was not enough. He turned his anger toward Solís.

"So! You disobeyed orders."

"No, my colonel. I got to the consulate just as the machine left, but we could not catch it. No horse can catch a motor car."

"Did you or did you not provide an escort for the gringo major?"

Solís glanced nervously at me and said, "Yes, my colonel."

"What?" Rubio shouted.

"I brought him back, personally."

"True," I said. "And the search they made for clues was very thorough."

"You looked for clues?" Rubio eyed Solís as if he were a corporal found dressed in a general's uniform.

"Yes, I did."

"General González will be glad to know that," Rubio said ominously. "You are under arrest, confined to quarters until I decide on an appropriate punishment. *Appropriate*," he repeated, savoring the word. It must have been a favorite of General González.

"The American ambassador," I said, inventing as I spoke, "would like to interview him. He suspects collusion. Perhaps the bandits were part of the military itself."

"Shut up, Tell," Riley hissed.

"Interview the *cabrón*, if you want," Rubio snapped. "But I can tell you that he is going to tell me everything that he knows before I have the *cabrón* shot!"

I opened my mouth to protest, but Solís said hoarsely, "Don't help me any more, *compadre*," an old Mexican saying that means, roughly, "Stop helping me down the chute to hell!"

I clamped my jaws tightly together and marched out with Solís on one side and Flaco on the other. Not until we were outside and the door shut behind us did I realize that Riley was still with Rubio. Alarmed, I turned to go back in, but Flaco barred my way.

"Only with the signal," he said. He turned to rap on the door and almost rapped the beaming Rubio escorting Riley out.

He ignored Flaco and flashed a golden smile at Riley, said, "Adios, *Weel*," and went back inside singing a verse from *Adelita.*

"What was all that about?" I asked Riley.

"He likes me," Riley said.

Chapter 8

· · · · · · · · · · · · · · · · · · · ✈

The champagne was ice-cold. There were cases of thick, dark Mexican beer and bottles of French wines and brandy and one lone bottle of Armagnac with a tag on it marked, "For Johnny Ávalos."

The embassy had come up with the ransom money, and those of us who had put up the actual cash had been repaid. To celebrate that, as well as Will Riley's freedom, I had thrown a party. Colonel Green could not attend, but he had sent a dozen cases of champagne. I had ordered and paid for the rest.

A long buffet table had been set up in the far end of the hotel restaurant. It was loaded with Tamiahua oysters, small buckets of crabs from Tampico and platters of the big, right claw from the Moro crab, an accommodating crustacean that, after his claw is removed, obligingly grows another. There were stacks of corn tortillas wrapped in heavy, heat-retaining cloths, yellow local cheeses and white woven balls of cheese from Oaxaca. I had invited all my new friends. Willard Riley, of course, was the guest of honor. His ear had been artfully bandaged, and he seemed to be fully recovered. He was at his best, witty and accommodating to all. He had brought an attractive blonde. He called me over to meet her.

"Tell, this is a New York journalist. Helen Anderson. Helen, Tell Cooper."

She held a hand out to me. I took it to my lips and then, as I released it and straightened up, looked at her closely. She was near my age but seemed much more worldly. Her eyes were blue, constantly darting here and there as if she were afraid of missing something. The top two buttons of her dress were undone, revealing the deep cleft between large, white breasts.

"I knew you before, major, but then you were only a captain. Captain Tex Cooper."

"I hated that name," I said, startled. "You were in France?"

"I did the *Times* story on Raoul Lufbery."

"Oh yes," I said, remembering a tough blonde who drank with the pilots and bedded with some. "I saw the story. Someone had tacked it to the operation's board."

"It was a good story," she said defensively. "Not every one sees things the same way."

I shrugged. "I thought it was a good straightforward account of a fighter pilot as seen by a layman, ah, that is, a . . . woman. Oh, my God," I added quickly. "Did I say that?"

"You did, but I have heard worse. Only don't ask me what." She smiled and seemed years younger.

"I wrote about you once too."

"You aren't the one who started that Cowboy Cooper business?"

"No. Not guilty, although I did use it. Didn't you read the story?"

"I never saw it."

"But it came out in the *Times* just before the war ended."

"I was in the hospital when the war ended. Had been for a spell." I put on my cowboy accent. "Was I a heroic hillbilly?"

"I did not write it like that, and spare me the phony accent. I told the story of a young man who, when his companion's machine guns jammed, stayed by him and fought off his attackers until he himself was shot down."

"But you never interviewed me?" I was startled.

"No. But I knew Jack Lescault. I was his girl."

"Yes," I said, the memories flooding through my brain. "You danced on a table once."

Her laughter was as musical as a marimba. "You are too gallant." Helen nodded at Riley. "I wore a rose and little else, but we were all wild in those days."

Riley did not smile.

"I did visit you in the hospital but you did not recognize anyone then, least of all me. I would have come again, but that was when Jack was flamed. So I bought a case of absinthe and took a leave of *absinthe* for about two weeks, or I would have done another story on you."

"I wish I had read the first one," I said truthfully.

"Cowboy Cooper, the Texas Terror," Riley said.

We laughed together.

"I have a string book upstairs." She knew that we did not understand and added quickly, "You know, a collection of our big stories. The ones that were printed. A bunch of clippings in a notebook."

"Come up to my room and read my clippings. Ha!" Riley said, "Why don't you do a story on me?"

"I have. I sent it out by wire a few minutes ago. But I would love to do another. The real story. Will you give it to me, Willard?"

"I sure will," he said huskily. "What will you do for me?"

"If it's a good story, almost anything."

"Almost anything?" I said and then glanced up to meet Toña's flashing black eyes. She was holding on to Johnny Ávalos, who had evidently paid off his tailor, for his uniform was not only cut from the best material, but fit his slim, athletic figure perfectly.

Helen swung her head to see what had caught my attention and said, "My God! What a perfect couple. The girl is gorgeous. Sultry sex. And her escort is the most handsome man I have ever seen."

"Yeah," I said, playing Cowboy Cooper. "I reckon they is as purty as a picture."

"You got a burr under your saddle, partner," Helen said, smiling at me.

Toña waved then and smiled. She tugged at Johnny's sleeve, said something to him and he also turned, saw me and waved. They came directly to where the three of us sat. Riley and I got up.

"Hey," Helen whispered loudly, "is she your girl?"

"A friend," I said. Then, not quite so angrily, I added, "A special friend."

I took Toña's hand and, awkwardly, brushed it with my lips. I shook hands, then hugged Johnny and shook hands again in the *abrazo* ritual: handshake, pound each other's back, and shake again.

"Lieutenant Antonia Canela and Major Johnny Ávalos," I said formally. "Allow me to present you to Helen Anderson, journalist, and Will—"

"I know the major, and his aide," Riley interrupted. "We have done some business together."

"Business?" I said dully. "Toña is in procurement and Johnny is busy redistributing land."

"Giving it back to its rightful owners," Toña said. "And, Tell, I work for Major Ávalos now."

"Sorry, Helen," I said. "Toña said that—"

"I understand Spanish somewhat," Helen said, speaking fair school Spanish. "I don't talk so well, but I can get a story using my basic Spanish."

Toña held out her hand, and Helen, still sitting, reached for it. They barely touched finger tips. If there would have been a longer contact, I would have expected to see sparks.

Johnny bowed low over her hand and kissed it. "I am Juan Ávalos de la Vega. Please call me Johnny."

"I will, Johnny. How about a story on you?"

"About what?" He seemed genuinely surprised.

"I'll think of something," Helen said, and we all laughed. When Riley, surprising me by his ability in Spanish, explained Helen's comment to Toña, she stopped laughing.

"What was your business with Johnny?" I asked Riley, speaking English so that Helen could follow the conversation easily.

"Well, Tell," Riley said to me as if I were a group of voters and he was running for office, "you might not know this, but I have always been an admirer of Zapata. While an official of the foreign service I could not voice that feeling. I most certainly can and do now, Tell," he paused dramatically, waited until we were all looking at him, and continued. "I have resigned from the foreign service. I can now speak out and declare my wholehearted support for agrarian reform."

"You," I said. "Willard Riley for agrarian reform! Come on. You are even opposed to the Homestead Act in the States."

"That is there and this is here," he said stiffly. "For Mexico, agrarian reform is ideal. I have finally been able to borrow a little money—not much—but enough to help the González group buy the old Ávalos Hacienda so that we can give that land, as Lieutenant Canela would say, back to those that work it. And that is precisely what we plan to do."

"You are quite an altruist, Willy," I said, not believing a word. "What do you get out of it?"

"Very little. Of course, I must make a living. With the modest amount left over after the land purchase, I intend to buy the old sugar mill."

"Let me get this clear," I said, puzzled. "You buy the land, give it back to the workers, then buy the mill and keep it. They bring the cane to you and you buy it and process it and then sell the sugar?"

"Exactly."

"What will you pay them?"

"Whatever the market price for sugar is, that is what they will receive, in cash, for their share. The day they deliver the cane to the mill they will receive cash payment! No waiting for them!"

"I see," I said. And I did. The farmers would take the risk, but no matter how high or low world sugar prices became, Will Riley would make a profit. "But how is that different from the old days?"

"The farmers will own their own land," Riley said reverently. "The Mexican *campesinos* will own the sacred land." He stood up and raised his glass to the room full of people. "*¡Viva General González!*"

Toña raised her glass in answer, but she yelled, "*¡Viva Zapata!*"

The response was a loud and enthusiastic "*¡Viva!*" that could be interpreted as a response to either name. Also, it was politically safe to be pro-González. He was alive, in charge, and rabidly against the remnants of the Zapatista movement.

"Johnny," I said, when Riley was seated again. "You were a cane planter. Who bought the fertilizer, furnished the tools and seed and the draft animals? Who advanced the cash for expenses in the old days?"

"The owners, of course."

"Who will do it now?"

"That will depend on the new owners."

"They will be able to get loans against their land?"

"No, Tell. They are simple people and would be taken advantage of."

"What then?" I asked him. I had heard that the lands would be communal.

"We have plans for agrarian banks to finance the small farmers."

"Then," I turned to Riley, "your only risk would be that the world might suddenly stop using sugar."

"Yes, Tell," he frowned at me. "Now, could we get on with the party?"

"Right." I stood up and spoke loudly enough to override the other sounds. "A toast to my reborn friend, Willard Riley. He is alive and well and has a bright future!"

We all drained our glasses. I refilled mine and held up a hand for quiet and then lifted my glass again.

"To Willard Riley and agrarian reform and, yes, why not, *Tierra y Libertad*!" While it might have been dangerous to shout "*¡Viva Zapata!*" as Toña had, Zapata's slogan—"Land and Liberty"—had become a basic tenet of the Revolution, and all of the generals who had just ousted Carranza claimed it for their own.

"*¡Viva!*" The restaurant rang with the enthusiastic response to my toast just as an uninvited guest, Colonel Jorge Rubio, walked in.

His new rank also included two bodyguards. Two men, who might have been stamped out of the same piece of rawhide leather, followed him. Each scanned the room constantly with cold dark eyes and kept a thumb hooked next to the same model of .45 semi-automatic Colt that Rubio carried. Except, judging by the worn grips and quick-draw belt holsters, they were experienced gunmen.

Rubio marched up to me flanked by his bodyguards. He looked at me and then let his eyes slide all over Helen. He took a deep breath to pull his stomach in and talked in short bursts as he attempted to speak and keep a trim profile at the same time. He failed. He turned from Helen to speak to me.

"Gringo. You have a date with me and my General González tomorrow."

"Be still my throbbing heart," I said in English.

"What did he say?" Rubio looked to Johnny.

"He said that it will be exciting to meet the general," Johnny said quickly.

"Speak Spanish," Rubio said. "Your English is too American for me to understand."

"Try 'son of a *beech*,' " Toña said. "He only knows the obscenities."

His face clouded. He snorted at Toña and then, stepping back to give his gunmen room, looked straight at me.

"Sure, Toña. Maybe I could speak good English if I slept with a *gringa*." He kept his eyes on my left hand as he nodded. "How about it, *güera*," he indicated Helen with his left hand, using a favored Mexican word for a blonde, but his eyes never left me. "You want to have a real man, a macho Mexican?"

The bodyguards now had hands on pistol butts. They knew that I had little choice. In their elemental world it was shoot or shame, beg or die.

Johnny Ávalos saved my life, uncharacteristically, at the very real risk of losing his own.

"Colonel Rubio. You are using highly offensive language in front of the ladies, one of which is a most influential journalist from *The New York Times* who has come here to interview our own General González, who, as you all know, is the probable next president of the Mexican Republic."

The room erupted into a cheer for President González. Riley moved to one side, the better, I thought, to fumble for that toy pistol. Johnny moved away, too, but not, as I thought at the time, to get out of the field of fire but to block one of the gunmen from a clean shot at me. Rubio's fat fingers opened and closed spasmodically, but he did not reach for his pistol. I held my hands up, palms outward, as if to show that I was not going to go for my pistol. Actually my hands were in a better position for the draw from my shoulder holster.

It took long, long seconds for the cogs to turn in Rubio's slow brain, but he finally came to a decision and spoke to Helen in the best English that I had, so far, heard him use.

"You are a periodical?"

He had just asked her if she were a newspaper, but no one laughed. Not even me. I had used up enough of my life at that point.

"Yes," Helen said. "I am a newspaper . . . woman. However, I get so little practice speaking Spanish, would you forgive my bad grammar and let me try?"

"You speak Spanish?" Rubio said, astounded.

"*Sí, mi coronel. Me llamo Helen Anderson. ¿Y usted?*"

"Ha!" Rubio grinned widely. "I am Colonel Jorge Rubio Contreras, at your feet." He took both her hands in his and leaned forward to peer down her bodice.

"Don't fall in, colonel," Toña said.

Rubio straightened up, glaring at her and then at me. "The *güera* speaks better Spanish than you do and she has only a few days here in Mexico."

"She does a lot of things better than I do," I said.

"But I do not fly airplanes," Helen said, groping for the Spanish words.

"Neither does he," Rubio retorted.

"I will. As soon as my company is paid."

"That is up to *your* general." Rubio picked up a glass of champagne from our table and drained it. It might have been mine. "My General González has paid his part."

"What does González have to do with the airplanes?" I said, surprised.

"He has decided to split the cost of the airplanes, but your general has not sent the money yet."

"Obregón is to send you the cash to pay for his share of the airplanes!"

"Listen to me. Maybe you will get smarter, gringo."

"I could say the same for you."

"What do you mean? Speak, plainly, without hair on your tongue!"

"If you think that Obregón would let all that money run through your hands, then you are one dumb imitation of a colonel!" I said, speaking truthfully—with "no hairs on my tongue"—as he had asked. I was much too plain, I saw, unhappily, for we were back to guns.

This time Rubio held his hands up. His men kept their hands on gun butts, but did not draw.

"Never mind, boys. I think my General González will enjoy this

76

big-mouthed gringo's court-martial."

"Court-martial! On what charges?" I could not imagine an accusation against me.

"Be at my office tomorrow at ten, and be on time for a change." He spun around and teetered out, a black and purple Frog King on high heels leaving a small puddle for a bigger one. I had a sinking sensation that I might just be a pollywog in the vacated puddle.

Rage engulfed me. I picked up the glass he had drunk from and hurled it against a wall. The sound of the shattering glass seemed to release not only my tension, but that of everyone else as well. The reaction was an immediate cacophony of music and shouted conversations in English and Spanish. Johnny handed me a newly filled champagne glass. I drained it in two swallows and did not know until much later that he had filled it, not with transparent champagne, but dark, amber cognac.

Although there were still tables of food and drink, the party began to break up. I shook hands goodbye with everyone, but refused those at my table permission to leave until we had had the obligatory *penultimate* drink; the truly last one is the one that you drink and then, immediately, you die.

"What will they charge me with, Toña?" I asked as I refilled glasses.

"I have no idea." She seemed as mystified as I.

"Maybe the shooting?" I suggested.

"What shooting?" Helen asked.

"I was defending the Frog King," I said. I told her about the incident. She took no notes.

"The charge," Riley said, "will likely be malfeasance."

"Mal . . . what?" I asked.

"The misuse of public funds," Helen said.

"What misuse?" I asked.

"There was none," Toña said after Johnny had interpreted for her. "Tell did not even take full commission."

"That in itself is suspicious," Riley said seriously.

"All I did was take a cut for cash and then refuse a commission on the overcharge."

"Overcharge." Riley pounced on the word. "You agreed to an overcharge?"

"Rubio insisted that the estimate include a fee for custom charges."

"Duties on airplanes imported for the government, Tell!" Riley looked at me as if I were a school boy who had misspelled *cat*.

"I have copies of the contract signed by Rubio," I said.

"Where?" Helen asked.

"In the hotel safe."

"Are you sure?" Riley asked. When I nodded yes, he said, "Get them. Now!"

"Nacho," I yelled.

The young bellboy who knew everything was at the table in an instant. I sent him, with a note, to the hotel clerk. He was back in a couple of minutes with a large envelope. I took out the contract and gave it to Riley. He read each word, and twice he asked me to clarify the exact meaning of a Spanish expression. When he was through, he smiled bleakly, but said, "You are covered, Tell, but be careful."

"Could I see it?" Helen asked.

"Sure," I said, handing her the contract and the envelope with the other papers. "Why?"

"I might do a story on the airplane sale. Help me." She tugged at my sleeve until I sat down close to her. She took out her notebook and an automatic pencil from her purse and jotted down notes as I translated the Spanish she did not understand. When she was through, I raised my hand to signal Nacho, but Helen stopped me. "I'll take them back. I want something from the safe myself."

"Sure," I said. "Rubio will not have a leg to stand on, but if he does, I'll skin it, dip it in batter, and fry it, Louisiana Cajun style."

We all laughed, nervously, but we were more relaxed than we had been. And then Helen returned, and the old and deadly mating game began. If I had been gifted with foresight as well as the hot blood of youth, I likely would not have allowed Johnny Ávalos to step in and save my life, but would have gone down fighting. However, my first shot might not have been aimed at that gross parody of a frog, Rubio, but at the handsome lady killer, Johnny Ávalos.

The family musical trio, which had disappeared when Rubio and his *pistoleros* arrived, had come back to their deserted oboe, French horn and piano, and for reasons known only to them, began a Strauss waltz.

I caught Helen smiling at me and asked, "Why?"

"Why not?" she asked and took me by the hand. She pulled me to my feet and led me to the dance floor. She slipped into my arms and, before I realized it, we were dancing. I held her tightly, afraid that I would misstep and crush one of her tiny feet.

"Relax," she whispered. "You are strung as tightly as a wing wire."

I took a deep breath, relaxed my grip and said, "Sorry."

"Nothing to be sorry about. You were close to being shot. Who wouldn't be nervous?"

"It's not that. It must be you."

"Flatterer." She squeezed my hand. "Why did you never dance?"

I looked down into her eyes and raised my eyebrows in a question.

"At the squadron parties. You never danced."

"I don't know how."

"What is it that we are doing, then?" She looked up into my eyes, laughing.

"Dancing! By God we *are* dancing!" I twirled her so quickly that her skirt flared and caught a champagne glass. It fell and broke, musically, I thought, like her laugh.

Toña, dancing with Johnny, swept expertly around the shards of glass. I suddenly felt as clumsy as a bear in a Russian circus.

"I need another drink," I said, releasing Helen. "How about you?"

"No. Not now. Would you like to see that story?"

"Sure. In a bit."

Back at the table, Riley was busily writing on a napkin.

"Are you figuring out your profits, Mister Riley?" Helen asked.

"No, just thinking with a pencil."

"What kind of pencil have you got, Will," I asked, "that writes on cotton?"

"Would you care to dance, Miss Anderson?" he asked, ignoring me.

"Of course," she said, When he stood up, I reached for the napkin, but he stuffed it into a pocket and led Helen off to dance.

I watched Toña and Johnny glide across the floor like one graceful shadow. How I envied him his build and looks and, above all, that infernal self-confidence. That self-assurance with women. With my woman! I slammed my big left hand down onto the table. All of the bottles, full and empty, jumped inches into the air and clattered. Two glasses fell to the floor but did not break.

I was picking them up when Toña and Johnny, the music still playing, came back.

"Is something wrong, Tell?" he asked.

Yes! I wanted to shout. You are what is wrong, you goddamn handsome lady-killer! What I said was, "No. It was just clumsy old Cooper at work. Care for a bubbly?"

"No," he said.

"No," Toña said, adding, "You have had enough too, Tell. Come and have a coffee with Johnny and me."

Johnny and me. Come along with Johnny and me!

Then she turned to him and asked, "Okay, Johnny?"

Johnny. She might as well have said "sweetheart" and been done with it. I was unreasonable, I know, but it is a sweet torment that lovers seem to seek.

"No, Lieutenant Canela," I said. "I would not intrude on a tryst, not even in order to sober up."

Johnny laughed, but when he looked into my eyes, he stopped. "It is just for coffee, Tell. Come along."

I weakened and would have agreed, but now Toña was angry.

"If Major Cooper would rather drink and dance with his blonde countrywoman, let him!" She spun around and flounced away.

Johnny looked at me, then shook his head sadly and followed Toña.

I was trying to pry the cork from a new bottle of champagne when Helen and Riley came back to the table. She picked up her purse, shook her head ruefully and said, "Great party, Tell, but too much champagne."

"Right." I stood up unsteadily. "Let's go see that story now. The one about Cowboy Cooper."

"*Mañana*," she said.

"Okay." I sat back down heavily. " 'nother drink, Willy?"

"No, thanks, Tell. I will see Helen home."

"But she lives right here in the hotel," I said stupidly.

"Yes, Tell. I know."

I watched them go and then brayed for Nacho. He came running and then left just as fast in search of Memo and my car. Maybe I had another glass of something before Memo arrived.

"Yes, my major." Memo stood in front of me, but he seemed to move in and out of my line of vision.

"Take me to the *Bandida's*."

"The Bandida whorehouse?"

"That very bandit," I said, lurching to my feet.

"Sure," Memo said. He slipped my arm over his shoulder and helped me. We went up a lot of stairs and then he helped me into a room. My room.

"This is not a whorehouse," I said, and fell onto my bed into oblivion.

Chapter 9

· · · · · · · · · · · · · · · · · · ✈

The worst of hangovers is either that brought on by an excess of champagne or the one occasioned by an offended morality. I had both. I could not bear to think of my behavior the night before nor dwell on what Toña and Johnny might have done—no, very likely did. I finally dressed, but I had trouble with all of the buttons that somehow seemed larger than the button holes.

I was on my way to the dining room, my mind set on hot chiles and ice-cold beer, when the soldiers stopped me. One of them told me, respectfully, that I was to report immediately to his Colonel Rubio.

Puta madre! I thought. Goddammit, the appointment with Rubio! My brain wobbled from one thin wall of agony to another. The threatened court-martial!

"Let me just drop off my room key," I told the soldier and hurried to the desk. I spoke quickly, in English, to the clerk. "Call Riley at the consulate and tell him to hurry to Rubio's office and give me the papers from the safe."

"There are no papers left in the safe."

"Of course there are. I looked at them last night."

"Colonel Rubio came back for them," he said sullenly. "He confiscated them for evidence."

"How could he know about them?"

"He has spies everywhere," the clerk said angrily. "Maybe one of them told him."

"I'll bet on it," I said.

The soldiers would not let me call for my car, so we walked. About halfway there, Memo, breathing hard from his run, brought me a cold beer. I stood in the middle of the intersection and drank it. I could almost feel blood being pumped through my body and, more importantly, into my brain.

"Find Colonel Hernández and tell him I am in trouble with Rubio and need his help."

"Yes, sir." Memo saluted, but he did not wait for my usual wave of dismissal, and left at the run.

Twenty minutes later we were in Rubio's office. This time the door was open and I saw him pacing up and down the hallway.

"You are late."

"I was on my way when the soldiers arrived," I said, looking to them for confirmation.

"Yes, my colonel, he was on his way," one of them said, looking at me sadly.

"Then you *cabrones* were late," he said. The soldiers said nothing, but their eyes flashed hate. They did not answer, realizing, as I did, that it was not a real question.

"We could have been here a half an hour ago," I said, "if you had allowed me to use my motor car."

"That vehicle has been confiscated," he said, in good humor again.

"Why?"

"All of your property is confiscated because of mal . . . mala . . ."

"Malfeasance?" I asked.

"Yes. That one. And we caught you at it."

"Who are the *we* that caught me?"

"Toña and me."

"No. Not Toña."

"*Teniente Canela*!" He yelled. He nodded at the soldiers and they herded me into the big office, over to his desk. Toña came over slowly, from the other side. She would not look at me.

"Is it true, Toña? Did you say that I misappropriated funds?"

"No. Not that. But you did the other."

"The other?"

"You told that blonde all about our plans. Secret plans. All night long you told her. I know you did."

"I must be guilty of something," I said, hurt rather than angry. She avoided my eyes. "Are you going to bother with a court-martial to find out what, or just shoot me?"

"Why not?" Rubio said. "We don't have to have the *pinche* trial."

"No. He must have a fair trial. Remember?" Toña said. Rubio shrugged but did not say no.

"Thanks, Lieutenant Canela," I said. "It is comforting to have a friend in court."

Rubio simply could not keep from grinning. He tried to impose an impersonal, wise, and stern but benign look upon his features, but he could not suppress the grin. He must have thought that he would never again have such an enjoyable time.

They sat me next to the corporal. He nodded hello, sat his old typewriter down onto the floor and produced a notebook. He would be

82

the court reporter. Rubio and Toña sat facing me, a long narrow table between us. There was a bottle of mescal, salt bowl and cut limes in front of Rubio.

The corporal swore me in and then sat back down, his pen poised.

"Do you admit your guilt?" Rubio asked formally.

"What is the charge?"

"Mal ..." Rubio gave up. "You tell him lieutenant."

"Malfeasance," she said.

"What happened to espionage?" I asked.

"What? What is that?" Rubio asked, interested.

"Shut up, Major Cooper," Toña snapped. Her voice was angry but her eyes seemed frightened.

"Yes," Rubio agreed. "Shut up and plead guilty."

"Not guilty," I said.

"Yes you are!" Rubio shouted. "Bribery too. You tried to bribe me and then you stole the money I gave you to give to the owners of the airplanes."

"I did not."

"You did too."

"Colonel Rubio," Toña said. "We should have at least one more officer to conduct this hearing."

"Sure. Sergeant!"

Flaco came in on the double and saluted.

"Bring me an officer."

"Which one, sir?"

"Anyone. The first one you find. Hurry."

Flaco saluted and ran out. Within two minutes he was back, a bewildered Lieutenant Solís trotting behind him.

"No, you dumb *cabrón*! Solís is under arrest. How can he be a judge?"

Flaco shrugged, then said, "He was the first one. Besides," he added hopefully, "the *cabrón* can read and write."

"Out!" Rubio yelled.

Solís shot me a look of compassion and scurried out along with his one-time comrade-in-arms.

While we waited, Rubio gloated. Toña, looking as miserable as I felt, sat still, staring down at the table top.

The sergeant was back quickly, a major with him. He was a thin man and wore eyeglasses over soft, reproachful brown eyes. His hair was thin and graying.

"Who are you?" Rubio said.

"I am Major Alberto Meléndez González."

"Major Meléndez," Rubio said sweetly, "are you related to my General González?"

"No, sir."

"Okay. Sit down. Over there, *cabrón*."

Meléndez looked at me apologetically and took the indicated seat.

"You know what you are here for," Rubio said to him, glaring.

"To be court-martialed?" Meléndez said in a small voice.

"No, *idiota*. We are going to court-martial that one, the gringo. What do you do for me?"

"I coordinate the statistics for the agrarian reform. I am a *licenciado* of—"

"Good. Now we can convict this gringo legally. We have a *licenciado*."

Although the title *licenciado* usually means the man is a lawyer, it also means that he might have a degree in some other field of study, such as in the case of the unfortunate Meléndez.

"I am a *licenciado* in economics, not law," he pointed out.

"Shut up. Are you or are you not a *licenciado*?"

"I am, but—"

"No buts. Now, you ask the questions."

"Not I," Meléndez said painfully.

"Yes. You! Now!" Rubio's roar almost blew the economist off his chair. He was trembling when he turned to me.

"Why did you do it?" He glanced at Rubio for approbation, and then continued in a low, hesitant voice. "Have you confessed to something?"

"No. And the charges are ridiculous. I stole no secrets, gave no bribes and pocketed no cash that was not mine."

"Then prove it, *cabrón*." Rubio took over.

"Ah. Yes, ah . . . you, *cabrón*. You must prove your innocence." Meléndez knew a cue when he heard one.

"All right," I spoke to Rubio. "Let me have the receipts you confiscated from the hotel safe last night."

"Sure," Rubio said happily. I knew something was wrong.

The corporal brought me a handful of papers and laid them in front of me. I took a chance. "Careful, hombre. That fresh ink might smudge."

"No, major. I typed these hours ago," the corporal, soon to be a private, said innocently.

84

"I ask the court for a mistrial," I said.

"On what grounds?" Meléndez seemed interested.

"*Licenciado*, these documents, as you have just noted, are forgeries." I permitted myself a small smile. "I rest my case."

"What do you rest it on?"

Instead of answering, I checked the documents. Of course, I had signed a receipt not for the cash that I had actually received, but for the full amount which, of course, included the phony customs charges.

I knew that my employers would never believe that I had stolen money from them, but I did not relish the idea of months in a Mexican jail.

"Witnesses," I said. "I have witnesses who saw the real documents."

"What witnesses?"

I told him.

"No civilians or plain non-commissioned soldiers," Rubio admonished, "but we might call Major Ávalos."

"We could call Ávalos," Meléndez said.

"Get him," I said, relieved.

Rubio banged the mescal bottle on the table. Flaco came at a trot, left quickly and was back in a minute with Johnny Ávalos. He must have been waiting outside. I was grinning from ear to ear. Johnny would not look at me. My stomach heaved.

While Johnny was sworn in, I scanned the documents again. They were badly typed, even for the corporal, with many erasures and smudges. They were all signed by either Rubio or myself with the same awful purple color that Rubio so admired. My signature had been so hastily traced that lines overlapped or did not even meet.

"You have a new pen, Colonel Rubio." I pointed at the large pen protruding from his shirt pocket.

"It is one *chingón* of a pen. It came from New York in the United States. You want to sign your confession with it?"

He held it out to me. It was, of course, purple. I unscrewed the cap and on the reverse of one of the documents wrote a pair of words: Toña Canela. The ink was more purple than lavender. It was the same ink.

"Purple ink," I said, acting impressed. "Did it come from New York too?"

"Sure. Came in from Veracruz yesterday. Give him the confession." He turned to speak to the corporal.

The corporal handed me a rambling document in which I had committed every crime from torturing the last Aztec emperor to

85

shooting Carranza.

"Okay," I said and wrote in ink on the back of the unsigned confession: Jorge Rubio signed all of the falsified documents with pen and ink received two weeks after the true documents were issued to Tell Cooper.

"Here." I threw the confession to Rubio. I cringed, mentally, expecting a deluge of obscenities. All I got was a big toad smile.

"*Licenciado*, ask the witness if these are the same documents he witnessed yesterday," Rubio ordered.

Meléndez did and Johnny mumbled yes. Rubio laughed out loud.

"Major," I asked, "should you not examine them before you say yes?"

Rubio threw them at him contemptuously. Johnny fumbled with the papers but I knew that he was not seeing them.

"Are they the same?" Meléndez asked, looked quickly to Rubio and was rewarded with a smile.

"Yes," Johnny said in a tired voice, "they are the same."

"Okay, beat it."

Johnny looked at me then, his eyes filled with anguish, spun on his heel and almost ran out of the room.

"Major Cooper," Toña said, "I know that the court will allow you to leave the country immediately if you plead guilty."

"I am not guilty of nothing," I said, using the correct Spanish double negative.

"And the blonde. You did not tell her of our order and other facts about the airplanes?"

"No, not anything that is not already printed in our catalogue."

"We caught her at the telegraph office, you know." Toña shook her head sadly. "She was sending the story. Every detail."

"She saw the contract, like everyone else at the table. You were there."

"I," she said icily, "was not in your hotel room."

"Neither was she," I said, "although what difference does that make to you? You were off with Johnny—"

"Enough," Rubio said. "I don't care if he screwed the blonde or not. Or about the secrets. We can only shoot the gringo *cabrón* once, anyway." He found that thought so hilarious that he laughed until he had to stop to gasp for breath.

Meléndez tittered along with Rubio, and he stopped instantly with Rubio. The corporal waited until they both stopped and uttered two sharp barks meant to be laughter. I did not join in, nor did Toña.

"No, colonel," Toña said in her no-nonsense voice, "that is not funny. He is not to be imprisoned, let alone shot."

"No?" Rubio said.

"No!"

Rubio's grin grew and grew. If I were a fly, I thought, I would never get near that mouth. Finally, reluctantly as if loath to break up a lively party, he cleared his throat and said, "The court-martial finds you guilty of all charges and sentences you to be shot tomorrow at dawn."

"No!" Toña cried out. "I vote that he is innocent. Innocent!"

"Write that down. The ex-lieutenant Canela votes that the gringo spy did not do it— except to the blonde."

He had another laughing fit. He was certainly in a good mood.

"The court must also grant a stay of two weeks so that my General González can review the court-martial," Toña said, almost pleading.

"Don't beg," I said to Toña. "He enjoys it."

"No, amigo Cooper. And to show you I am not so bad, I give you the two weeks. Let the general decide."

"Thank you, Jorge," Toña said.

While I did not thank him, I breathed easier. Surely in two weeks someone would get me out of Rubio's clutches.

Rubio rapped hard on the floor three times with a boot heel and the sergeant came in, on the double.

"Take him away," Rubio said, nodding at me. Then he looked directly at me and said, "*Hasta la vista.*"

Spanish is a polite language, so I said, "*Adios,*" but I certainly meant only goodbye and would never have said to him, as he had to me, "until we meet again," unless he meant in hell.

I nodded goodbye to the clerk, who surprised me by not only nodding back, but giving me a smile and wink as well.

"I wish you had stuck to economics," I told Major Meléndez.

"Me too," he said.

Outside, waiting with the sergeant for my escort, I heard the click of high heels and caught a whiff of the perfume that meant Toña to me. The door opened and she came out as uncertain as an ordinary young girl.

"Tell, do not judge me too harshly." She looked at the sergeant who obligingly moved up the hall and pretended not to listen.

"When we came back, you were on your bed, passed out, bright red lipstick all over your face. I was angry."

"Lipstick?"

"He was going to shoot you. I made him promise only to scare you and make that blonde stop writing bad stories about the agrarian reform. You know, the sugar land and mills."

"But what's that to do with me?"

"Nothing, Tell. That's why he'll keep you in jail a few days and then let you go. He'll even give you your money back. And the motor car. Maybe."

"And lose the eighty thousand he plans to steal from Obregón?"

"That he will not do." Her lips were set in that tight line that meant trouble for someone.

"I only hope that he doesn't shoot me anyway."

"No. He gave me his solemn word before God."

"But you don't believe in God."

"No, but Jorge does."

"Jorge Rubio who brags of shooting priests?"

"Yes, but he believes. He made a priest hear his confession once, in Tabasco, and then shot him."

Somehow, I did not find that reassuring.

"He's coming out," the sergeant hissed, and moved quickly to grasp my arm.

Toña looked up at me, her eyes soft and warm. "I have some things to do, including a talk with your blonde, but I will see you sometime tomorrow."

My two soldiers arrived as the door opened so I did not see Rubio come out or Toña go back in. Now that I was officially a prisoner, my hands were tied and I was marched a half a mile to the provisional military prison. It had once been a storehouse for grain. The walls were two-foot-thick adobe bricks. It had two windows, head-high for cross ventilation, and one huge door that could admit a wagon. It had been bolted to the floor, and a smaller door, complete with barred window, had been cut into it.

The jailer took my purse, my penknife, cigar case and match safe. I had two twenty-dollar gold pieces and three silver dollars in my purse.

"Give me a receipt," I said pleasantly, "for forty dollars and please return my cigars and matches."

"Of course, sir. A gentleman must have his cigars." The jailer, a large amiable man with the soft hands of an office worker, slipped the knot in my bonds and then opened the door to the cell for me with the deference of a headwaiter ushering a favored client into the dining

88

room. When I was safe inside and the door locked, he passed my things through the bar along with a receipt and a pen. I signed it, but held on to the pen, asking, "I really need the knife to cut the ends off cigars?"

He shrugged and gave me the knife. I returned the pen and the signed receipt.

I had been aware of a thin man clad in a dirty uniform sitting on a bunk in the cell. He stood up to meet me. He wore the insignia of a staff officer. He reminded me of one of those large thin dogs the Russians use to hunt wolves.

"You are an American from the United States?" His deep resonant voice should have come from someone with a barrel chest.

"Yes, I am."

"Are you here for long?"

"I think not."

"Nor I." He smiled sadly. "I leave at dawn."

"Good," I said, preoccupied with my own troubles. "*Que le vaya bien.*"

"Thank you. May things also go well with you."

I drew a cigar from the case. His eyes followed my fingers and his nose twitched, reinforcing the canine image.

I offered him the cigar. His hand trembled. and reached out involuntarily, but he caught himself, swallowed hard and said, "Do you have another for yourself, sir?"

"Yes." There were four more in the case.

He plucked it from my fingers, bit the end off and waited, cigar pressed between thin lips, for a light. I shook a match loose and lit it for him. He held the first puff so long that I forgot the match and burnt my fingers. I dropped it onto the chaff-covered floor and stomped at it energetically to keep it from igniting.

"How long have you been here?" I asked, after I had cut and lit a cigar for myself.

"Just two days here. I was taken up at Tlaxcalantongo and kept there until I was well enough to be brought here."

"You were with Carranza?"

"Yes."

"Was he killed in combat?"

"He was shot in his blankets. I do not know if he even woke."

"But how was that? Where were the sentries?"

"Traitors and more traitors."

"But I do not understand. If you are . . . were a Carrancista, how is it that they are releasing you tomorrow?"

"Because I am an officer. Forgive me, I am General Pedro Rivera Martínez, your servant."

I introduced myself and asked him to continue.

"Because of my rank, my wound was attended to there, before I was brought here to testify that President Carranza shot himself."

"Oh," I said, trying to keep the disdain from my voice. "That is why you leave tomorrow."

"I am leaving tomorrow because I will not say that. Tomorrow, at dawn, I shall have the honor to give the order to fire to the squad of riflemen that will execute the General Pedro Rivera Martínez."

"You? You are to be shot tomorrow?"

"When I give the order," he said, puffing casually on his cigar.

I tried to think of something to say. Anything at all. I could not come up with one appropriate word. We sat in silence on the one wooden bench and smoked silently. At last I was forced by the proximity of fire to my lips to gingerly remove the cigar butt between the tips of thumb and forefinger and crush it out on a bare spot in the floor. Rivera, by some superior technique, had managed to make his last several puffs longer. Perhaps that is why he was a general. However, I certainly did not envy him the rank that enabled him to preside at his own execution.

I was saved from uttering some inanity to the general when there was a sound of voices, some of which were familiar. Before I could rise from the bench, the door was flung open and Lieutenant Solís, blood trickling from one nostril and one eye almost entirely closed, limped into the cell.

"Lieutenant Solís," I said, standing up, "what happened?"

"I got court-martialed."

"For what?"

"I'm not sure," he said slowly, barely moving his lips, as if he might be afraid a tooth would fall out, "but it must have been serious, for I am to be shot tomorrow."

"You? Tomorrow?"

He nodded yes and said wistfully, "*Puta madre*. How I would like a drink."

The general nodded sympathetically.

"But they can't do that," I said. "You get two weeks so that General González can review the sentence."

"Is that true? Did they tell you that?"

"Yes," I said, relieved. I was sure that in two weeks I could get Solís off.

"The trouble is," Solís said, "that General González is one fast general. He doesn't need two weeks."

"You can't mean that he has already reviewed and upheld your sentence?"

"Yes," he said sadly and cocked his head to look at me out of his good eye. "Yours too. Colonel Rubio is going to give the order tomorrow, personally, to shoot us both."

The shock was worse than diving into an icy mountain pool. I turned my back quickly to mask the tears already forming in my eyes. Tomorrow morning! At dawn.

I breathed slowly, in and out, then expelled the air. Then, wet-eyed, but in a normal voice, I called out to the jailer, "Hey, amigo. I want you to give me a new receipt for an empty purse. We only have one night left and we need a drink. See what you can find."

Chapter 10

· · · · · · · · · · · · · · · · · · ✈

The jailer brought us each a black clay pot with mescal from Oaxaca. It was not as smooth as the kind called tequila from Jalisco, but that night it tasted like fine French cognac. I caught the worm in my teeth and spit it onto the floor. The general deftly caught his between thumb and forefinger and he gave it to Solís, who ate it with as much gusto as a gourmet dining at Delmonico's might eat an oyster.

"Sorry," I said. "I should have given you mine."

"Don't worry," Solís said. "How were you to know that they had not fed me?"

"Rubio is an animal," I said. It is a grave insult in Spanish.

"And González is a beast," the general added.

"I never liked Carranza either," Solís said, cocking his head toward the general. We sat like the three wise monkeys on the narrow wooden bench, shoulder to shoulder, Solís in the middle.

"Still," the general shrugged, "he was the First Chief."

"True," Solís agreed, cocking his head toward the general. "But why did he shoot my General Felipe Ángeles? Ángeles never shot prisoners. Not even the officers."

"What?" I said. "A Villista general who did not shoot officers!"

"My General Ángeles did not. I guess all the others did."

"The First Chief could be vindictive," the general mused. "When López Hermosa, who had defended Ángeles at the court-martial, delivered a message from Ángeles—three months after the execution—Carranza ordered López shot."

"What was the message?" I asked.

"He who lives by the sword, dies by the sword."

"But it was just a message," I said. "Keeping a promise to a dead man."

"Yes."

"And for that Carranza had him shot."

"No. I said that Carranza ordered him shot. A friend recognized López, interceded, and López was exiled to the United States."

"How do you know all that, general?" Solís asked.

"I was the friend."

"I would rather be exiled to the United States than be shot," Solís said, then added pensively, "I think."

We sat quietly for a few minutes, and then both the general and Solís spoke at the same instant.

"The hour?"

I slipped my watch from its pocket where it had gone unnoticed by the jailer.

"Three minutes before midnight."

I did not have to say three minutes before the last day of our lives. They knew as well as I. We had tried to persuade the jailer to get us paper and pen, but he had bought himself a jug of mescal and was sleeping soundly, if drunkenly, with no dread of the dawn.

"Do you have a family, Major Cooper?" the general asked.

"No," I said sadly. "My parents are gone and I have no wife. There is a girl who might miss me."

"That is sad. A good young man like you." He turned to Solís. "And you, lieutenant?"

"I have a girl, right here in Puebla. But she will be all right. My friend Florencio will take care of her. He will let my parents know. They live in a small *ranchería* west of Chihuahua."

"And you, general?" I asked.

"My dear wife will mourn me. I have a son so young that he will not remember me. I have an older daughter who will be heartbroken. I wish that I could write a last letter to them."

"They will surely know how you feel, general—"

"It is surely now past midnight," he said interrupting me. "This is the last day for the three of us. Let me suggest as an older man that we be dear friends, intimate friends, for these last few hours. My name is Pedro."

"And mine, Tell."

"Juan, my general."

"No, compañero Juan. You must call me Pedro and say *tú* to me."

"*Don* Pedro," he said, blushing with embarrassment.

He was able to say Pedro, provided that he put the honorific *Don* in front of it, but he could not bring himself to use the *tú* form, not even with me. So it was *Don* Pedro, *Don* Tell and Juan that sat on that short bench together, taking comfort from our mutual misery; our shoulders, rubbing one against the other, reminding us that we were still living beings with hot blood in our bodies and brains with vivid memories. But in spite of the talk and the jokes—yes, we even joked up until before dawn when the hours changed to minutes—my pocket watch ticked faster and faster and louder and louder. I put it away, but then the cocks began to crow, challenging the dawn.

All too soon the room lightened until a bright shaft of light came through the east window. We rose as one man to look through the small window to the inner patio. Solís had to stand on the bench to see over the sill. The patio was deserted, but we could see the ugly pock marks in the adobe wall where a stray bullet had missed its softer target. I wondered if it was just bad marksmanship or a last minute revulsion at shooting a defenseless man.

"Some of the riflemen always miss," the general said, reading my mind. "I, myself, have had to administer the coup de grâce."

"When he had plenty of time and ammunition," Solís said, "Fierro shot them on the run."

"I could not do that," I said. "I suppose that there must be executioners, but I could not be one."

"You were in the Great War," the general said. It was not a question. We had spoken at length that night about ourselves. "You killed many men. At least eight."

"Yes, but in battle."

"I suppose there is a difference," the general said, not really agreeing with me.

"Sure," Solís said. "*Don* Pedro, I could go easier if I could have a loaded revolver in my hand. And if *Don* Tell would keep his big hand off its hammer."

We smiled at one another and then laughed. A squad of riflemen marched into the patio and we laughed even louder. So loudly that we had to sit back down on the bench. And that is how Rubio found us, arms around each other, laughing until the tears came.

"What kind of *cabrones* are you?" Rubio was amazed.

The general recovered first. I supposed that he had more experience than we in controlling hysteria. He nodded disdainfully at Rubio and spoke to us.

"Shall we, gentlemen?"

We rose together, and I insisted that the general precede us as if we were on our way to a formal dinner. I laughed again, but I was under control and did not even smile when Solís insisted that I be next after the general.

"You *cabrones* been smoking *mota*?" Rubio turned to yell at the jailer, still half asleep, an old serape wrapped around him.

"You buy these *cabrones* some marijuana?"

"No. Never, my Colonel Rubio. None."

"Ha," Rubio snorted, but waved us on.

We moved slowly, but in step out onto the bricked-over surface of the patio. For one long agonizing moment I was sure that I would wake from the too-real nightmare, but I did not. An ugly fear wrenched at my intestines. I was afraid that I might defile myself.

"It will be nothing," the general said, noticing. "Would you like to stand with me while I give the order?"

"No!" Rubio shouted. "First the General Rivera, then Lieutenant Solís and then, last of all, the gringo Major Cooper."

Rubio sounded like a man badly in need of a drink, forcing himself to wait to heighten the pleasure.

"I would like to die with the general," I said.

"Me too," Juan Solís said. "I would be proud to die with you, *Don* Pedro and you, *Don* Tell."

"No," Rubio repeated happily. "I made a promise to my General González to allow General Rivera the honor of ordering his own execution. I am a man of my word, as you know, so I fulfill that promise. But, I made another promise to me, Colonel Rubio, to give the order personally to shoot *Don* Tell." He lisped my name and rolled his eyes, imitating, he thought, one of those born male by mistake.

"You may have the title of colonel," the general said in a loud ringing voice, "but in my army you would not have been a corporal. Now let us get this over with. I am tired of you and your traitor general, González."

"You cannot talk to me like that!" Rubio said, angrily.

"What will you do, shoot him?" I said, complacent, uncaring now, and, like the general, just wanting to get it over with.

Rubio yanked his pistol from his belt. The gold and silver inlay glittered in the early light. He pointed it at my chest and pulled the trigger. There was no explosion. He had forgotten to thumb the safety off.

I laughed in his face, then turned to the general and Solís for approval, but they did not smile. I knew then that each one had retreated into himself. It no longer mattered whether or not we stood together holding hands or died one by one. Each man would have to die by himself. No one could really ease that path or help open that fearful door. I wondered if there were such a door and, if there were, what might be on the other side?

"Proceed, general," Rubio said, returning the pistol to his belt. He carried it well back on his right hip now so that if he did shoot himself, it would be through one of his fat buns rather than a testicle.

Solís moved away from me and stood by the general. I stepped up beside them.

We ignored Rubio's yells and marched to the wall, did a precise about-face and then embraced each other and held hands. With the general in the center, we faced the firing squad.

"*¡Listos!*" the sergeant in charge of the firing squad called out the ready command.

The rifle bolts clicked as each round was jammed into the breech and the firing pin cocked.

"*¡Apunten!*"

The rifle barrels swung up and steadied and my eyes went out of focus. I could not see the muzzles of the modern Mausers pointing at my heart, but I could hear the slightest sound, even my watch ticking away in its pocket.

"No," Rubio interrupted. "Stop. Get the other two out of there."

The blurred firing squad became a group of individual soldiers. My legs began to dance. I could not keep them still. The sergeant understood and held me tightly by the arm and whispered that I would not be shot. Behind me, Juan Solís was led away. He walked easily with no apparent change. I wondered if he were still in the world that I had just left and almost yearned to return, but the reality of the reprieve wrenched me back into the real world.

"Now, General Rivera," Rubio said, "the squad awaits your order."

"Tell, do you have one of those fine cigars left?"

"Yes, General Rivera. I do."

"Might I smoke one?"

"Of course."

"Sure, General Rivera," Rubio said. "Show the gringo how a Mexican dies."

I took out the case and let the last one fall into my hand. I cut the tip off, handed it to Rivera and, after he sniffed it and rolled it between thumb and forefinger, lit it for him. He puffed on it three times and then, holding it casually in one hand, snapped out the orders.

Before they had been typically indifferent civilian soldiers. Now they snapped to his command like Prussians.

"*¡Listos!*" They were all experienced soldiers and knew, without a doubt, that their rifles were loaded and cocked, but to a man they ejected the old cartridge and seated a new one.

"*¡Apunten!*" The rifles snapped into line at the same second.

"*¡Fuego!*"

The volley was as one very loud shot. I think each one struck him. He dropped like a puppet with its strings cut, blood spouting from his chest. Not one bullet had marred his face.

Rubio strode over to the fallen man, peered down at him and holstered his pistol.

"That is the best shooting you *cabrones* have done this week," he said. Rubio meant it as a compliment to a Mexican general who knew how to die.

"And now," Rubio said, "we shoot the other two."

Ambrose Bierce's best story was about a man who dreamed of escaping the noose in the instant before it broke his neck. I might have had that dream. I looked directly at the sergeant and willed my voice to be steady. "You killed my friend cleanly. Please do as much for me."

"Hey, gringo," Rubio said jocularly, "wait your turn." He spoke to the sergeant. "Shoot the little one."

"I would rather not," the sergeant said. "We fought together. We shared blankets and *viejas*."

"*Viejas*," Rubio grinned. It amused him that the two had shared women. "Okay. I'll give the order."

Solís walked back to the wall and turned to face the firing squad. He stood a bit unsteady on his feet, peering into the rising sun, his good eye watering.

"Hey, lieutenant," Rubio said. "You want a blindfold for the one eye?" When he stopped laughing and realized that not even one of the soldiers had joined in, he called out angrily, "Okay, ready!"

Suddenly there was a sound of boots and a door banging, and then a large gray-haired man ran into the patio. He called out angrily, "Stop. Put the rifles down. Now!"

It was Rodolfo Hernández, wearing the stars of a brigadier general. He looked quickly at Solís, then saw me. He walked straight to me, ignoring Rubio. "It is all right now. I have an order for your release."

The patio spun around me. I spread my arms out and held on. "Do not let them shoot Solís. He is Obregón's man."

I stumbled then and would have fallen had not Hernández caught me. I held on to him tightly until my vision cleared. The early morning sky was blue now. A blue so intense that my heart ached. I heard the beating of each separate wing of a dragonfly somewhere near, and the sweet mixture of wood smoke and tortilla aroma filled my nostrils. I could stand by myself, I decided, yet when I looked for someplace that I might sit, there was none.

"I have an order to shoot Major Cooper," Rubio said. "It is signed by a major general. My General González."

"And mine is signed by my General Alvaro Obregón."

"General González will likely be the next president of the Mexican Republic and I have his written order."

"So do I," Hernández said and thrust a paper at Rubio. "Put down those rifles!"

The soldiers lowered their rifles. They did not bother to safety them, but stood waiting, stolidly, for the officers to make up their minds. Solís had backed to the wall and was leaning against it.

"This is signed by my general," Rubio finally said, after lip-reading every syllable, "but it does not mention the other *cabrón*, Lieutenant Sol–"

"It does not have to, *burro*. It is enough that I reclaim this man, Solís, for General Obregón. Or would you like to tell González that you shot his companion, and now Obregón's favorite lieutenant?"

"*¿Compañero?*" Rubio was as surprised as I. It was common knowledge that the generals hated each other.

"The senate and the *diputados* voted yesterday for a new provisional president. De la Huerta got 224 votes, but your General González could only gather 28. So until the regular elections are held, we are all *compañeros* under De la Huerta, and, you hollow-headed idiot, you should know that my general, Alvaro Obregón, will one day soon be the president of Mexico!"

While Hernández talked, Rubio had gradually come to attention, and, except for his protruding belly, was ramrod straight, staring stonily straight ahead.

"Lieutenant Solís," I called out loudly. "Juan! It is over. Come here!"

He turned his head dreamily to stare in my direction. I was sure that he heard my voice as he might a half-forgotten piece of music that he could no longer identify. My legs were still unsteady, but I walked over, took him by the arm, and led him back to life.

Hernández stared at Rubio for a long minute as if he were examining a horse that he might buy, then shook his head as if he had discovered a disqualifying defect and said loudly, "Dismissed."

Rubio saluted. Hernández returned the salute and then, glancing at the body sprawled on the brick floor, snapped out an order. "Have

General Rivera's body attended to immediately and interred as he desired."

"He was not allowed pen nor paper to write a last letter," I said. "A man should be able to write a last letter."

Rubio turned to go, but the steel in Hernández's voice brought him back.

"Why was he not given pen and paper?"

"I guess that stupid jailer could not find any."

"Do you not keep written records for the jail?"

"Sure. Anything that Obregón does we do better."

"Naturally. Like racing horses."

Rubio's teeth clicked shut. González was sometimes called General Racehorse by his detractors. González was known for his proclivity to precipitous and rapid retreats.

Hernández spun on his heel, leaving Rubio gulping for air like a voiceless toad. I followed quickly, still leading Solís by the hand.

My car was parked outside. I looked at the doors quickly, afraid that Rubio's name would be painted in gold leaf. It was not.

Hernández had also arrived in a motor car. He patted me gently on my arm, then pulled Solís, unresisting, from my grasp. "He will be safer with me. I will see you later, Tell."

I nodded numbly and someone, Memo, I thought, opened the back door and helped me inside. I felt a soft thigh as I slid into the seat and saw I was next to Helen Anderson. Next to her, Riley, grinning wolfishly, talked loudly about something I did not understand and waved a paper at me. I leaned back, the excited bursts of conversation washing over me as soothing as warm water, and I closed my eyes. I was asleep instantly.

Chapter 11

· · · · · · · · · · · · · · · · · · · ✈

Only vaguely, as if flying through a thick, white cloud, do I remember being half-carried up to my room, and then helped out of my clothes and into bed. I slept through that day and night and woke to a clean, new dawn. From that day on I invariably rose with the sun, watched it light the world, remembered, and was a much humbler man.

That morning I stopped hating Rubio as a man. I thought of him as a poisonous reptile. One with a tremendous ego. Even when Riley formed his infamous alliance with him, I understood Riley's reason. Also, when I did have to deal with Rubio, hate did not cloud my mind. It gave me a big advantage, and Rubio, somehow understanding that, hated me even more—so much, that later, when he might have ordered me killed, he did not. Although it might have been fear of Will Riley, I thought that it was because he had not yet been able to revenge himself of all the wrongs he fancied I had done to him.

I bounced down the stairway that morning listening to the songbirds just outside the open stairwell, whistled back at them and went in to breakfast smiling.

Across the room, sitting alone, Helen Anderson waved at me and indicated a chair. I hurried over and kissed her on each cheek in the French manner and then sat down. Among Mexicans, the custom calls for a single kiss on the right cheek.

The ashtray by her coffee cup was full of half-smoked cigarettes.

"Have you had breakfast?" I asked.

"No. I have been waiting for you." She reached across the table and placed her tiny white hand over my big, rough brown one. "You look so much better."

"I am great," I said, not able to stop smiling. "Just great."

I spotted the old head waiter, the one that had helped me prepare the dinner for Toña. I waved at him, but he made the pinched thumb and finger sign at me that, in theory, means "wait a minute."

Had Helen been a foot taller and twenty pounds heavier, she could easily have passed for a Minnesota Swede on her way to help her brothers stack hay. Her hair was so blond that it was almost white. She would have been what we called a tow-head when she was young. Her cheek bones were high, but her face was more flat than angular, and her eyes, while as blue as a northern sky, had an odd oriental cast to them. I learned later that it was a trait passed on to her by her Finnish mother.

"Well, Major Cooper, will I pass, or must I also be inspected by the regimental veterinarian?"

I tried to be serious, but I could not change my wide and foolish grin.

"Open your mouth," I said.

She did.

I cocked my head, reached over and tilted her chin slightly with my fingers and said, "Not bad. Still a lot of wear left." I leaned closer yet and then brushed my lips to hers. Her lips were soft and sweet from lipstick.

"Why did you do that, Tell?"

"I guess just to get even. You kissed me, that night after the party, no?"

The delicate blue veins in her neck disappeared in a pink flush. She looked down at the table.

"I came into your room to give you the receipts back. I swiped them. When Willard left, well, I peeked in to see you, but you were . . . asleep."

"Passed out," I said. "But you did kiss me?"

"Yes, she said defensively. "I did."

"More than once?"

"Tell!"

"All right, sorry. But if it was because of what I did for Jack, you didn't have to kiss me. Anyone of us in the *Escadrille* would have done the same."

"That, you obtuse Texas cowboy, is not why I kissed you twice. Now, may I order breakfast?"

I picked up a menu. "Sweet tamales," I said, and I thought to myself, "She kissed me, twice!" I laughed aloud.

"What is so funny?"

"Sweet tamales and chocolate," I said. "For breakfast."

She looked at me quizzically and then, smiling, said, "I never could understand juvenile humor."

"Me neither, mam. Then it will be sweet tamales for you, hot for me, and chocolate beaten to a veritable froth for both?"

"Could we have coffee first?"

I signaled a waiter with a coffee pot in his hand and he hurried over. The *café de olla* had been brewed in a clay pot with cinnamon and *piloncillo*, a sort of unrefined brown sugar. It was delicious.

Helen lit a cigarette. In the States it would have caused a furor. A woman smoking in public! In Mexico the ladies had been smoking in public for years. Likely before the Spaniards arrived.

I lifted a hand to call for a cigar and clamped my teeth shut immediately to keep the bile inside. I waited until the wave of revulsion subsided, turned my head away and drank a glass of water. All of it.

"What is it, Tell? You look as pale as death."

"It was the general. The one they shot. I was going to ask for a cigar and I remembered." I described the whole macabre scene to her.

Her eyes softened and misted over. Then she took a small notebook from her purse and wrote furiously for several minutes. She put the little book back and said, "It is over now."

"It most certainly would have been if Memo had not found General Hernández," I said.

"Would that be the little man that was your driver?"

"Was?"

"Is. I mean he wouldn't let them take the car so they beat him. He is recovering from a concussion."

Of course, I thought. He would never have given up our motor car without a fight.

"But then, how did Hernández know?"

"A skinny sergeant with a face cut from an old board came looking for a friend of yours. Someone sent him to me."

"Flaco," I said. "A buddy of Juan Solís."

"Yes. He kept saying that a man named Solís was for Obregón and should not be shot."

"Your Spanish is better than I thought," I said, impressed.

"Nacho helped me."

"The bellboy who knows all the English," I said, smiling, remembering Memo's awed description of the hustling bellboy.

"Then you went to Hernández?"

"No. I went to the consulate. He was gone, but Riley was there cleaning out his desk, I guess. Anyway, he thought he could get González to rescind the order. But the general was away."

"They lied. González countersigned the execution order *before* the court-martial. I really believe that."

"So did Riley, then. He seems to be privy to a great many shrouded events. He is a fascinating young man."

"Yes," I agreed, "but he knows too much about González to suit me."

"Still, you would not be here without him. He located Hernández at eight o'clock on a Sunday morning." Her laugh was like Navajo wind chimes. "I had never been to a mass before. But in we barged, me without a head covering and Riley, who knew better, running down the aisle, yelling in Spanish and waving those papers I had taken from you." She shook her head in disbelief. "An ex-assistant consul in a church yelling at a general!"

"Then Rubio never found the contract."

"He thought that he had. I copied it and gave the copy to the hotel clerk."

"And my signature?"

"I forged it." She looked up at me and shrugged helplessly. "I do things like that sometimes."

"I kiss the hand that forged my name," I said. "Besides, the first thing Rubio did was to destroy the real documents and forge his own."

I was still holding her hand when I heard the shivery, husky voice of Toña behind me.

"Please pardon me. I hate to intrude on such an intimate breakfast. After last night you both must be very tired."

I jumped to my feet and turned, my arms open, ready to forgive. She stepped back.

"Toña. You don't understand. They were going to shoot me yesterday at dawn. There was no two-weeks delay for me."

"I know. I am ashamed. Rubio lied."

Then she did come to my arms, spilling hot tears on my shirt and then on my hand as I touched her cheek and murmured, "Don't cry, little *Toñita*. Don't cry."

"Do you like tamales and chocolate?" Helen asked loudly.

Toña, drying her eyes with the back of a hand, looked to me for a translation. I repeated what Helen had said.

Toña nodded yes and smiled.

Helen said, unsmiling, "Good. You can have mine."

She left before I could stop her. I turned to Toña and said, "That woman, at times, mystifies me."

"Not me," Toña said, sitting down in the vacant chair. "I understand. But I want something else. Not tamales. Before I eat that blonde's breakfast, I would eat snails."

"Snails—escargot with garlic and—"

"Stop. I know. Johnny tried to get me to eat some. But they are loathsome."

"Johnny. Johnny?"

"At work it is Major Ávalos. Outside it is Johnny."

"But—"

"No buts. I don't ask you about the lipstick or the gringa, and you don't ask me about Johnny. Okay?"

"No!" I said. Her lip trembled and her eyes flashed.

"Well, I guess it is all right," I added, "But don't use that other expression. It reminds me of Rubio."

"Okay," she said, puzzled.

"That is the one. For me *okay* is snails."

She looked seriously at me, but her eyes betrayed her as she answered, "Okay."

With no trace of humor in my voice, I called our waiter. "The mademoiselle wishes a special order of escargot for breakfast."

"Tell!" She shrieked. "No. I will never use that word to you again. Okay? Oh, *¡por Dios!* I mean: all right?"

"Okay," I said. We laughed and laughed and held hands under the table until the food came. It was of course hot tamales, spiced with chile, and sweet, pink ones. Toña ate the hot ones.

"Do you know that De la Huerta is the provisional president?" she asked.

"Yes, I heard."

"He is not going to shoot anyone. He said that. Rubio believes him. He says that De la Huerta is a *maricón*."

I winced at the coarse word for a homosexual and thought that De la Huerta must be a real human being.

"No," Toña said, misunderstanding my reaction. "He declared amnesty. Even for the Carrancistas."

"General Rivera was shot yesterday," I said.

"We only got the telegram today."

"If he had only been sentenced to be shot one day later," I said.

"He was to have died today, but Rubio wanted you to see someone die first. He is a pig."

"A venomous toad," I said. A waiter brought me more coffee. I asked for a *piquete* in it.

"Liquor? At nine o'clock in the morning?"

"To settle my nerves. I liked General Rivera."

"But he was a Carrancista!"

"He was a man and I liked him."

"Thcy killed General Emiliano Zapata." Her eyes blazed.

"Well, what about your General González?"

"He is not my general. I am now, officially, an *Obregonista*. Next week, I go to Mexico. Besides, it was really Guajardo who killed Zapata."

"Sure. And I suppose if we go far enough down the chain of command we might find the one soldier who fired the first bullet to explode Zapata's heart."

"All right! It was Carranza, first." She glowered at me. "Anyway, I am going away, clear to Mexico, and you do not care."

"Wait a minute. You mean to stay in the capital?"

"Of course, you *burro*, to stay."

"Congratulations," I said, miserable at the thought. "What is your new job?"

"It is not new, but I can't be an officer any more. I guess I never was really. But I don't care. It is a man's job and I am a woman, but I can do the *pinche* work!"

"Hey, I'm on your side."

She looked around at the other diners and then shook her head ruefully. "I get mad. Anyway, now I do land reform. And we are really going to give the land back to the campesinos. Obregón will see to it."

"But Obregón is not president."

"He will be in six months. Everyone knows that he will be elected president. So we move to the capital."

"Major Ávalos is still in charge?"

"Yes, Johnny too." She smiled so sweetly that I was tempted to wring her lovely neck.

"How about your other dear friend, Jorge? Will the Toad be going along too?" Her face crumpled and I could have torn my vicious tongue out, but it was too late.

"No, not him. Not that I will want for lovers. There are thirty men in the office. I will have to rent a house with a very large bed, no?"

"I am so sorry. I did not mean to speak like that. I have no claim—"

"That is exactly right, *Don* Tell. You have no claim on me. None!" Her eyes flashed dangerously. I wondered if she still kept that thin stiletto hidden in her hair.

"I can only beg forgiveness. I have the sin of jealousy."

"Jealous. You are jealous of me?"

"Yes," I said. "Sorry."

She smiled enigmatically and held her cup out. "Order a *piquete* for me too, Tell."

When the waiter poured a splash of cognac into her cup we clinked them together and drank to our armistice.

"When must you go?" I asked.

"Tomorrow. We have a railroad car loaded with files and furniture. We have an office downtown, just off Juárez Avenue. The soldiers will be quartered in some old house. I will have my own rooms not far from the office."

"Where will major—Johnny—stay?"

"Right here." She laughed at me. "He and Rubio have been allowed to resign from the army. They are all partners now. Johnny and Rubio and your friend Riley. All partners."

"With Rubio? No! Partners in what?"

"You do not know about the *ingenios*?"

"Sugar mills. What about the sugar mills?"

"The three of them made a company to buy sugar mills. They have a concession to buy any non-functioning mill in the area controlled by General González. It is the best sugar cane land in Mexico."

"But the capital. Where will they get the money? Riley spent all he had on the first land deal and mill."

"He is selling shares in his new company. What do you call it when a company is owned by many people?"

"A *sociedad anónima*? We call it a corporation."

"That is it. He will sell shares and rebuild the mills, and when the company is producing sugar, he will pay the government. Not until then will he pay. Just the repairs."

"But," I said, thinking of Riley's perilous financial status, "the repair of a ruined sugar mill could cost a fortune."

"Maybe, but some of the mills I have seen do not need one more thing than some *cabrón* who knows which lever to pull to start squeezing juice from the cane."

"I see," I said, and I did. They would "buy" the mills that were for all practical purposes undamaged. Some of them might even have cane stockpiled waiting to be processed. Then the enormity of it struck me. There might even be raw sugar sacked, waiting at the mill to be shipped to Veracruz and then on to a sugar-hungry world.

"Let me guess. Besides Riley, Ávalos and Rubio, General González would be a major stock holder. Right?"

"Correct. I am not supposed to know, but I do. Also there is another famous gringo who is a stockholder?"

"Who?" I asked, completely at a loss. "Is it Colonel Green?"

"No," she laughed gaily. "It is you, Tell. You have a thousand shares of the company."

Chapter 12

· · · · · · · · · · · · · · · · · · · ✈

I came to the meeting, not early in the gringo tradition, but late. Later even than a Mexican might. I almost did not go at all. I was not sure that I could meet Rubio face to face and not shoot him. But then, my old nemesis, curiosity, got the better of me and I did attend the first official stockholder's meeting of what was to become the fabulously powerful corporation, Cornucopia, S.A.

The company symbol, suggested by Johnny Ávalos, was the legendary *horn of plenty* with brown sugar pouring out of it. The horn was designed by a young art student that Rubio was sleeping with and then badly executed on the office door by a sign painter. It looked more like an old, yellow human ear with brown wax running out of it, rather than a ram's horn.

Three men lounged against the near wall, smoking and eyeing each other suspiciously. When I neared the door, they turned their suspicion to me.

"What do you want?" the largest one, taller than I and a foot wider, asked.

"I came to see Señor Riley."

"Who wants to see my *patrón*?" asked a thin, swarthy man as clean-shaven as a priest.

Before I could reply the big man reached out to pat me down for weapons. I have always detested such loutish behavior and he reminded me too much of Rubio. I stepped back, flicking my revolver out as I did.

The big man stopped, frozen, his one hand still out toward me. The thin man had a short-barreled pistol in his hand. He was a quick draw. The other stood still, his hand under his coat flap, his eyes darting back and forth between the two of us with pistols in our hands.

"If you shoot," I said, "I will of a certainty kill the burro in front of me."

"Who cares?" he said, then added casually, "You have a name?"

"I am Tell Cooper."

"Major Tell Cooper?"

"Correct."

"And of what are you a major?"

I controlled my temper and answered evenly. "I am an aviator attached to the staff of my General Obregón."

He flipped his pistol back into a belt holster under his coat and said politely, "Please enter, Major Cooper. We had thought you were not coming."

I nodded and holstered my own weapon.

The big man cried out then and went for his gun. The third man drew at the same time, but pointed his pistol barrel at the ceiling. The dangerous one—as thin as a stiletto and with the pistol again, magically, in his hand—touched its barrel to the big man's neck.

"Put it back, *idiota*. He is a friend of my boss and my boss is the boss of your boss. Neither one of you would be mourned. Besides, the major would kill you before you got that pistol out of your pants."

The big man shoved the half-drawn pistol back into a waist holster. I caught a glimpse of a silver-inlaid barrel.

The other bodyguard sighed and replaced his own pistol. Then he opened the door for me. I entered and then paused and spoke to the man that in my mind I had dubbed as Stiletto.

"You would be the *guardaespaldas* of Will Riley, and you," I spoke to the big man, "watch the back of the Toad." I nodded to the man who had opened the door and said, "Thanks. And you would work for Major Ávalos?"

The man I called Stiletto smiled faintly. Ávalos's bodyguard looked nervous. The big man crossed himself and made the sign of the horns, I suppose, to ward off my evil eye.

An anxious Riley met me at the door, his tiny pistol in one hand and his other hand cupped protectively over his mutilated ear.

"The cavalry to the rescue," I said, grinning. "How are you, Willy?"

He dropped the pistol in his coat pocket, then, one-armed, embraced me. Johnny moved away from the long, green felt-covered table to shake hands and give me an *abrazo*. I kept Johnny between myself and Rubio, who waited, hand inside his coat, back against the far wall.

"It's good to see you, Johnny," I said, still speaking English.

"Me too, Tell. Toña asked me to—"

I turned away from him abruptly but with an eye on Rubio. "How is the ear, Willy?"

"It hurts, Tell. The pain in the top is excruciating."

"I know," I said sympathetically. "I had friends who lost limbs say the same thing."

"See," Riley said angrily to Rubio. "Tell knows. You are an ignorant savage."

"I never heard of it before," Rubio grumbled. "And I knew a lot of *cabrones* who lost extremities."

"Me too," I said. "I knew one *cabrón* who almost lost a testicle. Does it still hurt?"

"I never did lose . . ." He stopped, swallowed and seemed to wait for the flush in his face to subside. For a few seconds the room was very silent. Then he opened his mouth wide in a grin. He threw his arms open and advanced toward me.

"I am happy our little differences have been settled, my old friend." He stopped a few feet away, his arms still open to receive me. "That *cabrón*, the one who told me all those lies about you, amigo Tell, I had him shot!" His nostrils flared as he looked about him, daring anyone to deny that he had performed that heroic deed.

"I find that I can talk to you, *Sapote*, without a gun in my hand, but it is not easy, so do not tempt me." I added the "ote" ending to the word for toad to give it an extra meaning of size and coarseness.

His face twisted with a battle between what I thought was rage and greed. Greed won.

"You always make the jokes," he said.

"No," I said and turned to Riley.

"Come on, Tell. Come and sit at the board."

Riley sat at the head of the table. Rubio and I by tacit agreement sat facing each other. Johnny sat alongside me.

"Tell! I have done it." Riley could not contain himself. "We are on our way to a million dollars."

"We?" I said.

"We, Tell. We. All of us. You too."

"I did not buy stock in your company, Will." I glanced meaningfully at Rubio. "I am still trying to get the rest of my property back."

"You will get it all back, but do not talk of pesos. I am talking of millions of dollars."

"I bought no stock, put up no money."

"Yes, you did, Tell. When there was no money to ransom Willard Riley, who put up all that he had and shamed the rest of the Anglo-American community into doing the same?"

"I put up five thousand dollars. But I got it back. At least for a while." I glared at Rubio.

"You backed me with every cent you had, Tell. Did you think that I would forget that?"

He was dead serious. He took his hand away from his ear to pound on the table. I saw that his ear had some sort of a flesh-colored cloth patch, like an eye patch that some people wear over a blind eye. He put his hand back over it quickly and I looked away.

"I cannot accept the stock, Will."

"I will give you five thousand dollars in gold for it," Rubio said quickly.

"I wonder," I said, "where you got five thousand dollars in cash?"

"It is not your money," he said too quickly. I shook my head to show disbelief. He looked at Riley and Johnny, then said, "I asked first."

"I would rather light my last cigar in front of a firing squad with it than sell it to you, Toad."

"There will be no talk of selling," Riley said. "We do not want the shares thrown around willy-nilly."

"How many willy-nillys do I have?"

"A thousand. You each have a thousand," Riley said. "The rest are split up among a number of people."

"You didn't keep any for yourself, Will," I said.

"Of course I did. For God's sake . . ." He broke off and then said, "Rubio is right. You do joke too much."

"How many shares did González get?"

"None."

"What? Not one share?"

"Not one. Now let us get down to business."

"Hold on. Before we move on I would like to know the names of the stockholders and how much each one has."

"Outside of two thousand shares held by another investor, we are the stockholders. I control the remaining six thousand shares."

"Who is the other partner?"

"He prefers to remain anonymous," Riley said, irritated.

"Come on, Will, I am a stockholder."

"All right. It is Abelardo García."

"A brother-in-law of González," I guessed.

"No, hombre!" Rubio snorted at my ignorance. "His son-in-law."

Riley shot a venomous look at Rubio who shut his mouth with an audible snap and began to draw figures on a stack of paper. Note paper had been placed in front of each stockholder's chair.

I picked up the pencil in front of me and wrote down the names and shares. "It does not matter," I said to Riley, "who votes what. Willard Riley controls the vote."

"That is right and proper," Riley said. "And I want everyone here to remember that. Especially you, Jorge. Do as you are told and you will be rich and powerful. Double-cross me and I will erase you."

I found myself erasing the names from my note paper. I smiled to myself. The first name I had rubbed out was that of Rubio.

"Now we shall get on with the meeting." Riley dealt out papers from a pile.

"Jacks or better?" I commented.

"It is like poker," Johnny said, "but for bigger stakes than any of us have ever played for."

"No marked cards or stacked decks?"

"This is the real world, as I have told you before, Tell," Riley said intensely. He rubbed his hand gently over his ear, his hair almost long enough now to reach the mutilated tip.

"Are you going to let your hair grow long enough to cover the ear?" I asked.

"I might!" His voice was shrill and angry.

"See this scar," I said, tracing it easily, feeling the ridge running from eye to lip. "My lip looks like hell without the hair over the scar. But you do what you want with your ear. It won't bother me."

He looked at me suspiciously, then, slowly, removed his hand and pressed both of them down hard on the table.

"Hell, Willy boy," I said, putting on my West Texas accent, "it ain't but a cut like you'd get from shaving. It's red. Needs a mite of curing."

"Tell is right, Will," Johnny said. "I never even notice it any more."

"Who cares?" Rubio said, disgusted. "Will a whore go with a man with no ears and ten pesos, or some good-looking *cabrón* with only five?"

"You are right," Riley said.

Johnny and I smiled congratulations to each other.

"You are absolutely right, Jorge," Riley said. Rubio beamed at us. I shrugged.

To keep from looking at Rubio, I picked up the financial report. It took me a while to realize that it was in a language I knew, Spanish.

"Look at the bottom line, Tell," Riley said proudly.

I found the bottom line and knew enough to look for the red ink used to show the loss. But there was none. The report showed a profit of ten thousand pesos.

"It shows a profit," I said, thinking that I was pointing out an error.

Riley grinned at me. He was enjoying himself immensely. "No

error, Tell."

"But you have only been in business for a couple of weeks."

His grin widened. "True. However, Cosa has made a profit."

"Cosa?"

"Cosa is short for Cornucopia, S.A."

Cosa also means "thing" in Spanish. That is how I thought of the company thereafter. But not as Riley did—a "thing" to do his bidding—but rather as an indefinable "thing" wreaking mindless havoc, like something out of what would later be called a horror movie.

"Clever," I said. "Now explain how Cosa, just in business one week, made a profit out of ruined sugar mills?"

"One of the mills we acquired had a pile of processed sugar. We bought burlap bags, packaged it and sold the lot to the army."

"General González," I guessed. "He bought the sugar so that soldiers could sweeten their already sweetened coffee."

"Right!" There was a note of triumph as he added, "And they paid in advance."

"They have not received the sugar?" I asked, incredulous.

"Oh, they will," Riley said quickly. "They most certainly will. This is no fly-by-night, get-rich scheme. Railroad cars are being loaded right now, each sack carefully weighed and verified by an inspector."

"General González is sending out an inspector to verify the shipments?"

"The inspector is not exactly a González man," Riley said, looking at Johnny Ávalos.

"Then who pays his salary?"

"The Cane Grower's Cooperative," Johnny said.

"The cane workers organized a cooperative," I said, smiling. There was hope.

"They had some help. After all, they are illiterate farmers with no experience in such matters."

"Who helped them?" I asked.

"I did," Johnny said modestly. "With some good advice from Will."

"They have a leader?" I asked even as I knew the answer.

"Yes. They all voted for me." Johnny had the grace to grin sheepishly. Riley was as stony-faced as if playing poker. Rubio yawned, doodling pear-shaped breasts and circular feminine buttocks on his note paper.

I nodded. There was no need to ask who selected the inspector to make sure that the army got its proper quality and quantity. I decided to plunge right in.

"What is the total value of the company?"

"Total net worth, on paper?" Riley asked.

"Yes," I answered.

"Our paper value is ten thousand dollars." His eyes clouded over.

"Cosa made that much profit!"

"Yes. But for the official records, one must enter other costs and reclassify payments and capital flow."

"You surely don't have to pay any taxes?"

"My God, no." Riley was aghast. "But who knows about the future. It is always best to show as little as possible."

"I guess so," I said. "This has been an enlightening experience. I have thought of entering the business world, but I think my machine gun is not synchronized with my propeller."

"It is not so difficult," Johnny said ruefully. "It is like diving into cold water. You soon get used to it."

"Enough," Riley said. "The main function of this meeting is to elect the officers. I will function as the chairman until a president is chosen. The nominations are open."

"I nominate Señor Willard Riley," Rubio said, not looking up from his drawing.

"Seconded," Johnny said.

"All in favor raise your right arm," Riley said.

Three hands shot up, but mine was not among them.

"What about González—I mean Abelardo García?" I asked.

"I have his proxy," Riley said, looking injured. "Did you think that I would be so gauche as to vote for myself?"

"Sorry, Willy, but then," I grinned at him, "you won't need my vote then, so I guess I'll just abstain."

"Tell, I think that you owe me a vote. I would like my first election to the presidency of Cosa to be unanimous. It would mean a great deal to me. Tell?"

Johnny cocked his head to look at Riley from a different angle, as surprised, I supposed, as I to hear him express so much emotion. Even Rubio stopped drawing to look, first at Riley and then at me. I wondered why my approbation meant so much to him and what profit it could mean. Actually, I came to learn that at that time not only did he consider me to be his best friend, but his only friend.

"All right, Willy." I raised my right hand.

"Let it be so recorded," Riley said, delighted. He wrote the results,

114

in ink, into the Cosa ledger and then looked up, smiling. "I now nominate Tell Cooper for the office of secretary and treasurer."

Before I could voice my objection, I was voted into the office.

"No," I said, looking directly into Will Riley's cold blue eyes. "I will not be an officer in Cosa. Not secretary, nor treasurer nor janitor."

"I will do it, *Don* Will," Rubio said eagerly.

Riley looked at me sadly, then accepted my refusal without anger and turned to Rubio.

"No, Jorge. You do not have the mind for it. You would be wasted there. You will make a perfect frontman. Someone to see that my orders are carried out and that others understand my— our position."

"Like what?" Eyelids the size of silver dollars blinked over Rubio's protruding eyeballs.

"Well, I read an article in *The New York Times* about the importance of a new field, public relations. You will be charged with our relations with outsiders."

"I got it," Rubio said, nodding gravely. "I bribe the *cabrones* or I shoot them. That is public relations?"

The question was directed at Riley, but I answered. I had read the same article. "That is it in a nutshell," I said to Rubio.

"I would have put it differently," Riley said, but he did allow himself a thin smile. "But that will do for the present."

"What do I do first?" Rubio asked happily. It was the kind of work that appealed to him.

"First you must work closely with Johnny. Make sure that all of the cane workers join the cooperatives. There is a man in Morelos, Pablo Lavín, who is trying to get all of the independents to join a syndicate. You must deter our people from joining him. Point out to them that Lavín is just feathering his own nest."

"Wasn't Lavín one of Zapata's officers?" I said.

"Good point, Tell." Riley turned back to Rubio. "Offer him double, triple, what we gave that other labor leader."

"And if he doesn't want to join us?"

"He will," Riley said impatiently.

"But if he won't," Rubio said stubbornly.

"Then persuade him, idiot!" Riley glanced at me and then threw a folded newspaper at Rubio. "There, read it yourself. You must convince him."

"Yes, *patrón*." Rubio made a pretense of reading the *Times*, but I doubt that he could have read it even had it been in Spanish. A few seconds later I caught him busily retouching the bust of a woman illustrating an advertisement for typewriters.

"Do you want me to persuade anyone?" I asked, joking. "I report next week to the aerodrome in Mexico. Maybe I'll meet Obregón. I could give him a *cañonazo*." I referred to Obregón's famous statement of suborning rivals with a cannon shot of money.

"No," Riley said seriously. "We do not have enough money to bribe a president. Not yet."

I waved my hands as if in surrender and asked, "Then you are sure that he will be elected?"

"Of course. No doubt about it."

Rubio looked up from his drawing. "Hey, *Don* Will," he said, bubbling over with good humor, "if that one-armed *cabrón* can be president, I guess a one-eared man can own the whole *pinche* country, no?"

I winced. Johnny began to study the report assiduously.

Riley's left hand flew to his ear. His right leg stamped spasmodically, in anger, I thought, until the door opened and the man I thought of as Stiletto ran into the room, pistol in hand. It was then that I noticed the wire running from rug to wall and realized that there must be a bell outside.

"Kill him!" Riley shrieked hysterically. "Kill him, Pepe!"

"The gringo?"

I hunched up but kept both hands on the table.

"No!" both Riley and Johnny cried out in unison.

Then Johnny spoke quickly, earnestly, to Riley. "We need Rubio. He is González's man. Without him we will have nothing. Maybe after the elections we won't need him."

"*Por Dios, Don* Will. ¡*Patrón*! I meant nothing. Forgive me." Rubio rolled his eyes back and forth from Riley to the thin man with the shoe-button eyes and a pistol held loosely in his hand. He turned to him and said, "Pepe, ¡*hombre!* It was just a joke."

"What is it to be, *patrón*?" Pepe asked, no emotion at all in his voice.

"You loathsome toad! You poisonous frog!" Riley screeched. Then his voice changed. I thought for a second that he might cry. He did not, but there were tears in his voice when he did speak again. "You would make fun of a blind mother or her crippled daughter. You are detestable."

"What would you do, Tell?" He turned to me.

116

"Well," I mused, taking my bit of revenge. "If Pepe will gig him, gut him and yank the skin off, I know a great recipe for toad legs."

Rubio gaped at me in horror. His tongue flicked out nervously to lick at his lips, and his eyes bugged out even more. I thought him never more toad-like and ludicrously funny. And so did everyone but Pepe. Had I known him better. I would never have made such a suggestion, for he was capable of carrying out any Riley order, however bizarre.

Johnny led off with a burst of high-pitched laughter. My own contrived laughter sounded unnatural to my own ears. Then Rubio managed a feeble croak and, I believe, that saved him. That sound set us all off into hysterical laughter, including Will Riley. Rubio was the last to finish with short bursts of air, much the way a steam locomotive stops. Then he turned to me, completely serious, and said, "You are a very funny man, but you should not tell jokes that might hurt people's feelings. What if I really looked like a frog or a toad?"

I exploded into genuine laughter, and I was still fighting it when the iced champagne was brought in by Johnny's bodyguard. I looked at him closely and remembered. He had worked for Johnny some time before—after Riley bought the first mill, but before Cosa. That is one way I kept track of Johnny. Johnny before and after Cosa: B.C. and A.C. Except their Christ was Cosa.

"How is your bride-to-be, the Señorita Virginia García, Johnny?" I asked.

"She is very well. We expect you at the wedding."

"I thank you. And Toña?"

"You should see her, Tell. Talk to her."

Yes. I should. But my mind darkened and I merely shrugged, and said, "Thank your bride for the invitation." I stood up. "I drink to the future Señora Ávalos." Johnny stood up, but he would not meet my eyes. Will said something, as did Rubio, but no one mentioned that she was much older than Johnny, or that she was the maiden daughter of Abelardo García, confidant of General González.

Riley got to his feet and said, "And on that happy note I would like to drink to the company that will make us all rich: Cosa."

Rubio sprang to his feet and held his glass up, his eyes fixed on Will Riley.

"To Cosa!" Riley said, standing.

"To Cosa," we chorused and drank.

"I should like to propose another toast. One to each of you," I said, holding my glass out for more champagne. "But you must promise not to become angry. Agreed?"

They did and waited with refilled glasses for me to speak.

"First, to the man with the golden tongue." I lifted my glass to Rubio, who took it as a compliment and swelled with pride. Johnny almost choked on his drink, and Riley grinned.

"Next, to my old friend, the master of the boudoir, the nemesis of virgins, Johnny Ávalos, the man with the golden cock!"

Rubio guffawed. Riley chuckled apologetically. Johnny shot me a hurt look and did not even smile.

"And now, a toast to the genius behind Cosa." I held out my glass to Riley and there was the musical click of crystal against crystal. "To my dear friend and future millionaire, Willy Riley, the man with the golden ear."

Riley's eyes filled with tears immediately.

"Not you, Tell. Not you."

"I am sorry, Willy. Sincerely sorry. I never meant—"

"Pepe!" Rubio yelled.

"Shut up, Jorge." Riley said. "The meeting is adjourned."

He sat his glass, still full, on the table and walked out quickly, refusing to talk or even look at me. In the years that followed he never again referred to that incident, but he never forgot it. And I never again called him Willy.

Chapter 13

· · · · · · · · · · · · · · · · · · ✈

Mexico City, 1922.

There was no light in the one window that I could see above the eight-foot wall, but then it was barely dark. I found a dangling rope and yanked it. The bell was loud enough to compete with one of the smaller churches, but no one answered. I was at the right place. A tiny pink house with a bougainvillea-covered wall next to a huge, gray-stone residence across from the tobacconist's shop. I reached for a cigar and discovered that I had left both case and matches at the hotel. I shrugged and crossed the street.

I waited while an elderly man dressed in an expensive but much-mended suit searched for a mild cigar. He gave me a long thin one that crinkled and smelled sharply fresh.

I nodded assent, borrowed his clipper to slice off the tip and then lit it from the gas jet that was his only advertisement.

"Excellent," I said. "I'll take a box."

I could see that he was grateful for the sale, but puzzled.

"There are twenty in a box, I think, and three pesos a box, so one cigar . . ." He shook his head angrily and said directly to me, "The box is three pesos. The first one is courtesy of the house."

I thanked him and gave him a five-peso coin. He took it between thumb and forefinger and dropped it into an empty cigar box. I could see his lips move along with his fingers.

"You do not happen to have three pesos?" he asked hopefully.

"No," I said. "But that box is full of change." I pointed to another, near the empty one.

"Yes," he said helplessly. "I know."

"Just give me two pesos back," I said, understanding.

"Yes, sir," he said happily. He picked out two silver pesos and handed them to me.

I thanked him and left, wondering how he, and many like him, would make the other more difficult change—from rich man to struggling merchant.

The moon had risen, its light forming a checkerboard on the brick-topped street. I stepped from a light square to a dark one just as a

119

carriage drove up and stopped in front of the house where my Toña lived. I stood still, grinning foolishly, waiting to see her step down into the moonlight. But instead, Johnny Ávalos stepped down from the carriage and, like an actor on a softly lighted stage, stood there, an arm extended.

Toña took his hand and allowed him to swing her down onto the walk. Now that she was no longer an army officer, even by her own criteria, had she become more feminine? Or was it because of the handsome and charming Johnny Ávalos?

I know that I should have rushed over and claimed her. Fought with Johnny, perhaps. But I procrastinated until they dismissed the cab and went inside. The hurt and anger flooded through me.

It took a long time for a light to come on, and then it was not a bright or large one. I rehearsed what I would say and do after Johnny left. I would be proud, but obviously heart-broken, until a tearful Toña begged forgiveness. Only then would I take her into my arms and declare my eternal love. I liked the scene and dialogue I improvised while I smoked my cigar. But then, as I lit another from the first, the light went out in that despicable house. I felt lost, betrayed. My insides shriveled and tears came to my eyes. I dropped the box of cigars onto the street and walked blindly away, seeking the brighter lights like a muddled moth.

Not far away, a door swung open, a well-dressed man entered, and I caught a glimpse of a man standing behind the bar, looking sadly outside. Misery loves company, I thought, and went in.

"Good evening, sir." The barman, about my age, was a pudgy-faced cherub with soft brown eyes and an upper-class English accent.

"Evening. Whiskey."

"Yes, sir. Whiskey, it is." He took the first glass within reach, a water tumbler, and half filled it with Scotch.

"I would prefer bourbon," I said.

"Of course you would." He looked somewhat desperately at the array of bottles behind him, stacked on a dozen shelves.

"The one with the picture of the crow will do." I pointed out the bottle.

"Right." He half filled another large glass, sat it in front of me, said, "cheers" and he drank down the Scotch.

"Cheers," I said, and I drank the bourbon.

"Another?" he suggested.

"How much do these cost?" I asked, suddenly a bit wary of the strange bar—I was the only client now—the other had disappeared.

"What do you usually pay?" he asked anxiously.

"I think a peso," I said, trying to remember the last time that I had ordered whiskey in Puebla.

"Good. That is what I—we—charge."

"You are the owner?"

"Goodness, no. I often drink here, or upstairs, when in funds. And I help out at times." He stuck his hand out at me and added, "I am George Richmond-Jones. Call me George."

"Tell Cooper," I said, taking his hand. He had a surprisingly muscular hand.

George had just poured us each another drink when a middle-aged man, who looked more like a banker than the owner of the most exclusive bordello in Mexico City, walked in from the street.

"George, I told you no more drinks on the cuff." He might have been scolding a mischievous puppy.

"But Ramón. You know my money will not be in until Tuesday next."

"I most certainly do, George. It is you who forgets."

"Excuse me," I said. "The drinks are to be put on my bill."

"Of course," Ramón said, extending his hand. "Welcome to the International House."

George slipped out from behind the bar to my side. Ramón took his place, refused my offer of a drink and mixed himself a lime and mineral water.

"I will get even with you after Tuesday," George said, "Ramón is right. I always forget and then I suffer terribly from being too thirsty and hungry–"

"And horny," Ramón interrupted jovially. "The girls never extend credit. Not even to George."

"Too true," George said somewhat sadly, but without a trace of embarrassment.

"What do you do?" I asked, wondering about his income.

"Do? Oh, yes. Employment. I sell bridges, and canals as well, I believe."

"I can see how they might go together," I said. "Do you sell many?"

"Not one!" Ramón broke in. "In the year that I have been privileged to know George he has not sold one solitary bridge."

George merely smiled shyly. Ramón had not spoken in ridicule but with affection. George had that effect on people.

"What is upstairs?" I asked, suspecting the answer.

"Gambling on the second floor. Not legal of course, but then not illegal either, right, Ramón?"

Ramón merely shrugged.

"And on the top floor, the third, are the girls from all over the world."

"Shall we have a drink up there?" I asked. "I have always wanted to be a world traveler."

George led at a trot. The door at the second floor landing was ajar but not open. I heard the rattle of a ball clicking around a roulette wheel and a slow southern voice speaking in English, "Call three and up five."

There was no door at the third floor. The stairs opened up into a warm, dark area that might have held anything nocturnal.

I stopped to lean on the rail at the landing and let my lungs catch up to my pulse.

"Sorry," George said guiltily. "I seem to be inured to living at somewhere between seven and eight thousand feet. It takes a bit of getting used to."

"I can match you, foot for foot," I said, stung at my implied infirmity.

"Of course you can," George said. "Shall we sit at one of the tables?" He waved a hand at a sea of blackness with two or three flickering lights that might have been fireflies, stars or even flickering candles.

"Yes," I said and followed close behind him while he walked surely to a table, lit a match, lit a candle stuck in the neck of a wine bottle, and then indicated a chair. I sat down, trying not to breath too audibly.

"Georgie! Your check came early."

The voice from that unknown dark sea outside the circle of our one candle was pure East Side, New York. Once you have heard that accent it is as definitive as, say, West Texas.

"No," George said. "But come out anyway, Marie Antoinette."

There was a jangle of a dozen bracelets and bangles and a bare-footed, bare-legged and bare almost-everything-else girl danced into the circle of light. Later, when George and I were staid members of the Mexico City Chamber of Commerce, I would recall her as a big-assed, large-breasted, red-headed sapsucker.

"What's your name tonight?" George asked.

"Lotus Blossom. I'm a Chinese Princess from Bombay."

122

"Bombay is in India, love," George said.

"It is?" She shut her eyes tightly and concentrated. She opened them, smiled brightly, and said, "Right. Last week I was an Indian Princess. This week, I'm from Peekin, China."

"Of course you are," George said. "Blossom, I want to present you to an old friend, Tell Cooper."

"Pleased to meet you. Any friend of George's, with money, is a friend of mine."

"I hope so," I said. "Will you have a drink with us?"

"Sure. Champagne." Her voice was strident enough to level the candle flame. When it was vertical again George held a hand up for silence from Blossom and attention from me.

"Tell, these girls, particularly Blossom, can drink champagne like camels getting ready for a three-month caravan."

"It matters not a whit," I said. "I had planned to spend a great deal of time and money on a lady tonight. She chose not to be available, but I still have both the time and money." I pulled my purse from a coat pocket and upended it onto the table. There were over a hundred pesos and one bright, gold fifty-dollar Eagle.

"That will certainly do it," George said. "But will you have enough apart to live until your next remit—I mean until you receive new funds?"

"Likely," I said as carelessly as I felt. "I expect to get close to five thousand dollars from the Obregón government any day."

"Five thousand dollars!" Blossom said sitting down in the chair next to me. "You could move in with me."

"No," George said seriously. "You must invest that money in a good, solid business. Something with its feet on the ground."

"Like an airplane taxi service?" I said.

"Exactly. But you would have to have one propeller here to take a big bite of the thin air and another at sea level to turn faster and get the machine up in the air."

"Of course." I pointed a finger at him. "You are an aviator."

"Guilty as charged. Sopwith Camels."

"Spads, and now, de Havilland Scouts."

"De Havilland? Why, Geoffrey is an—"

A clash of cymbals interrupted George. The girl that undulated into our little world of dim light was as full-breasted and wide-hipped as Blossom, but half the size, and where Blossom was light, she was dark. Her hair was black and her eyes but a shade lighter. She swayed in front of me and pivoted her hips, and then, just as she spoke, thrust her pelvis at me. One taut breast slipped from its silk sheath and quivered a few inches from my eyes. Her skin was almost the same dusky brown as that of Toña.

"I am Tombola, African slave girl," she said in English heavily accented, I suspected, by Cuban Spanish.

"Sit down," I said. "I am a slave buyer and this is—"

"George," she said. "I know George." She patted him on the cheek. He might have blushed, but with George I never knew. His cheeks were always red.

"They have private rooms," George said. "Little suites with, ah, . . . two bedrooms and a . . . ah, commode."

"Can we have our drinks in one?" I asked.

"You certainly may," George said, then turned to Blossom and asked, "Is there one open?"

"Sure," Blossom said. "Limbo or Paradise?"

"Which?" George asked.

I got to my feet and pulled Tombola to hers. "Come on," I said. "Let's all go to Paradise."

Chapter 14

My student, Paco Escobar, a captain in Obregón's fledgling air corps, lined up with the runway, checked the drift, lowered the right wing just enough to counter the slight crosswind, brought the nose up, leveled the wings again, and then stalled the big de Havilland. It dropped, no more than a foot, to a three-point landing on the tarmac at the new landing field near Mexico City.

He had been nervous before the flight, but when he took the controls, he became an integral part of the machine, completely in control, planning ahead, flying the airplane, never allowing it to stray from his control. He knew that the airplane was larger and more powerful than any he had flown before, but still, an airplane.

Escobar taxied back to the takeoff point, swinging the nose back and forth in wide S turns so that he could clear the blind spots in front of the long nose and avoid the occasional interloping cow or burro.

When he swung into the wind at the end of the runway, I turned to look back at him. He patted his helmet to indicate that he still had the controls and then mimed a takeoff. He had just made the difficult unassisted landing and now wanted to make the relatively easy takeoff. He was so surprised when I waved a negative finger at him that he pushed his goggles up onto his helmet and opened his mouth to argue. I forestalled his argument by clambering out onto the wing and, crouching over the after cockpit, spoke into his ear.

"You don't need me any more. Bring it back in a half an hour or so and I'll buy you a cup of coffee."

His wide grin was answer enough. I waved and eased myself down from the wing, my parachute under one arm. I could remember when we were forbidden parachutes because it might tempt a pilot to prematurely abandon his airplane. Raoul Lufbery might have lived to shoot Richthofen down had he carried one.

I resisted the temptation to look back and walked away quickly to the small adobe building that we used as a squadron utility room. I slipped out of the harness and handed the parachute to the supply sergeant.

"You have a new student," the sergeant said. Something in his voice alerted me. The new student would not be an ordinary one.

125

Likely the son of a powerful *político* or a very wealthy man.

"Where is he?"

That husky voice still had power over me. I did not turn around to face Toña until I had mastered my emotions.

"You said, Tell, that one day you would teach me."

"Yes, we said several things to each other." I could not keep the hurt out of my voice.

She looked at me strangely, then moved toward the door. "Could we talk outside?"

"Of course."

I watched Escobar land that big, awkward biplane like a feather and knew that he would be one of the really good ones.

"I have some news. Maybe good news, Tell."

"Johnny is going to marry you instead of that rich García girl?" The anger in my voice surprised me as much as it did Toña.

"What are you blabbering about?" Anger breeds anger.

I could not tell her what I thought. I could not bring myself to say: 'You took another lover. You loved another as much—maybe more—than me.' So I said angrily, "I am talking about Mexico and a bunch of crooked *políticos* that will not give me my money back. I have been here a month and—"

"You have been here a whole month and you did not come to see me!" Now she was shouting.

"I thought that you would be too busy with Johnny to see some ugly gringo," I said, turning the knife in my own wounded pride.

"What has Johnny got to do—"

"Besides," I interrupted, turning the knife outward. "I have been seeing a lot of Helen. You remember the blonde?"

"I remember!" Her eyes were still flashing with anger, but were wet now, and I felt ashamed.

"I know about you and Johnny," I said, my anger spent. "I wish you both well."

"Sure. So do I wish you well. You and the blonde that does not carry a knife or act like a man."

"Helen is just a friend," I said.

"Like Johnny," she said. "He is just a friend too. My friend."

"Of course," I said, angry again. "A close friend."

"If I want to sleep with Johnny, I do it. He is a handsome man. Suppose I try him out like you did the French girls?"

"But they were just whores," I said.

"And Johnny is not?"

"Did you pay him?" I could not cut the words off quickly enough. I felt an intense dislike for myself. I tried to unsay the words, but of course I could not.

"Maybe *he* paid me. What is the difference? Does it matter who pays? I am a woman and a human being. I think and I get hurt. Just like you. Maybe more. Oh, you are just like the rest of them, the petit bourgeois." She burst into tears. I tried to take her into my arms, but she spun away from me and cried out, "No! You have shamed me enough."

"I am sorry," I said with complete honesty. "I did not mean to be your judge. And I do hope that Johnny will marry you."

"You just do not understand." She turned to face me, no longer crying, but her face was wet with tears.

"I guess I cannot. But be my friend?" I held a hand out in supplication.

"Yes. I suppose that we had better be friends." That rather cryptic statement made no sense to me then, obtuse as I was, but I was relieved when she took my hand for a second before releasing it.

"What about your news. The good news."

"Yes. Of course. Well, I will have a post in the new Federal Bureau of Aeronautics. I must learn to fly and the general said you are to teach me."

"Of course. I will be delighted. We will have to borrow another airplane."

"Why?"

"The de Havilland is such a large airplane. Just to move the stick and rudders requires a great deal of physical strength."

"I am not a weakling!" She stood, legs apart, hands on her hips, waiting for my argument. "You once thought I could fly those very airplanes."

"I still think you can," I said, surprising both of us. "At least it is worth a try."

I led her back into the squadron room and showed her a model of the de Havilland. I moved the aileron, the rudder and elevators, and explained how the air rushing over the wing drew the airplane up into the air, and that if not enough air rushed over the surface of the wing, it would shake and lose its lift and the airplane would stall.

For a minute or so she was pensive, then her eyes flashed with insight and she said, "Of course. It is like sailing a boat."

I had forgotten that she had grown up on the coast.

"It is the same thing. When you sail too close to the wind, the air no longer rushes by the sail. It just flaps and you have to work the bow around to get the wind again."

I almost began to correct her and then thought better. Likely it was as good a definition of a stall as my own.

"Makes sense. A sailor should make a good aviator."

I was prophetic. Within the week she soloed. I pretended not to watch her first flight, but I stood outside the adobe squadron room, ostensibly reading a newspaper, following her every movement. My feet and hands moved with every flutter of a wing or change in attitude. And then she made her turn into the field and floated the big airplane down. It was a perfect three-point landing, and as often happens, it would be her last perfect landing for a long time. She was ecstatic and when my prize student, Paco Escobar, pretended not to know that she had landed the de Havilland and instead congratulated me on a perfect landing, she laughed in pleasure and kissed me.

I had heard the motor and thought that it would be Helen in her new Model T Ford that her newspaper had financed, but in the spontaneous gaiety of Toña's solo flight, had forgotten.

"Hey, if I take up flying, may I get kissed too?" Helen called out from the doorway.

"Of course," Escobar, who spoke idiomatic English, chimed in, holding out his arms and smiling. "I have an opening in my school."

"*Hola,*" Toña greeted Helen. "I have just soloed!"

Helen, whose Spanish was improving daily, replied, "I see. So what do you get when you graduate?"

Toña slipped out of my arms and held out her hand to Helen, then, a look of astonishment erased her smile and, avoiding Helen's out-thrust hand, ran for the bathroom. She slammed the door behind her, but we could hear her retching.

"She never got airsick before," I said.

"It was not rough today," Escobar said.

"Toña has put on a little weight lately," Helen said softly as if she might be talking to herself.

"What?" I asked Helen.

"Never mind," she said. "I'll look in on her." She rapped on the door, whispered and then opened the door halfway and slipped in.

We waited. Escobar, already late for a meeting with a superior officer, finally climbed on his old but reliable motorcycle and roared off.

I banged on the door. "Hey! If you are all right, why don't you come out?"

"Shut up, Tell," Helen yelled. "We will damn well come out when we are good and ready."

I shrugged for my own benefit and walked outside just as one of the duty de Havilland Scouts roared over the field. I could not recognize the helmeted and goggled pilot, but I had undoubtedly checked him out in the machine, so I waved. He saw me, waved back, and then flew over even lower. His observer threw out something streaming a white banner behind it. I ran over and picked up a manila envelope with a thin cotton cloth tied to one corner. I opened it and found that it was weighted with a .30-caliber bullet. I lifted the packet high to show the pilot that I had it and waved. The pilot waggled his wings and turned back to fly east, towards Puebla.

The note inside the envelope was not from a general or even a military man of any rank. It was from Will Riley.

> *Dear Tell,*
>   *I need your help. It is vital to both of us that you meet me at the Metropolis Restaurant at eight o'clock this evening.*

Toña and Helen came out of the squadron room laughing and chattering, arm in arm. I wondered what had changed an apparent dislike of each other to a schoolgirl intimacy.

Memo drove up, greeted Helen and then spoke to Toña.

"You are looking good, lieutenant. Flying agrees with you."

"It does, Memo. But I am no longer a lieutenant. I am now only a señorita."

That, for some odd reason, set them to giggling again.

"Are you feeling all right now, Toña?" I asked.

She ignored me and spoke to Memo.

"When are you resuming your own flight lessons?"

"When the Pope shakes hands with the Devil," Memo answered promptly and crossed himself at the same time. He had bailed out of the airplane as it taxied to the takeoff point on his initial flight. There had not been another.

"I have bad news, ladies," I said. "I won't be able to take you to dinner. I have a life-and-death kind of message from Will Riley and I have to meet him tonight."

"We are not invited," Helen mocked me. "I thought that Riley liked girls."

"He does. But this is business of some kind, I think."

"I do not know whether I would rather miss dinner with the great Willard Riley or an appointment with my executioner," Toña said.

"I guess we will have to fend for ourselves," said Helen, who also detested Riley, but was fascinated by him at the same time. "Let's celebrate your . . . solo flight."

"Yes. Of course." They were amused, again by something I could not understand.

"All right," I said, irritated. "Be here early tomorrow, Toña."

"No, Tell. I think I will suspend the lessons for a while."

"But you feel all right now?"

"Yes, but who knows about early morning."

"The morning? Why the morning?"

They both broke into laughter again, exchanging arcane looks. When I drove away, riding in front with Memo, they were still laughing like schoolgirls planning mischief.

Chapter 15

· · · · · · · · · · · · · · · · · ✈

The man I called Stiletto sat at a corner table with a petite redhead, likely an American girl, judging by the bobbed hair and mannish coat. But as I approached the table, the redhead swung around to welcome me. It was Riley, his hair cut in the style of the little Dutch boy, with bangs in front and trimmed long to cover the tops of his ears.

He wore new expensive-looking clothes: white silk shirt and English cloth. Likely English tailoring too, I thought, and wondered if he was using Johnny's Mexico City tailor. We embraced and pounded each other on the back. Stiletto stood up, expressionless.

"It is good to see you, Tell. What has it been, six months?"

"More, I think," I said, wondering if I had lost track of time.

"Right. I have been so busy, Tell. My God have I been busy!"

I turned away for a brief handshake with the bodyguard, Pepe, who hesitated, then gave me the tips of his fingers, Indian style, to touch. He nodded and moved to another table where he could observe the room and its only entrance.

"Good man," I observed.

"Yes. Now, what will you have: cognac, whiskey, bourbon?"

"I'm not exactly on the wagon, Will, but I think I'll stick to beer or wine."

A waiter appeared and took our order. Riley suggested the pepper steak and a French wine. I agreed. The wine was a vintage Beaujolais. He sniffed the cork, tasted the wine and offered to pour me a sample.

"No, if it's good enough for you, fill up my glass."

"Good, Tell. Excellent."

We clinked glasses and drank. Then, idly, I asked, "Now, what is so important? Whom do I have to kill?"

"Who told you? How do you know?" There was no color in his face.

"Hold on. That was a joke. What's wrong?"

"Some lunatic tried to kill me last week, Tell. A man shot at *me*. Had it not been for Pepe, he would have killed me."

"Who tried to shoot you. Why?"

"A crazy man named Barrera. Rubio shot his father and the idiot blamed me."

"But why you?"

"Because of Jorge and a theater."

"The Toad killed a man in a theater?"

"No. Jorge was trying to buy his theater and they got into a fight over the price."

"Rubio shot him because he asked too much?"

"It was self-defense, Tell. Everyone said so. Even the attorney general."

"Would that be the one that is the cousin of Johnny's rich fiancée? Or is she the ex-girlfriend now?"

"Yes, that one. And yes, she is an ex-fiancée all right. Johnny married her last week."

"But he and Toña—"

"Toña has no money, and besides," he added distastefully, "she is a socialist if not an outright Bolshevik."

I decided not to mention his championing months ago of the down-trodden, landless peasants. "But if Rubio was buying the theater, what did it have to do with you?"

"He was not only buying it for himself, but for me and you too. Cosa made the offer. Tell, have you seen a moving picture lately?"

"Yes, I have. Now tell me what the hell you are talking about."

"Jorge made that theater owner an excellent offer, more than he could have gotten anywhere, what with his union trouble. But the man went crazy."

"Do you by some odd coincidence have something to do with a labor union of theater employees?" I asked, sensing the connection.

"No. Of course not. That is Jorge's job."

"Then you do control the union?"

"Jorge helped the workers organize a union, if that is what you mean."

"Then why did the man shoot at you?"

"He found out that I am the president of the company buying the theaters and the dead man was his father so—"

"Hold on Will. You say theaters. Plural?"

"Yes. We have five now, but the one in Puebla was the only real hold-out. The rest will sell now on our terms. We will make a great deal of money, Tell. All of us."

"You want me to shoot a few more to lower the price even more!" My anger came out in my voice, and I noticed Stiletto snap his head to stare directly at me.

"No, you idiot. I only want your proxy. We have run out of cash,

132

even with the financing the theater owners allowed us. We are going to offer the shares of Cosa as security for a huge loan. Enough to finance the purchase of many more theaters."

"How many?"

It was a moment Riley chose to savor. He twirled wine in his glass, held it up to the light and sipped it before answering.

"All of them," he said joyously. "All of them, Tell!"

"Every one?"

"Every single one."

"My God, Will. What's next?"

"The studios, Tell. The factories where they turn out the movies themselves."

"Send the stock over and I'll endorse it back to you, Will. I got my five thousand dollars back, eventually. Jorge Rubio cheated me out of one thousand dollars."

"You will get your money within the week. I promise. But I will not take your stock. Here." He handed me a printed form authorizing himself to vote my stock on a specific date and for the reason given. I signed and dated the release.

He replaced the document carefully in an inside pocket and then applied himself to the food. I did the same. We said little until I lit a cigar to have with my coffee. I was careful to keep my smoke away from his sensitive nostrils. He hated cigars. I think it was because his father smoked them.

"Your contract will be up soon," Riley said. "What then?"

"I am an aviator. I will find a flying job."

"Find a war somewhere?"

"No," I laughed. "I might open a flight school. Maybe fly passengers on emergency trips where time is all-important. Or deliver something to a place where trains don't go. There are cities in Mexico that not even horse-drawn wagons can reach during the rainy season."

"But you could?"

"I would need just a few hours of decent weather and a place to land. A pasture with good drainage."

"I endorse the idea," Riley said seriously. "And, if you will take your place in the company, as a director, we will finance your air train."

"Aerotrain," I said. I liked the name. I still do, but I am almost alone in that opinion.

Unbidden, after an excellent chocolate mousse, the waiter brought cigars and a bottle of Martell to the table. I would have refused the cigar, but Riley said, "Go ahead, Tell. Just smoke downwind of me." I might have refused the cognac, but he had been gracious about my cigars, so when he swirled the golden liquid around the bottom of a wide-based snifter glass, I accepted both.

"Will, when you have your million, what will you do?"

"Start on the second."

"But when you have many millions?"

He shrugged.

"How many more?" I asked.

"All of them," he said humorlessly.

I laughed, but seconds passed before he finally smiled.

"You are in one big poker game and you won't quit until you have all the chips."

He dismissed the idea with an impatient wave of a hand and said, "Tell! Do you have any idea what the real worth of Cosa is?"

"Let's see," I guessed. "I own ten percent that was worth—at least you figured my loan was worth—five thousand dollars. Someone is willing to loan money for it as collateral so it must have appreciated in value. Say seven thousand?"

"Should your share be sold for its rock bottom value based on tangible assets, it would bring ten tomorrow. In a week I could sell it for twenty and would pay thirty for it myself."

"Sold." I stuck my hand across the table and grinned to hide my surprise.

"Do not be such a fool, Tell." He ignored my extended hand.

"Well, *Don* Willard, forgive your humble servant. But maybe the stock could be collateral for a loan for my aviation company."

"I will see to it. Take your time. Study the market place. Buying and selling. Find out what licenses are needed and whom to pay off. Then come and talk to me."

"Maybe," I said, tiring of the game.

Riley said nothing, but he must have made some kind of a sign, for the waiter was there with the bill in his hand. Riley, who had in my presence haggled over the price of a three-penny box of matches, flipped the paper over without reading it and signed the back.

"I'll leave the tip," I said, reaching for my purse.

"No, the tip is included."

I glanced at the bill. He had written in above his signature a huge tip, nearly as much as the bill. Both signature and tip were in violet-colored ink. I tried to remember what it was that I disliked about ink

134

that was not black or blue in color, but could not.

"Thanks for the dinner, Will. Can I drop you—"

"The night is not over and it is still my treat."

I protested, feebly, I admit, for I was as nearly broke without actually being in debt as I had ever been. And Riley must have known.

Stiletto left first, then ducked back in to nod at Riley before, shrugging into overcoats against the cold winter night, we followed him out.

"Leave the car," Riley told his bodyguard. "Come on Tell. This fabulous place I want to show you is just around the corner. It is called the International House."

He waited expectantly for my laughter so I did not disappoint him. But when we reached the door into the bar where I had met my future partner, George, Riley took me by the elbow and steered me on past the door, around a corner and into an alley back of the building. There, by an outside staircase softly illuminated by gas jets, stood Stiletto.

"All the suites are taken, except one," Stiletto said.

"What is left?" Riley asked.

"Hell," the thin man said, his voice, like his face, expressionless.

Riley turned to me, his thin eyebrows arched like twin question marks.

"Sure," I said. "Why not?"

Chapter 16

· · · · · · · · · · · · · · · · · · · ✈

Willard Riley

Hands folded demurely in her lap, her long-lashed, almond-shaped eyes downcast, my future bride sat demurely between her dusky Mexican mother and her blond, blue-eyed Italian father, Alejandro Balboa.

At the moment he did not look the wealthy and powerful banker, but more the supercilious weak and doting father that he really was. His lovely and obviously sensual daughter was several months pregnant and would not or possibly, I thought with amusement, could not identify the father.

So Carmencita must have a husband and soon, or the scandal would shatter the world of Balboa in which every man is sworn to defend the virtue of his women with his life, even as he risks it in pursuit of someone else's sister or daughter.

And I must have a huge loan and soon. We both had about three months before we would be extremely embarrassed by our miscalculations. I could understand her dilemma, for I too had been fucked. However, mine had given me no pleasure whatsoever. It had not even been personal, but it had been administered by the bank, run and largely owned by Alejandro Balboa.

After Jorge Rubio killed that recalcitrant theater owner in Puebla, we had no more problems buying, at generous terms, the remaining movie houses. We immediately tripled the price of tickets. We lost about a third of our audience but made twice as much; within three months we were selling as many tickets as ever.

I soon realized that those who made and distributed the movies made more money out of the increased revenue than Cosa did. So I again put up our stock as collateral and borrowed enough capital from the Balboa group to enter the moving picture business, creating CosaCine Films.

We tried to take control of the actor's union, but its head, a stupidly stubborn man who had been with Obregón at Celaya, Emilio López, refused to deal with us. When Johnny Ávalos gave up, I sent Rubio to reason with him. Rubio ambushed the union leader outside his home one night, but Rubio, who knew that López carried a pistol, must have been nervous, for his shot did not kill—and he got a bullet in the gut. Luckily I had sent Pepe to back him up. He killed the union man cleanly, but then, instead of doing the same for Rubio, he brought him back. The bullet had passed through Rubio's huge belly without touching an intestine. He was in the hospital for two weeks and, were he not such a hypochondriac, would have been out in one.

We spent a fortune in bribes—Obregón remembered that stupid union leader—and even the newspapers charged three times their regular rates to print our version of the incident. We could have done the job cheaper and better without the pistol, and barring unusual circumstances, I will not countenance its use again.

The costs on our first picture were horrendous. We had to pay standard wages and buy material at highly inflated prices. So I must go, hat in hand, to ask for an extension. I fully expected to pay a much larger interest for the short-term loan. I was completely unprepared for the demand that we give them a percentage of the gross income—not of the net profits, but total revenue. Perhaps Jesse James would not have been as notorious had he managed banks instead of robbing them, but he certainly would have been richer.

So far I have learned little about the actual making of movies, but I have learned a great deal about the financing and deceptive bookkeeping involved in the production of just one simple film. I was determined to control that phase that I did understand: the financing. And I was at last ready to begin that phase.

"Alejandro," I said, using his first name but not preceding it with the honorific *Don* as befitted his exalted position and his fifty years of age, compared to my twenty-five. "You were to give me the note tonight."

His thin nostrils flared and he clenched both hands. He did not like me to call him Alejandro. I smiled and waited for his answer.

He looked quickly at his daughter. She noticed his glance, but her large brown eyes were on me. She might not have understood the code words, but she knew that she was being sold just as surely as if she were one of the girls at a Puebla bordello.

"Yes, of course, ah . . . Willard." He drew a folded paper from an inside pocket and held it out to me. I stood up and took it from him.

"It is signed, notarized and stamped."

"Of course," I said. I read it carefully, slowly, enjoying myself as the red moved up from his tight collar into his jowls. I refolded the note and thrust it into my inner pocket before I sat down again.

I folded my arms and waited. Alejandro squirmed, glanced again at his daughter and then turned to his wife.

"Could I see you in the library for a moment, my dear?"

"What? Oh, yes. Of course, but to leave Carmencita alone . . ."

"A few seconds," he said and stood up.

"As you order," she said uncertainly and stood up. He took her by the arm and led her out of the room. I did not hear a door close and assumed that they were listening. I hoped so. It would make our future relations easier.

"We will be married by the civil this Friday and in the church—"

"In the cathedral?" She interrupted me, a smile curling her full lips.

"No. Not in the cathedral. In a church. And that only after paying a great deal of money to a priest in Puebla who is starting a home for fallen women—"

"Prostitutes," she said in English. I hate being interrupted.

"Whores," I said loudly enough to be heard through a door. I listened for an outraged gasp, but heard only a low moan that might have come from either parent.

"If I am a whore then you must be a . . ." She threw her blond hair back and looked upward as if seeking the unfamiliar word and then, unable to find it, said, "*padrote.*"

"Your English is quite good," I said truthfully. "The word is pimp. But it would not apply to me. To your father, perhaps, but I am the client. And you were not cheap."

The amber hidden in the brown of her eyes flashed and her large breasts pushed out as she took a deep breath. She was a most attractive girl, and had she been a real whore, experienced and subservient, I might have had her checked for disease and then taken her into a back room. As it was, I would have to wait, but I intended to recoup a part of my investment before she became too distended with her bastard child.

"How much did you pay?"

"Besides giving you my good name?"

"Riley. A gringo from Boston. Shanty Irish. I know Boston."

"And so do I. And I know Puebla. And Mexico. And this city is no different. Except the power is closer here. I can feel it. And I will be a part of it. You Italians think you know power. But you are wrong."

"I am Mexican."

"So am I."

She burst into laughter. When I did not join in, she stopped and

138

then asked me seriously, "Were there other bidders?"

"I think not," I said. "At least no one socially acceptable to your family jumped forth to offer his name to an unborn child."

"But you did."

"Yes. I did. I agreed to marry you and to accept the child as my own."

"You mean that? About the child. And if there should be another?" She blushed and looked away. "I mean, yours."

"I will want sons to carry on an empire, but the firstborn will be just that. With the prerogatives that go with it."

"I will make a bargain with you," she said, the hardness absent from her voice. "I am not a stupid woman. I speak Italian and French as well as Spanish and English. I know a little about the banking business. I will sleep with you, care for you and be loyal to you. All this I will do if you will be kind to me and the child."

"Of course," I said and stood up to call Alejandro. But when I looked at her, her eyes were wet with tears. Of course, I thought, she is only a woman, after all.

"And will you marry me, then?" I asked.

"Yes, Willard. Yes, I will."

She burst into tears and the parents came rushing in to play out the charade. We talked of many things, none of which I ever remembered, for I was to busy formulating a timetable for the takeover of the Balboa Banking Group. I thought it would be difficult, but I knew that I would find a way. I had not an inkling of how easy, thanks to Johnny Ávalos, it would be.

Chapter 17

· · · · · · · · · · · · · · · · · · ✈

Mexico City

The day of the civil wedding, a week before the formal affair, I was at the studio watching a scene from our new film. It was to be a three-reeler, an ambitious undertaking for our neophyte company.

The director was screaming through his megaphone for silence so that the actors could hear him. When it was quiet, he called out to the two actors dressed in the loose-fitting white shirts and pants of the Mexican peon.

"All right. You two *cabrones* stay in front of the camera and bang the machetes together. Okay?"

"Sure, Señor Romero," one said and lifted his machete threateningly. The other eyed the blade and then held his up to it.

"Action!" Romero yelled and they began to clang the blades together. The shorter one was moving his lips as he fought, counting silently, one, two, three and four. At the count of four they reversed places, each missed with a wild swing, and then they repeated the numbered movements.

"At three, you get him, Manolo!" the director shouted.

Manolo, facing the camera, flung his machete in the air and screamed in agony.

"Bleed, you *cabrón*, bleed!" Romero shouted.

There was no blood. Manolo, his face still contorted with agony, fell to the ground.

"Cut," Romero yelled. "What the hell is wrong with you Manolo? You grab your neck and break the blood bag and *then* fall down."

"Manolo. My God!" The other actor knelt down and cradled Manolo's head in his arms. "I lost count and I killed my best friend. What have I done?"

"Done? You *hijo de la chingada*, you have broken my collar bone." Manolo pushed the other actor away with one hand and rubbed his neck with the other.

"*Puta madre!*" Romero was furious. "Fuck, what a waste of time and film." He heard the cameraman still grinding the camera and shook a fist at him. "I told you to cut, idiot!"

140

"And I motioned to him to continue," I said. Romero stared at me. An orange would have fit in his mouth.

I nodded at the cameraman. "But you can stop now."

"You do not understand," Romero said nastily.

"I understand," I said, "that if *you* have not fucked up on your reflectors or the camera angles, we have likely got the best scene on film since I got into this miserable business."

"You cannot talk to Romero like that!" Romero was a tall, thin man with thin eyebrows and a moustache to match. All three features jumped up and down as he talked.

"I will talk to you any way I want, as long as you work for me!" I used the *tú* form to address him, which is considered insulting between equals who are not close friends.

He flung the megaphone across the set and stalked out.

"Does anyone know what this story is supposed to be about?" I asked.

"No," the cameraman answered. "But I don't think it matters as long as one *cabrón* kills the other one and there is plenty of blood."

"Of course," I agreed. "There should be blood."

"We could kill the director," the cameraman said.

"That is not amusing," I said. I was not sure but that I might have to bring Romero back to finish the picture. "Try to get closer with the camera to the man lying on the ground with his shirt full of whatever it is you use for blood."

"Okay, mister. Luis, you lie down and squeeze that condom until all the ink runs out. Okay?"

"No. It was Manolo that was killed. I want the other actor, Luis, to hold him just the way he did before. Remember?"

No one did, so I had to tell them how. Then the cameraman cranked, Manolo bled, and I yelled, "Cut!"

"That will be a good shot," the cameraman said. He eyed me appraisingly. "We threw away some pretty good shots of a real doll last week. They might still be in the scrap barrel."

"So?"

"We could run them first and then show the fight. She shows a lot of tit and leg."

"Show me," I said, interested.

The cameraman was not as tall as I, but he was almost as wide. Flat-faced and button-eyed, he reminded me of photographs I had seen of canoe Indians in the northwestern United States. We walked out to the barrel. It must have weighed fifty pounds, but he lifted it, one-handed, to tilt it and run through the scrap film. He found a strip of film and handed it to me.

I held a strip against the sun. He was right. She looked like a girl that had just been ripped out of her clothes and ravished—or was about to be. She would have tempted any man. She was one of those high-cheekbone Indian girls that have always seemed more exotic to me than the ones with more of an oriental cast to their features. So it was there, in a trash barrel of discarded film, not in a small fishing village on the west coast of Oaxaca, that I first saw the girl destined to be Mexico's Theda Bara.

The difference being, of course, that every man that saw Lilly lost all thought of protecting the defenseless female and simply wished that he could tear her clothes off and rape her.

Her large, pointed breasts slipped in and out of the torn blouse, and her long brown legs—wondrously long for an Indian girl—were bare to the thigh.

"Here's another shot," he said.

The first frames were of the back of a man dressed in Indian white. He ripped open her blouse and tore her skirt half off.

"Of course," I said. "Do you not see? We will open with this, then cut to the fight and then back to the last few frames where you can see one whole tit and the curve of the ass. We could leave it on the screen for a full second?"

"Sure. And we could title it *The Sister's Shame.*"

"No. It will be *The Brother's Revenge.*"

"Good." He nodded approval, and I felt a warm surge of gratitude at his understanding. "Maybe if we called it *The Sister's Shame* or *The Brother's Revenge* we could get both ideas across. Sex and blood."

"Yes," I said, seeing the strategy clearly. "That is the way we will advertise it: sex and blood."

"Perfect, *patrón.*"

I flatter myself on my ability to pick up new ideas. I am not averse to taking them from any source. Besides, the cameraman seemed more aware of what he was doing than did the arrogant director.

"Why did Romero not use that footage?"

"Lilly wouldn't put out."

"What?"

"She wouldn't lay him. She was living with a Gypsy bullfighter at the time, so she wouldn't. So, Romero, he wouldn't use it. But he

142

should have."

"He certainly should have. My God!" We both shook our heads at the folly of the director.

"What is your name?" I asked, arriving at a decision.

"Timoteo Morán de la Garza, at your orders."

"All right, Tim. We will work together for now, but after this film, you will be the director."

When Romero came back the next day, he found us busy finishing off the film. His old canvass folding chair had a new name tacked to its back: Tim Morán. He went at his replacement tooth and nail, but Tim shoved the wide end of his megaphone over his face and then knocked him silly with one quick chopping blow to his ear. Tim gave him back the battered megaphone and even helped him brush the dirt off his cashmere sweater before he led him off the set. I never saw the man again.

Within a week we had made enough copies of the film to send to all of our movie houses. By the end of the month, we were deluged with mail addressed to the "Sister" in care of CosaCine Films. So the girl known to me at the time only as Lilly and as the "Sister" to the audience, became an overnight sensation—what would later be called a star.

But of course, on that day, the day I was to be married, all I knew about the film was that I had forged another link in a financial chain that might hold an empire together. I seldom sing or even whistle, but I caught myself doing both on the ride back to my new apartment near the American Embassy.

Tell was there, pacing the floor, more nervous than I.

"Relax and have a drink," I told him. "It is only the civil ceremony. The religious one will be next week, in Puebla."

"Why be married twice? Once ought to be enough for anyone."

"One must have a civil wedding now to be legal. Ask your friend Obregón."

"My friend?"

"You always praise him."

"The man has something," Tell said in his rumbling voice. "He really believes in Mexico. But he isn't one of your fanatical, humorless *políticos*."

"No," I agreed. "Most certainly not."

"You ever hear how he got his arm back? The one that was shot off at Celaya?"

"No," I lied. Tell loves that story.

"He told it to me, himself, straight-faced, completely serious. He went back to the battlefield, full of dead and dismembered men and horses, and he walked through the carnage holding a gold coin in his good hand. Suddenly, his missing forearm and hand leaped out from a stack of corpses and snatched the golden coin!"

Tell barely finished before going off into a paroxysm of laughter. He is a good mime and tells a story well. If he were a handsome man, he might be useful in the film industry. He might make an excellent villain.

"Wonderful," I said, after I had laughed in genuine pleasure, not at the old story, but at Tell's obvious delight. "However, our president is a devious man."

"Yes, but are there any other kind?"

I shook a negative finger and turned to the liquor cabinet. I poured cognac for both.

"Maybe I better not drink," Tell said. "I don't want to show up for your wedding drunk."

"I have never seen you drunk," I said.

"Never?"

"Well," I reconsidered. "Not staggering drunk."

"Will, it's almost four now."

"The bride will wait," I said, lifting my glass.

"In that case I will have a quick one." He lifted his glass to me and said, "To a happily married life."

There was a sadness about him, and I wondered if it was because of his notion of the Johnny and Toña bond.

"To the bride and her family, the banking Balboas," I said.

Tell drank and then said, "I have never met the lady."

"Well," I said defensively, for I hate to be pinned down to dates, "you left Puebla and came here ages ago."

"You have been here over a year, Will."

"I have been busy," I said, bristling. Tell can be so damned self-centered at times.

"How did you meet her?"

"Cosa does a lot of business with banks." Before he could continue, I asked, "Do you have the ring?"

"Ring. What ring?"

I let him search his pockets desperately before I laughed and said,

"You do not have the ring. Nor do I need one until next week at the church." Then I added casually, "I want you to fly me over."

"No! Not Will Riley in an airplane!"

"You have invited me before. This time I accept. If I am to invest in Aerotrain, I must have some knowledge of flying. Also, that morning I want to see the edited prints of the new film."

"Sunday morning?"

"Yes. The wedding is scheduled at twelve. We can leave the studio at eleven."

"That is a tight schedule. We might be late."

"They will wait. The family treasures me."

Tell did not laugh as I had expected. Instead he put one of his huge hands on my shoulder and asked, "You do want to marry the girl, no?"

I almost blurted out the truth and even my reason, but then thought better. A wise man keeps his own counsel.

"You know that I am not supposed to sleep with the bride until the church wedding?"

"Right. So you suffer another week."

"I didn't wait. You know how these hot-blooded Italian women are." I winked. It would not hurt for the story to get around that I had knocked her up. In a few months some of those old bitches would notice her belly and count the months.

"I guess it makes no difference as long as you get married," Tell said and consulted his watch again.

"All right," I said. "Did you borrow that black sedan from an undertaker?"

Tell touched his forehead and said, "Yes, esteemed one."

"All right," I said, "take me to my wedding in your hearse."

Both of our cars were out in front. His chauffeur was eyeing Pepe uneasily. Pepe frightened most people. I motioned Pepe to follow and got in back with Tell. As I knew he would, he placed me to his right. It was an instinctive move to keep the other rider where Tell could draw, and bring his pistol to bear immediately on the danger.

"Were you ever, outside of that fracas in Puebla, in a face-to-face gunfight, Wild West style?" I asked, thinking of the cinematographic possibilities.

"Yes."

I waited for him to elaborate. When he did not, I questioned him further. "I am thinking of filming a gunfight for our next moving picture. I would like it to be realistic."

Tell nodded, closed his eyes and was quiet. I knew he was remembering a brief instant of fear and triumph.

"If you can get Rubio in front of a camera, I will be pleased to shoot him for you." He spoke in that infuriating Texas drawl.

"Tell, goddamn you, I am serious."

"So am I, Will," he said, fighting not to smile. "But if it would make you feel any better, we could load his pistol with blanks."

"Tell!" I was angry now and he knew it.

"All right, Will. I remember the first time, in Texas. It was like everything was magnified, except time, and time stops. It shatters like a pane of glass on a brick patio. My dad was a cool sure shot, and he taught me to watch a man's eyes to see if he meant to draw, and if he did, then I was to draw first. He told me to draw slow and shoot sure at the center of the man. The average drunken cowboy will yank his revolver out and shoot as fast as he can thumb back the hammer."

"But what happened in that first fight?"

"I got off the first shot."

"But if you drew slowly . . ."

"He snatched that pistol out so fast that he dropped it. Then, when he bent down to grab at it again, he kicked it with the point of his boot. Then I shot."

"You killed him," I said with some satisfaction. I knew that Tell could be ruthless.

"No. I was a bit nervous too. I damn near shot the toe off my boot."

"But what happened to him."

"The cowboy? He fainted. He thought he was dead. When he came to he was so happy to be among the living that he bought me a whiskey. We were good friends until he was killed a few years later in a gunfight."

"He dropped his gun again?"

"No. He practiced his draw a lot. He got real fast. He got off three shots before some little old gunfighter left over from the frontier days shot the pistol out of his hand."

"But that surely did not kill him."

"No. That soft-talking old man took a better aim and put a round through his heart."

After pondering over Tell's story and discounting at least half of it as fantasy, I said, "I think you can do the moving picture industry a great favor, Tell. Stay away from it."

146

He shook his head sadly, but smiled all the same, so I was never sure how much of his story was true. In fairness I must say that even Rubio admitted that Tell had behaved with extraordinary coolness during that shooting in Puebla.

There was a line of cars, and groups of chauffeurs and bodyguards were gathered together to smoke and, I suspected, to compare wages.

When I presented Tell to Carmencita, he came close to stuttering. When he raised her hand to kiss it, she smiled radiantly. She is beautiful, I thought with some surprise and pride.

"I had no idea that your *novia* was so beautiful," Tell said, grinning. "I'll bet my saddle there's not one girl in that cinema business of yours that can match her."

"Keep your saddle," I said. I looked at Carmencita again and realized that she was likely as lush as my sexy movie star, Lilly. "The Balboas are noted for their beautiful women," I said.

"Yes," Carmencita said. "That and oppressing the peasants. I take after the Mexican side of the family."

A waiter brought champagne. We drank toasts to us and to Tell, and then a thin young girl with large luminous eyes greeted Carmencita.

"I have not met your *novio*," she said, but her eyes were on Tell.

"Mary Rivera . . . my intended, Willard Riley; and our dear friend, Tell Cooper."

Our dear friend? I would have spoken, but the girl merely touched my hand before she turned to Tell.

"Major Cooper, I am the daughter of the late General Pedro Rivera Martínez."

"Then you did get my letter?" Tell said.

"Yes. Forgive me. I could not answer. Yet I knew that one day I would meet you and thank you. It was all I had. The letter."

Tears suddenly welled in her eyes. Thank God the girl had sense enough to trot off to one of the bathrooms to cry.

"What was that all about?" I asked.

"Mexico. The Revolution. I spent the night with her father, the general, before he was executed by a firing squad."

"That night in Puebla?"

"That night."

A small bell tinkled and my future father-in-law called out as cheerfully as a songbird.

"Everyone is here . . . now." Alejandro paused for the laughter at the one person who should have been on time: me, the gringo *novio*.

"The registrar is here and I have enough for the fee." He paused again for the perfunctory laughter and then said, "So, if the bridegroom will come forth." Again he waited for laughter. My mother-in-law laughed dutifully. He continued. "And the bride, of course."

Carmencita snatched another glass of champagne and drained it, then almost tripped and fell before Tell caught her. She must have had several drinks before I arrived. I filed the information away. I knew that I would have to discipline that unruly girl. Like Caesar's wife, she should be above suspicion. The thought pleased me, and that is why I smiled as I signed the register.

"I would be smiling, too, if I were marrying the beautiful daughter of Alejandro Balboa." A pudgy man with a voice as resonant as an Italian baritone spoke. He was a banker who controlled three financial institutions.

"I am indeed lucky," I said, and thought that I would have been just as fortunate had she been as ugly as sin.

Alejandro joined us. He beamed at the other banker, then spoke to me. "I see that you are getting along famously with Arturo. That is good. The Balboas and the Perrugias have been allied for centuries."

Likely true, I thought. They might have farmed the same miserable piece of rocky land in Italy until one of their more ambitious relatives—or just the odd one on the run from the law—had worked his way over on a freighter. I said, "I hope to have a long and rewarding talk with Señor Perrugia after the wedding."

"Of course, but, young man, please call me Arturo."

"Thank you, *Don* Arturo," I said. He was likely several years older than I, but I let him have the little meaningless title, the feeling of superiority. Let him smirk and be condescending. One day I would take over his banks.

Carmencita left Tell and walked without a trace of a stagger to my side. We received the good wishes of all of the guests, about half family friends and the others business friends, mostly Perrugias.

Finally, with the ceremony over, the crowd thinned. Querulous wives nagged the last drunken husbands out of the room, and I was left alone with the Balboas, Tell, and Mary Rivera, who was, I discovered, a house guest on a visit from the state of Sonora.

"Major Cooper," Alejandro asked, after we had settled down around a coffee table to drink coffee and cognac. "What will you do now that you have finished training the pilots?"

148

"I don't know—"

"He is going to form a company called Aerotrain," I interrupted.

"Aerotrain? What is that?" Mary asked.

"A train of airplanes," Tell said, grinning, "but no rails."

"It will be a fleet of airplanes, like ships at sea," I said impatiently. "They will carry essential cargo and a few elite passengers through the skies over mountain barriers and impassable swamps."

"I'm going to do all that?" Tell looked at me in mock horror.

"I like the name, young man," Alejandro said.

"So do I," I said dryly.

Tell had the grace to tell them that the name was my idea and even disclaimed the fleet of airplanes. Then the talk turned to weddings and deaths and centuries of bogus family history. I think that Carmencita was as bored as I, or maybe just sleepy from too much champagne.

"It is time to go." I stood up and eyed Carmencita speculatively. "Are you ready, love?"

Carmencita laughed, but neither her mother or father cracked a smile. Finally Tell laughed nervously and they permitted themselves a wintry smile at my coarse humor.

"Where will you go on your honeymoon?" Mary Rivera asked.

"I do not know." I turned to Carmencita. "Shall we use your bedroom or mine?"

Mama Carmen covered her face with her hands; Alejandro turned pale, then red, and stuttered when he did talk.

"You are not yet married. Not in the church. No. It is not—"

"Señor Balboa," Tell broke into the conversation. "Will knows that. He has a very dry sense of humor. It takes some getting used to. Do not take offense."

"He will not," I said. "I have promised him that I will take better care of his daughter than ever he did. Is that not true, dear father-in-law?"

He nodded, looking at his hands, and then reached for the cognac.

"And you, Mama Carmen?" She peeked out at me from between fat fingers.

"Mama Carmen!" I called out loudly. She gave a little shriek and flung her hands away from her face. She knocked over her husband's glass and it shattered on the tiled floor. No one looked at the shreds of glass.

"Yes, Señor Riley," she whimpered. "Yes, yes."

"You must call me son, now, Mother Carmen," I said. I should not have baited her, but she was such a mixture of abject religious fear and middle-class propriety that I could not resist. Besides, she reminded me of my own mother. Even old Alejandro might have been a successful version of the ward-heeling drunk who had fathered me seven months before the wedding. Or—the thought was a red slash in my brain—had he?

"Of course," Mama Carmen sniffled, "I will, after the wedding. The real one in Puebla."

A warm red haze drifted into the room. The others did not seem to notice. Carmencita laughed up at me. I could see the deep golden cleft between her breasts as firm and larger than those of . . . was it Lilly? No. La Martinique. The French-speaking octoroon from Martinique, or so she claimed. I had paid her price and more and she had been worth it.

"Stand up," I said.

Carmencita got to her feet, but she seemed puzzled. Why, I thought. I paid for her just like the other. Except more. She pivoted, shoulders bare, golden hair brushing the skin that gleamed with just a touch more of brown in it than did her hair.

"I'll take this one," I said and moved to take her arm, but she shrunk back, peering at me fearfully.

"Will! Stop it. It is no longer funny." I heard Tell speak as if from a lower story of a very high building, but he brought me back. The color ebbed and was gone. All of the actors were frozen in their positions, as if at the finish of a play, waiting for the fall of the curtain.

"I am sorry," I said. "I wanted a good look at my bride. A week is a long time."

I turned to go. "Come on, Tell. I guess I have had too much to drink." I pretended to lean on him as we left; all of the others were glad to have a pretext to avoid a confrontation. Most people will. I have used it to great advantage. If there is no chance of physical harm to me, I revel in any confrontation.

"You know," I said so loudly that Tell shushed me even as we closed the door behind us, "I think Carmencita has bigger tits than La Martinique."

Chapter 18

· · · · · · · · · · · · · · · · · · ✈

Just before dawn, when night is at its darkest, the nightmare strikes; the truth blazes in my brain. The death of Will Riley is as inevitable as that of an ant. The voice that condemns me to death is sweetly familiar. But then as the bullet smashes into my heart, I summon up my last bit of strength and jerk free from the perverse umbilical cord dragging me down into the black depths of oblivion. Then, heart pounding, I wake. There are a few seconds of panic, which I conquer by repeating a litany that I taught myself when only eleven years old: "I, Willard Riley, will live forever. Willard Riley will forever live."

When I looked down from the cockpit, high above the valley of Mexico, I saw that same deadly cord reaching for me. I screamed, buried my face in my hands and crouched as low as I could into the cockpit. And for the twenty-odd minutes of the flight from Mexico to Puebla, I repeated the litany over and over, else I would have gone mad. It was my first and, I thought, my last flight. I realize now why there are so few aviators and why there will never be any great use for airplanes except for war and special cargo deliveries. At Puebla I was barely able to crawl out of the cockpit, down onto a wing and then slide off into a heap on the ground. Tell had the effrontery to congratulate me for not being airsick! Alejandro and Perrugia rushed forward to help me. I struck out at the groping hands and got to my feet. I snatched off my helmet and threw it at the airplane.

"Who has a drink?" I asked loudly, my ears still clogged from the altitude changes.

Perrugia produced a small, thin silver flask. I lightened it by half. My heart beat slowed.

"Willard," Alejandro said nervously, "it is already twelve o'clock."

"A Mexican worried about time? But I forget. You are an Italian, a race preoccupied with time since they reconstructed the calendar."

"I, for one," Perrugia said stiffly, "am always on time, be it the English hour or the Mexican."

"So am I," I spoke curtly, for I was still upset by that fearful flight. "And if this wedding were in London or New York, I would have been on time. As it is in Mexico, I am an hour late. Or am I still too early?"

Perrugia snorted his displeasure and turned away. I knew his type.

More Mexican than the Mexicans. He donned golden and silvered charro costumes on Sundays and rode through the park. My temper cooled. I needed his support—for a while yet.

"Forgive me *Don* Arturo," I said quickly before he could walk away. "I have a great fear of flight and it befuddled me, but I am all right now. I am late and I apologize." He did turn to stare at me; there was no sign of friendship in his eyes. I searched my mind frantically for the correct combination to unlock the man. It was so simple.

"I have a favor to ask, *Don* Arturo?" I said.

"Yes?" he answered sullenly.

"I need a close friend to stand up for me."

"But you already have your friend, Major Cooper," he said, puzzled.

I put an arm on his shoulder and lifted to my toes so that I could look straight into his eyes.

"Tell is my good friend, but then, so are you. I thought it would be more appropriate to have a Mexican, who is not only an old friend of the Balboa family but also a distinguished banker, to act as my best man."

I turned my head, caught Tell's eye and winked. He did not even smile. He removed the small box that held the ring and held it out.

Perrugia embraced me. When he spoke his voice trembled with emotion. "Of course I will do this for you, amigo Willard. After all, as you say, our families are interrelated."

Perrugia pocketed the ring and insisted that I ride with him in his limousine. I heard a peal of high-pitched laughter and saw the American journalist, Helen Anderson, walking arm-in-arm with Tell. We all got into the back seat except for Perrugia, who surprised me by riding, democratically, in the front with his chauffeur.

Tell was strangely quiet, but Helen was full of questions.

"How are you able to market your sugar? There are so few railroad cars available."

"We have been fortunate. The government buys and transports most of our sugar."

"Of course. And is the business as profitable as expected?"

"It will be," I said carefully, for she was an accomplished, resourceful reporter. "But it will take a long time to amortize our huge capital investment, rebuilding, replacement of heavy machinery, new housing for workers, and the cost incurred in buying the land to turn over to the cane growers."

"You mean the communal farmland, the *ejidos*?"

"Well . . . yes, I suppose you could call them that."

"But I thought that the land was distributed free by the agrarian commission."

"Yes, except that the original owners did receive compensation."

"Johnny Ávalos?"

"Yes, among others," I said, "but why do I have such a feeling of déjà vu? Did we not discuss all this once before?"

"We did." She smiled. "I am bringing myself up to date. I have been asked to do a series on successful American businessmen managing to do business in such a turbulent country. You are one of four—"

"Who are the other three?" I interrupted, not bothering to tell her that I was actually a citizen of Mexico.

She ignored my question. "How many theaters do you own?"

"Around fifteen," I said.

"I would have thought thirty," she said. Cosa actually owned thirty-one.

"Do you think they will catch the man who murdered the leader of the actor's union, Emilio López?" She meant to take me unawares. Perhaps she thought that I might blurt out some revealing knowledge.

"Yes," I said, nodding my conviction as well. "Our own company has offered a reward of five thousand pesos for information leading to the arrest of the assassin."

"I have heard from reliable sources that Jorge Rubio was wounded at the same time. Do you think it might have been the same man that shot both of the moviemakers?"

Tell said, "Moviemaker!" and snorted.

"What reliable source told you that Jorge was wounded?" I asked, annoyed.

"Jorge Rubio. He even showed me the scar."

I grimaced involuntarily. The smart little whore must have gotten Jorge into bed and then talking, which would not have been difficult. Not with a good-looking blond gringa with big blue eyes and big tits.

"Would you like to see my scar sometime?" I said, staring at her cleavage.

She colored immediately, but said nothing. She regained her composure in seconds. I was impressed. Someday I might need someone as good as she was in her field.

"He showed me his scar in a public restaurant. He was proud of the scar. He said he got it in a gunfight."

"Perhaps he did," I said. "I wonder if you would like to do some writing for Cosa. A history of the company along with its plans for expansion. Do it in your spare time and collect from Cosa and the *Times*."

"Something that might attract international investors?"

"Well," I shrugged, "all companies, large and small, need capital. I am thinking of issuing stock in CosaCine Films."

"Do you intend to make full-length movies?"

"We are about to make one with Lilly and Raúl Camargo."

"I saw a lot of Lilly in *The Sister's Shame*. What will you call the new one?"

"How did you like it?" I decided to play her game.

"Not much. But then, they are made for children or over-sexed men, aren't they?"

"No. We make them for the whole family. The next one will bring them all in."

"And what will it be called?"

"*Bloody Lust*," I said without thinking. Of course she laughed. So did Tell, and even that idiot in the front seat, Arturo Perrugia, who spoke no English, laughed. Helen looked younger when she laughed, not as hard, even innocent. But then she must have changed bed partners as quickly as she did the sheets. A young girl like that, alone in Paris. What would her morals be? I felt a quivering of my loins, which I quelled immediately. It would not do to bed Tell's girl, even if she were a whore.

"That will bring them in, Will."

I laughed with her to show her I held no malice and nodded agreement.

"Jorge told me that Raúl Camargo will only work through the Artist's Labor Union."

"Jorge knows nothing of the movie business. Write your story as I told you. Lilly will play opposite Camargo."

"All right. What is Lilly's last name?"

I could not remember her family name. "She has none. That is, she refuses to reveal it. She was found on the doorstep of a mission in Chiapas. The nuns who raised her said that she was the daughter of an Indian princess and a Swedish nobleman who disappeared into the jungle never to return."

"You should write for the magazines, Will," she said. "There is a great market for short fiction."

154

"Very funny, Helen," I said, smiling, but I vowed that I would find a way to buy that girl one day if for nothing else than the sheer pleasure of bending her to my will.

Although everyone seemed to be more or less where they were supposed to be, the ceremony still seemed to take an eternity. Carmencita seemed dazed. Her eyes were dull and the skin around them was dark. She mumbled so badly that the priest not only had to repeat his questions but also prompt her. At the culmination he hissed, "Say yes, *mi hija!*"

She did, and it was over.

Outside, I looked for Tell, but he was nowhere to be seen.

"They must have gone ahead in another car," Perrugia said.

"I suppose it was too much to ask of the organizers of this spectacle that my best friend ride to the reception with me."

"But Willard, he would be welcome—"

"Oh, come on," I cut him off, and, dragging Carmencita along with me, got into Perrugia's automobile, just the two of us, for Carmencita's wide-skirted, virginal-white wedding gown took up most of the room. I called to the driver to proceed before Perrugia could catch up and ride in the front again.

"Where is Tell?" Carmencita asked.

"Forget Tell. He already has a bed partner. That good-looking gringa is his."

"I saw her. She is lovely, but maybe too old."

"Old and virginal," I said. "Or do you think that Tell would invite a whore to our wedding?"

"Do not do this, Willard. I will do my part, but you must—"

"Must? Must!" I meant to acquaint her to a few of the rules of conduct that she would conform to, but the driver pulled over, jumped out and opened the door for Carmencita.

The reception was in a huge, statue-filled garden. There must have been a hundred people there that I had never met. I searched for Tell, but all of the unknown ones would stop me and propose the same banal toasts, and I would have to sip champagne and so would my already tipsy bride.

I found Jorge Rubio in a corner of the garden, his coat and shirt unbuttoned, as he exhibited a roll of brown fat with a puckered white scar dancing on it like a sail on a muddy river.

"Why not take your pants off too, Jorge?" I asked.

He laughed, then saw Carmencita and turned away to button up.

"Have you seen Tell?"

"Not since the wedding."

"Where is Johnny?"

"He was at the wedding with his old lady."

"I know he was there with his wife. Where is he now?"

"I don't know. I was telling these *cabrones*—I mean caballeros—about the Revolution and the time the *federales* shot me in the—"

"Balls!" I said. "Find Ávalos for me. Now!"

Rubio turned his reproachful toad eyes on me and began, "*Patrón*, I was only—"

"Now!"

"Sure." He trotted off without looking back at his companions. They, in turn, nervous as altar boys serving a visiting bishop, muttered congratulations and moved away.

"I never thought I would feel sorry for that Toad," Carmencita said.

"You may have another occasion soon," I said and stopped, for I could hear his croak all the way across the hundred-yard-long garden.

"Hey, *patrón*! I found him."

I made angry motions for him to come to me, for all other conversation had ceased. Half way across he halted, flung his arms in the air and yelled again, although I think he meant to whisper.

"*Don* Willard, do I have news for you!"

I made one hand signal for him to shut up and then a palm-down gesture to come closer.

He trotted the rest of the way, belly swaying, scattering waiters with champagne filled trays, costing Alejandro a small fortune in spilt champagne. He stopped in front of me, beaming.

"Will, guess what?"

He had gone from "boss" to "*Don* Willard" to old-pal "Will" in one short walk across the garden.

"Tell and the . . . ah . . . gringa . . . they—"

"Stop. Count to ten, if you know that much arithmetic and . . ." I saw Johnny, his wife not with him, walking through the crowd, stopping every few steps to embrace someone and take a sip of wine and then move on, like a prince at court.

"Tell Cooper and the gringa—"

"Go bring Johnny to me. No, just send him to me and then go show your scar to some of the older, more experienced ladies. Go. Now!" I pointed with a finger toward Johnny, and Rubio slunk off like a disobedient dog.

I had to smile and embrace Johnny before I could ask him about Tell.

"He is likely half way to Veracruz," Johnny said.

"But the wedding was over just a few minutes ago," I said.

"Your wedding, yes."

"That's what I was going to tell you, *patrón*." Rubio spoke from behind me.

"Will you leave me?" I spoke softly, but I was furious and he knew it. He walked away, shooting me one venomous glance before he marched across the grass, shouldering aside those who got in his way.

"Be careful of that one," Johnny said. "He will sting, you know."

"Yes," I agreed, for I did know. Still, Rubio did have his uses. "He is a back shooter, but I have Pepe to watch mine."

"*Sí, patrón?*" Pepe, unobtrusive, but near, had thought I called him. I never even look for him any more. I knew that he would be watching over me. Each year his salary was to be doubled. If I died, he would receive nothing except a quick death. It would not matter how I died, for the killer known only to me would be paid a magnificent sum from Cosa to kill Pepe. As a result, besides being a very professional killer himself—Tell had once commented on him, called him the Stiletto—he was very concerned with my health.

"I did not call you, Pepe. I merely mentioned to Señor Ávalos that you are a most vigilant bodyguard."

"Thank you, patrón." He was dressed as well as most of the guests, and standing there, with a glass of champagne in his left hand, no one would have guessed that he could draw his hidden pistol and shoot a would-be assassin through the heart, and never spill a drop of champagne.

"He has the coldest eyes," Johnny said. "He gives me chills even on a hot day like this."

I nodded impatiently, agreeing with him for brevity's sake. "Now tell me, what is this Veracruz thing?"

"Tell and Helen are on their way there to get married. She knows a registrar there that will do anything for her."

"I wager he will. But we must stop the marriage. What general should I wire?"

"Why must we stop the wedding?"

"She is not a virtuous woman, Johnny."

"She is just as virtuous as anybody else," Carmencita said loudly.

She had been standing behind me, quietly drinking champagne from every passing tray. "Not a whore." She glared at me. "Not a whore at all."

I took her by one elbow and pointed her toward a group of older guests, including her mother, and shoved her. She tottered off, still muttering about virtue.

"They will be there by now." Johnny clicked the face of his pocket watch open. When he snapped it shut, the cover sparkled in the sun. A year ago the diamond- and ruby-encrusted timepiece had been in a safe in the National Pawn Shop in Mexico City.

"Impossible," I snapped. "Even if the train was on time they would have left just a few minutes ago."

"But they did not take the train. They went the way you came, Will, in the airplane."

"They skipped out on my wedding to fly to Veracruz in a stinking, dirty airplane?"

"They were at the wedding, Will. Maybe it was catching. Anyway, I drove them out to the airfield, still in their wedding clothes, drinking champagne. They took a bottle each in the machine. Helen said that they would drink toasts to all of the volcanoes: Popocatépetl, Iztaccíhuatl, and Orizaba. Some way to get married!"

Johnny sounded wistful.

"Would you run away and get married to a girl you scarcely know?" I asked.

"No, I guess not. But then Tell has known her on and off for a long time. Why, you have only known Carmencita a month or so."

Of course. That was the reason! I laughed out loud and said, "Just another shotgun marriage."

"Another shotgun marriage?" Johnny asked, his black brows almost meeting as they did when he was perplexed.

"Sure, Johnny," I said, sure of myself now. "The first baby only takes eight months, after that, nine."

158

Chapter 19

· · · · · · · · · · · · · · · · · · ✈

We had embraced, patted each other on the back, drunk two cups of that muddy silt the Italians and Spaniards dote on, discussed my bastard son Alejandro, and I had refused one of Perrugia's twisted, poisonous cigars. Only then was Arturo Perrugia ready to talk business. He wiped off the tolerant smile and assumed the pursed lips of the all-powerful banker dealing with a humble borrower.

"You have requested an enormous loan, Will."

I shrugged, blew some of his own stinking smoke back into his face, and waited. He began to fidget and then spoke first. I had won that little game.

"Your collateral does not justify such a loan, Will," he said stiffly.

"*Don* Arturo, with all due respect I must say that you do not understand the moving picture business."

"I know that your company, CosaCine Films, makes an excellent profit. I also know that it does not have the physical assets to justify such a loan."

"I will, as has been customary, assign you the negatives."

"For a half-a-million-peso loan!"

"My last picture made double that."

"You made a net profit of exactly $600,200 pesos and forty-three centavos," he said.

"How in the world did you know that?" I asked, shaking my head in awe. Actually when Arturo had suborned my head accountant, I had been delighted. So was the accountant. He received two salaries and did not have to purloin the information. I furnished it to him. The profits were as represented by our books, but the costs were actually half of those listed.

"*Don* Arturo," I continued, "we need new equipment, a studio of our own. Then I will show you profits that even you will not believe."

"We just might accept the movie houses as collateral," Arturo said casually, as if the thought had just occurred to him.

"You read my mind," I admitted ruefully. "However," I added, "what I have in mind will be even more profitable for us both and will also, so to speak, keep it in the family."

"Continue." He leaned back in his chair, his fingers interlaced over his blossoming belly and his eyes fixed on the ceiling. He must have seen the film of the banker rejecting a loan to the valiant young agronomist, and he picked his own hero.

"I suggest a simple exchange of collateral stock," I said. "We will allow you to hold, as a guarantee for present and future loans, say, a million pesos. You will do the same for us with a block of equivalent stock."

"Give you our stock?"

"No. Not give. Place in our surety until the day that we both return each other's stock. It will be our guarantee that you return our stock. Of course, if we do not repay a loan, the CosaCine Films stock will be yours."

"It does sound tempting, Will. I will have one of my assistants check—"

"No. Either we have a deal or we do not. I thought to offer the opportunity to the family first. But," I waited until I saw alarm register in his eyes, and added, "I can always strike a deal with Félix Montemayor at the Banco—"

"Will. Please." This time he interrupted me and I knew that I had him. "You are too impetuous. Of course we have a deal. However, we must work out the details."

"Of course," I repeated gravely, laughing inside. "I will send Johnny Ávalos over to deal with your people. As a personal favor to me, would you watch over him for a few weeks? Show him the ropes. If we are to work as closely in the future as I envision, I want a man in my organization with a knowledge of banking. And the only one I would trust to train a man for me is you, *Don* Arturo. Please do not mention this to *Don* Alejandro Balboa."

We both smiled at my little joke. We also both knew that Alejandro was getting dotty. "It is not just my opinion. I have talked with others. And the consensus is that you are the banker's banker, *Don* Arturo. Will you do it?"

"You exaggerate," he said, but if he had been a parrot, which he did at times resemble, he would have preened his feathers. "I will help Johnny. He is a fine boy. I knew his father well. He controlled most of the sugar production in the state of Puebla, you know."

"Really?"

"Oh, my yes. They were one of the really wealthy families before the . . . the . . ."

"Glorious Revolution." I finished the sentence for him.

160

"Yes. Before."

"I will send Johnny over tomorrow with a copy of our books."

"Do that." He grinned slyly. "Send the ones with the government stamps and the other set as well, hmm?"

"You sly old fox," I said, standing up.

He closed the door behind me. I could hear him humming happily as I walked away.

Pepe moved in behind me like the shadow he had become. The chauffeur not only had the door open for me, but was scanning the street both ways. Pepe had assured me that he was as familiar with automobiles as he was with firearms.

The automobile drew up at the entrance to my private elevator at the rear of the Cosa office building. Pepe got out from his front seat and was gone the three minutes he needed to check out my small, semi-secret apartment and return. We left a guard to watch over the car and the elevator entrance, then went on up to my apartment. Pepe used his key to open the door just outside the elevator, and then locked it behind us. He opened my apartment door with another key. After I entered, I heard the lock click again. He would wait for me in the outer chamber.

I was slipping out of my new silken underwear, cut above the knee in the French fashion, when the bell began to ring incessantly. It would be Lilly. She was the only one that could lean on the doorbell and get away with it. She was the only one that Pepe would allow to enter unannounced.

I slipped into a blue silken bathrobe, pried my feet into slippers of the same material and walked slowly to the door, tantalizing myself with the thought of the golden-brown body on the other side of the door. I paused with my hand on the doorknob and could smell her musky perfume. My erection was instantaneous. I slipped the latch and threw the door open.

"Son of the bitch! I been out here pushing that *pinche* bell for a week!" Lilly spoke fluent if ungrammatical English mixed with an occasional Spanish oath. She had learned both in bordellos along the northern border.

She flung coat and purse onto a coffee table and began to peel off her clothes.

"Hold it." I was excited, breathing hard, but I knew Lilly. "Let me see the medical report."

"Here, you bastard." She drew a slip from her brassiere and thrust it at me. It was warm and scented from her breast.

The note was signed by Doctor Guzmán, and dated, including the time: eleven a.m. The golden kitty is clean.

"You are clean."

It was not a question, but she took it as one.

"What the hell! It's eleven thirty. You think I got laid in the car on my way over?"

"My God!" I said. I had not thought of that.

"For Christ's sake, Will! I swear on the *pinche* Bible I didn't even shake hands with Jorge."

"You have a voice," I said, irritated, losing my erection, "like an irritated seagull."

"Don't I know it," she said cheerfully. "When you going to put in the sound?"

She was a gross, nearly illiterate, amoral bitch. But she was a realist and not unintelligent.

"Soon," I said, my mind on her tits instead of business, and then I added quickly, "maybe next year."

"Sure. Next year. And that's why I get no new contract." She stepped out of her skirt, drew her blouse over her head and then unfastened the brassiere and let those gorgeous golden breasts free. They sagged more than a finger's width for they were the shape and size of pineapples. She wore transparent white silken bloomers. The black curly pubic hair showed through at the crotch, and a black garter belt crossed higher on her hips to hold up the sheer silk stockings.

She turned her back to me, then smiled at me over one shoulder as she stripped off one stocking. I could stand no more. I half-tore the other stocking off, then guided her foot back into the special shoes I had designed to make her long legs look even longer. She turned around, the pubic hair glistening darkly through the silk, now inches from my eyes.

"All right, you cunt-hungry, cock-pushing son of a bitch!" She drew a fist back menacingly. "Take that huge, hot cock and get up on the bed!"

I made sounds of alarm and scrambled over to the bed. I leaned back against the over-sized pillows while she swayed and twisted her pelvis at me, moving closer and closer. I threw my robe open and touched my penis. It seemed to burn my fingers.

"Now. Come here!"

"What is it you want, sir?" She assumed the look of apprehension

162

combined with an overwhelming sensuality that had made her famous—and had made our company a fortune.

"I want you, you bitch. Get those tits and legs and ass up here where I can—"

"No. No more, *Weel*."

That refusal was not in the scenario. I sat up straight. "What are you talking about?"

"I want to marry Jorge."

"Jorge Rubio. The Toad. You want to marry him?"

"Sure. He owns a lot of the company."

"He has one wife."

"A man can get a divorce now. He don't care about the church."

"Jorge wants to screw you so badly that he will marry you?"

"Yeah."

"What do you want? My permission."

"Jorge told me I had to. He's scared."

"What would I do to you and Jorge?" I asked, interested.

"Maybe disappear us?" It was not quite a question.

"What a thought," I said, and then, "Go ahead. What the hell. You will never make it in talking pictures anyway. And now, do something for me."

"Sure. I can't fuck you anymore. At least not until after the wedding, but I'm going to do something for you I never do before, except with my best lover."

Before I could respond she took my pulsating cock into her hand, squeezed it hard with a rhythm that constricted my lungs and made me gasp for breath, and then took the head into her mouth and with a flickering tongue and soft, red caressing lips drove me into the wildest orgasm that I had ever experienced.

When I could breathe again, Lilly was dressed as carefully as when she had entered. Her hair was not mussed. Only her stockings were missing. She bent over the bed to kiss me goodbye. I realized, barely in time, her intention, and hastily averted my face, controlling the urge to vomit. My God! The thought was horrendous. Could she have done that to another man and then come here to lie with me, to kiss me with lips that, for all I knew, were sticky with semen? I barely made it to the bathroom before I was sick.

"*Weel*," she called to me from outside the door. "You all right?"

"Yes. Just go."

"Sure, *Weel*." And then the clever bitch had to add, "Maybe it was something I ate."

Her harsh laughter faded with the sound of the apartment door slamming. Laugh, away, I thought. You will marry Jorge and you will tell me everything that he does, and whenever I want one of those French specialties, you will do it for me. I was no longer sick and almost sorry that she had not stayed to do it again. But, I promised myself, I will never again kiss you on the lips. Maybe I might nibble on the tip of a golden breast, but never again would I touch those lips except, I permitted myself a small chuckle, with an erect cock.

Chapter 20

Tell Cooper, Mexico City, 1923.

"I have almost six thousand dollars," I said, "but I will need to keep out enough to take care of the family until we have established an income."

"You must need a large amount," George said.

"We could get by on two hundred a month."

"You mean that you and Helen and the boy could manage on two hundred? With a chauffeur, a gardener, a cook and a maid?"

"We would have to cut expenses. But we can do it. I know Helen is willing."

"Extraordinary," George said. "Imagine, the three of you living on such a small amount."

"How much do you have, George?"

"Not much."

"How much?"

"Well," he said defensively. "If it had not been for that American girl, Babs what's-her-name, I would have made it through the month easily."

"You are broke?"

"Yes, but Tell, I only have a few days to go before the post will bring me my check."

"You don't have any capital?"

"No. None that I can get at."

"But you do have an income. I have capital but no income. We'll use my capital and live on your income. How much is it?"

"Not much. The bank gives me almost four hundred pesos for the sterling."

"Well that's it," I said full of enthusiasm. "We can get a couple of slightly damaged de Havillands, rebuild them and start a Mexico-Puebla-Veracruz route."

"I don't know a soul in Veracruz."

"We'll get all of the urgent, light freight and an occasional passenger."

"What about your flying school?"

"Paco Escobar will take over my students. All one of them. He can do that and fly for the Army at the same time."

"How about the airplane? You could sell it to him and get more capital." He smacked his lips over the last word.

"He already owns it. That's where my capital is coming from."

"Oh," George said as if disappointed, but then added brightly, "All right. I shall do it. Where is my half of the capital?"

"Where it will stay until we need it, in the bank."

"I must have a checkbook."

"Of course. And you will sign checks, along with me. It will take two signatures to cash any single check."

"Oh, I say, Tell!"

"I will be the manager and treasurer. You will be the engineer and bookkeeper. Flip a coin for the job of chief pilot?"

"I suppose." George shrugged disconsolately. I tossed a gold *Centenario* in the air, caught it with my right hand, and held it hidden, covered on the back of my left hand.

"*Águila*." George chose the eagle image on one side of the coin.

"Sorry," I said, showing him the coin.

"This is not one of my better days," George said.

"Here is an advance on your first month's salary," I said and gave him the coin.

"Thank you, Tell. I shall nurse it through this period of famine." His brown eyes brightened and he smiled. "An advance on my salary. I have never had a real salary. I have never even had a real job before."

"How about the bridges?"

"I was to get a commission, but I never sold one."

"Didn't you get paid for flying Sopwith Camels?"

"I only flew them towards the end. Actually I flew the de Havilland Scout mostly. And I did get paid, but I don't remember if I spent it or not. Would it matter?" he asked anxiously.

"I doubt it," I said, eyeing him suspiciously. He had already caught me with some stories that would have done justice to a Texas trail cook. "But then you will know more about the de Havillands than I do."

"I doubt that too. But I really am an engineer, you know? Now, what's the name of our company?"

"*Transporte Interamericano Aéreo*, or 'TIA' for short. Means 'aunt' in Spanish. Easy to remember."

"I'm sure it is. I was wondering if flying to Veracruz was inter-American enough."

"Think of the future, George. El Paso, Texas, to Mexico."

"I am thinking of changing propellers from here to there and back again."

"That will be later. Think of twin engines and easily changed propellers."

"Breathtaking," George said. "We will have to pay the employees daily, you know. It is the Mexican custom."

"We will pay the employees daily, the executives monthly."

"And I," George said sadly, "am an executive."

"Yes, but do not feel too badly. I think that in your case we might make an exception and pay you daily if only to keep our engineer from starving to death."

"Ripping! Never could budget, you know."

"Your share will be, roughly, three pesos." I hesitated and then said, "Daily."

"Three pesos!" George was horrified. "Half of four hundred is two, and that divided by, say thirty, is a bit more than six—that will scarcely pay my rent."

"But George, we are not splitting our income down the middle. There are three of us and only one of you."

"But Tell, Helen is a wee thing and Tell Junior is a very little boy. Answer me, Tell, how much whiskey does he drink every day?"

"You have a point," I agreed. "We will count Helen one half and Tell number two as a quarter. Done?"

We shook hands on it.

"Now, where do we get the slightly damaged de Havillands and where will we repair them?" George was all business now that we were bound by the handshake.

"Actually they will rebuild them where they are, in El Paso. We should be off soon to see that they are properly repaired. Particularly the airframe."

"God, Almighty, Tell. One of the frames must be repaired?"

"It crashed, George. Did you never crash an airplane?"

"Never."

"Never?"

"Never, except the one time and that was the fault of my observer."

"How did the observer cause you to crash?"

"He shot away the bloody rudder."

"How did you survive?"

"Oh, I was in the front cockpit. The rudder's in the back, you know.

Never touched me."

"George! Airplanes do not fly without rudders. They spin."

"How right! We spun, but only a half a turn."

"How did you get it out with no rudder?"

"Didn't, you know. I was trying to get the bloody thing up in the air again, but that Boche on my tail thought to scupper us. There was only room for the half a spin before we ploughed into the runway. The Hun sailed right over us and crashed up ahead."

"My God," I said, completely taken in. "A German scout right down on your own field and shot you down on takeoff?"

"Not really. It was his field, you see. It looked a lot like ours. Except for the flag. And the German aeroplanes," he added ruefully.

"You didn't do it, George. You did not get lost and land at a German aerodrome and then try to takeoff again!"

"I rather think I did, Tell. I definitely remember getting very drunk with the pilot that shot us down. It seems to me that we both were credited with shooting the other down. I got a medal out of it," he added, a note of gratification in his voice. "A cross of some kind."

"You received a Military Cross?"

"No. It was an Iron Cross, second class. If he had drunk just a bit more, I think that the German pilot would have given me his first-class one."

"George! Is there one single word of truth in that whole story?"

"Of course there is. Remember when I said that I had never crashed an aeroplane?"

"George," I gasped, trying to control my laughter. "You are a bastard!"

"No, that would be my cousin Harold. He would have been next in line for the title otherwise."

"What title?"

"Earl of something or other."

"And who is the present earl of something or other?"

"My father, I expect."

"Then, one day you will be the earl of something?"

"I suppose so, but I would rather be the flying bookkeeper of TIA than an earl. Besides, it likely pays better."

I gave up and roared with laughter. George, pleased with himself, joined in and that is how Paco Escobar found us, sitting on the floor of an empty office that I had rented only because it had two telephones for each of the lines that connected the two halves of the city. If you asked for a telephone number, you had to note whether it was the Ericsson or the Mexican exchange and then use the appropriate telephone.

"What are you idiots laughing about?" Paco spoke excellent English with an accent somewhere between mine and George's. He had been educated in New Orleans and London.

"It's George," I said between gusts of laughter. "He flew for the British and the Germans gave him an Iron Cross."

Paco looked at me blankly and repeated, "You are both idiots. Now what is this about me taking over your flying school?"

"Maybe you can make it pay," I said. I told him about TIA and mentioned the Aerotrain. To my great surprise, he liked my ideas. Paco was the practical one of my friends, not a dreamer but a doer.

"You should not fly those de Havillands down here. Dismantle them, crate them and ship them by rail."

"Why?" I asked.

"He's right," George said. "The ones built in the States with the Liberty motors have about a two-hundred-and-fifty-mile range. I think we would have to refuel twice. God knows where."

"Then ship them," Paco said.

"It's a matter of economics," I explained. "It will be costly to send them. We need every *centavo* to use for a rented hangar, extra parts and—"

"And you have barely enough to cover basic expenses," Paco interrupted.

I shrugged agreement.

"What you need is more capital."

I shrugged again.

"I have five thousand dollars in a bank in Laredo, Texas."

"How did you make five thousand dollars, Paco?" I asked.

"Did you steal it, Paco?" George asked.

"Of course not!" Paco said.

"Then, Tell," George said, "what the deuce do you care?"

"When you are right, George, you are very right," I said. "We really need three airplanes, one as a spare, and there is a third one available in El Paso."

"How many shares do I get?" Paco asked.

"How many of you are there?" George asked plaintively.

"Have you been drinking mescaline cocktails?" Paco said, eyeing George suspiciously.

"No! It matters how many of you there are. To each according to his numbers, I think. It's the capitalistic system."

"What George is talking about, only he knows for sure," I said. "But he is paying his share monthly. We'll use that to live on, splitting it up between George as one unit and Helen, Tell Two and I as two units."

Paco stared at me. I might have been an airplane with a half a propeller.

"How many shares, Tell?"

I knew something about how companies were set up and stock issued because of my experience with Riley and Cosa. When I had asked how stock was priced for sale to the public, Riley had said, whatever the market will bear.

"We will, eventually, all invest five thousand. So we each get a third. Thirty-three shares each."

"Three times thirty-three is ninety-nine," Paco said.

"Likely took a first in mathematics," George said, his eyes pleading with me. "He'd make a superb bookkeeper."

"I want to give the odd share, as an incentive, to our maintenance engineer."

"Who?" they both asked.

"Guillermo Gómez."

"Memo?" George said. "Your chauffeur?"

"My ex-chauffeur? He is at work right now preparing the hangar for our airplanes."

"Memo is sweeping out the hangar?" George asked.

"No," I said, remembering how Riley had handled similar questions. "Our Maintenance and Operations Chief is readying the hangar so that the Chief Mechanic—"

"I think I have it," George interjected. "That also would be Memo."

"Also," I said. "When Pat Mahan left after training all of the mechanics, he said that Memo was by far the best."

"Pat said that?" Paco asked.

"Yes."

"Okay, then," Paco said.

"George?" I asked.

"What?"

"Shall we give the odd share to Memo?"

"Will I still be paid daily?"

"Yes."

"All right, then. Certainly. I vote that we deliver a share to good old

Memo."

So it was that good old Memo, who was a year younger than George, got a share of TIA, the company that because of its acronym he always called *Tia Tell*, or Aunt Tell. Of course, none of us, least of all Memo, ever dreamed that his one share would one day be worth almost a million pesos.

Chapter 21

· ✈

Willard Riley, 1928.

General Obregón is dead, assassinated by a religious fanatic posing as an itinerant caricaturist. Obregón would have been installed in office shortly for a second term. Now, an interim president, Emilio Portes Gil, elected by the Congress, presides in his place. How long he stays will depend on the new strongman, Calles. He was Obregón's man. The two of them had connived to change the sacred no-reelection statute so that Obregón, after an interim term filled by Calles, could be reelected. No doubt they planned to trade the presidential office back and forth until one of them died. One did.

However, it little mattered to me which one controlled the country as long as our access to the ministries remained unchanged. I believe that our lines to the important ones are as strong as ever.

Tell has begun an air service from Mexico City to Puebla and perhaps Jalapa in the state of Veracruz as well. They have three airplanes but only two aviators. A third partner, a Captain Escobar, plans to resign his commission and enter the company actively if the venture is successful. Of the three, only Tell has the most minimal idea of the business world. However, his mind is so cluttered up with puritanical mores that he will likely go bankrupt without my help.

And that is the basic reason for this meeting. To help Tell help himself. Tell would not consent to a formal meeting, so we held an informal one at my home. I did not tell him that Jorge would be there for fear that he would refuse to attend. However, he did not leave when he saw Jorge and if he was unpleasant to him, it was no more than Jorge deserved. It is not possible to be affable with the Toad, as Tell calls him. Jorge has no peers, only superiors and inferiors.

I had just poured brandy for Johnny Ávalos and myself and pointed out the tequila keg to Jorge when Tell arrived.

"Hello, Tell," I called out gaily. "I haven't seen you in ages."

"Not since your wedding," he said.

"But that was over five years ago." Could it have been that long?

"Closer to seven," Tell said, eyeing the cut-glass decanters as well as the Monet on the far wall. I glanced down at the Persian rug underfoot. His eyes followed mine. He grinned and said, "Should I take my shoes off?"

"No," I said. "The very expensive ones are on the walls in the library."

"How are you, Tell?" Johnny got up and opened his arms.

I moved up to Tell, quickly, before Johnny could hug him and shook hands.

"*¿Qué tal?*" Jorge asked.

"I'm okay," Tell said. "Shot anybody lately?"

Tell referred to a stupid newspaper story—the reporter had been fired the same day it came out—about a mysterious killer called the Toad who worked for a gringo robber baron named Riley. Neither description was accurate. For some time I have not been a gringo, and Jorge is now used mainly for intimidation. If a man must be "erased," as the Mexicans say, then Pepe sees to it. Sometimes he takes Jorge with him if the task is not too complicated.

"No," Jorge said, grinning. He likes to be thought of as a dangerous *pistolero*. "How about you?"

"No," Tell said, eyeing Jorge speculatively, "but I have thought about it."

"What about that artist that plugged that old *cabrón* Obregón?" Jorge said.

"That old *cabrón*," Tell said angrily, "in spite of his faults, was a better man than anyone in this room!" I had forgotten how attached Tell had been to Obregón.

"He did understand power," I said truthfully.

"That he did," Johnny said, moving around me, his arms open again. "It's good to see you again, Tell."

I stood aside and let them get the silly *abrazo* ceremony over with. When they had finished, I said, "We have new contacts. Obregón thought that he would live forever, but one must always plan for a transitory life and its effects on—"

"I'll have to believe you, Will, but I was fond of Obregón the man. Do you remember his story about the Spanish ambassador?"

"No," I said. "And I thought I had heard them all."

"Some *cabrón* stole the *gachupín cabrón's* watch," Jorge said, using the pejorative term for immigrant Spaniards.

"You should give recitals on the stage," Tell said.

"Sure, I can tell a good story," Jorge said, pleased.

"You certainly condensed that one," Johnny said.

"Will someone tell me what happened?" I said.

"I might add a detail or two to the Toad's version," Tell said, smiling. "It seems that the Spanish ambassador was seated at a table between two generals, one of them being General Obregón. The ambassador discovered that his expensive watch was missing. The general to his left was missing his right arm. When the ambassador turned to Obregón, Obregón lifted his right stump to demonstrate that he could not have picked the ambassador's pocket. The Spaniard grew furious and began to curse. At this point, Carranza, seated across the table from the ambassador, flung the watch at him, saying, 'For the love of God. Stop making such a fuss about an old watch.' "

I laughed along with them even though I had heard the story many times.

"Did the general ever confirm that story to you, personally, Tell?" I asked.

"Yes. And when I stopped laughing I asked, 'General, surely Carranza did not steal that watch?' "

" 'No,' the general said. 'Like I told you, he got caught. Just like with the provisional government. He tried to steal it too, but he got caught.' "

After another burst of laughter, Johnny said, "I suppose that he did, but the old man paid for it with his life."

"So did the general," I said. "He got caught trying to steal another term."

"I don't think so," Tell said uncertainly. "It was just that young fanatic."

"Yes," Johnny agreed, "both Obregón and Calles have been harsh with religion."

"We have to shoot the bloodsucking priests," Jorge said, and then crossed himself hastily.

"Yes," I said, speaking seriously for Johnny and Jorge, but smiling slightly for Tell so he would not take me seriously. "I speak for all the liberal Catholics when I say that the epitome of evil is that embodied in a depraved priest."

"Sure," Jorge said. "I know a good story about a nun, a burro and a priest—"

"Shall we get on with the meeting?" I said before Jorge could get into one of his gross, pointless stories. Both Johnny and Tell immediately said yes.

"Good," I said. "An opportunity has come our way. One that we

174

little dreamed of when we agreed to help the agrarian movement by regenerating the sugar industry." I motioned to Johnny. "Please continue."

"Alcohol, gentlemen," Johnny said, lifting his glass to us. "Shall we sit down?"

When we were comfortable and Tell had his brandy snifter, Johnny continued. "The one most important byproduct of cane is alcohol."

"Sure. You get *aguardiente* from cane. But," Jorge added, "it's mostly rotgut. I drink tequila."

"Yes, Jorge. I am aware of that phenomenon."

"But he is right," Johnny continued. "That raw alcohol that they flavor is awful, but it can be the base for an excellent rum. With expert supervision it could be the basis for whiskey."

Johnny leaned forward to place a hand on Tell's knee. "Tell, I just spent a month in the States. People are drinking more than ever before. Some who never even drank beer before prohibition are making gin in their bathtub. Every year some misguided soul strains wood alcohol through a loaf of bread. Some of them die. Only the wealthy can afford a bottle of genuine liquor."

"And that," I stepped in to clinch the sale, "is why Cosa is building a distillery to produce a good, safe alcohol that can be easily converted into a palatable rum, gin or whiskey. We will ship barrels by the carload to Ciudad Juárez."

"But there is nothing in the North," Tell said. "Here is the real market. The capital. Maybe there would be a market in Guadalajara and Monterrey as well."

"But, Tell," I said, delighted at his thinking, "north of Ciudad Juárez is El Paso and the United States of America. And that is *the* market."

"But the sale of liquor is prohibited there."

"Precisely."

"You want to bootleg alcohol in the States?"

"No," I said, "but Johnny does. What I would do is sell alcohol, legally, at border points with good access to whomever has the funds to buy it by the barrel."

"Like the arms maker in *Major Barbara*?"

"Exactly," I said, delighted with his insight. "We will be most moral and sell, without prejudice, to all those able to buy."

"But what has this to do with me?" Tell asked.

I waved a hand at Johnny.

"We need your airplanes, Tell," he said. "If we were to set up landing fields a few miles apart on each side of the border, how many trips a night could you make?"

"The fields would need some kind of light."

"Oil lamps to mark the boundaries," Johnny suggested.

"Yes, that would do. I suppose that you might make a dozen flights a night in good weather."

"And in bad?"

"None."

"How many barrels could you carry on each flight?" I asked.

"Will, I fly airplanes. I don't drive trucks."

"But we sell barrels of alcohol."

"A barrel weighs about five hundred pounds," Johnny interjected.

"Then the de Havilland could carry one barrel a flight. We have modified two of our planes to carry cargo by rebuilding the front section where the forward cockpit was located. Like the ones that carried the U.S. mail."

"Then," I asked eagerly, "you could haul twelve barrels a night. If you averaged sixty barrels a week, your company could gross at least three thousand dollars a week. Also, you would, of course, share in the much higher profits accruing to the parent company, Cosa."

"I'll pass on the offer to my partners."

"But have you decided?" I said, sure that Tell made the important decisions in his company just as I did in mine.

Just then the door to my study banged open and Carmencita lurched through, yanking her son, Alejandro, along by one hand. Our daughter, Sofía, tottered uncertainly after her.

"Hello, Johnny," Carmencita mumbled, and then, seeing Tell, she dropped Alejandro's hand and staggered over to wrap her arms around an obviously embarrassed Tell. Johnny looked away. Jorge eyed the slit in her robe, hoping that she would flash a piece of thigh.

Finally she stepped back and said, "I didn't know you were going to be here, Tell, or I would have come in before. I had a drink with Helen last week."

"Sit back down, Tell," I said. "Carmencita must put the children to bed. Now."

"Hello, Johnny," she said, allowing him to kiss each cheek. Then she turned to me, a smile flickering on and off like a lamp in a lighthouse.

"It's about Alejandro. He got a gold star today. Look." She pointed dramatically at the boy. He is thin and blond with an oversized head. His eyes are as bright as glass marbles. Most people point out his resemblance to me. A gilded paper star had been stuck to the center of his forehead.

"Remarkable," I said truthfully. The boy was a troublemaker. Always fighting. I had ordered a weekly report from the school on his transgressions. Who did the boy remind me of?

Alejandro smiled at what he took for approbation.

"And what did you do, Sofía?" She peeked out from behind her mother's robe. She was as light as her brother, but her hair had a reddish tinge to it, like my own.

"I was good. Very good. But not Alejandro. He was bad."

"And what did he do?" I asked.

"He stole a star out of the teacher's desk."

"Alejandro stole a gold star!" I roared with laughter. There might be some hope for the boy after all. But, disappointingly, he burst into tears and ran from the room.

"You shouldn't laugh, Willard," Carmencita said, slurring her words. "He adores you. But you laugh at him. Me too. You laugh at me. You laugh at everybody, but they don't know it."

She was a discerning woman. Alejandro was bright enough. But I must know the father. Carmencita would never give me a clue. Not even when in a drunken stupor. I must know for sure who the father was. "Goodnight my dear," I said.

"Goodnight," Carmencita said and hurried out, not a trace of drunkenness showing in her walk. Sofía smiled at me, and while I did smile back, I pointed sternly to the door, so she trotted after her mother.

"They are lovely children," Tell said. "You should brag some on Alejandro, Will. He needs a boost to his ego."

"You have been reading Freud."

"No," Tell said, a bit defensively, I thought. "Helen reads everything and then she puts it into language that I can understand."

"She is an astute lady. I have offered her a large sum to write a series of reports on Cosa for the New York newspapers."

"Like the one she did when you first started?"

"No! Exactly *not* like those stories. I want to sell some stock at a higher, not lower, price."

"I didn't think you were selling any more stock."

"We have sold stock a dozen times since I first started Cosa. Every time we form a new company, I see the need for more capital, so I issue stock. Do you have any idea how many shares of how many companies you own?"

"Yes," Tell said, looking straight into my eyes. "I own thirty-three shares of *Transporte Interamericano Aéreo*."

"Your stock in Cosa makes TIA look like an ant alongside an elephant. But we will talk about that another day. Will you work with us?"

"I will pass on the offer to my partners, but my vote will be no. I want to build an aerial transport service, not head a squadron of flying bootleggers."

"I am sorry," I said. But I was only sorry that Tell would not work with us. I had never liked the liquor idea. It was too much like children playing at pirates. Now Johnny would do as I had suggested. Sell the alcohol directly to our American contacts. Let them worry about the border crossing. And we would sell truckloads, not barrels.

Tell swirled the cognac around the bottom of his glass, but when I reached for the bottle, he sat his glass down and stood up.

"No, thanks. I have to be going. Helen is waiting supper for me."

"You eat a large meal at night?" I asked, surprised.

"No. Just hot chocolate and rolls. But I get a chance to talk to the kids."

"You talk with children." I was amused.

"Sure. Don't you?"

"Of course I do. You heard me talk to them. But it only takes a minute. What can a six-year-old talk about?"

"I got a kid six years old," Jorge said suddenly. "He is a smart little *cabrón*. He asked me yesterday why I did not live at his house any more. I told him I had found a new mama with a bigger ass." Rubio laughed and laughed. I allowed myself a chuckle. If Tell had not been present, I would have laughed more. At least Jorge is an honest lout.

"If I had a child," Johnny said, "I would treasure it. If anyone does not want to keep his, I would raise it as my own."

Tell shook hands goodbye with Johnny and said, "Could I see you at the bank this coming week?"

"Of course, but why the bank?"

"I need a loan."

"Better turn it over to Torres," I said to Johnny, "You just might be called in to see the president tomorrow."

"Portes Gil?"

"No, I meant Calles, the one with the power. He has two cabinet

178

positions open. Both will need undersecretaries. Which would you like, Labor or Treasury?"

"*Hacienda*," Johnny said quickly. Of course, the treasurer controls the purse strings. Johnny will go far.

"*¿Hacienda?*" Tell asked. "You mean Johnny has a choice?"

"He does, my doubting friend. Calles has a high opinion of our Johnny."

"How about labor for me," Jorge said. "I got a lot of experience with unions. Remember that *cabrón* that tried to organize the sugar mills? Hombre, did I ever bust his balls!"

"Maybe," Tell said, speaking to Jorge, "you could organize all of the whores and become the Secretary of Pimps and Whores."

"Hombre: What a *padre* idea. There must be ten thousand good-looking *putas*. I could pull in ten thousand pesos a day, easy!"

"A great idea, as you say, but I am sorry to disillusion you, Jorge," I said. "There is already a union that they all pay their dues to. It is called the police."

"That's it." Jorge's eyes glittered. "I could be the head cop. Why not?"

"Why not," I answered. But as my answer echoed in my ears, I thought, fearfully, why not, indeed?

Chapter 22

Willard Riley

They were all seated around the conference table, the Balboas and the Perrugias: sons and sons-in-law, cousins and nephews. Arturo, still slim except for his cannonball belly, at age fifty, represented the Perrugias. My father-in-law, Alejandro, represented the Balboas and—unknown to him—myself as well.

"Gentlemen," I said. "Let me restate my proposition in simpler terms. A formal merging of our interests will not only be approved by the Treasury Department, but encouraged. Our business will increase and we will all benefit immensely."

"I agree, Will. We all agree. What we cannot accept is the chairman of the board." Arturo looked everywhere but at me.

"With all due respect, Will, you are still a young man with little experience in banking. Some of us here have over thirty years in this business." Arturo flicked his eyes at me.

"Then the only objection is to me as chairman?"

"Yes, Will," Alejandro broke in excitedly. "Not that we do not all esteem you highly."

"Very well, then." I smiled for I knew that I had them. "I withdraw my name and place in its stead the name of a man who has had much more experience, who has indeed held the highest of executive positions, a man older than I. I propose the ex-Undersecretary of the Treasury himself, Juan Ávalos!" The silence was so complete that I felt its weight. Arturo's mouth twitched but no words came. From the far end of the table, his son Arturo, called Junior by the others, spoke.

"But Ávalos is your man."

"Then," I said, "it is to me that you object after all."

Junior stood up, his chest puffed out like a fighting cock. "If you wish to take it that way."

I stood up, fastening a smile to my face. "In order to avoid dissension I would like a short recess to confer with my father-in-law, Alejandro Balboa, and my dear friend, Arturo Perrugia. Agreed?"

There was a murmur of assent. I turned to Arturo.

"Might we use your office, *Don* Arturo?"

He smiled at me tolerantly, thinking the victory his. He waved me and Alejandro into his office. We sat down. They lit cigars.

"I want Johnny Ávalos," I said, "as chairman of CosaBanco. Not for my own sake as much as for the sake of young Alejandro, your grandson, and," I turned to Arturo, "your son."

"My son, Arturo Junior, needs no help from you. He has been manager of the central bank now for three years."

"True. Junior has been sleeping through meetings for the past three years," I said. "Let me speak plainly, Arturo, without hair on the tongue, as we say in Spanish."

"*Don* Arturo," he said indignantly, "if you please, and I do not like your manners."

"I speak of your son named Alejandro, not Arturo."

Arturo fell back in his chair, waxen-faced, his lips bloodless. His smoldering cigar fell on the thick rug. I stood up to stamp it out and to look down on the two men.

My gamble had paid off. I had not been absolutely sure until that second.

"I assume that you did not know, dear father-in-law, that the poor little love child, whom I named Alejandro after you because he had no father, was sired by your compadre, Arturo Perrugia."

Alejandro sat clutching the arms of his chair so tightly that the tendons stood out from his plump wrists. His eyes were squeezed shut.

"Look at him, Alejandro," I said harshly.

"No. He could not have seduced my little Carmencita! No!" His eyelids fluttered open. His expression was one of reluctant horror. A living nightmare. "Did you do it, Arturo?"

Arturo shook his head negatively, but he could not speak. Nor could he look Alejandro in the eye. He struggled to sit upright and reached for a decanter. He poured a water glass nearly full of cognac and drank it down.

"Well," I said, "Arturo, old family friend, did you impregnate Carmencita?"

"Maybe I did," he mumbled.

"Maybe! You mean it might have been someone else. How many other men screwed her?" I asked quickly.

"Beast! Animal!" Alejandro flung himself on Arturo, who covered his face with his hands and began to sob. After Alejandro had flailed away with his puny fists for a moment, I pulled him away.

"Calm down. Both of you. Arturo does not deny that he is the father of Alejandro, my adopted son. I accept that. But I also demand that the boy's future be assured. I would not want to continue this discussion at the meeting. Would either of you?"

"No. My God, no!" Arturo said, horrified.

"I will kill you, Arturo. I will get a gun and kill you!"

"Now, Alejandro," I said, "think of the boy that bears your name. Would you not want to see him grow up and take his proper place as head of the banking chain?"

"Of course," Alejandro said and burst into tears.

"Will you vote for Ávalos?" I asked Arturo.

"No," he said defiantly, tears streaming down his face.

"All right. Then I will go tell Junior that his baby brother will be the future president of CosaBanco."

"No," he said shrilly. "I forbid you."

"You forbid. You?" I laughed at him. It was theatrical of course, but Latinos understand those things.

"I ask. I beg." He opened his arms.

"I also ask a favor," I said.

"I will do it. I will do whatever Alejandro tells me to do. Even kill myself." He ripped his shirt open to expose a hairless bony chest. "Shoot me, Alejandro. Shoot me!"

Of course they both knew that Alejandro never carried a weapon of any kind. Nor did Arturo. But it was the gesture that counted.

"Kill me, or forgive me, compadre. For the love of God, forgive me. I will make it up to you and the boy. I swear."

Alejandro, the old fool, opened up his arms and they hugged each other, sobbing like babies. When they were all cried out, I helped Arturo run his tiepin through tie and shirt, and with his coat in place again, ushered them back to the meeting in the conference room.

Although they all eyed us curiously, it was Arturo Junior, his lip curled in what seemed to be a permanent sneer, who spoke.

"Are you prepared to vote now?"

"I have proposed Juan Ávalos. Do you have someone of like stature to nominate?

Junior looked with venom at me. He turned to his father for support, but Arturo had closed his eyes. He turned to his maternal uncle, Alberto Sánchez. "Would you put a name in nomination, *Don* Alberto?"

"Of course, nephew." He stood erect, a handsome man in his sixties, silver hair and bronzed skin. He wore a red rose in his boutonnière. "I propose a son of the founder of the Perrugia Banks, a graduate of the

182

school of . . . that is, a graduate student of economics at several of Europe's most prestigious universities and an executive in our own banking family for some time. I nominate Arturo Perrugia Junior."

While the others did not actually cheer, the emphatic nods and muttered approval along with a few outright angry glances at me made clear their preference.

"I second that motion," a younger version of *Don* Alberto said. "And I would like to point out that my *compañero*—"

"Could we get to the vote," I interrupted, tiring of the charade.

"Your candidate has yet to be seconded," Junior said happily.

"I second the motion," Alejandro said. Then, speaking in a stage whisper audible to anyone within fifty feet, added, "But we don't have the votes."

"Our gringo friend would like to vote," Junior said. "So we will vote. I cast one hundred and fifty votes for myself."

"And I have fifty votes for Arturo Perrugia Junior."

"We control only forty percent, even with Arturo's stock," Alejandro whispered this time softly enough so that only I heard.

"Forty-three," I whispered back.

And so it went around the table until it was up to Alejandro, who cast his five hundred shares for Ávalos. Then, Arturo, his eyes on the stock certificates in front of him, croaked, "I vote five hundred and thirty-five shares for Ávalos."

"What!" Junior screamed. "You said Ávalos!"

"Yes. Ávalos."

The room burst out in torrents of Spanish and Italian, punctuated by terrible expletives. I waited for a lull and then called out for a count.

Alberto, the dandy, turned out to be the secretary. He held his thumb and forefinger almost touching to signal me to wait a bit, and then he consulted his notebook.

"I have 1,840 in favor of Arturo Perrugia Junior to 1,435 in favor of Mister Riley."

"You have made two serious errors, *Don* Alberto. One, I am not in nomination, and two, you have not counted all of the votes."

"Ah, yes, the votes are ostensibly for Señor Juan Ávalos." He snickered at his own wit and then added sternly, "but I have, of course, counted all of the votes."

"You have not. I do not think you did so with any criminal intent, but fraud is always a possibility."

His mouth popped open and then shut again. "But I have a list of the shares. I could not have missed any."

"I have five hundred shares in front of me."

"Might I look at those shares?" Manuel Balboa, a young cousin of Junior, asked. I agreed, thankful that someone there thought to confirm their authenticity.

He scanned them and said, "But these are not your shares. While they are voting shares, they were only given to your company to hold as surety for the shares in your company delivered to us as collateral for your last loan."

"True. It is also true that the note attached to the top share is a proxy signed by the Perrugia Bank's president, Arturo Perrugia."

"Never," Junior screamed. "Never will we turn our beloved company over to a foreigner. Our lawyers will send this arrogant gringo back to his country!"

Manuel Balboa waited until the hate group led by Junior had cheered itself out before he said, "Our lawyers will not be able to change that signature. In any case, I withdraw my votes for Arturo Perrugia Junior, and vote, instead, for Juan Ávalos and let the record so read."

"Traitor!" Junior yelled. "You are siding with the *yanqui* invader!"

"I would like to point out," I said, speaking slowly, enunciating carefully, and speaking my very best Spanish, "that I am a Mexican citizen of Irish extraction. The leader of the Saint Patrick's Battalion that fought so valiantly against the North American invaders of Mexico was also a Riley and," I added, perhaps even truthfully, "a direct ancestor of mine. I know that the son of the Italian liberator Garibaldi fought for our Revolution and bled for Mexico, as did my ancestor, Riley. Gentlemen, I see no reason why we Irish Catholics and Italian Catholics cannot both become the best of Mexican citizens."

By the time I had finished, they were all nodding affirmatively, with the exception of Junior, of course, but even he said nothing critical. When I called for a recount, one by one they changed their vote. And then it was up to Junior.

"How do you vote, nephew?" Alberto asked.

"I suppose that I must vote for Mister Riley."

"No," I answered. "Indeed, you cannot. You can, and should, vote for yourself, Signori Perrugia; pardon me. That was rude. I beg your pardon, Señor Perrugia."

Of course, he voted for himself. His pride would not let him do otherwise. And now he would be remembered as the only stockholder

184

to oppose the majority and vote for himself.

Now that it was all over, they elbowed each other out of the way to congratulate me. Manuel Balboa waited until the last to shake hands with me. I asked him to call on me at my offices. I had plans for that young man. The very last one was Junior. He forced himself, jerkily, to offer me his hand. I took it, pressed it firmly and said sincerely, "I congratulate you too, Junior. You are a shrewd antagonist."

"You congratulate me?"

"Of course. No hard feelings?"

"No," he squeaked the word out.

"I admire your spirit and your knowledge. I would like you to stay on as an adviser to the chairman. I am sure that Johnny Ávalos will feel the same way. With a substantial raise, of course. What do you say?"

"Johnny?"

"Juan Ávalos. I call him Johnny, the English name, as a sign of affection. As I might one day call you Art."

He peered at me suspiciously, but I gripped his hand all the harder and smiled wider.

"I do not like gringo nicknames."

"Of course you do not. I wonder if another five hundred a month would be satisfactory, Art?"

"Five hundred! *¡Por Dios, hombre!* I mean, yes. Quite satisfactory, *Don* Willard."

It certainly should be. It would double his present salary and enable him to move his mistress out of a tiny one-bedroom apartment into something more becoming of a banker. He would not earn his salary. Not now nor ever, but he would be in my debt as he would be under my thumb until the day that I turned my thumb down and squashed him.

Chapter 23

· · · · · · · · · · · · · · · · · · ✈

Memo Canela, 1935.

"But, Mama, I do not want to go to school with the gringos."

"You will do as I say, and you will not use that word. It is a rude *grosería*."

"Still, the gringos stole more than half of our land."

"True. But also remember had it not been for that monstrous traitor, Santa Anna, we would have driven the gringos back into the sea at Veracruz."

"But then why must I go to the gringo school?" I asked, and then, as an awful thought came into my mind, I added, "They do not even speak *cristiano* there. Only pure English. I can only speak pure Spanish."

"That is why you will go to the *grin* . . . to the American School. To learn their language and how they think."

"But Mama," I pleaded. "I have no friends in that school. They will beat me."

"They will not!" My mother's black eyes glinted. When they did, I quailed. "You will not allow that! Your father would not have been afraid. He feared nothing."

"Not even when he was just a boy, like me, in Tabasco, before the gringos killed him?"

"Memo! It was not the gringos."

"You said it was General Green."

"General Green was not a gringo—not the kind of gringo that comes from north of Mexico. He was a Mexican. He came from one of those old pirate families from Campeche. They were barbarians, but I think their descendants are Christians."

"Are we Christians?" I knew the answer, but I did not wish to talk more about the fearsome American School.

"Of course not. We do not believe in the blood-sucking clergy and the sermons that are opium for the poor. We speak Spanish. However we do call it *cristiano* because—"

She must have caught a gleam from my eyes, for I know that I did not have a trace of a smile on my lips. Nor did she when she continued grimly.

"All of which you know very well and none of which will get you out of registering tomorrow at the American School."

"They will put me back a grade," I said, desperately. "They put Pancho Muñoz back and he is so smart that sometimes the teacher asks him to answer tough questions."

"Nonsense. What question would *maestro* Román ask that boy, Pancho?"

"What makes an airplane fly?"

"And what does make an airplane fly?"

"The wind pushes it up in the air, like a kite."

"That is idiotic!" I was careful not to glance at her, for she had taken the bait. "The vacuum created over the curved surface of the—"

I was suddenly standing on tiptoe, my mother's strong fingers twined in the short hairs at the back of my neck. She left me with my nose in a corner.

"You will wear the ears of a burro! You are not nearly as smart as you think you are."

"Mama." I tried manfully to stifle a sob, but not enough so that she would not hear me. "When will I learn to fly?"

"When you are old enough," she answered automatically, forgetting that I was being punished.

"I will fly the biggest airplane in the world and I will bomb the Jews!"

This time I was up on the balls of my toes, dancing and screaming with pain. I could hear her anger and almost feel it, like the lingering odor of firecrackers.

"Bomb Jews! Where did you get that from?"

"Please, Mama. Let loose. I'm sorry. I won't bomb any Jews."

"Where?" I lifted my head as high as I could.

"From Miguel and Enrique. At school. They bomb Aaron, the Jew."

"Aaron Goldstein?"

"Yes. He is a Jew and they are not any kind of a Christian. Enrique's father is German and he says—"

"I will speak to the director of your school and Miguel and Enrique too."

"Aaron too. He will feel badly if he is left out."

"He likes Enrique and Miguel even when they *bomb* him?"

"He likes being bombed."

"How do they bomb Aaron?"

"They fly over like this." I gave my best imitation of a huge bomber dropping bombs on Aaron and then I changed into Aaron and said, "Now you dirty Germans, take that!" I did my rat-a-tat machine gun sound, which even Aaron, the school expert, thought was very good.

Mama let loose of my hair and even patted it back into place. She did not mention punishment again and I, in my innocence, thought that she had forgotten. But it was no accident that a few days later, when I did register at the American School, Aaron, to my surprise and relief, was there. Mama had been to see his father.

"Hombre," Aaron said, "am I glad to see you!"

A lanky boy with pale blue eyes and pink skin heard us speaking Spanish and asked timidly if we knew where to register.

"Sure," I said, pointing. "That table over there. See, the sign is in *cristiano*."

"Thanks. Do you speak English?"

"No, do you?"

"No, just Spanish and German."

"German! Why don't you go to the German school?"

"Because we are Von Ivens and the Von Ivens are not Nazis."

"There are Nazis in the German School?" I asked.

"Too many, my papa says."

"Are you Jewish?" Aaron asked me.

"Of course not," I said. "We speak *cristiano*, but neither I nor my Mom is a Christian."

He thought about my statement before he finally asked, "Are you Nazis?"

We laughed and hooted at the idea.

"Well, then," he said. "I guess it doesn't matter." He stuck his hand out. "I am Klaus Iven."

"You said 'Von Iven,' " Aaron reminded him as he shook hands.

"We only use the 'Von' to impress stupid Nazis."

That seemed reasonable to me. We shook hands and, braver now that we were three, I led the way and we marched over to the table and enrolled. For the next few days we moved as one unit. When one of the teachers noticed, he called us the Three Musketeers. When we learned that they were fierce French soldiers, we were proud.

The school had clubs, and wonder of wonders, an aviation club. I was in a frenzy to join, so the others signed up too.

We built model airplanes out of thin sheets of feather-light balsa wood and tissue paper. Using old safety razor blades snapped off at one end to form sharp points, we cut ribs and long, thin stringers from the wood. We dripped quick-drying glue into the slots on the wing ribs and then pinned the stringers to them. The body was fastened together the same way. A whittled balsa block held the propeller, which was fastened to a heavy rubber band stretched and anchored to the tail. We covered the whole body and wings with tissue paper. With a wet toothbrush, we flicked water on the paper. When it dried, the gauzy paper had shrunk as tightly as the fabric of a real airplane. We glued the French tricolor on the upper wings, for it was, we had decided, the top fighter plane of the war, a French Spad. We would have attached the landing gear, but the bell rang, so we had to leave that step, and its maiden flight, for the next day.

Our class bully was a larger, older boy whom we called Bobo the clown, but only to his back, for he knew Spanish and we were all afraid of him. His real name was Bob Rowley. He belonged to the aviation club, but he could never make anything, not even a simple glider. His fingers were too thick and clumsy. He should have been in the eighth grade, but he had been with his father in Chiapas for two years and had practically no schooling. He said that he did not want to go to a "dumb Mexican school anyway" and would not learn anything until his father took him back to what he called God's country.

Whenever a teacher was late to class, Bobo would play his favorite game. We would all line up, like soldiers, and he would swagger in front of us, sneering at our posture and poking us in the chest with his huge finger. The first day, out of wounded pride and bravado, I turned to the boy standing next to me and whispered, "I am not afraid of that clown." Except I had said Bobo, which in Spanish means "clown" or "fool."

To my horror the boy immediately called out, "Hey, Bob. This guy says he ain't afraid of you, and he called you Bobo, a clown!"

Bobo stamped, then glaring and wrinkling his upper lip like a gangster in a movie, which is where he had learned his sneer, he said, "You ain't scared of me?" He doubled his right hand into a fist and waved it at me. And I, poor innocent, had my eye on that threatening right hand when his left buried itself into my unsuspecting belly.

From that day on until our final confrontation, I stood ramrod straight with the rest and kept my mouth shut. So did Aaron and Klaus.

Bobo sneered at our airplane, as he did at anything that he had no part in. When it finally began to take form, he would make pistols with his hands and pretend to shoot it down.

Our club leader and science teacher, Mister Jones, an older man, maybe as old as my mother, was proud of our airplane. For it was the first, and as it turned out, the only model airplane completed that year.

"You boys can be proud. It is done to scale, well built, with a strong landing gear. I believe that it will fly. However," he walked to the window and peered out, "I don't like the look of the weather, men."

My chest filled with pride. The three of us grinned at each other.

"I know that you nervy fellows would risk it; however, I think it only prudent to wait for better weather until tomorrow for the test flight. What do you say?"

We agreed.

"It's only a paper airplane, for cripes sake," Bobo said. "It ain't The Spirit of Saint Louis."

"Yes it is, Bob," Mister Jones said earnestly. "That is exactly what it is. Any one of these boys, maybe even all three, might very well make an important contribution to aviation."

Bobo farted. Mister Jones reddened, but he pretended not to hear and then the bell rang. We three skirted Bobo expertly and, chattering excitedly, ran out of the room to our next class, which would be given in Spanish, a welcome relief after a morning of pure English.

At home late that afternoon, we held our weekly meeting of the Three Musketeers Society. We met upstairs in the tiny rooftop room that would have belonged to a maid if we had one. "The minutes are that we made a law that if any member gives away secrets and gets caught, he will be killed and fined a pack of *chicles*," Aaron spoke—so rapidly that his words ran together.

"I am going to be an airplane engineer," I said before Aaron could catch his breath.

"I shall be a pilot and fly over the oceans," Klaus said.

"I will be a fighter pilot and shoot down the Nazi bombers." Aaron said the same thing he always said. But then, so did Klaus. And so did I.

"One for all and all for one," we shouted, holding out imaginary swords.

Klaus, looking troubled, held up a hand for recognition.

"You may speak, Klaus," said Aaron, who was the society's president that week.

"I have been reading *The Three Musketeers*, but—"

"Bring it here," I interrupted. "I want to read it too."

"All right. But, Memo, there are four musketeers, not three. There are Aramis, D'Artagnan, Athos and—"

"It must be a bad translation," Aaron said.

"It is in French. The author wrote it in French."

"You read French?" I asked.

"Certainly, don't you?"

"Only *cristiano* and now, some English, like you and Aaron."

"I can read Hebrew, and I speak Ladino too," Aaron said.

"What is Ladino?" I asked.

"Spanish Jews speak it. It mostly is Spanish. My father says it is as old as Spanish."

"Then it must be *cristiano*," I said.

"I guess so," Aaron said and then turned to Klaus. "Anyway, if there are four, we will take in another member. No problem."

"Sure," I said, enthused. "How about that skinny boy who plays right wing on the football team. He is fast, and he is not afraid of Bobo."

"Would he join?" Klaus asked doubtfully.

"Who wouldn't?" I replied.

"You ask him, then."

"I'll do it. You write it down, Aaron."

The big, fat white clouds that Mister Jones told us were called cumulus were just beginning to bubble and churn. It would be afternoon before they would turn dark with water and then pour down into the valley of Mexico. But now the sky was mostly blue and so clear that the twin snowy volcanoes, gleaming white in the sun, seemed close enough to fly a kite over.

Mister Jones had not yet arrived, but most of the club members were standing around waiting, including the skinny kid we called *güero* because he was so light complexioned. His hair was blond and he had gray eyes.

"Hey, blondie," I said. "You ever tangle with Bobo?"

"No, Memo. He backed down."

"Bobo backed down? No!"

"He sure did."

"Hey man, would you like to join us Musketeers? We got a secret password and a place to meet and talk about flying."

"Okay. I got a book about fighter pilots and my dad is in it!"

"Wow!" Aaron said. "Could we see it?"

"Sure. I'll bring it to the next meeting."

"Did your papa fly bombers too?" Klaus asked.

"I think so. He flew de Havilland Scouts in Mexico. They might have carried bombs. When are you going to fly your airplane?"

"As soon as Mister Jones gets here."

"Hey," a boy yelled. "The door is opening."

And the door to the classroom where our club met did open, but it was not Mister Jones that stepped out—holding our precious airplane in one hand and a lit match in the other—but the detestable Bobo.

While I watched, heart pounding, paralyzed with dread, he touched the match to the paper and balsa-wood model, released the tightly wound propeller, and let our airplane, burning like a torch, soar up over our heads. As if it were a real airplane in some miniature war, it spun down to the ground to burn itself up in a clump of grass.

I sensed my mother's presence. She had not promised to be there, but she was. Her eyes glinted like obsidian jewelry in the sun, and her lips were set in what might have been taken by a stranger for a smile. I knew better.

I walked slowly up to where Bobo stood, gloating. He pretended to quail, covering his eyes with his fingers, but grinning widely.

"Bobo," I said, using the hated nickname to his face the first time. "Not only are you a real live *bobo*, you are a *pinche* Nazi!"

I swung. He dropped his hands contemptuously to block my punch to his stomach. But I had struck purposely much lower. He grabbed for his testicles, screamed and fainted dead away.

"You hit him below the belt," yelled one of Bobo's toadies, who, while looking me in the face, turned and ran straight into the arms of Mister Jones.

"He hit Bobo—Bob, I mean—right in the nuts," the boy shrieked, looking back at me fearfully.

"Watch your tongue, young man," Mister Jones said quickly, looking around to see if there were any females present. I expected a comment from my mother, but she had disappeared and would never admit, even years later, that she had even been there to witness my showdown with Bobo and, as it turned out, my last day at the American School.

And so it also happened that Blondie Cooper, whom I might have known as a friend, if not as a brother, never joined the Musketeers.

Chapter 24

............................✈

Tell Cooper, 1938.

The clouds, dirty gray sponges dripping water, rolled in from the ocean, adhering wetly one to another, and then, as if by the added weight, sank even lower. I glanced upward through the right section of the windshield from the copilot's seat, estimating the cloud base at a thousand feet. While Bill Crowley taxied the twin-engine Douglas to the down-wind end of the runway, I uncaged the gyroscopic instruments, the Sperry artificial horizon and the compass. I set the compass on ninety degrees, the reciprocal heading of the takeoff strip we were paralleling.

Bill swung the DC-2 around to the takeoff position and ran through the takeoff checklist. He then called for and received radio clearance from the tower. He looked at me, holding up a thumb up in question.

"The ceiling is no more than nine hundred feet now," I said apprehensively.

"It doesn't matter. With the radio range system a pilot can ride a beam into the airport, locate the landing beam and glide on down until he can make visual contact. Hell, Jimmy Doolittle took off and landed blind not so long ago."

"All right," I said, answering with a thumbs up, "but I would rather have a Fokker Dee Seven on my tail than fly blind."

Bill ignored me and pushed the throttles forward.

"What if the radio doesn't work?" I said, but he was too busy taking off to answer, or, perhaps with the roar of two engines at full throttle, he did not even hear me.

We had installed gyroscopic instruments in our own old de Havillands when we rebuilt them, but the radio system of positioning an aircraft for a bad-weather landing was something brand new. If it lived up to my expectations, I planned on opening a passenger service from Mexico City to San Antonio. Good old TIA would become a poor relation of such huge air transport companies as Western Air Transport or United Aircraft.

At Bill's signal I levered the wheels up. I scanned the instruments—engine and flight—while he adjusted the engine controls and control tabs to climb up into the cloud cover. He leveled off at fifteen hundred feet. He could easily have flown on up and through into the bright southern California sunshine, but he was demonstrating the new blind-flying landing system, so we would stay on instruments.

At cruising power, with the powerful engines throttled back, we could talk easily. Those fortunate flyers who have never been exposed to the mad symphony of sound produced by an explosive engine and whistling air of an open cockpit airplane have no idea how comfortable the modern ones are.

"We'll fly out to sea three miles, make a ninety to the north and then fly back on a reciprocal heading."

"How far north?"

"Three minutes."

"Then we should come in about five miles north."

"Yeah. If the wind holds."

"Why don't you take over now, Tell? After all, it is your airplane, one way or another."

"I have it," I said, tapping my head. I tightened my hands on the wheel as he removed his own hands, and I took up the pressure in my legs as I sensed his feet leaving the rudders. There was no change in the little white airplane within the artificial horizon panel, nor in the new and precise Kollsman altimeter. The speed indicator held steady at one hundred and ten.

"Odd, Tell, me teaching you something."

"You must have had the best of instruction in Scouts," I said, using the word for what we called fighter planes a long time ago, "or a minimal talent."

"It must have been the instruction," he said, grinning.

All I had done was to check him out in a Spad and indicate a few basics of the trade. He then had gone on to shoot down twenty-two German aircraft, only four short of Rickenbacker's record.

"Let's switch seats. It will be a bit easier for you, flying from the left side. You might get a little tense as we near the ground, still on instruments."

He slipped into my seat as I vacated it and held the controls until I was in his seat. I might get a little tense. How could I get any more nervous? I was to find out shortly.

"Three miles out," I said.

"Make your turn."

I swung the nose and watched in the instrument panel as the right

194

wing of the little white airplane dropped as I banked. I straightened out on the zero heading, watched the compass swing from the turn, and as it steadied, corrected the heading. I lifted the earphones and adjusted them to my oversized head. I heard nothing, not even a buzz.

"Shouldn't I be hearing something?" I said, tapping an ear phone.

Bill frowned and clicked the radio switch several times. "It was all right a moment ago."

"Goddamn all innovations," I said, and turned the nose back to the western heading and began a gradual letdown.

"What are you doing?"

"I will lose altitude ever so slowly over the ocean until one of us spots a white cap. Then I shall ease into contact flying, make a shallow turn back and fly just above the water until we reach land and that field where that wonderful little transmitter is sending all of those signals that we cannot hear. Then I shall turn it over to you. You have landed it before, I believe?"

Bill's laughter was genuine, not nervous, as mine would have been. I smelled a rat.

"All right. What the hell is going on?"

"Go on back up to altitude and take the reciprocal back to the field. I'll fix the radio." He reached over and flipped a master switch. There was a shrill metallic dash followed by a metallic dot: an electronic, high-pitched Morse code signal for the letter *n*. It repeated incessantly.

"So?"

"So you passed a test. We need a chief pilot. One who checks the others out."

"So that's what you meant, my plane, 'one way or another.' " Then I added, not angrily, but emphatically, "Bill, I have my own air company!"

"Calm down, Tell. I want you with us. You'll get some stock and maybe we can even take over your company as an extension."

"Could I answer you later, assuming we do not both die in a fiery crash?"

"All right." He folded his arms. "Take me home."

I leveled off at a thousand feet, now well within the cloud cover and headed due east. I knew the theory and had worked out several range orientation problems in my hotel room the night before. I had enjoyed the process. It reminded me of that new American diversion, the crossword puzzle.

The radio transmitters at an airfield send out a steady stream of

Morse code signals. For example, a dash-dot, or *n*, is sent north and south, while a dot-dash, an *a*, is sent east and west. The stream of letters is interrupted only by an occasional but different signal to identify the airfield itself. Where the *a* and *n* signals overlap, the result is a steady sound, like a constant whistle. This is the beam. The beams intersect and form an *x*, or four legs. This particular airfield, because of the prevailing winds, had its beams arranged to run northwest by southeast, and directly east and west.

I felt for the volume control and turned it very low. It built up immediately, which meant that I was approaching the field. A drop in volume would have meant we were headed away from the airfield and the radio signals. I was in the *n* sector. Next I heard the uninterrupted whistle as the dots and dashes became one. As I crossed the beam, I began to hear the clear dot-dash, the *a* signal. On a scratch pad buckled to my knee was a diagram of the four legs and their compass headings. I penciled in the track and confidently made a ninety-degree turn to the right to intercept the eastern leg of the east-west leg. I waited one minute, then two, but the signal grew weaker. Something was wrong. Sweat stung my eyes. I stared at the pad without seeing it. I shook my mind and focused on the approach legs and their headings. Suddenly there was a blessed light of understanding.

"The wind has shifted," I said happily. "We are in the southwestern *a* signal sector, not the northeastern!"

I knew that the frustrated Bill Crowley wanted to cheer, but all he did was pull on his unlit pipe and say, "Right."

I began to breathe normally and swung right again until the compass swiveled to due north. I held that course until I crossed the western leg. I turned right, holding a few degrees north of due-east to allow for the wind drift.

Bill called in for clearance and landing instructions. The wind was indeed from the northwest. We were instructed to take the southeast leg and then land on runway 340.

I turned right onto the southeastern leg of the solid radio beam, entering the expected cone of silence directly above the transmitters, where there was no signal and the earphones went quiet. I looked at Bill.

"Drop your wheels and flaps and then make your turn back. You know what to do."

Sure, I thought. But can I do it?

When I had made the turn to three hundred and ten degrees flying at one thousand feet, the wait for the cone of silence seemed like an hour, but it was just a few minutes. I throttled back and set the rate of descent at five hundred feet. If all went well, I should hit the cone soon. I did, but there was no break in the thick white fog running past our wings.

"Should I take it back up?"

"Yes. No! Look."

The field lay before us stretching out northward toward the ocean. We were at no more than a hundred feet with the cloud base brushing the cabin top. Now that we were back over land and close to the ground, the uneven heat sent up currents that bounced the big airplane around just as it would have done to one of our de Havillands.

But it flew like a charm. I eased it down, dropping the left wing slightly to keep from drifting across the runway. I lifted the nose and eased off the throttle until I felt the wheels touch. Then I cut the throttle off completely, but still shouted over the non-existent noise of the engine.

"My God, Bill! I thought that the new gyros were something, but this is a marvel. It will be the making of passenger air service."

"It is and it will."

I braked, turned off the runway onto a taxi lane, and brought it slowly over to the tie-down area in front of the hangar.

I cut the throttles on signal from the mechanic and flipped off my seat belt.

Before I could leave my seat, Bill grasped me by an arm and said, "Sign on with us, Tell. We need this airplane too. We'll pay you a bonus for it."

"You must want the airplane badly," I said, smiling.

"We are back-ordered for three," he said seriously, "but it's you that we want."

"Do many of the large fields have the radio landing systems?"

"They do, or they soon will."

"At no cost to you?"

"One way or another, we have to pay for them."

"I suppose," I said, voicing my thoughts, "that we will have to pay for them in Mexico City and Monterrey."

"I take it, Tell, that you are turning me down?"

"I guess I am," I said, surprised that the decision had been so easy. "I guess I am."

Chapter 25

· · · · · · · · · · · · · · · · · · ✈

Helen Anderson de Cooper

"*¡Telegrama!*" The maid called out in excitement, brandishing in one hand a twig broom for sweeping cut grass. I walked quickly to the gate in the wall that kept out the other world. The messenger boy was a step inside, grinning at our young flirty maid. I took the coarse yellow envelope from him and found a *tostón* coin in my apron pocket. It was a large tip, but then he had ridden his bicycle all the way from the center of the city up the steep Reforma Avenue to our new home.

It would be my father. I had not been to see him for almost two years and now I would never see him again. His kindly face, the one of thirty years ago, flashed into my mind. Tears formed instantly and overflowed.

"It is bad news," María wailed.

I shook my head negatively to rid myself of her and then, that evil envelope clutched in one hand, stumbled blindly back to the corner of the garden where I had been pruning a small lime tree. It was the second one I had tried to grow.

I ripped the envelope open with the tip of the shears and drew out the sheet of cheap paper and held it at arm's length, but I could not make the block letters out. They would swim in and out of focus.

"What's the news?" Tell came out of the house, part of the Sunday Excelsior newspaper folded in one hand. The tip of a brown beer bottle protruded from the other.

I thrust the telegram at him, sobbing with fear.

"Hey, sweetheart, what is it?"

I buried my face against his hard chest. I liked the bony feel and hoped that he would never turn into one of those old men that sat around the American Club drinking whiskey and talking about the good old days.

I heard the bottle fall to the ground and then his pretend angry voice.

"Helen, for God's sake! You scared the bejeezus out of me. I thought you were crying sad, not glad."

I backed up far enough to see his face. Tell is a foot taller than I. He was grinning at me, his eyes soft with joy.

"I knew it. I absolutely knew. Wait until Will hears."

"Will. Will who?" I did not have any relatives or close friends in New York named Will.

"Will who? Hah! Will Riley is who. He will cut his other ear off. Seriously, sweet, if anyone else had written that book, he—or even she—would not have been safe in Mexico, or maybe even in New York."

"The book? It's about the book!"

"You didn't even know what the message was and you were crying your eyes out."

"I thought it was Daddy. I thought he had died and I would never see him again."

"I know that feeling," Tell said sadly.

Of course he did. He did not even have a grave someplace that he could decorate. Not that he would have. Tell is just short of being a pagan. I was a rebel myself, but as I grow older I think more and more about religion. I was brought up Episcopalian.

"I think that I could find out about your father; maybe even locate his grave," I said, crying again. I am hopeless.

"Honey, it doesn't matter. Villa is dead and likely the ones that killed my father are too. Sooner or later, we all die. When you look into that final rifle barrel, our routine worries disappear."

"Tell, you must go to church with me next week. The new pastor expressed much the same idea in his sermon this morning. You should talk to him."

"Well, if you really think I can help him, bring him over after church," Tell said, grinning just in time to avert my anger. "Any way, before I get saved, maybe you better answer that wire. Assuming that you accept their terms."

"I accept," I said. I handed the shears to the gardener, who had been eyeing my attempts on the lime tree with trepidation, then took Tell by the arm. "Come along and talk to the telegraph people for me."

"Okay, you poor little befuddled tourist."

I do, of course, speak fair Spanish, but sometimes the nuances escape me and I get into trouble.

"We could be there in two days," Tell said as we went into the living room.

"Be where?"

"New York." Tell pointed me toward my study and his at-home office and gave me a gentle shove. "The city where your publishers are.

Get the operator and I'll be right there."

Publishers! What a magical word. Of course. Helen Anderson de Cooper would have a book printed. Maybe they will have it for sale in the big American bookstore on Juárez Avenue. Laughter welled up inside me, but damned if it didn't get mixed up with tears. But they were happy ones. I was giggling when the operator spoke.

"Tell!" I yelled. "The operator is on the telephone. Do I use Ericsson or Mexican?"

There are two telephone companies and you have to know which one to use because they do not interconnect. Because of the airline, we have both lines running into the house, each with its own apparatus. I was never sure which one I was using, but the operator spoke up and said, "Ericsson."

"I guess I want to talk to *Telegramas Internacionales*."

"No, operator," Tell said, taking away the telephone. "Get me long distance, New York. Charley Goldberg. He is in the telephone book. Tell him that his favorite client, Helen Cooper, the famous author, wants to talk to him. One hour? Fine. She will be at this number."

"What will I say to Charley?"

"Just tell him to call the publishers and say that you must have two thousand dollars advance, but if they won't pay that, you will take a thousand."

"Why not just send a telegram?" I said, thinking of the cost of an international call. It might well be several dollars. Perhaps as much as twenty pesos.

"Because I want you to tell Charley to keep the contract there, and call your father to warn him that the Coopers are coming and to explain our reasons to celebrate!"

"Oh, Tell. Can we afford it?"

"Why not? Our flight to San Antonio leaves tomorrow. I'll likely get a discount from there on."

"But Tell, TIA is not even making expenses."

"No matter. I'll fly copilot and you can take whatever seat is available."

"I'll use my advance to buy stock in TIA."

"We can use the cash," Tell said. "But if I were you, I would invest in Rickenbacker's airline. That is, if you want to get a return on your money."

"If money was all that I wanted," I said happily, "I would have sold the manuscript to Riley. I think that he would have paid more than I will ever get from royalties."

"Sure," Tell said, that thin, white scar extending his crooked grin. "And he would have to pay you every year not to publish. And if the price of paper should go up, he would have to pay even more to cover the higher costs of not publishing."

"Tell, you are outrageous!" I pulled him down onto a sofa alongside me. "But can you really go with me?"

"Yes. I need to raise a hundred thousand dollars soon, or go to work for Bill Crowley as the world's oldest copilot."

"But, Tell, how about your stock in Cosa?"

"I do not own stock in Will Riley's company."

"But you do," I protested. "I wrote the book, remember?"

"Goddamn it, Helen! Do not tell me what I own. I refused that stock in twenty-one."

"It is still registered in your name."

"Then I shall go demand the printed shares and burn them in front of the Presidential Palace."

"Be careful," I said, only partially in jest. "President Cárdenas just expropriated the oil. TIA might be next."

"No. Never. Underground resources, like petroleum or gold are different. But private business is another thing."

"Strange," I said, trying not to smile. "I had an odd idea that your airplanes used gasoline. What do you do, wind up large rubber bands?"

He opened his mouth to retort, caught my smile, and swung me easily up onto his lap, his big hands clasped around my waist, fingertips almost touching. Not bad, I thought, for a forty-five-year-old woman with two children. And then he moved his hands up higher to caress my breasts.

"Tell. The maid or the cook might walk in any minute. And the kids are liable to pop in for—"

"And you are the indecorous little rebel that used to shock me out of my pants." He paused to laugh; of course, I joined in. "Anyway," he continued, "you always got me out of trouble somehow. An Eastern city slicker having her way with a country boy."

"That country boy better be careful," I said, my voice changing deeper the way it does just before we make love, "or he might have to make good on his threat."

"What threat?" he said innocently, but I could feel his hardness pressing up against my thigh.

"I better go change clothes," I said throatily.

"Me too," Tell said.

We stood up together just as the front door slammed.

"Hey. Anybody home?"

"Here," I said.

Our son had Tell's piercing gray eyes, but his hair was as blond as mine. True, he looked more like an Anderson, but inside he was Cooper: stubborn, fiercely independent and being nearly seventeen, out to prove it. He burst into the room with a ray of sun, his hair reflecting in the glass doors like a halo. My heart expanded every time I saw him, and I yearned to hold him again, cradled in my arms.

"Hi, Mom." He brushed me a kiss on the cheek before he turned to chatter, excitedly, to his father.

"Dad. Guess what? Smoky Brant is back from Spain. He shot down five planes and got a thousand dollars a plane, and he says that the new German Messerschmitt is the best fighter plane in the world and he might go to Finland to fight the Russians unless the big one starts in France before—"

"Hold on." Tell held his arms up protectively, like a fighter in a ring. "I surrender. Who is Smoky Brant?"

"Who is Smoky Brant!" His tone and expression implied that such a question could come only from someone with an abysmal ignorance of worldly affairs.

"Oh," Tell said, grinning. "*That* Smoky Brant."

"My God!" Tell Dos said. "Dad, you really don't know!"

We named our son after his father, but I could not bear to call him junior, so I took to calling him Tell Two. But that, besides being a confusing alliteration, is also too near the sound of the Spanish familiar *tú*, meaning "you," so Tell and I switched to the Spanish for two: *dos*.

"Perhaps my number two son might enlighten his poor ignorant father," Tell said.

"Besides Spain, he *only* flew the Hughes racer. He should have had the world record, but it wasn't official because Hughes wouldn't let him fly it over the F.A.I. course. He flew the F4-B and he also once did an outside loop."

"Does he need an airplane to fly, or does he just give his halo a spin and takeoff?" Tell said, his smile slipping.

"Did you ever do an outside loop?"

"No, not even when I flew aircraft with wings stressed for that dangerous maneuver, nor did I want to rupture my eyeballs as did a friend of mine."

202

"Was that Orville or Wilbur Wright?"

"His name was Jack Lescault," Tell said softly. "He was a gentleman and a great aviator as was Orville and as is Wilbur and I would thank you not to mention them in context with your imaginative friend."

"Sure. Your friends were all aces. What did Jack Lescault ever do?"

"He shot himself," Tell said, openly angry now.

"So?" Tell Dos shrugged.

I would never have struck the boy, but I lifted my hand so quickly that Tell caught my wrist.

"He was in a burning Spad so he shot himself," Tell said.

"Why didn't he bail out?"

"We were not allowed parachutes, so we carried pistols, instead," Tell said coldly.

"Smoky has bailed out many times."

"Tell," I said, ignoring my son, "you never told me about Jack." I was crying again. I wonder where my tears come from.

"I'm sorry, Helen. Truly. It just slipped out."

"You knew this Jack guy, Mom?"

"I was his girlfriend. In Paris."

"You had a boyfriend before you met Dad?"

"Yes, believe it or not. I was once twenty-five. I danced on a table top and I kicked wine all over your father."

"But you were the other guy's girlfriend?"

"Yes."

He shook his head as if he were trying to rattle the idea around inside his head until it found a place to fit. "But Dad never had a girlfriend. I mean, besides you?"

"Yes, he did," I said quickly before Tell could answer. "She was a beautiful girl. Still is. You were in her office when you got the application form for a student pilot."

"That was the aviation department . . . the official mayor's office." He shut his eyes tightly the way I do when I try to remember. "Canela's office. She works for Canela?"

"No, she is the official mayor, the number two. Her name is Antonia Canela."

"Oh, yeah. I remember her. She must be forty years old."

"She will be thirty-six," Tell said, wrenching my heart, "on her next birthday."

"If she's an old flame of yours, how come we had so much trouble getting the San Antonio flight?"

"Because she is an old friend, and honest."

"But you had to pay someone off. You always have to pay someone off."

"No," Tell said, lying unknowingly. "I paid the legal fees, period."

Tell did not know what I had done, on my own, when Rubio had tried to block the permit. Toña had turned her head while I sent the money on, and then blocked Rubio neatly.

"That old gal is a flier?"

"Yes. That lady is a pilot and in a dogfight she would shoot you down."

"Flame me! In a pig's—"

He broke off, glanced at me, colored, then added lamely, "ear."

"You speak English the way a Tepito *pelado* speaks Spanish. Guys and gals and flame—and pig's ears. Is this the way your new friend Smoky Barbecue talks?" Tell's voice was growing louder by the second.

"Brant. Smoky Brant," Tell Dos said sullenly.

"You need a change. A new school," Tell said.

"No. Not another school, Dad."

"Somewhere where they speak English properly. Somewhere that you can learn a bit about airplanes."

"But Dad, you said airplanes." That was the magical word. Maybe Tell Dos did lack that intangible quality that made his father such an incredible pilot, yet he was enthralled with airplanes and often pointed out flaws and solutions for them while working on our own transport planes.

"I did. Do you remember when you were small and we rebuilt those de Havillands to carry mail and general cargo?"

"Sure, I do. De Havillands, all right, but built in the States."

"Right again. And I have received permission for you to attend classes at the school and factory."

"Where? New York?"

"No. The school will be at Farnborough, about twenty-five miles from London."

"No!" I startled them both. "Not Europe. Tell Dos can't go to Europe!"

"Why?" Tell Dos asked.

"The war. There will be a big war. Spain was just a testing ground. Hitler will never be satisfied until he has all of Europe and that means another war as horrible as the other."

"He will back down in a hurry when the French and British call his bluff," Tell said.

"Besides," Tell Dos said. "I'm going to England, not Germany."

"I wish you wouldn't," I said, but I could see that he was desperately eager to go. Tell must have arranged it with Geoffrey de Havilland himself. I forced myself to say, "If go you must, I guess a tired old mom will have to let you leave the nest so that you can learn aviation from the best." It was not very funny, but the way the two of them laughed I might have been Charlie Chaplin.

"How come you know so much about Hitler?" Tell Dos asked me.

"I read. You should try it yourself sometime."

"Like what?"

"*Mein Kampf.* He wrote it himself. There will be war. It is a matter of when. However, if one breaks out while you are in England, you must come home immediately. After all, you are an American."

"Yes, I am. Also a Mexican. I guess one day I will have to decide which citizenship to choose."

Tell looked at me uncertainly, then said, "You have time to think about it."

"But," I said, "maybe you should travel on a Mexican passport. Mexico will not get into a European war. You could sail from Veracruz."

"He could," Tell said, "but I can get him a free ride all the way to New York and then he could sail directly to England. The best he could do from Veracruz would be one of those island-hopping German steamers."

"New York, then," I agreed, thinking of Tell Dos stranded in Hamburg.

"I'll send a cable to the de Havilland people."

"That will be a long cable," I said. "You had better send a letter with all of the pertinent information about Tell Dos. It could be sent air mail by the Clipper."

"I sent the letter . . . about three months ago."

"What?" Tell Dos and I cried out in unison. His was one of elation; mine, dismay.

"I know that I should have told you both, but I was afraid they might not take him and I wanted to be sure—"

"You mean I'm already accepted." My son tried not to smile, but he could not help himself. Suddenly I could see all of the smiles: the little curved toothless one, then the buck-toothed grin and the missing teeth, and finally the wide, grown-up grin he wore now.

I grabbed the poor boy and hugged him. Of course I cried all over his shirt, but I laughed too.

"When must he leave, Tell?" I asked.

"He can fly with us," Tell said.

"With you? Where?" Tell Dos asked.

"Your mother has sold a book to the biggest publisher in New York and they insist that she fly up to sign the contract."

"Tell Dos, the book is incidental. I wanted to see your grandfather. And they are not the biggest publishers in New York."

"Dexter and Peters. Of course they are. Dexter is well over six feet and Peters must weigh two hundred and fifty pounds."

I made a fist at Tell and he cowered.

"Hey," my son asked. "You wrote a book, like Hemingway, and those fat guys are going to print it?"

"No. Not like Hemingway. My book is factual, and those two publishers are not fat."

The telephone rang. Tell picked it up, speaking Spanish so rapidly that I could not follow him. Then he handed the telephone to me.

"Who is it, Tell?"

"Charley Goldberg in New York."

"Yes, Charley. Of course, I accept. I am overjoyed. Will you get rooms for three at Delmonico's? Thursday. Yes, we will fly, of course. My husband owns an airline." I replaced the receiver on its hook and sat the telephone down on its table. Tell and our son were both grinning now, all animosity gone. Tell squeezed our son's arm. I know he wanted to hug him, but Tell Dos was too adult to hug his father, except in Mexican ritual, so I held out my arms and hugged them both.

"Well, Tell Dos?" Tell asked, "Will you go?"

"To study aeronautics." He threw back his head and let loose with a Mexican yell, the kind that sounds like a coyote yodeling. I think that it must have been the basis for the famous rebel yell of the Civil War.

"I take it that means yes?"

He bobbed his head up and down, his still boyish features split by a huge grin.

"We will have a *despedida*," I said. "We cannot send our son off to another continent without a going-away party."

"Of course," Tell said exuberantly. "We will have a big fiesta, a real Mexican *pachanga* tomorrow night for the world renowned aircraft designer and his mother, the Nobel Prize-winning author."

"Great, Dad. I'll call the Metropolis."

"The Metropolis Hotel?"

"Yeah. That's where Smoky is staying."

"Good," I said quickly before Tell could speak. "And I'll call some of your other friends."

"I think I'll put in a call to the Ritz in Paris," Tell said.

"Why?" I asked suspiciously.

"Because," he shrugged innocently, "that is where your pal, Ernest Hemingway, is staying."

Chapter 26

· · · · · · · · · · · · · · · · · ✈

Tell Cooper, 1940.

The metamorphosis of Elena was, to my eyes, so sudden that at times I did not realize that the breathtaking beauty with the laughing blue eyes and golden hair was my daughter. I still would call out to her, "Elenita," attaching to her name the "ita" suffix that indicates both affection and youth.

"What is it, Daddy?"

"I just want a hug from my number one daughter." I would get an impatient hug and a brush of lips on my cheek, along with a delicate aroma of clean hair and a touch of perfume, and then she would be gone, dancing into another room, singing one of the latest hits. That day it was, "*Solamente Una Vez*," soon to be transformed by New York's Tin Pan Alley into "*You Belong To My Heart*."

When I heard the postman's whistle, I strode to the door before the maid, broom in hand, could reach it. He had a registered letter for me, so I had to go to the outside gate. The stamps were British airmail. It was from Tell Dos. I found a silver peso and gave it to the mailman. His mouth opened wide in surprise, then widened with pleasure. He left whistling.

My son had been gone for more than a year and I missed him sorely. I smiled at the memory of telephone calls that I had answered, only to find a giggling girl on the line, and the times that he had to listen to an irate banker let off steam until he could politely call me to the telephone. Finally, when called to the telephone, we learned to sing out: "Is it for Tell one or two?"

"Tell," Helen called to me from the doorway. She had heard the whistle too. "What's the mail?"

"It's from Tell Dos," I said.

Helen reached for the letter, looking myopically around the room for her forever-lost bifocals.

"No. Let's sit down and I'll read it to you. Then you can read and reread it as long as you like."

"Read it, Tell. Hurry."

"Dear Mother and Father." Somewhere along the way "Mom" and

208

"Dad" had disappeared. I read slowly and carefully. "I have something important to tell you. First, this war is not a phony one, the way the newspapers say. It was not for the Poles, anyway. I know some Polish pilots that are now flying under the aegis of the Royal Air Force. You might not believe some of the stories they tell, for they sound like propaganda horror stories. But they are true horror stories. I know. I read Hitler's book, Mother, all the way through. He will strike us when he is ready, no matter what he says. I do not think that we have very much time. Neither does Mister Geoffrey de Havilland. And neither does Tommy Wright, my roommate. England is terribly short of both pilots and aircraft. Tommy has already written home for permission to join the RAF. He is from Renton, Washington. His father works for the Boeing plant there. His father signed for him. Of course, Tommy is twenty and in a year wouldn't need permission. But that might be too late. I know that I am only eighteen, but I am needed."

"Tell," Helen interrupted me fearfully, "read the end. Tell me now! Does he want to join the air force as a combat flyer?"

"I think so, but let me finish the letter."

"The RAF have formed a new squadron for Americans." I smiled and then repeated, " 'have formed.' He is picking up *English* English." Helen shook her head impatiently, motioning for me to read on.

"They already have one for the Poles and, I think, some Czechs. The American volunteer group will be called the Eagle Squadron. I have already been accepted provisionally—with aid from highly placed, important people.

"Father, I wish that I could tell you about the new fighter planes that the RAF will be using. I ache to fly one. I have over a hundred hours of flight time, while many of the volunteers like Tommy have no more than ten hours solo in small planes.

"I do not mean this as a threat, but one of the Polish flyers told me that he could get me into the Polish Squadron easily. All I have to do is pretend to be Polish and speak Spanish to the English liaison officer. He will never know the difference. The English are not linguists as a rule."

I had to stop and laugh. "George must read this letter," I said.

"Finish it, will you, Tell!"

I shrugged and continued. "Please sign the form and airmail it back to me right away. I guess I did mean that part about the Polish Squadron as a threat. I must fly with the British. Tell Elenita that I want her to write to Tommy. He saw the picture she sent me and thinks that she is a 'real hot tamale.' His very words. Also I send her a kiss and a hug, and to you both too. Also to María. I miss her *enchiladas* and *mole* and everything. Abrazos to the chaps at the hangar and love to you all."

It was signed: Tell (Dos) Cooper.

Helen sat still, looking out toward the far wall where the bougainvillea had turned the adobe bricks crimson. Her eyes were wet, but not a single tear trickled out. I put my arm around her. "He will be all right, sweetheart. He is a good pilot."

"So was Jack. So was Lufbery and Ball and—"

"We all need luck just to get through one day. Tell Dos will need some luck, but he has a head start. He already knows something of fighter tactics."

"What about fighter tactics?" Elenita materialized in front of us. She seemed to float through the rooms and, unless she was singing, moved as silently as a glider.

"Your brother wants to be a fighter pilot," Helen said, looking resentfully at me.

"No," I corrected. "What he wrote, was that he wanted to fly for the RAF."

"Tell Dos wants to fly in the war?" Elenita said fearfully. "Could he get killed, dad?"

"Anyone might be killed, honey."

"But," Helen said bitterly, "if you want to hasten the process, take to the air."

"A fighter pilot," Elenita mused. "My brother, a fighter pilot!"

"Hold on," I said. "He may not even pass the physical. It is a strenuous one. And if he does, he may be sent to fly transports, or even to instruct. After all, he has over a hundred hours, and he was taught by one of the best pilots still alive."

"Who was that, Daddy?" Elena asked innocently, but the twitching corners of her mouth gave her away.

I burst out laughing. Elenita giggled, and finally Helen smiled.

"You did teach him, Tell," she said. "Did you teach him to be a good fighter pilot? One that cannot be killed?"

"I did not teach him to be a good fighter pilot, Helen. I taught him to be a good, careful pilot."

"He'll be the best fighter pilot in the war," Elenita said. "I know he will. I hope the British win. I don't care what some of the Mexicans are saying about the Germans."

"So do I, honey," Helen said. "So do I."

210

"What do you hear?" I asked.

"Oh, Daddy, you have heard them." A born actress, she struck a pose. " 'The Germans are not stand-offish like you Americans. They are musical and mix right in. They all speak Spanish and they never took Texas and Arizona and New Mexico and California away from us, and they never chased Villa around Chihuahua and they never bombarded Veracruz!' "

"Yes," I admitted. "I have heard them too. The ones that run the big hardware store downtown. They were bragging how quickly Germany overran Poland. Poland, for Christ's sake! I asked them if they thought that was as valiant a conquest as that of their confederate, Mussolini, over Ethiopia. Wait, I told them, until you meet the French and the English on the battlefield. That will be another story."

"Daddy, you didn't!" Elenita said proudly.

My chest swelled as I nodded yes. The truth was not so heroic. It had been the owner's dull son-in-law who bragged, and I suspect that he had never heard of Ethiopia.

"Daddy, is the American president's real name Rosenvelt and is he Jewish?"

"That one is right out of Goebbels's propaganda factory," Helen said. "Which one of your little fascist chums told you that?"

"Jorge heard his father say that, but he didn't believe it."

Helen looked at me. I merely shrugged, so she answered the unasked question.

"*Roosevelt* is not Jewish, but suppose he was? What difference would it make? What does race or religion or even culture have to do with whether or not we accept a good person?"

"Mexicans hate Spaniards," Elenita said, looking sideways at me. "They call them *gachupines*. They say they cheat them in business."

"Likely they do," I said. "And probably some gringos cheat them too."

"Mexicans trust Americans." She never used the word gringo; I often do with friends.

"Who is this Jorge?" I asked.

Before Elenita could answer, Helen spoke, hurriedly, "What will we do about Tell Dos?"

"What do you mean, do?" Elenita asked. "Tell is going to be nineteen years old. Goodness, he could even have a child himself. That is if he were married," she added hastily and turned pink right down to the neck line of her blouse.

"I agree," I smiled at her. "He is a very old Tell, but he still needs a signature before he can legally enlist in the RAF."

"Let me see, Mom."

Helen handed her the letter and the legal forms. She scanned everything in seconds. She could read as swiftly as her mother. Either one could finish off a novel in one afternoon.

"Polish Air Force?" Elenita looked at me.

"Part of the RAF," I explained.

"Wow. My own brother a fighter pilot. I wonder if Tommy is cute?"

"I fervently hope so," I said. "I also hope that he has good reflexes and steady nerves."

"Sure, Dad, but he could be cute too, no?"

Both Helen and I laughed.

"We don't have much choice, Helen. Tell Dos is every bit as stubborn as you. If he wants to be an RAF pilot, then an RAF pilot he will be."

"Then you sign that ugly document. I will not touch it."

"Done," I said. "Now, who is for lunch at the Catalán Restaurant?"

"I will want a martini," Helen warned.

"A double if you like."

"They make lousy martinis," Elenita said.

"How would you know?" I asked.

"Jorge says so."

"Jorge! Just how old is this martini connoisseur?"

"Eighteen . . . almost."

"Stick with the martinis, sweetheart," I said.

"And I shall have a *sangría*," Elenita said, pretending not to look anxious.

She smiled happily when I shrugged assent. After all, the wine cooler was more fruit juice than wine.

"Will José drive?"

"No, Elenita, I think that I can manage to steer the car all the way down the hill and even back up again. Then José will not have to wait around while you two decide what dessert to order."

"You hardly ever use José to drive, Daddy. Why?"

"José thinks a car is some kind of burro."

"José is not Memo," Helen said.

"True. Memo was one of a kind."

"Why doesn't he still work for you, then?" Elenita asked.

"He does. He is in charge of aircraft maintenance."

"Señor Gómez was a chauffeur?"

"He was. I taught him how to drive and I would have taught him to fly as well, but airplanes terrified him."

"Don't tell your customers, Daddy."

"I won't. But he has to fly now on every plane after every major overhaul."

"Should I have a drink before we go?" Helen asked.

"If the ladies can be ready in fifteen minutes, I will meet them at the gate with the Cooper limousine."

I sent María to have José take the car out of the garage and park it at the street entrance. I was almost dressed. I went in to the study and slipped into my old shoulder holster. I caught a glimpse of myself in a mirror. I looked like a movie gangster. I slipped into my jacket, but it seemed to me that I could see the bulge. I took the coat off and removed the holster. I thought I looked slimmer without it. I took a flat .380 Browning from the desk drawer, checked the clip and then, feeling foolish, put it back into the desk. I heard the telephone click as someone dialed the outside telephone, then I heard Elenita, speaking Spanish, slangy with schoolgirl expressions, invite someone to meet her at the Catalán restaurant.

The telephone rang and, luckily, I took it on the first ring. It was Charley Goldberg calling from New York.

"We got the manuscript back from those gutless schmucks," Charley said, dispensing with formalities. "They give a big advance, sit on the book until it damn near hatches, and then don't print."

I said. "How much does Riley pay?"

"Enough," Charley said. "But we won't take one more contract without a penalty clause that will kill any publisher dumb enough not to print the best fact book to come out in the last ten years."

"Will you sell it?"

"Sure, I will. You want me to tell Helen?"

"No, not today. She just found out that Tell Dos is going to join the RAF."

"Somebody has to stop that madman, Hitler," Charley said, "I just wish it wasn't always the kids."

"Daddy," Elenita called. "We're waiting for you."

I said goodbye and trotted out to the car. I slid behind the wheel, checked the rearview mirror and patted my right side. Of course there was no pistol there. I had noticed that in the capital everyone who wore a tie and a wristwatch was also sure to have a pistol tucked away somewhere.

"I am the exception that proves the rule," I said out loud as I eased the big car away from the curb. The three of us sat in the ample front seat. Helen in the middle, Elenita by the window.

"What rule are you testing?" Helen asked.

"Not testing," I said, "proving."

"What that saying means, Tell," Helen said, lecturing me, "is something that *tests* the rule. If there is an exception to a thesis then one had better have a good, hard look at the thesis, or rule."

"Well, what the hell," I said sadly, "I don't even have a watch."

"You have several at home and at work," Helen said. Then, as my nonsensical sentence registered, added, "Whatever are you talking about?"

"Watches and ties and pistols."

"What?"

"Never mind," I said. "I think you are an exceptional rule that needs testing constantly."

"What on earth does that mean?"

"Hah!" I chortled.

"It means he doesn't know," Elenita said.

Chapter 27

· · · · · · · · · · · · · · · · · · ✈

When we reached the stairway leading to the upstairs restaurant, a group of excited Spaniards were yelling insults at each other. Typically, no one listened. I finally found a Mexican waiter who told me that there had been a shooting, minutes ago, between two rival Spanish refugee groups. Two men had been wounded, one a Stalinist, the other a Trotskyite.

I positioned Helen and Elenita behind me and plowed my way through the crowd to the door. A waiter I had known for years met me there.

"I am sorry, *Don* Tell," he said sheepishly, "but I must take your pistol. It is the rule now."

I shrugged and held my coat open. His eyes widened.

"But you are not wearing your big revolver."

"No," I said smugly.

He opened the door and waved us on.

"You left that awful pistol at home," Helen said, hanging on to my left arm, by habit, as we climbed the stairs.

Why have I continued to wear a gun in modern Mexico? I decided that it must be habit, but I said, "It didn't match my tie."

"I have a friend," Elenita said, "who wears a tiny pistol, this big," she held up thumb and forefinger to show its size, "in her garter."

Helen nodded pleasantly as if to say that was where most sixteen-year-old girls carried their pistols. I yawned, but when Elenita peered at me, worried that she had failed to shock either of us, I burst into laughter.

"Daddy," she wailed. "I am not joking. She really has one."

"One," I said innocently. "I thought they came in pairs."

"Pairs?"

"Sure, legs and—"

"Stop right there, Tell," Helen warned.

When we were seated at our Sunday table, half hidden at the far end of the large dining room by several huge potted rubber plants, Elenita, glancing slyly at me, continued.

"Of course girls have two—"

"I know," I interrupted. "I knew a French girl that hid a large Le

Mat revolver between hers."

"Stop! Both of you," Helen said, smiling, but serious all the same. So, Elenita and I, chastened, did so, but whenever our eyes met, she would giggle until I had to laugh with her.

Our drinks suddenly appeared. Helen had somehow communicated in her special sign language that every waiter in the city seemed to understand. How she used her fingers to order a wine cooler, I did not understand at all.

Of course, Pablo brought our drinks almost automatically. A dry martini—four to one—for Helen, a double shot of tequila *añejo* with a slightly larger glass full of tangy red *sangrita* to chase it with for me, and the mild sangria for Elenita.

"Pablo," I spoke to the waiter, "how did you know that I would allow my daughter to drink alcohol?"

"It is not really alcohol, *Don* Tell. Just a touch of wine in a magnitude of fruit juice. Besides, look at me. I grew up on pulque."

"You have a point, but I heard a rumor that you are not a day over seventy years old."

"A lie. A huge prevarication. I am almost eighty years old. My third wife is over sixty. Why, even my horse is thirty."

"And they all drink pulque!"

"Certainly. Shall I get one for you?"

"I'll take another tequila instead," I said, smiling. There would be no milky pulque served in this restaurant, and we both knew it, but it was a game we enjoyed.

"Pulque has many vitamins and is most healthful."

I looked up, for the voice was vaguely familiar, but the young man was not. "So Pablo claims," I said, "but it looks too much like milk to suit me."

"Yes, Señor Cooper. But it does not taste like milk."

He did not smile, so I replied seriously, "No. It tastes to me more like that slimy trail that a snail leaves when it crawls over the grass."

"But, no, Señor Cooper—"

"I know," I said, standing up. "You would be Jorge." I glanced at Elenita waiting for a proper introduction, but she kept her eyes on the table.

"This young man is Jorge . . . Montejo," Helen said.

I nodded and indicated a chair. "Sit down. A drink?"

He shook hands with me, then Helen and last of all Elenita and then sat next to her.

216

I could almost see the thoughts churning in his mind. Should he order the same thing as his girlfriend's father to show him that he was a man of the world, or ask for a soft drink to impress him with his sobriety?

"I will take the same as the Señorita Elena," he said.

"Good choice," I said and then, while we waited for his sangria, asked, "Are you of the Yucatecan Montejos?"

"Yes, sir. Except that we are from Tabasco."

"Of course. I have a friend from Ciudad del Carmen. One of the old pirate families, Raymundo Macdonald."

"I went to school with his son."

"What do you study now?"

"I am in the school of law at the national university."

"You plan to practice law here in Mexico City?"

"No."

"In Tabasco, then?" I asked, surprised. Two attorneys should be enough for Tabasco, one for the defendant and another for the plaintiff.

"I do not intend to practice law."

¡Puta madre! I thought in disgust. Another cradle-to-grave politician. Aloud I said, "Politics, then?"

"No. I will go into business. Law is a good background for business, no?"

"Of course it would be," I said, liking the young man. "I wish that I had a background in law." I looked at him closely. He was heavy-shouldered, but lean in the flanks and hips. His eyes were closer to gray than brown, and his face as flat as that of Memo. He was altogether an engaging young man that another man would take to, but a woman might not. I grinned. I had likely described myself.

"Haven't we met before?" I asked. "There is something about you—"

"Here come the drinks." Helen interrupted me. "And why are you cross-examining the boy? One would think that *you* were the lawyer."

"Sorry," I said.

"It is nothing," Jorge said, grinning for the first time. "Señor Cooper, I would like to ask your permission to invite the Señorita Elena to the annual ball of the law students at the university."

"Permission?" I asked, stupidly.

"My mother would, of course, accompany us. Also, of course, you and the Señora Cooper are most cordially invited."

Perspiration was beginning to bead on his forehead. The boy was scared to death.

"Yes, you have my permission to ask the Señorita Elena." The Señorita Elena! Yesterday she was in kindergarten.

Jorge sat back in his chair and reached for his sangria. He drank the better part of it, then looked to Elenita for comfort but got none.

"Are you going to ask me?" I said.

"But you already said yes." Jorge looked at me guiltily. "I asked her, sir, if she would go, if I asked you and you said—"

"No, please. You have lost me. Just ask Elenita again."

"Yes, sir. Señorita Cooper, would you do me the honor of accompanying me to the ball for the law students of the national university?"

"I'll think about it," Elena said. "How about another cooler?"

"Elenita!" Helen said, an edge to her voice.

"All right. I'll go."

"Thank you. I will call for you at eight o'clock in the evening next Saturday, English time." He meant that he would actually arrive at eight instead of nine or ten.

There were four courses served before the Sunday specialty, paella, Barcelona style. I barely tasted each one, for if I was not careful, I would not do justice to the golden heap of rice with its hidden treasures of tiny clams still in the shell, shrimp, chicken, and whatever else might have inspired the cook that morning. When the paella arrived, I was overjoyed to find a large claw from a Moro crab. That uneasy wanderer of the Mexican east coast is often interrupted on a nighttime foray by a crabber, who rips the large right pincer from its body and then releases the crab, which is able to grow another claw.

We drank a good white wine from Andalusia. I wondered if the Catalán owner had stockpiled a great many cases, for Mexico had broken diplomatic relations with Spain and was not, to my knowledge, importing anything from the fascist regime. For dessert we decided on slices of candied quince or *membrillo,* served with slabs of yellow cheese made by the Mormon colony in Chihuahua. Jorge and Elenita ordered hot chocolate, while Helen and I drank coffee and sipped Grand Marnier. I asked permission to smoke and took out one of my mild cigars.

"Damn," Helen said, fumbling in her purse. She had forgotten her cigarettes.

Jorge offered her one of his. When she accepted, over one end he carefully dripped wax from one of those tiny matches made with cactus

218

quills. When the wax hardened, he gave it to her with a flourish. Elenita was impressed. He lit the cigarette for Helen and watched anxiously as she took a puff. Her eyes went out of focus and were wetly luminous. She said, "Good tobacco, but strong." She sat it in an ash tray and let it burn itself away.

Jorge, after the wax ritual, lit one for himself. It was easily twice as strong as my cigar.

"You did not offer me a cigarette," Elenita said.

"You do not smoke," Jorge answered.

"She most certainly does not," I said, just in case.

"Mama does," Elenita pouted.

"No," Helen said. "Mama does not. Mama has just quit for ever and ever."

There was a sudden clamor of angry voices, the sound of bottles falling and scuffling, and then three loud shots followed by a brief but complete silence.

I spoke first. "Helen, take Elenita and go to the ladies room. Now!"

Before they could do more than rise to their feet, three men were in front of our table waving pistols wildly. One man, his belly quivering like a purple balloon inside his gold-trimmed charro jacket, planted himself in front of me, his bulging eyes bloodshot.

"Hello, Rubio," I said, standing up.

"Tell Cooper! What are you doing here?"

"I used to eat here."

"Those *cabrones* tried to take my pistol and I sent them to *chingar a sus madres*!"

"Watch your language, Toad. There are ladies present."

"It's all right, Tell," Helen said and turned to the Toad. "Please move along, Jorge."

"Huh? Oh, the gringa writer. You got married to Cooper and . . ." He broke off in confusion as he stared at the young man.

"Jorgito. What are you doing here?"

"He is my guest and need not answer to you," I said.

"No, sir. I must answer. He is my father."

"You are Jorge Rubio's son!" I spun to face Helen. "You knew and did not tell me."

"We, Elenita and I," Helen said hesitantly, "thought it would be better if you judged him for himself, not by his father."

"Who is this gringo *cabrón*?" asked the thin, sallow man wearing rimless glasses standing next to Rubio.

"He is Cooper," Rubio said. "The one that shot that *cabrón* in Puebla. Riley likes him."

"Oh." The thin man slipped his pistol back in its belt-clip holster.

The other drunk, shorter and wider even than Rubio, slipped his little pearl-handled pistol back in his coat pocket. He waved a pudgy finger at me in warning.

"Watch what you say, Señor Cooper. Jorge is a famous killer. He is a dead shot."

"True," I said. "And if he does not get away from me, that is exactly what he will be, a *dead* shot."

"Daddy! Don't anger them." Elenita began to cry. I saw Rubio hazily as if through a thin screen of red silk. I lifted my left hand and Rubio flinched.

"No. Do not draw. I have no quarrel with you. I don't care if my son picks your daughter for his *novia*."

"You do not mind! You slimy toad. I mind. Apologize and go, or shoot. One or the other."

In my extreme rage, I spoke without thinking, but even if I had reflected on the lack of a weapon, I would have done the same. And somehow I believe that I would have killed him before I died. And Rubio sensed that.

"Sure, Tell, hombre. Whatever you say." He spoke using the familiar *tú* to me as if we were old friends. He holstered his pistol next to his bloated belly and turned to go.

"No. Not that quickly. You will apologize to the ladies."

"Sure," he said, a swagger in his voice. "Drank too much. You know how men are."

I might have let him go then if he had not leered at my daughter and said, "Adios. my skinny *gringuita*. Don't worry, one day you're going to have as much meat on you as your mama."

"No!" I cried out. I put the fingers of my left hand inside the right lapel of my coat. His two friends backed away and lost themselves in the crowd of curious spectators. "Down on your *pinche* knees and ask for pardon!"

"No!" He recoiled from me in horror.

"Then draw and shoot."

"I am not a gunfighter." He looked around the room for support or comfort and found neither. "Not like you. It is not fair."

"Which is it?"

He fell to his knees. "I beg your pardon, ladies." His eyes filled with tears.

"Papa," his son was standing over him. "Let's go."

"Help me, *Jorgito*," Rubio said. His son gave him both of his hands, lifting him to his feet. Then he turned to face me.

"Maybe my father has done things that I do not approve, but he has been kind to me. You are a cruel man, Señor Cooper. Far more cruel than he. It would have been kinder to have shot him."

"How could I?" I said, an insane hate still searing my soul. "I am unarmed." I held my coat open to show them. Rubio screamed like a wild animal and went for his pistol, but his son, quicker than his father—and also sober—got it first.

He showed it to me, the barrel pointing at my feet. "I could kill you, now, easily. But I will not. Remember when you brag to your friends of your great bluff, that it was the son of Jorge Rubio that spared your life."

Slipping the fancy gold-engraved automatic pistol in his pocket, he spoke directly to Elenita. "I am truly sorry. I will never forget you. Adios."

"Wait, *Jorgito*," Helen said.

"Adios, Señora Cooper," the boy said sadly, then took his father by an arm and walked him away. The other two gunmen came out from the crowd and accompanied him down the stairs. There was a long silence and then an instant uproar. I recognized a reporter for Excelsior; I wondered what kind of a version Rubio would pay him to write.

"You destroyed that man in front of his friends and his son. Tell, I never knew you could be so vindictive." Helen looked at me much the same way she had when she first saw a man beating a burro half to death.

"Daddy." Elenita was deathly pale and her eyes unnaturally wide. Her voice was cold enough to send a shiver into my brain. "I hate you and I will never forgive you. Never!" She burst into tears and fell into her mother's arms.

I began to shake so hard that I had to sit down, but even then it was not until I had drunk a half a snifter of cognac that I was able to keep the chair from rattling. When I looked up, they had left, taken a cab, and with it, a part of my life.

Chapter 28

· · · · · · · · · · · · · · · · · · ✈

Letters

Dear Tell,

I was ever so sorry to leave Mexico, but even an old codger like me must go home to help when the Hun is once again threatening to sink our little island.

I cannot tell you all that I am doing, but it involves the "Big Boys" as they call the heavy bombers over here. And big they are. I have flown a Lancaster. Four engines and the wingtips reach to the horizons. My reserve commission was that of a captain, but they are so short of officers that they have made me a colonel. My old squadron mate, Pinky Harris, says that he will put me up for brigadier as soon as I learn to salute properly.

Alas, I am also an earl and I suppose that I will perforce assume that role, which means that even after we have defeated the Boche, I will stay on in England.

Also, I have been put to stud with one of the Balder sisters, the middle one, I think. Not one of them is sure where Spain is, let alone Mexico. But one must leave an heir I suppose. In any case, I have decided to turn my stock in TIA over to Tell Dos. He was reluctant to accept, but when I pointed out to him that the value of a real de Havilland-trained aeronautical engineer and a hero of the Battle of Britain is infinitely greater to the long-term future of TIA than any amount of capital, he agreed. I will keep one share so that I will not feel guilty when I journey to Mexico during one of our dreary winters to attend a stockholders meeting. I will, of course, vote for a change in management.

Now for the big news. Tell Dos, or Whitey, as his mates call him, is flying our new magnificent Spitfire. I cannot go into detail, but its top speed, for example, is three times better than the latest model Spad that you flew.

The lad has already been in combat and has shot down an enemy plane, a Messerschmitt fighter. He followed the Hun down from fifteen thousand feet to the channel and flamed him at a thousand. The pilot had an option denied us, a parachute. He bailed out and was picked up by one of our rescue boats. In the old days he would have been brought in to the squadron mess and treated to a party before being shipped off to prison. It is different now. We hate them so intensely that there is even talk of shooting them in their parachutes. I know it sounds barbarous, but if you could see the havoc worked by the Germans' indiscriminate bombing of London, you might understand.

I am adding this note two days later because Tell Dos, temporarily, cannot. First of all, he is all right. He is burned badly about the face and head but will recover completely, the surgeon assured me, and will have only a few fine lines around his eyes and mouth, to show to his admirers. He had followed another Messerschmitt down from on high, but this time there was another behind him. They dove through a cloud layer and Tell Dos's wingman lost him in the clouds, but the Hun did not and his incendiaries set Tell Dos's Spitfire aflame. He bailed out, his chute opened, unburned, but the boy was already badly burned. He will be out of the hospital in a few weeks and will tell you the details.

I wanted to be sure that I wrote to you before the American lad, Tommy, who is his leader and his friend, did, and perhaps, unintentionally of course, alarmed you. Your son is okay. My special love to Helen, a kiss for Elenita and an abrazo to my old and special friend, Tell.

George

Dear Father,

George was in to see me, but I was still floating in the arms of Morpheus—no more pain, one just drifts dreamily away—so he left a note. When you got his letter, I hope you read it first and then broke the news to Mother. The truth of the matter is that I am a competent fighter pilot, but no more, which is better than a bad one, I guess. But I think the Germans flying the new ME 109s are a couple of notches above mediocre.

Now I understand why you carried a pistol in case of being set aflame in the air, as I was. At least I had a parachute, else I would not be here. But had I known the pain would have been so intense, I might have used a pistol. It was the morphine that saved me. Blessed relief! I can understand why there are people addicted to its use.

Somehow I used to think that a fighter pilot would spend his combat time doing pretty loops and Immelmanns instead of making one tight turn after another. Turns so tight that sometimes you nearly black out and can scarcely see the wing tips. I think that when you occasionally do meet head on, like knights jousting, the winner will be the pilot who turns tighter and shoots better. I remember you shooting dove, one after another, with that old double-barreled twenty-gauge, while I blasted away with the big twelve, missing as often as not. Maybe I should have been in bombers. I get along well with the crewmen, the mechanics. They come to me for advice when they run up against technical problems with one of our birds. And lovely birds they are. Rolls engines and a wing load you would not believe for a fighter plane. And eight, count them, eight machine guns!

I have resolved to keep my head on a swivel, as they say here. The German that got me followed me down from at least five thousand feet and flamed me before I knew he was on my tail. I wonder how often that happens? After we win the war, I want to come home and not fly for a while. Just work in the shop. Tell Memo that I won't get in his way and I really am an excellent engineer. Mister de Havilland would have given me a post at the factory, but then, Tommy, my roommate, joined up and I got keen on the idea and, well, here I am. But Mother, you were so right about Hitler, even if one discounts half of the stories I hear first-hand. How is it that you knew when so many others did not? Are the clues always there for people like you to find?

Also in the category of big news: I might have a girlfriend. Although when they take the bandages off my face, she might not be my girl any more. I always thought I had a baby face, so a scar (or likely a dozen) might even be an improvement. Anyway, as she faithfully pens this letter for me, she is about to promise to have dinner with me the first time I am allowed to leave the hospital.

Tommy has written to Elenita for me. He must have a two-pound package of letters that he carries with him even when he flies. All from my little sister. Did she go to Los Angeles?

Abrazos to María and José and my love to you and Mother.

Tell Dos

Dear Mister and Mrs. Cooper,

This note, tacked on to the letter from Whitey—that is, Tell Two—is from Susan Blakely. I am a volunteer who helps the sisters at the hospital. I have been reading to your son and I offered to write the letter for him; his hands will both be perfectly well once they take the bandages off. He called me his girl and asked me out to dinner as he dictated the letter. But he has never even seen me. I am doing this awkwardly. I am sorry. His eyes will be all right, but he still has bandages over them. I am a rather plain, ordinary girl about his age and I have accepted his invitation, but I am afraid that once he sees me he will think just that—an ordinary girl—and forget my "gentle hands." Whatever does happen, your son is a personal hero to me—one who has sacrificed much for a country not even his own.

Dear Mother and Father,

Maybe I shall become a journalist, like my mother, after the war. I have a natural talent, for I ferreted out some information that one Susan Blakely tried to keep from me. Namely that she is madly in love with me, but conspired with you to keep the secret from me. (His sense of hearing is so acute. He heard me scratching away, writing the postscript to you and tricked me into admitting it. Susan Blakely.)

She broke down and admitted to certain affection for me, so I don't give a hoot if I never see again as long as I have the loving hands of the lovely Susan to tend me. On Friday next I have reserved a table at a posh restaurant, which, because of its strategic location in an almost bombproof cellar, is much in demand. We shall dine and I will drink to Sister Suzy only with "thine eyes and I'll not lack for wine." (I had to stop and go asking through the ward to find out if the quotation was correct. The head surgeon who knows everything said that it was close enough, so we can continue. This is going to be a strange letter.)

I still do not drink much. Remember when, emulating my dashing father, I threw down a shot of tequila and then spent the rest of the day pounding my head and drinking water? As you know, my mates call me Whitey—they should have seen the color of my hair under the Mexican sun—and the newspapers call me "the indestructible Whitey Cooper." But I am also sometimes called half-pint. Not for my height, which is a respectable 5 feet, 10 inches, but because I often order a pint at the pub and leave it half finished.

I would like to ask you, Father, something that has been on my mind, and were I not lying here in the dark, safe and secure with Suzy at my side, I might not ever have had the nerve to ask.

I have shot down only two planes. I know that you had eight confirmed and who knows how many shot down on the wrong side of the lines. But one or a dozen, the question must be the same. I wonder about the ones I kill. Might we have been, in other circumstances, friends? Might someone write a letter to his family, not like Sister Suzy is doing for me, but in the third person past, advising his family that he died quickly and painlessly? (I am not a sister, just an assistant to any nurse that needs me. SB) Was this as painful a thought for you as it is for me?

I know that Suzy is getting writer's cramp, for I can hear her fingers making little whimpering noises, so I shall say goodbye for now to my father who was an Ace in France and my mother who danced on a table and kicked wine all over him during that other war.

Your loving son, Tell Dos.

Postscript: I am adding this to the letter outside the wardroom, in the hall, where not even clever Tell will know. He is the bravest man I have ever known. It is possible that he will never see again, and although he has never been told this, he knows. He is the most admired man in a room full of heroes. Sometimes the awful thought flashes in my mind that he may never see again, but it is not pain that I feel, but relief, for then I know he will be mine. I do love him so. Forgive me, but I felt I must tell you. Susan Blakely.

Dear Mr. and Mrs. Tell Cooper:

You will have received the cable concerning the death of Flight Lieutenant Tell Cooper II. The cable would have read: lost and presumed dead. There was no doubt as to his death. I personally saw his plane explode upon contact with the water. Death would have been instantaneous. I made several low-level, slow passes over the area and saw nothing but small pieces of debris. There must have been two German fighters in that melee for every one of ours. If it is of any consolation to you, I shot down the plane that got Whitey, as we affectionately called your son.

I have collected his personal things and will hold them until they can be sent to you. It is numbing to lose a mate, any one of them, but Whitey was special for all of us. He had been offered non-flying duty and then, alternately, a spot in the training command. He refused, saying that he could not leave the rest of us to fight against such terrible odds. He thought that one experienced man might make a big difference, and I am sure he was right. Which one of us might he have saved? And how many times? We will never know. Had he not been there, perhaps the plane that got him might have shot down someone else. But he was there, so that someone *will* live to fight again. If I am that someone, I promise you that my resolve is so strengthened by the death of Whitey that I will fight the Germans with all my will until I can fight no more or we have won.

Yours in sorrow,

226

Charles Berenson,
Wing Commander, Eagle Squadron. RAF.

Dear Mom,

My heart is broken. I got a copy of Berenson's letter to you. Tommy Wright, Tell Two's roommate, sent it along with his own letter. Tommy has been writing to me for more than a year now, and every letter mentions someone he knew that was missing or dead. I cannot bear to talk—or even write—about Tell Dos yet. Perhaps when I see you next.

I cannot write to Daddy yet either. I never knew that he could be so hard, so cruel. I know that Jorge's father did some terrible things to Daddy, but even so, to humiliate him in front of his son! Even if his father was an evil man, should the son be forced to bear the sins of his father?

I didn't tell you, but I called Jorge the next day. His sister, Amelia, answered the phone. I could hear his voice in the background telling her what to say to me. He would not talk to me. He said he couldn't. He told her to tell me adios and sent his love. What is going to happen to me? I am only eighteen years old and I have lost my only brother and my sweetheart.

I like living with your old friend, Athena. She is so sweet and knows everything about the college. However, I have been invited to join a sorority. If I join, I would move into the house. It is just off campus. All of the girls say that it is a keen place and everyone is best friends.

The girl that asked me told me that I would have been "rushed" sooner, but they thought I might be Mexican and Catholic. Do you think that if I had been one of those beautiful *tehuanas* with black hair and golden skin and a Protestant, they would have asked me? Why are Americans so conscious of race? And why are they against Catholics and Jews? I think I'll ask Athena. I would like to belong to a sorority for I am lonely. Maybe now that I am starting classes I will make friends.

I suppose that I will write a note to Daddy after a few years when I am over my great sorrow. But then, he probably doesn't care anyway. My classes are almost all girls. Some of the boys who would have been here were drafted, and others volunteered. Even my favorite professor (Ancient History, also my favorite class) says that he may accept a commission. He is a full assistant teaching fellow and looks younger than twenty-three. He also looks a lot like Cary Grant. He is terribly anti-fascist, but he is also anti-war.

So many of the boys are in uniform now, although no one thinks that America will enter the war actively. Still, we see the newsreels with our sailors protecting the convoys that are delivering all kinds of war material to the British.

Of course, there are those who boo and hiss and call Roosevelt a war monger. I get mad and cry and even curse, but do so in Spanish so most people won't know. Besides, as Tell Dos says . . . said, it is much more satisfying. There, I did it again. I had to stop and let the paper dry, and now I can write no more.

With love,
Elenita
P.S. You can let Daddy read this if you want.

Chapter 29

.... ✈

Tell Cooper

The thunderheads, which had churned themselves up high enough to cool, burst and gave the valley of Mexico its afternoon drenching—just as my old Renault coughed and died.

I got out and folded up one of the hood covers to check the carburetor. Within seconds an interested crowd had gathered, and soon there was no room for me to peer under the hood. Men began to quarrel over what should be done. Then one of them waved a hand and announced imperiously: "I am a real mechanic."

I heard several derogative remarks, but he ignored them and produced an aged, wrinkled business card which he handed to me with a flourish. "Tomás Durán Hernández of the Durán Automobile Repair Service." I half expected him to click his heels. "Also," he added, "we have the use of the telephone just next door."

"Take the car," I said, handing him my card. "But before you do, call the number on the card, ask for Señor Gómez and tell him what is wrong. He will procure any part that you may need."

He took my card, but released his own reluctantly. I suspected it might be his only one, so I decided to return it once I got the car back.

I waved down a cab and jumped in. I felt uneasy, as if I had forgotten something important. I told the driver my destination and when he paused, waiting for the normal discussion of price, I merely urged him to get me home quickly. He did. He also punished me for my lack of social graces by charging me twice the going rate.

Helen was curled up in her favorite chair, her head resting on the padded arm, watching the fluffy white clouds alternately expose and hide the volcanoes. She held a martini glass in one hand. Our old-fashioned photograph album with its thick covers and a silver clasp lock lay open on a side table. I knew without looking that it would be turned to the last page, the one that held a picture of Tell Dos in his RAF uniform. I glanced at it before I spoke. He was so young and vulnerable. I could see the boy who at ten had sobbed uncontrollably when his younger, pragmatic sister had proved to him that there was no Santa Claus. When he stopped crying, he had lashed out at the little girl, stating with adult superiority, "Of course. I knew that. It is the Three Kings that always bring the presents in Mexico. Santa Claus is only for the gringos."

I felt tears in my eyes even as I laughed, softly I thought, but Helen looked up then. She had that same look as Tell Dos in the photograph.

"I will never see him again? Will I, Tell?"

"Sure you will. And you do. I see him every day."

"But not that way. I want to touch him."

"All I can tell you is: work. Keep busy. How is the rewrite coming?"

"I am talking about our son and you ask about a silly goddamn rewrite?"

"You have to go on, Helen."

"Why?"

"Because of Elenita. Because of me and because of you."

"Oh, shit! You sent him there to die and now you tell me to go on. Keep a goddamn stiff upper lip. What!"

Helen never even said "hell" unless she was extremely angry and lashed out at whatever or whomever was closest.

"I sent him to England to be an aeronautical engineer," I said, trying to keep any trace of anger and frustration out of my voice.

"You sent him to a country about to go to war. I told you and still you sent him."

I sat down abruptly in the other chair next to the side table. I hefted the martini pitcher. It was light. Nothing but a little ice and melted water.

"If I could have done it differently, Helen, I would have."

"But you didn't. You sent him to be another Tell Cooper, daredevil fighter pilot and gunfighter. Only he was not a cold-blooded killer. He was just a little boy trying to emulate one—his father."

Anger and guilt choked up inside me and almost cut off my breath. I lurched to my feet and slapped the palms of my hands over my ears hard. But still the phrase rang inside my head. You sent him. You!

I had my hand on the front door knob when Helen caught me, sobbing as hard as had Tell Dos that Christmas so long past. She held me tightly around my waist until she could speak.

"No, Tell. It wasn't you. It was them. And us. All of us. It was the goddamn world that killed my boy."

"Wash your face, sweetheart," I said as calmly as I could, although my voice sounded thick to my own ears. "Let's go out. There is a new bar at the Regis."

230

"Go out? What a good idea."

I released her. She took two uncertain steps and then said, "I'll just look in on the children."

"Helen," I cried out involuntarily. "There are no children here."

She looked up at me puzzled and said, "Then, where are they?" and crumpled to the floor.

I picked up her dead weight and carried her into our bedroom. There was a half-empty martini glass on the night table. I undressed her clumsily and drew her puppet-like limbs into her pajamas. I did not want her to think that she had passed out in the living room. She had never been a heavy drinker. The last few months and the pitcher of martinis were too much for that petite body. But now, I thought, the painful sliver has festered and forced its way out. She will be all right now. The tissue will harden and scar over and we will be as we were before. I was wrong.

I left her there, snoring gently, her face childlike in repose, framed by hair with a touch more yellow in it than had my son, whose mates in the RAF had called Whitey. I picked up a bottle of tequila and a shot glass, then sat down in Helen's chair, staring at the clouds covering the volcanoes. I sat alone, as the sky darkened, isolated, peering into myself and wishing that somehow I could have been a different man.

For an instant I saw and heard my father, swung up behind him, on his big, brown gelding, and then I turned and gave the thumbs up sign to Tell Dos in the student's cockpit in the old Meyer's biplane. There was another second of what I can describe only as spiritual serenity, and then my tears came. I cried as hard as I ever had, even more so than as a boy, when I was told that I would never see my mother again until I died and went to heaven.

As I sat there in the dark, sobbing, the album still lying open to the picture of Tell Dos, María, that gentle little Indian woman from the mountains of Michoacán, padded softly up to me, a candle in one hand. She thought the electricity had gone off, as it often did during thunderstorms, and had brought me light. When she saw the tears running down my face, she made a moaning sound and then spoke.

"Ah, señor. It is good to cry. It cleanses the soul. But you must remember that Tell Dos was such a good boy that he surely lives with the *angelitos* and in less time than it takes a cock to crow, we will all see him."

That simple, sweet woman spoke with such conviction that I nodded agreement. I willed myself to believe and stood up, the tequila bottle untouched, and walked quickly into the bedroom. Once in bed, alongside Helen, I fell into a deep sleep such as I had not known since the death of my son.

I awoke to the sun and to Helen humming to herself, a happy canary loose in the house.

"Hurry! María has made *menudo* and she has some cold beer for you."

"But I didn't—"

"If you dance, you must pay the piper."

She was sure that I was suffering from a hangover. So be it, I thought, as long as she was in good spirits.

"Maybe," I said, smiling tentatively, "I'll shoot the piper."

I groaned loudly for her benefit and went in to shave. The new electrical shaver that she had given me last Christmas was still locked in its case. I had used it but once. It had fastened on to my moustache with the tenacity of a bulldog. I had been forced to scissor off part of my moustache to cut it loose. It still held a clump of reddish-brown hair in its teeth. I shaved with the same old safety razor that I had been using since college, showered in hot and then ice-cold water and dressed quickly. When I got to the table, Helen was sipping orange juice and working a crossword from the English language newspaper.

The menudo was spicy hot. It had more chile than tripe. María had used those deadly little red *chiles de árbol*. I sprinkled salt on a tortilla to combat the chile. When that didn't work, I drained the cold beer María had placed by my plate.

Today was payday and I had to get to the office early. I grabbed my coat, paused briefly at the study door, thinking about my pistol, but then, seeing what I took to be apprehension in Helen's expression, shut the door and turned back to kiss her.

"I have to run. See you tonight."

She took my kiss on her cheek, but I still caught a strong scent of gin.

"Kind of early for gin," I said in what I meant to be a light bantering voice.

"But it's all right for you to soak up beer." She jerked away from me angrily.

"Sorry, sweetheart. Sure, a little hair of the dog that bit you."

She glared at me.

"Will you be working on the rewrite today?"

"I don't need to write one goddamn line. I don't know what's wrong with that goddamn Jew anyway."

"Hey," I said, astonished. "That's your friend, mine too, Charley Goldberg, you're talking about."

"Why did he have to die?" Helen wailed.

"Charley died?"

"No, you idiot. My boy died. Maybe the Jews did start the war."

I grabbed her by the shoulders and held her at arm's length until finally she stopped struggling and looked up at me.

"Helen. Our boy, Tell Dos, is dead. It is not something that can be blamed on me or you or Charley."

"Oh my God, I do know that, Tell. I love Charley and I know the book needs rewriting. I wish that they would get a good writer to do it."

I released her and said, "They have one. The best. Will you get started on it today? As a favor to your adoring public?"

She smiled suddenly and threw me a smart palm-outward British salute. "Yes, sir, major, sir."

I paused at the door and instead of saying "Stay off the juice, Helen," I blew her a kiss.

While I waited out on the tree-lined extension of the old Reforma Avenue for a cruising cab, I thought of Helen and Paris and our early Mexican years. When a cab with a *libre* sign pulled up, I was whistling *"The White Cliffs of Dover."*

The big hangar with its converted offices was blazing with light. I checked my watch, thinking that I was even earlier than I thought. The door was locked and I suspected that someone had left the lights on by mistake, but when the door swung open there was the familiar clatter of drills and lathes and rivet guns. Everyone, including the maintenance chief, Memo Gómez, were as busy as ants.

"Hey, Memo!" I yelled over the machine concerto.

"Good morning, boss. What are you doing here?"

"My question to you, Memo." I pointed to the wall clock. It was within five seconds of my own watch. "It is not even seven o'clock."

"Better to work early than late."

"But I authorized no overtime. We simply cannot afford to pay overtime."

"I know, but we got to get that DC-3," he jerked his nose at the plane in the middle of the hangar, "ready for the flight tomorrow to San Antonio."

"But it was up yesterday."

"I know, but it didn't rev up right and then—"

"No. Don't tell me. How will I raise the money for the overtime?"

"But you and me and Paco, we all work overtime and we don't get no extra pay."

"True, but we are executives and stockholders."

Memo worried that fact around his head awhile. Then the solution reached his eyes and golden lights danced in them.

"We'll make all of those *cabrones* executives too."

"We can't make all of the workers executives . . ." I broke off as the thought struck me with pristine logic.

"No," I continued, "we cannot make them all executives, but we can make them all stockholders."

"Good," Memo said, looking impatiently at someone waiting at the airplane for him.

"We will put all of their overtime in a special book and when they get enough to pay for a share, it will be credited to them and issued in their name."

"Okay, but it won't make any difference. These are good *cabrones* and they know they got good jobs."

"Tell them anyway," I said.

I waited at the rail separating the offices from the workshop area to hear the excited chatter and maybe even a cheer or two, but there was no reaction. None. It was beyond their experience. Years later when an old employee brought in a share to sell so that he could send his son to Mexico's top engineering school, the Monterrey Institute of Technology, I asked why it was in three pieces, like a jigsaw puzzle. He said that it tore apart when he scraped it off a wall where he had pasted it to cover up a hole.

I like to think that from that day on TIA made a profit. It took longer, but with the load of the excessive payroll lifted from our backs, Paco and I took a few more chances, and within a year we were running the largest independent airline in Latin America. And when the crooked union, which was wired into the top echelon of the government labor bureau, tried to take over our shop, they could not. Not only could we prove that TIA was owned by the workers, but that it had paid dividends regularly.

Memo stopped by my office a few hours later, leaning inside to yell that my car was ready. I could pick it up whenever I wanted.

I worked straight through the lunch hour and then, the payroll dispersed and my correspondence caught up, I begged a ride with an advertising salesman for XEW, the national radio network. I sent him to see Walter Thompson de Mexico, our advertising agency, but only after he had dropped me off at a lean-to with a crudely lettered sign proclaiming that it was the Durán Automobile Repair Service.

A half an hour later I drove up to our gate in a driving rain and honked the three short, three long and three short sounds that was the Morse code for SOS, the international distress call. Everyone on our affluent block had their own signal. Mine was one of the shorter ones.

José—the gardener, occasional chauffeur and husband to the indispensable María—wearing one of those finely woven serapes from Saltillo to keep the rain out, swung the gate open. I dashed through the rain into the kitchen and called out to Helen.

She did not answer, but I could see light filtering through the cracks of the door to the study. But when I opened the door, the room was empty. The manuscript was still in the unopened package with Charley Goldberg's logo stamped on the outside. The cover was off the typewriter and she had left a note, still on the roller, for me: *I had to go to a party at Susan's for Jim. Come on over, if you want*. She had not bothered to put my name or hers on the note.

I called Sue. Her husband, manager of the City Bank, answered.

"Yes, Helen was here. But she left about an hour ago."

"I was supposed to have gone with her," I lied, "but I had car trouble and missed her. Maybe Sue knows where she went."

I heard Sue call from somewhere near the telephone. Too near, unless she wanted me to hear. "She was pretty sloshed. I think she was going with Donald Billings and Rodrigo to the Lincoln Grill, or maybe it was the Country Club."

"I guess she went with a group," Jim said, doing a little lying of his own, "to the Lincoln Grill or the golf club."

I thanked him and then called both places. She was not at either one. Neither Donald Billings nor his buddy Rodrigo were married. I hoped that they had their own girlfriends along.

I brought out the tequila bottle that I had left unopened the night before, and called María to bring me lime and salt. I settled down to wait. At ten o'clock I began to pace myself at one drink every half hour, so I was not quite drunk when I heard the car drive up out front. Neither was I quite sober.

I opened the front door and heard loud voices; then a car door banged shut. I had left the light on over the outside door, but whoever was trying to open it could not seem to find the keyhole. I opened the gate and Billings, an exaggerated surprise on his lipstick-smeared face, fell into my arms. I lifted him up, stepped outside and then threw him up against his fancy new Cord automobile.

"Hey," he screeched drunkenly. "I'm just bringing her home. I ain't the guy that screwed her."

I reached instinctively for the pistol that I no longer carried. The car door flew open and Rodrigo yelled, "Get in, you dumb shit! He shoots people." He gunned the motor and then, as Billings stumbled in, careened away, the door still open.

"Yes, sir," Helen pushed herself away from the wall to stand uncertainly in the dim light. "He shoots people all right. He sends them to get shot too. Don't you, Major Tell Number One?"

"Get in the house!"

She snorted and almost fell. I caught her by the elbow and half-lifted, half-drug her into the house. I shoved her through the open door into our bedroom. She fell and looking up at me, her face ugly with hatred, said, "Don't you even want to know which one it was that screwed me?"

Chapter 30

She would not fly. My wife, Helen, who had flown with me in the old open-cockpit de Havilland from Puebla to a makeshift field near Veracruz to be married, would not fly to San Antonio in a twin-engine DC-3.

Tell Cooper, manager and partner of TIA airlines, was seeing his wife off on the Mexico City-Laredo express train. I turned off Insurgentes Avenue into the Bellavista railroad station.

We arrived early and would have to wait at least a half an hour—if the train started on time. It took two porters to carry her luggage into the compartment. I tipped them and then sought out the conductor and insisted that he accept twenty silver pesos to watch over my wife who was "ailing and nervous."

If anything, overzealous, he insisted on rearranging her luggage personally. When he bent over to lift her overnight case, his fingers jerked loose. He stood for a second gaping in astonishment at the mysterious bag, then took a firmer grip and, flexing his knees, lifted it from the floor to the pullout shelf with its steel basin and mirror. The bag clinked like a dozen people banging beer stems.

When he excused himself and left, I tried to thumb the bag open. It was locked. We never locked our luggage; we laughed at those fearful souls that did.

"What's in it?" I asked.

"I brought along a bottle of gin for the trip."

"Is there anything else in it besides gin?"

"Of course there is." Her voice rose in anger. "Every goddamn other thing that I need."

"There is a club car on the train."

"Good! Let's have a drink while we wait. Or would you rather leave now?"

"Would you rather I left now?"

Her face blurred and became an angry mask of the woman I loved. "Sure. Take off. Besides the gin, I got a guy stashed away. Soon as you leave, we'll have a little drinkie together."

She could not have been drinking that morning, I thought, but I was not sure. I was never sure any more. That was what I had told Charley

Goldberg. Maybe he could reach her and help. Or know someone who could.

"I could stow away," I said.

"No. I want to go alone. You promised, Tell."

"Sure. It's all right. Charley will meet your train in New York. He'll see you to—"

"Charley," she interrupted. "Why?"

"I thought that it would be a good idea for the two of you to get together on the rewrite."

"So he meets me at the station and we sit down on the sidewalk and go over the galleys?"

"Helen, please. Your father can't leave the apartment. Not for a while yet, so Charley volunteered."

"All right, Tell. You did your good deed for the day, go on back to those goddamn airplanes. They all have snakes wriggling out of their nacelles." She giggled shrilly. "The Medusa Airline."

I tried to take her in my arms, but she wrenched free. She took a deep breath and then spoke in what she meant to be a normal tone, but it was not. "You are a nervous Nelly. I am only taking the train to New York. People do it every day."

"Sure. Some of them even take airplanes."

"I know that." Then her voice did break. "Tell, please. I don't know what is wrong with me. I feel really rotten. Let's go to the club car. Please?"

There were a few men in the car, drinking coffee and smoking cigars. We sat in a booth by the window.

Helen ordered a silver gin fizz—for her hangover, she told the uninterested waiter doubling as the morning bartender. When he asked what that was, she switched to a martini. I ordered coffee with a tot of cognac.

"Will you work in New York for a while before you come back?" I asked, affecting a nonchalance I did not feel.

"That is the reason I'm going there."

"You said to see your father."

"That too."

"Then you will work on the book?"

"I said so, didn't I?"

There was a warning whistle and the car jerked for a few feet when the engineer took up the slack. My coffee sloshed over.

"Then I won't see you until Christmas?"

238

"I thought maybe Elenita could fly to New York and spend Christmas with Daddy and me. You never know when it might be your last Christmas with someone." She smiled brightly at me, but her eyes were wet. She held the empty glass up for the waiter to see.

Then there was the second whistle, and this time a conductor came through warning the visitors to leave. It was leave the train or go to Laredo. I have often wondered what might have happened had I elected to go.

"Time to go, Tell." She turned a cheek for me to kiss, her eyes on the waiter.

I kissed her and stood up uncertainly.

"Tell, you must get off!"

The train bumped ahead a few feet. "What if I stay?"

"Tell, goddamn you!" Her blue eyes bored into mine, seeing something that I obviously could not, but which was hateful to her.

"All right," I said reluctantly. "But I'll see you at Christmas time."

"I told you that I would not be in Mexico for Christmas."

"Me neither, mam," I said, speaking "cowboy," as Helen used to call my West Texas accent. "I reckon I'll saddle up old Paint and ride on up to the big city in time for Christmas."

She laughed perfunctorily, glancing outside nervously as the train moved again, this time steadily. I leaned down, cupped her chin in my big left hand and kissed her full on the lips.

"Goodbye, sweetheart," I said, turning quickly away so that she would not see my own tears. I walked unsteadily to the outside door. I had to take two quick steps to keep my balance and when I turned to wave, I caught no more than a pale, somehow wistful face of the woman I loved and who seemed to have lost her way. That face would be engraved in my mind. As would be the casual wave of the glass, as if in a last toast—which it was, for I was never to see her again.

Chapter 31

All but one of the iron-and-tile cafe tables were taken. I scanned the room, table by table, but could not locate Rodolfo. I smiled at myself. Twenty years in Mexico and I still arrived at an appointment on time. I would likely have to wait at least a half an hour before my old revolutionary comrade from Sonora showed up.

The buzz of Iberian Spanish, harsh and sibilant, identified the cafe as a favorite among the Spanish population of Mexico, now greatly increased by the influx of refugees from Spain.

I sat down, opened my paper and ordered a cup of coffee disdainfully called Americano because, in my opinion, it was not thick enough to float a spoon on as was the *exprés* favored by the Spaniards. The news was good. The weather had turned bad. The Germans would not invade England this year.

"Hiya, Tell. Long time no see."

I looked up to see a plump man who reminded me of the cartoon character, Porky Pig, that was being shown in Will Riley's movie houses just after the newsreel and before the feature film.

"Hello," I said uncertainly and stood up.

"Maybe you don't remember me. I'm Smoky Brant. I was at Tell Two's going away party."

"I know who you are," I said, remembering. "I thought you would have been a squadron leader by now."

"The fascists running the Army Air Corps blacklisted me or I would have been a major by now."

"The British are fighting," I said. "Tell Dos flew Spitfires for them."

"Flew. Past tense, right? I knew he would, once he read Marx and Lenin."

"He shot down two Messerschmitts."

"I shot down five in Spain." He stopped abruptly and looked nervously at the table behind him. "But that's all water under the bridge now. Sit down at my table?"

"For a few minutes," I agreed, curious.

There were two young Mexicans, Eduardo and Tomás, a Spaniard about my age named Emilio, and a man who might have played a German pilot in the movie *Wings* about fighter pilots during World War

240

I, as it is now called, and who said his name was Martín González. I found out a year later that his real name was Gunter Nikolaus and that he had been a squadron leader during the invasion of Poland. When I met him he was a key man in the Abwehr, the German Secret Service in Latin America.

"Señor Cooper's son was flying for the British," Brant told him.

"An unfortunate war," Martin said. "Brother Aryan against Aryan. Tragic." His Spanish was crude and harshly accented, but fluent, like my French.

"Your Russian allies are all Aryans too?"

"It is not a racial matter. The Russians are anti-war. They do not wish the conflict to spread."

There was a flicker of derision on the Spaniard's face.

"What do you think, as a Spaniard, of the Republican trainload of gold bullion being shipped to Russia . . . for safekeeping?" I asked.

"How is it that you know about the treasury?" he asked suspiciously.

"It is common knowledge among the Spanish expatriates," I said.

"That is a fascist lie, imperialistic propaganda by the capitalistic press," Brant said angrily.

"It must be true, then," I laughed. "I had thought it a wild rumor."

Brant's mouth snapped shut. The Spaniard said nothing, but he did smile faintly with what I hoped was approval.

"But," the German said, "your own son ceased flying when he realized the futility of opposing the great Germanic culture."

"No. He ceased flying because he was shot down. He died fighting Nazi culture."

"I am sorry for you, but it is the chance a fighter pilot takes."

"True. Of course, he had already shot down two of your Messerschmitt—three less than Brant here claims in Spain—but he died ahead of the game. I myself shot down eight confirmed in the other war. Then we called them Hun or Boche. We even drank with them in those days before we sent them off to internment. I remember the last one. He wore an iron cross and the star of David. I guess he must have been a Jewish Aryan."

"Brant got five Messerschmitts?" the German shook his head slowly, negatively. "Maybe he shot at five. But look Señor Cooper, I agree that there are some good Jews. It is the bad ones that we must remove from our society."

"Communists do not practice racial discrimination," Brant said. "Many Jews are active in our movement."

"So I understand. I believe the man Lenin picked to succeed him, Trotsky, a Jew, is trying to stay alive right here in the city, somewhere in the Coyoacán suburb."

Crimson-faced, Brant stuttered slightly as he spoke.

"Leon Trotsky is a traitor. A counter revolutionist of the worst kind. Do not talk to me of Trotsky."

"How many shots did the Mexican muralist, Siqueiros, fire into Trotsky's bedroom?" I asked the Spaniard.

"The papers talked about several hundred."

"The Trotskyites did it themselves," Eduardo, the younger of the two Mexican men, said. "Then they blame it on the real communists like our great artist, Siqueiros."

"How do you two young men feel about the German philosophy of the Aryan super race?" I asked.

"Well," Tomás, the elder, said, "the Germans never stole half our country and they never occupied Vera—"

"Yes. I concede that my country committed acts that I do not approve of, but, tell me, do you feel inferior to your friends?"

"No! Do you say I am inferior?"

"No, of course not. But the Nazis do, and"— I jabbed a finger into Brant's chest—"and the Russians and Germans are allied. Birds of a feather . . ."

"Still," Eduardo said, "the Germans are winning. They have taken all of western Europe and they will take England soon."

"No," the Spaniard said. "I think not. Nor do I think that Hitler and Stalin will share the same bed much longer."

"Emilio!" Brant snapped. "What you are saying is heresy. You are a heretic and a fool!"

"You call me a heretic and a fool. You, who collected a thousand dollars a month as well as a thousand for every plane you claimed to have shot down! While I fought without pay and often without food against the fascists." He put his left hand inside his coat, below the table level and said loudly enough so that all conversation ceased. "I, Emilio P. Ibáñez, shit on the tits of your mother so that you will suck that shit!"

Brant put both hands palm down on the table top immediately. "Emilio," he said, "please understand me. In the world conflict between materialistic capitalism and communism, sometimes we must make certain accommodations. I also sometimes become too intense in my speech. I beg your pardon."

Emilio shrugged noncommittally, but his hand did not move from his coat.

"You mean Stalin makes certain accommodations," I said.

"Comrade Stalin is our true leader."

"Now I know why you are in Mexico!" I said as the realization hit me. "Trotsky is your responsibility. You are after Trotsky!"

Somehow my brain, working like one of the new electrical calculators, had sorted out all of the numbers, totaled them up and come up with an answer, which surprised me when I blurted it out as much as it did Smoky Brant.

Brant sat rock still, and then in what must have been a reflexive action, reached under his coat. He was to my left. I thrust my hand under his coat, grasped his hand and squeezed hard.

There was an explosion, slightly muffled by his coat. "Mein Gott!" Martin exclaimed, eyeing the hole furrowing the back rest of his chair. Had he not been leaning forward, he might have needed a new spine.

"Take your finger off the trigger, or I will break it off."

"Jesus, I can't. Ease up."

I relaxed my grip, felt his hand withdraw, took the snub-nose revolver out from its holster, and dropped it in my coat pocket.

"Smoky! You all right?"

The nasal voice speaking Kansas English was to my back. I slipped my hand back in the coat pocket and turned.

"Do not bother, my friend," the Spaniard said to me. "He is no danger."

"It's okay, Barry," Brant said. "Little accident."

"That's right," I said, and switched to Spanish. "The señor's pistol discharged itself and made a small hole in a chair and a dent in the floor. He will pay for the damage and promise not to play with his gun any more."

It was not much of a joke, but with at least half of the men in the cafe, armed and nervous, it was greeted with bursts of laughter. The head waiter brought a bill to Brant. He checked it carefully, left-handed, and agreed to pay the whole amount, including thirty pesos damage to a chair. Years later I drank coffee at the same table. The chair with the furrow in its back was still there.

"You can have my chair," I told the redhead from Kansas. "I must be leaving anyway."

"No, thanks. I'm at another table." He left, tacking across the room like a sailboat against the wind so that he could keep an eye on me.

"I have to go also," the Spaniard said.

"I'll walk to the door with you," I said.

"I have to leave too," Brant said. They all stood up together like puppets taking a curtain call. "I want you to know I never saw that gringo before. He mistook me for a friend."

"Sure," I said.

He stuck his hand out. "My gun."

I shook hands with him. "Drop by my office and pick it up." He never did.

At the door I shook hands with Emilio.

"A pleasure," he said. "Watch yourself with those people. They might be dangerous."

I thanked him and we shook hands. As he turned to go, I said, "I have a doubt. Are you a Stalinist or a Trotskyite?"

"I am a reformed anarchist," he said, smiled and left. I never saw him again.

I glanced down the street at the Chinese Clock. It and my watch agreed. Rodolfo was a half an hour late.

"Tell, hombre!"

I spun around. He was white-haired now, and he was no longer taller than I, but his deep set eyes were as bright as ever and the voice unchanged.

"*Don* Rodolfo!" I cried out in delight and threw my arms around him. "How long has it been?"

"Since Obregón was killed."

"That long!" I stepped back to grin at him. "Shall we go someplace else. I feel like a change."

"But you don't change, Tell. You still take pistols away from angry men."

"You saw that?" I asked, embarrassed.

"Yes." He tapped the noticeable bulge under his arm. "I had the redhead and the little fat man on your left lined up for one shot."

"Are you still carrying that old cannon?" I asked.

"Yes, what happened to yours?"

"I don't know," I answered, puzzled. "One day I just stopped carrying a pistol."

By tacit agreement we walked as we talked. Soon we were at a corner table in a nearby restaurant.

"Are you going to stay in Mexico City for a while?" I asked.

"No. I really came just to see you."

244

"I'll fly you back, then."

"Not while I have a pistol," he said, grinning. He detested airplanes. "What is it? What is the problem?"

"It's the airline, TIA, again. It happened once before and I was able to stop it, but now, whatever we do is wrong. Someone highly placed in the government is after TIA. I can't fight that. They haven't even asked for a *mordida*, so I don't even know whom to bribe."

"I know. You will have no more trouble, for a while, from the government. Not from official sources, anyway. Your real problems are not from your enemies, but your friends."

"I know the old saying," I said. "When your best friend keeps helping you to go broke or gets you deeper in trouble, you say: 'Don't help me any more, compadre!' "

"That is what I would do if I were you, Tell. I would go to my compadre and I would say: 'Willard Riley, don't help me any more, please.' "

Chapter 32

The *Pacífico* Bar, softly illuminated from windows set several feet above my head, was pleasantly cool. The bar, walnut-planked and encased in teak, ran the length of the room. Glass shelves backed up by continuous mirrors reflected an infinity of bottles from a hundred countries. There was a door midway in one wall, separating the walnut wainscoting, that led to the restaurant. Mostly the clientele ordered and ate in the bar itself. However, if they felt like a more formal service, or were meeting a lady, they would use the dining room with large windows overlooking the busy street.

There were three bartenders. The youngest, called Chamaco because of his tender age, was sixty years old. He grinned as he spoke.

"Dark beer, tequila and *limón*, major?"

"*Por Dios*, Chamaco," I said. "I have not been here in three years. You have a memory like an elephant."

He smiled again and ran a stream of beer more black than brown into a liter mug. He sat the *tarro* of beer in front of me, and then he poured amber tequila into a shot glass that was close to my left hand. Quartered limes and coarse salt were in small clay dishes every two or three feet along the bar.

Chamaco waited patiently as I salted the back of my right hand, sucked a bit of lime, emptied the shot glass and licked the salt, paused, and then swallowed an inch of the dark beer. Then he spoke.

"It is the season for the maguey worms. Would you like a *taquito*?"

"Just one," I said. "I will be dining here later."

He brought me only *one*—but it was one *order* of three tiny tacos. The worms, fried crisp, taste to me like the brown skin on peanuts. They were in a sauce that brought tears to my eyes; however, like all of the free lunch items in the *Pacífico*, it was as tasty as Mexican food can be, which to me is somewhere just this side of perfection.

I was holding the last taco, squeezing the bottom between thumb and forefinger to keep the tasty sauce from leaking out, when I spotted Johnny's reflection in the bar mirror. I waved the last taco at him, finished it off in one bite, and turned in time for the abrazo.

"It is good to see you, Tell." He pounded me on the back with one hand and hugged me with the other. "You never change."

246

His voice was exactly the same, but he had changed even more since we had last met. He was running to fat, his eyes seemed to have faded and he was combing his hair from one side to the other to cover up a bald spot.

"It's good to see you too, Johnny," I said in English.

He glanced from side to side before he answered. There was no one but the bartender near us.

"How is my aunt?"

"TIA ... my airline?"

"The same."

"You mean you don't know?"

He looked away. "What do you mean?"

"Johnny, someone is causing me a lot of political problems."

"Tell. You can't mean me?"

"No, Johnny," I answered truthfully. "But you might be able to help me."

"Toña does not have the title, for she is a woman and this is still Mexico," he said, "but she exerts a tremendous amount of influence in the bureau."

"How about Will Riley?" I decided to go to the heart of the matter.

"Talk to Toña, first," he countered.

"I haven't seen her in years," I said.

"Since before her baby was born?"

"My God!" I said. "Has it been that long? He must be in his teens. Older than my own boy."

"Tell Dos?"

"Of course. What other boy do I have?"

"But, Tell, he is dead."

"I know that, goddamn it! Of course I know that." Tears stung my eyes. I turned away.

"Tell, my friend, cry if you like. I did. I also sent a card, but I did not think you would want visitors then."

"So," I said gruffly, "the boy must be some twenty years old. What do you call him, Juanito?"

"No," Johnny said. "Toña named him Guillermo. Why would she call him Juan?"

"After you."

Johnny looked directly at me, and this time I looked away.

"You thought the boy was mine?"

I nodded affirmatively, unable to speak.

"She never loved me, Tell. Never."

"But you lived with her. In Mexico. After she left Puebla."

"Who told you that?"

"What difference does it make now?" I said.

"She let me stay with her a few days," he said, pensively, "when I moved to the city. I was a lost soul and she helped me. To me Toña was—is special. She never gave a damn what other people thought. She was the most honest person I ever met. Maybe the only one."

"But you never . . . slept with her?" I blurted out and immediately blushed.

"Is that you speaking, Tell? You know she was a free spirit. She lived like a soldier then, and, for a while, slept with any one she fancied."

"Please, Johnny. Forget I asked," I said, ashamed.

"Forget what?"

"Chamaco," I called. "Bring this gentleman a drink."

Before I could finish the sentence the bartender sat a highball glass in front of Johnny.

"Scotch and soda," Johnny said. "All of us *políticos* drink Scotch now, although some of us," he added wryly, "drink it with Coca-Cola."

"Johnny, can you get Will Riley off my back?"

"Tell, he is a difficult man. More than before. He thinks you are conspiring against him."

"Me? With whom?"

"With Helen. She is in New York, trying to get that . . . exposé published."

"Helen writes what she likes. You know that."

"Yes, I know, but *Don* Willard does not."

"What she does is none of Will's business."

"But it is, Tell." He lowered his voice dramatically. "It is about his ear."

"Fuck his ear," I said.

"*¡Por amor de Dios!* Tell." He lowered his voice to a near whisper. "Never even think that word near Will."

"Do you know the working title of the book?" I began to chuckle. "Riley's Golden Ear."

Fear crossed his face and then, like a swimmer who has gotten over the initial shock of icy water, he grinned and said, "I hope that Helen's next book is not titled 'Who Shot Tell from Under the Apple.' "

It was good to laugh loudly and clink glasses with Johnny again.

248

Soon we were talking as easily as we had that day long ago when I bought the family limousine from him.

"Would you have ever thought that you would be a cabinet minister one day, Johnny, back when your room at the hacienda had a great view no matter which unglazed window you looked out of?"

"Wall-to-floor windows but no ceilings, at that. No, I never thought about a tomorrow then. It was day-to-day survival."

"And now they mention your name as a presidential possibility."

"They are fools, then. I will never be president."

"But, Johnny. Look what you could do. A real honest president. You could turn this corrupt government around. Make a real democracy out of the Revolution, instead of a big stage where wind-up politicians repeat the same old platitudes."

"Cárdenas is an honest man," Johnny said.

"Was he elected fairly?"

"Of course. We counted the votes." He had the grace to smile. The votes were counted and the process monitored by the top party officials who were always also the top executives of the governmental bureau in question.

"But he really won?"

"He really did. The party does not lose elections."

"Is Will backing both men, or did he give an edge to Calles?"

"I can honestly say that we always figured Cárdenas for his own man and backed him one hundred percent."

"After he kicked Calles out of the country?"

"The day before," he grinned.

"You could change things, Johnny. From the top down. Kick out the crooks."

"Calm down, Tell. Your puritanical ancestry is running amok."

"Do you condone such behavior?" I asked, curious now, not angry.

"Look at it this way. The top men are mostly honest. They do have certain—"

"Then why do the people call that street in Cuernavaca where Calles and his group—"

"Ali Baba and his forty thieves." Johnny finished my sentence. "I know the story. And it is true. But they work hard and they are expected to become wealthy. The traditional honest politician is one who does not steal too much."

"Who decides the limit?"

"His boss."

"And if he is the president?"

"It would depend on his conscience," Johnny said. "But what difference does it make? One man can eat and drink only so much. So he builds a few mansions and buys a few girls. The money is still circulating, working, building."

"If the actual stolen capital stays in the country and is used productively, I suppose that the impact on the general economy would be minimal. Still, corruption is pervasive and, in the end, will ruin any country."

"That puritan ancestry just reared again," Johnny said, then added, grinning. "If you meant what you said, you are the one who should be running for president."

"Would you steal, were you president?" I asked seriously.

"I would not have to. I am already a very wealthy man. So are you. If you would just come to a stockholder's meeting, you would find out. Also, Will Riley would be overjoyed. That is your real problem with Riley. He likes you."

"What happens to my supposed dividends?"

"They are carried on the books as operating capital loaned to the company and receive standard interest," he answered promptly.

"I wonder how much I might have?"

"Enough to finance a much larger airline."

A fleet of twin . . . no, four-engine airplanes flying south to Buenos Aires and north to Toronto. Maybe even to Europe and the far East as well. How Tell Dos would exult. My chest suddenly constricted. There was no pain, but I could hardly breathe for a few seconds.

"What's the matter, Tell?" Johnny peered at me anxiously.

"Nothing. I was just thinking about a worldwide airline and it depressed me."

"But that's the way to go. If the States does not get mixed up in the war—or even if they do—you will have a big head start in Latin America. You can finance a part of it and ask Will to okay the plan. Our bank will put up the rest."

"But what will Will want for his okay?"

"Be reasonable. Let him read the manuscript. Maybe delete a few minor things that would hurt his feelings."

"Like his butchered ear and the kidnappers?"

"Maybe. You can never really tell, with Riley. He might want to keep it in."

"It's Helen's book."

"Talk to her. She is your wife."

He was right, of course. She was still my wife. My long-gone wife. I could write. She would not take a telephone call from me.

"Will you, Tell?"

"I might. What about you, Johnny? How about a run for the top? If you can get Riley to release the money you say is mine, I will sign it all over to you on your promise to try for the presidency."

"Would you like Willard Riley calling the moves of the president? I think not, Tell. But thanks, anyway."

"No thanks needed, Johnny. Anything I can do for you?"

"Yes, there is. It's Memo—Toña's son," he said, using the affectionate nickname for Guillermo. "He is crazy about airplanes. Talk to him."

"Sure. One of these days."

"No, Tell. This week. I promised Toña."

"All right. I'll see him this week."

"I told him there was an opening in your company for an ambitious young man."

"It is not just my company and there is no such opening."

"Tell Dos worked for you."

"He knew a lot about airplanes. He was a pilot."

"So does Memo and he also pilots a plane, when he can afford it."

"Tell Dos was my son, Johnny. My son."

Johnny almost told me then, but he was too loyal a friend for that. Too loyal to Toña and to Helen and, in the bitter end, too loyal to Willard Riley.

"Do it as a favor for an old friend, Tell. Just see the boy. Talk to him."

"Okay. Have him call me this week."

"He thinks he has an appointment for tomorrow at eight o'clock."

"Johnny," I said, "you are a *cabrón*! All right, tomorrow morning at eight sharp!"

"My bill," Johnny called out to Chamaco, wrung my hand and, again glancing uneasily about the bar, left at a trot.

"Another taco, major?" Chamaco asked.

"Taco. Taco!" My God. We had completely forgotten about lunch. I ran out of the cool dim interior into a harsh sunlit and busy sidewalk. There was no sign of Johnny. I would not see him again until the closing chapters of the Riley saga took place in a suburb of Los Angeles, California.

Chapter 33

· · · · · · · · · · · · · · · · · · ✈

Memo Canela

The air is thin and cold in the winter months on Mexico's high plateau. There were patches of ice left over from hosing down airplanes, which crunched under my feet. But I was warm. I was wearing an old hunting serape, slit to let my head through and belted at the waist to keep cold air out. I glanced at my new wristwatch, a genuine Waltham my mother had given me when I graduated from prep school. It was fifteen to eight. I found a shaft of weak sunlight playing against the east side of the building, so I stood there, cupping my ears from time to time against the cold.

At the risk of looking like an Indian just in from the hills, I was loosening my serape to lift it up over my head when a paneled truck stopped in front of the big hangar door. One man jumped out, unlocked the heavy padlock and then slid the door open far enough for the truck to drive in. The driver, a dark man with a big cigar stuck between wide white teeth, waved at me to follow them. I trotted in after the truck and helped slide the door shut again.

One of the men pulled a master switch, and suddenly the whole hangar was illuminated. It was like a stage in a theater, but much more impressive to my eyes. There were two of the large, twin-engine Douglas airliners, several de Havillands altered for cargo, and one small, blue biplane that turned out to be a Meyers that the major kept for instruction in aerobatics.

"Hey, Memo, get the *pinche* fire going before we all freeze our *pinches culos* off!" The stocky man puffed furiously on his cigar as if he meant to heat up the hangar with it. He turned to me. "What do you want?"

"I would like to see the Major Cooper."

"No doubt. But, the thing is, does he want to see you?"

"I think he does," I said uncertainly. I had never even applied for a job before.

"You are called . . .?"

"Guillermo Andrés Canela, at your orders."

"Canela. Not a common name," he muttered. "I knew an Antonia

Canela once. She thought she was in the army."

"That would be my mother," I said. "But never say *she thought* referring to my mother."

He uttered a terrible blasphemy concerning the Virgin *María* and stuck his big square hand out for me to shake.

"I know your mother. And please don't tell on me. I am also a Guillermo. Guillermo Gómez León."

"A pleasure to know you, Señor Gómez," I said.

"No, you must call me *tocayo*, for we share the same name."

"I think I had better call you *Don* Guillermo," I said, "for I am looking for a job and you might be my boss."

"Might be? But you are the son of Toña Canela. How could I turn you away? She might come looking for me."

He grinned, of course, but I think that he was half serious, for she still was, in the words of one of her superiors, a live grenade with a loose pin.

"Then I might get a job?"

"Sure. Unless you want to get paid."

"I would like to be paid a little."

His heavy body, which looked like fat but wasn't, shook with laughter. "I'll fix that. I'll hire you and pay you damned little."

"But you will hire me?" I could not believe that I could just walk in from the outside world and be allowed to be around real airplane mechanics and airline pilots.

"Sure, *tocayo*—you're hired."

"Yes, *Don* Guillermo."

"Okay, kid. Here on the job you better not call me *tocayo* or Memo, but when you take your boss out and buy him a beer, you can call him Memo. Okay?"

"Sure, *Don* Guillermo," I said laughing aloud in sheer happiness.

"Okay, kid. You are now a skilled worker in the air transport industry. Here is your washrag."

When the major arrived, I was already at work, high on a ladder, scrubbing away happily on the DC-3 slated to fly to Monterrey that noon.

"You, up on the ladder. You are Guillermo Andrés Canela?"

"Yes, sir. At your orders." Even looking down at him, he seemed oversized to me. When I grew taller than he by a couple of inches, he still seemed the taller.

"I am Tell Cooper—"

A rattle of what sounded to my untrained ears like a machine gun drowned him out. He motioned for me to follow him and pointed to the far end of the hangar where I knew the offices were.

He held the door open for me, courteously, even if I was his employee, and then shut the door on most of the noise. He sat behind an old desk that had lost its rolltop. I sat on the visitor's chair in front of him.

His Spanish was fluent, but northern in accent. He might have been from Sonora. His face was craggy and wrinkled; a thin, white scar ran up from his rust-colored moustache nearly to his right eye, and his eyes were the color of a rifle barrel that has lost most of its bluing. However, when he looked straight into my own eyes, I did not feel that I had to stare him down or look away. Somehow, he made me feel at ease.

"You are Antonia Canela's boy . . ."

It was not a question, but I nodded yes.

"I knew her many years ago, in Puebla, when I was selling airplanes to General Obregón."

"She has often told me that you were the best pilot in the world."

"I managed to live through almost three years of aerial combat," he said. "I flew Scouts. What they call fighters today. I was young and skillful. But, above all, I was lucky."

I did not understand then, but one day, not too far away, I would not only understand but commiserate.

"What kind of education do you have?"

"I have my high school diploma, my *bachillerato*, and one day I would like to attend the technological institute in Monterrey. I would study aircraft design."

He nodded gravely in agreement, as if I had shared some valuable information, then he added, "Learn about flight instruments, radio, electronic technology."

"And one day," I said, "I would like to be a commercial pilot for TIA; I already have logged thirty hours of solo time, Major Cooper."

"Just plain Señor Cooper will be sufficient," he said.

"I could not. You are a famous man and you were the world's greatest fighter pilot and I must call you major."

He grinned at me then, and I felt the happiness building up again. "All right. You call me major and, if it's all right with you, I'll call you Memo."

"Please do. But," I said, thinking of the friendly shop manager, "you already have one Memo here. Maybe you could call me Memo

Dos." The color ran out of his face and his jaw slackened so that his mouth opened like a man who has run too far, too fast. He spun around in his chair, and with his back to me, he spoke angrily.

"I'll call you any goddamn thing I like. I'll call you Chamaco or Chato, but I most certainly will not call you Memo Dos!"

I was stupefied. His anger was real. I could almost feel its heat. I shriveled in my chair. But then I thought of Bobo who had destroyed my model airplane while my mother watched. I stood up as straight as I could.

"I am not a child to be called Chato, nor a prizefighter to be called Chamaco. I said that you could call me Memo. If that displeases you, call me Andrés, or Señor Canela."

He swung around to face me. "Please sit back down. I apologize for my rude behavior. May I call you Memo?"

"You may," I said stiffly, not ready yet to be placated. "As long as you remember that I am a man and must be treated like one."

"Done! You want to work on airplanes, be an airline pilot one day?"

"Yes."

"I can pay you little, practically nothing."

"Will I be permitted to learn?"

"I will make a deal with you. I'll not pay you one *centavo*, but once a week I will give you an hour's instruction, and later, on your own time, I will lend you an airplane for solo time."

I could say nothing. I gaped at him, visions whirling in my brain of myself at the controls of the big Douglas while an admiring copilot envied me my skill.

Finally he said, "Well, Memo?"

"Yes, sir, major. It is perfect." Then I allowed myself to grin in return. When he dismissed me with a wave of his hand, I trotted back to work, whistling.

Saturday at noon, while the others lined up in front of the pay table waiting for their salary in silver pesos, I changed clothes in front of the locker that I shared with Memo, the shop foreman. There was no confusion in the names. When they wanted him, they yelled out, Big Memo. I was, of course, Little Memo, even as I stood a head taller than he.

I was about to step out of the hangar door when the major called.

"Little Memo, how about your pay?"

"But I was not to be paid," I said.

"Not in cash." He was wearing a helmet and carried a parachute under one arm. My heart leapt. He turned to the foreman. "Find your *tocayo* a helmet that will do and a parachute. Make sure that the straps are adjusted perfectly."

A half an hour later we were at twelve thousand feet, about five thousand above the valley floor. Only the snow-covered peaks of the two volcanoes were higher. My helmet was too big, but buckled tightly, as were the goggles. I had a scarf wound around my face, the ends tucked into the helmet, and I wore fleece-lined gloves. Only my nose and my feet were cold.

The major spoke to me through the gosport tube. All of the instructors in open planes used them. It was nothing more than a flexible hose that led from a mouthpiece shaped like a funnel, which the instructor held, to the student's helmet, where it split into two smaller tubes, each tube leading into an earphone.

"Toña taught you wingovers and spins?"

Toña? He called my mother Toña!

"Well?"

I thrust my thumb up in the affirmative signal. I could not talk back. It was a one-way system, which was, I decided, why the instructors liked it so much.

"Pat the top of your helmet when you take the controls. Now take them."

He held up both hands to show me that he was no longer flying the airplane. I patted my head with my left hand, my right on the stick. I felt the wings tremble and then moved the rudder pedals slightly and the tail wriggled.

It was a tiny biplane, but it seemed large then, as large as the Hellcat fighter that I was later to fly in combat. I had learned to fly in a 65-horsepower, two-place Piper Cub. The Meyers, underpowered as it was, still had a 125-horsepower motor.

"All right, show me a wingover."

I nodded my head and yanked back on the stick. The airplane lunged upward. I shoved the stick forward to avoid a stall and then kicked the left rudder and skidded around in a wobbly left turn. It was so awful that I wished, fleetingly, that I might bail out and land somewhere so far away that I would never have to face the major again.

"That was a little rough," he said. "I'll do one now and you follow me through on it."

He patted his head to show that he was in control. I forced my

256

hands to unclasp and then hold, but not grip the stick and eased my feet back until just the toes were touching the rudder bars.

"This old Meyers does beautiful aerobatics, but it has a small power plant. Even with a propeller with a pitch set for this altitude, you have to dive a bit to pick up speed."

He dropped the nose briefly, then pulled up so smoothly that I felt no gravitational pull when he turned to come back and down. I glanced at the ball-bank indicator. The ball was dead center.

"Now you try one." He looked back at me. I nodded and remembered to tap my head. This time I was consciously relaxed. Although the simple maneuver was jerky and improvised, it was better by far than the first. I did more than a dozen. The last one, I thought, in my innocence, was perfect.

"Not bad," the major said, "but it needs work. Now do a two-turn spin."

I pointed the nose at Popo's peak which was likely no whiter nor colder than my own nose. I eased the stick back until the nacelle rose and covered the volcano's peak. I held it there, throttle off, until I felt the wings tremble before I kicked left rudder and snapped into a spin, twice as tight as the ones I had done in the Cub. I saw the landscape— mostly a patchwork of cornfields—whirl and whirl, then jammed on all of the right rudder and pushed the stick all the way forward. We came out of the spin cleanly. I added throttle as I eased the nose up to the horizon and leveled the wings. The mountain was not in sight.

"Did you line up on Popocatépetl?"

I nodded yes.

"How many turns do you think you made?"

I stuck up two fingers and then added a third.

I heard him chuckle before he spoke. "You made one and a half. Look behind you."

I did, and I saw the volcano directly behind me.

"You should line up on something you can see easily while you spin. A highway is good. Then count and start your recovery a quarter of a turn before you complete the last turn."

I shook my head in disgust.

"You did better than you think. If you stick with me, I will make you into a fine pilot."

I held up both my hands, thumbs up, because I knew he could not see my huge grin under the scarf.

"Good. I like an enthusiastic student. However, it does have its problems. For example, I wonder who is flying this airplane right now?"

I snatched at the controls, but he spoke quickly, and I eased off. "I have it now. But I want you to follow me through, firmly enough to feel everything, but not heavily enough to interfere with my handling of the controls. Okay?"

I bobbed my head again while he patted his and took over. He found a low, flat cloud where we practiced landing on its surface. Of course the second the wheels would touch, he would add throttle and fly back up through it, then turn and come back again. We took turns until I felt comfortable and sure of the stalling position and the feel of the Meyers in relation to the horizon and the simulated landing strip on a drifting cloud.

"All right. That last one was good. You take it on down to a thousand feet and enter the left-handed traffic pattern. This time I'll follow you on the controls. Okay?"

I nodded happily, gave him a thumbs up and patted my head. I throttled back, making a gentle descending turn toward the field. There was only one other airplane in the pattern; it was turning upwind on its landing approach.

"Look off our left wing, in front of our hangar. That will be our landing spot."

I glanced at it. When he looked back, I bobbed my head to show that I understood.

"Just about now we'll start an easy turn and then line up with our wing square to the field."

I could scarcely feel him on the controls, but then as we got closer to the ground, his touch was more obvious.

"With the wind straight on, like it is today, I use that big cottonwood off the end of the runway to line up on. I concentrate on keeping the wings level as we sink lower and lower, keep the nose straight by tapping rudder . . . a bit more right, then as we stall, the stick comes back all the way."

I pulled back, instinctively, along with him, and the wheels touched, bounced and then we settled down. I smiled to myself. Even the major can make a rough landing.

"Pull off the runway as soon as you slow down."

I tapped my head. When we had almost come to a stop, I turned and added throttle to keep the airplane moving.

"Stop in front of the hangar." I cut the throttle, coasted up to a point opposite our hangar, and set the brakes. "Would you like to try another

258

landing?"

I showed him a thumb up immediately. I wondered if he might be embarrassed by the rough landing and wanted to show me a smoother one.

To my complete astonishment, he stepped out of the cockpit onto the wing and bent down to yell into my ear. The speaking tube was left in the cockpit, buckled under the seat belt to keep it out of the way.

"Go ahead, then."

"But, major," I yelled, before he could jump down from the lower wing. "I have never landed this airplane before."

"Yes, you have. Rough, but safe. Did you ever see me pat my head to take over the controls?"

Before I could think of an answer, he was gone and I was left there alone, a decision confronting me. So it had been him, lightly, but on the controls. I had bounced the Meyers onto the runway. So be it. If I had made one landing, no matter how rough, I could make another.

I taxied in S-turns so that the nose, which seemed to have suddenly grown much longer, did not hide any obstacles as I moved to the head of the runway. I looked at the tower for a green light, got it, lined up on the same cottonwood that I had used for landing, then pushed the throttle all the way forward. I held strong right rudder to contain the torque, felt the airplane asking to lift off and eased the stick back like a rider lifting the head of his horse. I felt the airplane wrap itself around me like a protective blanket, an extension of my own body, like a beetle with its carapace.

I flew on up to a thousand feet, but I did not leave the pattern and came on around for my second landing. The tower flashed a green light. I glided down gently, turned upwind, eased back on the stick, tapped a rudder pedal to line the nose up on the cottonwood, and was on the tarmac, rolling along smoothly before I realized that I had landed. I had just made a perfect three-point landing. I would not make another until almost three years later—on an aircraft carrier in the Pacific Ocean.

Chapter 34

Tell Cooper

It took a sneak attack to force my country to fight the most despicable tyranny of modern times. Hitler's outrages against the conquered peoples and his racist policies were not enough.

George has nothing for me, says I am too old, and our government wants me to stay put. They are even going to send me a copilot that will be on my payroll, but will not cost me a cent. He will be some kind of a spy, I suppose, when he is not flying.

The latest copy of the *Times* carried an article by Helen on the roots of the war. She has not written to me in a year. I have written her almost monthly.

In that same edition of the newspaper I read an observation by the retired colonel who wrote the weekly military column. It seemed that the Japanese pilots were severely handicapped. They are myopic, uncoordinated and yellow.

Great athletes do not necessarily make great fighter pilots. Eyesight and coordination and instinct are enough. When the United States finally entered the last war, the administration finally and, I believe, reluctantly offered the Americans flying in the Lafayette or other French squadrons the opportunity to switch to the American unit.

When the physical examination was administered to our squadron, not one man could pass. While any one of their clean-cut youths could have outrun Hank Jones, who had flat feet and ran like a bear, or Indian-wrestled Bill Thaw's crippled arm down, not one of them would have lasted five minutes against either Bill or Hank in aerial combat.

Our leading ace at the time, Raoul Lufbery, could not walk a straight line backwards; I was afflicted with what is today called a deviated septum.

Thus, I would treat the combat-seasoned Japanese pilots with the utmost respect, were I a fighter pilot in the Pacific, until I learned otherwise. I would point this out to Memo at least twice and perhaps as many as three times. Young men are not good listeners.

He had asked to speak with me privately; he then insisted that we speak English, which was odd. Although his English is good enough to pick up American girls at the Sanborns restaurant, it is still far from fluent, so when we discuss something important, we invariably speak Spanish.

"No," I said anticipating the question. "You are not yet ready to fly co-pilot for Paco."

"That is not it. I want that you recommend me to the naval aviation."

"What?" I laughed, but when I saw the hurt in the smoky-colored eyes that I had thought were a blend of Johnny's brown and Toña's black eyes, I was sorry. I said so, but he shook off my apology and went doggedly ahead.

"My mother says they will take me if you approve and write the letter to the Navy."

"Hold on, Memo. You are not even ready to fly copilot for TIA, and now you want to fly airplanes from an aircraft carrier?"

"I am not a stupid, major. I will go to the flight school in the States and I will learn."

"Why the Navy?"

"They are the best."

"You mean those white uniforms and gold wings?"

He grinned, embarrassed. Obviously the fancy uniform had been a consideration. "They are the best," he said.

"Some of us army pilots were not too bad," I said, my pride stung.

"You was—were a best fighter pilot, major, but not from an airplane carrier."

I had to nod agreement. I wondered how it would be to come back, dead tired from combat, every nerve on edge, arms and legs aching from one tight turn after another, to find that your tiny landing field was pitching and rolling in a heavy sea. If you found it at all.

"No," I said, the thought strong in my mind. "You are not ready for that kind of flying. Besides, fighter pilots are born, not made."

"And why was I not born one?"

He was right. No one can know for sure. Not until the day he bores in, turn for turn, watching the big, orange tracers float by.

"If Toña—your mother—calls and asks me to write a letter of recommendation to send her son off to war, I will."

Likely, I thought with some satisfaction, she will not call. Even if she does, he will not be able to pass the reputedly near-impossible physical. Also, he would have to pass a difficult written examination in the English language.

At that moment, the telephone on my desk rang. My private line. I knew, somehow, as I answered that it would be Toña.

"*Hola*, Toña. It is me, Tell."

"So write the letter, *pendejo*."

The epithet crackled out of the ear phone and Memo and I both laughed.

"Schmuck," I said, following our custom where I would often pass on to Memo English equivalents to odd Spanish words.

"Smook?" Toña asked.

"It is often applied to naive young girls from Tabasco who use bad words over the telephone."

She laughed, as huskily as ever. I could see her clearly in that room in Puebla, smell her perfume, feel that firm, golden skin.

"Well?"

"Well, what?" I answered, lost in thought.

"The letter of recommendation."

"Do you really want him to join the United States Navy?"

"No. But it is what he wants. So do it."

"All right," I said. "But I must be paid."

Outside of the usual electrical noise of the line, there was not a sound from Toña. Memo looked worried. He knew that we were waiting approval for a new flight to Guadalajara.

"I guess dinner and drinks might be enough. How about meeting me at the Lincoln Grill?"

"You sure, Tell? You haven't seen me in years."

"Sure I am," I said urgently, suddenly realizing that I truly did want to see her again.

"Just the two of us?"

"Don't be so bourgeois," I said.

"Me? You imperialistic, capitalistic—"

She heard my chuckle, broke off and then she laughed too. "Okay, Major Cooper. I agree."

I sat there staring at the telephone, even after I heard the click as she hung up. Then, startled as Memo let loose an exultant yell, I dropped the receiver just as an answering yell from Big Memo sounded from the shop, and then the whole work force was yapping like a pack of coyotes under a full moon.

Big Memo brought out a bottle of tequila. I shook my head at him in feigned anger, but he knew me too well.

"Come on, boss. It's after work and a young man only goes off to war the first time once, no?"

262

"Your logic is irrefutable," I said, and drank from the bottle.

"The gringos will send those *chinos* running once they get some help from us *mexicanos*," Big Memo said proudly, one arm around Little Memo. All of us were out in the shop now.

"Those *chinos* are Japanese," I said. "The Chinese are on our side."

"Why?"

"Because they were already fighting the Japanese," I explained.

He shook his head in bewilderment, then passed the bottle to me. I took another drink, pretending to swallow twice. Memo looked at me, worry in his eyes.

"Would you type the letter, now, major?"

He did not say: "Before you get too drunk to write properly."

"Sure," I said. I moved over to my secretary's desk and inserted a sheet of paper. The paper rolled up double or triple on the roller, then I got the carbon in backwards, and then the keys kept jamming. Finally, Irma, who knew not a word of English, pushed me away from the typewriter. She ordered me to print the message, by hand, on lined paper. Then she typed it, error-free, in one single minute. I still have a copy of the letter.

> *To the United States of America Naval Air Service:*
>
> *Guillermo Andrés Canela is a natural pilot. I have taught him aerobatic maneuvers and basic combat tactics that I learned while flying Scouts in the last war. It would be a waste of time to send him to basic training. Place the young man in advanced training immediately.*
>
> *Tell Cooper, Captain, Lafayette Escadrille*

No self-respecting Mexican is ever on time for an appointment, so when I arrived on time, I figured that I would have at least a half an hour to drink a few beers and clear out of my head the cobwebs spun by a tequila spider. However, Toña was there, seated, smoking a cigarette, sipping cognac.

She sprang to her feet and we embraced. I held her tightly until she let her arms fall. Then I stood back to look at her. She was heavier, but in the places that I liked anyway. Her eyes were as black and shiny as ever, and her teeth flashed white against golden skin. There were a few lines and some gray in the hair, yet she was still as enticing as ever. I grabbed her again. She protested at first, but then she hugged me just as tightly.

Finally, after a burst of staccato throat noises from an embarrassed waiter, we moved apart so that he could set his tray of *antojitos*—tiny tacos and *sopes*—on the table.

A waiter brought me one of the quart-sized porcelain mugs of dark beer. We nibbled on the spicy, round *sopes*, and popped the taquitos into our mouths, and drank, and in between we played the "Do you remember . . .?" and "Whatever happened to . . .?" game. Finally, after a lull in the name-game that neither of us felt compelled to fill, she placed her hand on mine. Looking into my eyes, she asked, "What do you think of Memo?"

"He has some of your qualities. He is stubborn, opinionated, good looking and completely honest. I wish that he would have stayed with me."

"Me too." She set her mouth in that straight line that I remembered so well. "But he marches to his own drum. He will be the best of the fighter pilots. Better than . . ." She let the words trail off.

"Better than whom?" I prompted.

"Anyone. Richthofen. You."

"He is a crack flyer. Almost as good as Tell Dos."

Her eyes misted over immediately. What an ass I am, I thought—and then proved it.

"That was a stupid thing to say. Memo, right now, is not the technical pilot that Tell Dos is—was. But he has a flair that Tell Dos did not have. Anyway," I continued, floundering deeper and deeper, "a lot of it is just plain, old-fashioned luck. A so-so pilot shoots down a great one because he caught him at the right instant."

"*Puta Madre!*" I swore in disgust. I had never seen tears actually fall from her eyes before. "I am glad I am not a centipede. All of the feet might not fit in my mouth, huge as it is."

She was able to smile and say, "He talks a lot about you. He looks up to you."

"Well," I said, embarrassed, for I was genuinely fond of Memo, "I'll soon have to look up to him. He is as tall as I am, and growing while I seem to be shrinking."

I laughed, but she did not. Still, I continued.

Where did the height come from. Do you have any tall ancestors?"

"How tall are you, Major Tell Cooper?" Toña said loudly, standing up.

"One point eight meters," I said, puzzled, getting to my feet.

"I didn't know that you could pile shit that high," she snapped, spun around and hurried out of the room. I stared after her for a few shocked seconds, then threw money on the table and raced out after her.

Too late. I saw her in the back seat of a cab pulling away from the sidewalk. My own car was still at the airfield, waiting for new cylinders from occupied France.

There was no other cab, so I walked along in the cool night air. Tell was tall and therefore full of shit. Why? Memo was tall. Memo was—is—not as good a pilot as Tell Dos. And they killed Tell Dos, so they will kill Memo too. And I signed a paper sending him off to die in a war he need never have been involved with. That was it, of course! Toña had asked me to write the letter, for she had to. Her duty to the manhood of her son demanded it. But the mother, the real mother, that part of Toña, had counted on me not to give the boy a recommendation. I might have kept both boys from harm. I had failed Helen and Tell Dos, and now Toña and Memo. I ached with the desire to be once more a twenty-three-year-old fighter pilot with no duty in the world beyond dying in aerial combat on the morrow.

A cab pulled up. The driver leaned out the window to call to me. Automatically I held up three fingers and said the name of our Mexico City suburb, "Lomas."

"Okay."

I got in beside the driver.

"Home?" he asked.

"Yes," I said. God but I was tired. "Take me home."

"You Americans are good husbands," he said, seriously. "You go home at night to be with your families instead of whoring around until dawn."

Chapter 35

· · · · · · · · · · · · · · · · · · ✈

Memo Canela

Today, in less than twenty minutes, I shot down four Japanese aircraft. Not one of the pilots bailed out. Of course, two of the planes were Vals, which are copies of the old Stuka dive-bombers and are being used as kamikazes. Obviously, suicide pilots would have no use for parachutes. But the other two were fighter planes, a Tojo and a Zero. Probably they had no time, if still alive, to get out of their airplanes, for the huge dogfight swirled over and around the southern Okinawa shore, just above the support fleet, from two thousand feet right down to the sea itself.

I now have eight confirmed victories. As many as the major. Of course, each one of his had to be confirmed either by the downed aircraft itself, if on his side of the lines, or, if not, by three independent and unrelated observers. Here, the ocean usually swallows up our kills, or they smash into one of the coral islands, explode and burn into nothingness. So, another pilot's word is usually sufficient. Better yet, however, is the gun camera which cannot lie. No? Well, it certainly can exaggerate. At times four pilots will be shooting either simultaneously, or at intervals, at the same airplane. It might well be on fire at the time. Will each pilot get credit for a victory, or will all four receive one quarter—like a pack of wolves that have pulled down a deer?

Mine were all on film. Although I will not see the processed film for weeks, if ever, there was no doubt that each plane exploded into flame while my tracers illuminated the stream of ball, armor-piercing and incendiary projectiles that smashed into the unarmored Japanese planes.

The camera is a simple 16-millimeter, mounted so that its lens films through the same electronically illuminated orange rings and grids that are projected onto the Plexiglas windshield, which is what the pilot uses as a gunsight. The control stick itself is a pistol handle, with a trigger for the machine guns and a thumb button on the top for bombs or rockets. When I heard the first tallyho, an expression borrowed from the British to warn of sighted enemy planes, I flicked on the camera switch and left it alone. The trigger would activate it. The camera would film for three seconds after the trigger was released and then shut off. In a large melee like that one, it films almost continually.

Throughout our training we were taught to maintain our formations. Never break up the flight. In the extreme case where the four-plane fighter formation cannot stay together as a unit, then the two-plane element—leader and wingman—must not be separated. Never. In reality, when two masses of aircraft attempt to occupy the same space, everything comes unstuck and it is each man for himself.

I fell away from my own flight leader when he and his wingman suddenly pulled up to the stalling point to fire a burst at a Zero that was flying a few hundred feet above us in an opposite direction. I dropped my belly tank, and to avoid a red rain of tracers, I suddenly rolled violently to the left and lost my own wingman. I turned so tightly that I felt my jowls drop. The new "G" suit, which I had just been issued, inflated, pressing tightly against my thighs and stomach to keep the blood from leaving my head. I caught the Zero turning the wrong way for an easy thirty-degree deflection shot. Using all six machine guns, I fired one long burst that blew it apart. Pieces of the plane that looked as big as doors rushed back at me. I flinched and hunched into myself. Somehow, the prop wash must have deflected the residue.

The second plane, an antiquated Val with fixed landing gear, was in a shallow dive heading directly toward one of our destroyers. All of the ship's starboard antiaircraft guns were firing—and missing. I flew down into the barrage and swung my sight well in front of the Val—a full deflection shot—and fired a timed burst of no more than three seconds. The fire-control officer of that ship might well have saved my life. He identified my stubby-winged fighter as a friend and put his trust in me, for he halted the ship's barrage.

I kept the same lead and, timing the bursts so that I would not overheat and warp the gun barrels, held steadily, letting the Val fly into the destructive wall of .50-caliber lead, armor-piercing and incendiary bullets.

When I pulled up and over the destroyer, I could see the gun crews wave. I rocked my wings and turned, climbing back up out of the kaleidoscope of bursting shells, crisscrossing tracers and burning aircraft. I turned, cleared my tail—there were friendly fighters behind me—and then spotted a Zero high above me. I made a climbing turn to meet the Zero, but then I was engulfed in tracers. I dove straight down to keep the armor between my back and the lead stream behind me until I had built up speed. Then, talking into the microphone as I laid the

Hellcat over in a tight left turn, yelled: "This is Bengal Eleven. *¡Puta Madre!* Some *cabrón* is shooting at me. Knock it off!"

There were no more tracers. I had been right. Some idiot, thinking that I was a Zero because I had dropped the belly tank, had bushwhacked me. For some time after, whenever I would meet an old squadron mate, I would hear a different version of my radio message; variations of my Mexican swearing became a part of the squadron lore. I finished my turn, half hoping that I would get a clear shot at my attacker, Jap or gringo, but the only planes I saw were down lower busily fighting each other.

The major told me once that good fighter pilots were efficient predators. They invariably saw the prey before it saw them. Otherwise, the roles were reversed. Also, the successful ones were lucky. Above all, they were lucky.

And I needed all the luck I could get that day, for a crack fighter pilot flying a Zero had spotted me and turned toward me. He had the altitude advantage, so he would be able to turn even tighter. I had the more powerful engine; if the speed were kept around a hundred and fifty knots, I could out-turn him.

I pushed all the engine levers to the firewall and climbed to meet him, keeping one eye on the airspeed indicator.

The second he crossed above me, I whipped left, taking advantage of the torque that makes a left turn easier. So did the Zero. We met again on the turn, head on, no advantage to either and not even enough time to get a burst off. Next came a gut-wrenching right turn, and that time he dropped his nose for a second and fired a burst. The tracers seemed to float by me in slow motion even as I knew our combined speed must have been well over three hundred knots. On the third turn we were at the same altitude, but, as if by tacit agreement, he pulled up slightly, and I nosed down, leaving a few feet between propeller arcs as we met head on. It would appear that neither one of us was thinking of suicide.

Sweat stung my eyes. I wiped my forehead with the back of my sleeve. After two more turns, I had gained maybe ten compass points, and I was able to fire a burst just before we closed.

Then I made my first error. I became caught up in the tight turns and forgot about the speed until I no longer had the advantage. I added throttle, let the nose fall a bit, and as we bored in toward each other on the next pass, had fully decided to use my power to zoom up away and then come back down on him from above. But then, as we met again, my training and reflexes took over. Bore in. Make the enemy turn first. Get the split second advantage. It will put you back of him again with a clear advantage. What no instructor mentions is that if both pilots bore in, neither willing to give an inch, there is going to be one hell of a collision. And there was.

There is too much noise inside an airplane, including the constant radio noise of the earphones, to hear anything except the engine and the muffled bangs of the guns—unless you collide with another airplane. Then you hear and feel metal wrenching, tearing and scraping, and it is heart-stopping.

The stick was wrenched from my hand and my plane thrown to one side like a leaf in a gust of wind. An image of the Zero burned into my brain. The small fighter was whirling around in a death spin, with its fulcrum being the half wing left by the collision. I snatched the stick back, dropped the nose, and found that I had flight control. But I was no more than a thousand feet above the sea, barely high enough to parachute safely. Down below, burning pyres spiraled up into the air from both crashed airplanes and sinking ships. I scanned the horizon fearfully. Seconds ago I had been the hunter. Now I would certainly be an easy cripple for the first fighter to spot me.

"Bengal Twelve, this is Bengal Eleven. Over." I released the transmitting button and willed my wing man to answer.

"Bengal Eleven, this is Bengal Twelve, over."

I took a deep breath. I might live after all. "Bengal Twelve from Bengal Eleven. I have been struck by an enemy plane. I need a visual check. I am circling at one thousand feet. I repeat, Angels one, bearing one sixty from the destroyer. I am climbing to Angels three. Over."

"Bengal Eleven from Twelve. See you at three thousand feet. Out."

Thank God for Tex Houston. Often, we did not know the first names of our fellow pilots, only their nicknames, which were based on their last names. Other examples are Dusty Rhodes; Buck Rogers, the space traveler; and Snuffy—because his last name was Smith, like that of the cartoon character. I, being Mexican, had to be Pancho. Memo, short for Guillermo, would not do. Tex, my wingman, was not from Texas but from Oklahoma.

I saw the lone Hellcat slip away from the smoke and intertwining airplanes; it poked its nose up toward me. I maintained my slow climbing circle. When I reached three thousand feet, I leveled off. I looked down to see the dark-blue back of the Hellcat, climbing fast and turning inside my wide circle on an intercept. Then I saw the squadron identification on the tail. Seconds later, as the wing slipped inside my own, I saw his freckled face and wide grin. I could see him speak as he picked up his microphone.

"Keep on climbing, Pancho. Then at five we'll take a look at the damage. Maybe you can try your wheels and flaps and such. Over."

"Roger, Tex. Thanks."

Why had I not thought of that? My mind began to function then the way a flyer's mind should. I climbed until I was at five thousand feet, circling over what was supposed to be a provisional field on Okinawa. Then I leveled off and looked at Tex. He slid away beneath me, surfaced on the other side, then came back up on the right and gave me a thumbs up. I felt better. Maybe it was the air, cool at that altitude with the cover slid back, open all the way in case I might have to bail out.

I let the flaps down. The right wing lifted much faster than the left, but it was easily controlled. I trimmed the aileron and then dropped the wheels. They clunked into place. The panel showed them locked. I looked at Tex for confirmation. He gave me a grin and a thumbs up. I made the sign for the tail hook and got the same affirmative thumb. I took a deep breath, then throttled back until I was just a few knots above stalling speed. The left wing dropped and it took all of the right aileron I had to bring it back level. I tried it again with the same result. Only at ninety knots or more could I keep the wing up. I would not be able to bring in that airplane on the carrier at a few knots above stalling speed, bring my wings level with the axis of the pitching carrier deck, and then snap the plane into a tail landing. I shook my finger negatively at Tex. He nodded and showed me a thumbs down. I got on the radio.

"Bengal One. This is Bengal Eleven. Do you read me?"

"Bengal Eleven this is Bengal One. I read you loud and clear. Over."

"Bengal Eleven here. I have suffered some damage. I think I can land all right on the field at Nan Three,"—the code name for the emergency strip on the island—"but not on Bengal. Negative on Bengal. Over."

"Affirmative Bengal Eleven. Do you have a wingman? Over."

"Bengal One. This is Bengal Eleven. Affirmative. I do have a wingman. Bengal Twelve will see me down. Over."

"Go ahead and good luck, Pancho," Bengal One said, disregarding standard radio procedure. Bengal One, leader of the combat air patrol, was Bobby Cole, a full lieutenant, and at age twenty-five, the second oldest man in the squadron. I cut power to make a lazy spiral down over the airfield.

At two thousand feet, an anti-aircraft battery from the edge of the field opened up on us. We climbed up and away at full throttle. Tex pulled in close, his wing below but inside mine.

"Maybe you should just ditch alongside the carrier," Tex said angrily.

I must have looked dubious, even at twenty feet away. He did not wait for an answer, but said over the radio, angrily, "We'll try again. Maybe we can shoot our way down."

"Right," I agreed, wondering if they were reading our radio frequency. "Maybe we should pump a few rounds into the control shack."

Tex flashed the light-blue underbelly of his fighter at me as he peeled off to lead the way. If he went down at the field like a falcon, I bounced down, wheels and flaps still down, like a pregnant pelican. I might have been a sitting pelican, but my radio came alive.

"Unidentified planes approaching Nan Three, identify yourselves!" There was panic in his voice. Unfortunately it was made to order for Tex.

"Me Melican," Tex said in his best but totally inadequate Japanese accent.

"Fighters above Nan Three." The voice was almost hysterical. "If you are friendly, wriggle your wings. Over."

I wriggled my wings quickly just in case. Tex, up ahead, did the same and dropped his flaps so that he could ease back and fly wing on me again, now that it appeared to be safe. He was not through yet. Speaking in his own imitation of a theatrical southern accent, he said, "Towah! This is Bengal Twealve. If you all can heah me, waggle youah tower."

He waved goodbye and pulled up. I knew that he would be low on gas. I gave him a thumb up and tried to grin.

"Naval fighter planes." A new voice sounded. "This is Captain Hunter. You are cleared to land at Nan Three. However, exercise caution. Our field has been under attack."

"Roger, Captain Hunter. This is Bengal Eleven coming in from two seven zero descending from two thousand feet. Over."

"Roger Naval airplane, the wind is zero nine zero at 15 knots. Out."

I came in wide and slow. When no one shot at me, I dropped down to five hundred feet. I came into the little runway hot, setting the wheels down first and then letting the tail drop as I lost speed. I almost ran out of runway, yet by tapping the wheel brakes set into the tops of the rudder pedals alternately, I stopped before the runway ended—but barely.

I turned and taxied back. No one was in sight, but I saw what looked like some kind of a light plane tied down near a large Quonset hut. I spun the big F6F around by the other airplane, pushed the mixture forward, cut the gas off and let the motor cough to a stop. I switched the magnetos off, then I leaned back, drained. I was down, safe, and as tired as I had ever been in my life.

There was a hand on my shoulder.

"Sir? Are you all right, sir?"

I opened my eyes and looked up. A stocky, moon-faced man wearing a baseball cap peered at me anxiously.

"Yes," I said, languidly. "I am fine."

"Would you please get out, sir? Right away. Something loose was banging along behind you making sparks on the link chain, and your airplane looks like a sieve."

"The tail hook!" I exclaimed. "*Por Dios*, I had been carrier-ready."

"What?"

"Nothing," I said. I climbed out wearily, found the toehold and let myself down. I stood back and began to count, "*Uno, dos, tres—*"

"You talking to me sir?"

"Counting the holes," I said. "You are right. It is a sieve."

He eyed me warily, but said nothing. I kept quietly counting until I reached fourteen. I think in English now, most of the time, and everyone tells me that I speak like someone from some other part of the country, but I cannot seem to do simple addition, subtraction or even count easily in English.

"*Jeezus*, sir, look at that!" He crouched down and pointed. There were at least a dozen holes stitched across the belly of the Hellcat, crossing through the aluminum fuselage about a foot behind the seat.

"How many did you get, sir?"

"Four," I said and then trying to make a small joke, added, "I had to ram the last one."

"Holy mother! Look at the underside of this wing!"

There was a smear of greenish brown and a large blob of red on my airplane.

I glanced at his sleeve, as he had brushed the color onto his shirt.

"Sergeant, it looks like that last Jap gave me a decal. Better than gun-camera film for proof."

A plane flew over at a thousand feet. I knew without looking up that it was one of our incredibly sturdy torpedo bombers.

"We better get you in under cover, sir." He glanced at the sky fearfully. "We been under fire, you know."

"Under attack here? Why would any pilot attack the Quonset huts and the one lone observation plane when there were capital ships a mile or so away?"

"Well, some of the stuff might be from our own batteries. Stuff falling in. But it could kill you just the same."

"What were your guns firing at?"

"Why, Japs, sir. A couple of them came in just a minute before you landed. Bold as brass. One of them was one of those Jap dive bombers."

"A Val?"

"That's the very one. I identified him because of his fixed landing gear."

"Oh," I said, understanding. In his eyes an unfamiliar naval fighter plane with its wheels down became a Val dive bomber—intent on destroying him, personally.

He ushered me into the Quonset hut. It appeared to be the operations office—or a bar. It was both.

"I am Captain Rod Hunter." He looked like an actor playing the part of a combat pilot. His smile was dazzling and exuded camaraderie.

"Memo Canela," I said, sticking my hand out. He shook his head, still smiling, but a bit ruefully as if I had forgotten to bring him a birthday present.

"Are we not forgetting something?" His grin widened even more until I could see that all of his teeth were indeed perfect. "I am a captain. You are an ensign."

"Yes," I groaned inwardly. One of those. I stood at attention, my helmet in my left hand. "We do not salute, sir, in the Navy unless we are covered."

"Covered?"

"Wearing his hat," the sergeant said.

"Oh. Well, in that case, welcome aboard, Candle."

"Canela," I said. We shook hands.

"Hey," a red-faced, balding man wearing officer's pinks, but without insignia, called from a corner. The radio gear was piled onto a large crate; alongside sat a portable typewriter. "You, the guy in the monkey suit. You, the one who shot some planes down. The one they call Pancho?"

"I guess so," I said, wondering how he knew.

"Name's Jerry Andrews," he said. "Call me Scoop, Pancho."

"My name is Guillermo Canela."

"Sure, but you're Pancho too. I been listening to the action, kid."

I decided to try the captain again.

"Sir, is this bar open?"

"Sure, Pancho," Andrews yelled before the captain could answer. "Give the kid a good belt from my bottle."

Andrews walked the few paces over to me, with toes out as if he were going against a gale. He stuck his hand out, and said, "I'm the rep for the Richard Shaeffer chain."

The name meant nothing to me. If he had mentioned one of the twenty newspapers that Shaeffer controlled, I might have been more impressed. While he held my hand loosely with his right, his left toyed with the knobs of what looked like a professional camera.

"Here you are, Pancho," the captain said.

"My name is not Pancho," I said, but I accepted the tumbler full of wine. It had little taste, but it did warm me. I could almost hear my muscles relaxing.

"Pancho!" I looked up into a flash. For a few seconds I could not see, but Andrews never stopped talking.

"*Hombre*," he said, pronouncing the silent H loudly, "you drink that Irish whiskey like it was root beer."

"That was whiskey?" I asked, amazed.

Everyone, including the sergeant, roared with laughter. You would have thought that I had said something very funny.

"Sergeant," the captain said, "you might as well mix us all a drink."

The sergeant poured a stream of amber liquid into three glasses, and when no one was watching, except me, the stranger, he poured a quick shot into an open Coca-Cola bottle.

"Tell me," the captain asked, "why did you eat up all that runway? I thought you guys could land on a postage stamp."

I was puzzled. Army pilot's silver wings were pinned to his shirt and he had heard me talk to Tex. "I lost a piece of my left wing," I said.

"So?"

"Also a piece of aileron. At low speeds the wing dropped away on me, so I brought it in hot, over ninety knots."

"How did you lose the wing?" Andrews asked. "Did a Jap blow it away?"

"He smashed into that last one," the sergeant said. "You can see part of the red meatball on the bottom of the left wing."

"Jeezus and Mary, he did ram it after all." Andrews yanked his camera from the bar and ran outside.

"I usually land in the first third of the field, make a ninety and taxi straight over to the tie down area," the captain said.

"Good flying," I said and took a swallow of the whiskey. It brought tears to my eyes.

"Of course," he said modestly, "it is just a little spotting plane that I fly when I am here."

"What plane do you usually fly?" I asked.

"I think Scoop wants you outside," he said and led the way.

I posed in front of the big fighter, one hand on the lower blade of the propeller, while Andrews took at least a dozen photographs from as many angles.

"One more, kid," he said, lying on his back, "and pull that hose out of sight. You look like a Martian with a green dong coming out of his side."

The sergeant stuck my helmet back on my head and pinned the air pressure hose out of the way.

"Okay, kid," Andrews said. "Look noble and fearless. Me and my Speed Graphic will make you famous. Pancho, the Mexican Rammer."

"Name's not Pancho," I said, let loose of the propeller and swung at the newsman. The sergeant helped me back on to my feet. The sky seemed to be turning flatly, in one dimension.

"Come back and fight," I said. And then Andrews and the sergeant were helping me back into the bar. I think that I had more to drink, but I might have merely curled up in a corner and slept.

In any case, that is how the famous picture of the heroic Pancho, the Mexican Rammer, came to be published, first, in the twenty Shaeffer newspapers and later on in every major newspaper and magazine in the United States as well as some other countries, including Mexico.

For a while I was badgered unmercifully by the rest of the squadron, for every parent of every fighter pilot sent clippings that mentioned the squadron number. I was no longer called Pancho, but Rammer. I would have preferred the odious Pancho. For too long I did not make one flight during which someone did not cry out for help. "Rammer, this is Bengal one hundred. I am out of ammo and thirteen Zeros are after me. Please Rammer, come and ram 'em."

Finally, Tex Houston inadvertently took the pressure off me. He not only filmed the then-unknown piloted Baka bomb, but also shot it down and then caught the fleeing mother plane and shot it down as well.

He was then known by all, to his great disgust, as the Baka Bomb Baby, soon shortened to Baka Baby. Then, one day, to our great surprise, we were both summoned to Naval headquarters at Guam and sent back to the States, ostensibly to promote the war effort, but in reality to publicize naval aviation with an eye to keeping as large a peacetime navy as possible.

We were flown, two bewildered ensigns, amid naval captains and admirals, in four-motored C-54s to Kwajalein, Johnson Island, Hawaii, and, finally, San Francisco.

We spoke to auditoriums full of loud high school students, mess halls full of aviation cadets marking time while the war ran down, and to the workers at an occasional aircraft factory, which is why we were in Los Angeles when the war with the Japanese Empire suddenly—and inexplicably to me—ended after a mysterious "atomic" super bomb forced the Japanese military to capitulate.

And that is how on V-J Day I ended up in a mansion overlooking the beach at Santa Monica, attending a party that was hosted by a strangely frightening little man who wore his bright red hair long enough to cover his ears.

Chapter 36

· · · · · · · · · · · · · · · · · · ✈

Willard Riley, 1945.

From the veranda I could see the Santa Monica beach outlined by impromptu bonfires set for V-J Day. Down below on the coastal highway, cars moved slowly along, lights blazing and horns blaring, using up their gas ration, confident that with the end of the war there would be an abundance of gasoline.

"Will," Johnny called to me from the study. "Your call is through."

I hurried into the room just off my bedroom to take the receiver. Johnny left, shutting the door behind him.

"Yes," I spoke into the receiver.

"Mister ambassador," the long distance operator said, "your call is ready."

"Ambassador Real?" Helen Cooper said. "Do I know you?"

"Hello, my dear. It is Will Riley. You cannot get a call through now unless you have a title."

"Willard Riley!"

There was no warmth in that bitch's voice.

"To what country are you ambassador, now that both Germany and Japan have fallen?"

I reached up to cup my poor mutilated ear and waited a second or so until I could laugh. "I certainly have missed you and your wild sense of humor, Helen. I am ambassador to Paraguay. Of course, I never go there."

"What do I have to do with Paraguay?"

"Nothing, I hope. I called about your book. Our book, I should say."

"It will finally be published, Will, and when it is, I'll send you a copy."

"I have a new proposal, Helen. I will double your advance and your subsequent royalties. You keep your present publisher."

"In return for what?"

"Very little. A few minor deletions that might be embarrassing. Your book might even be more interesting. I can tell you a few things about some highly placed people that even you do not know about."

"Like what and whom?"

"For example, the president—" I stopped. The conniving bitch was trying to draw me out. Well, I had given her an opportunity.

"Do we have a deal?"

"No," she said. "No deal."

"Look, you drunken bitch," I said. "I wanted to spare Tell any pain, but you—"

"Hurt Tell?" she interrupted. "How could you hurt him? He sent his own son to be killed. Who's left?"

"The girl. You have a daughter to care for."

"What do you mean? What about Elenita?"

That took some of the slur from her speech. She should sober up soon.

"I have a daughter in school here too. The same school as Elena. Quite a coincidence. I worry about my daughter. So many awful things can happen to a girl alone in a big city like Los Angeles."

"You leave my baby alone, you goddamn sadist. You touch one hair of her head and I'll . . ."

"What will you do?" I smiled. I had the sneaky little bitch.

"I'll tell Tell," she said uncertainly.

"Tell Tell?" I laughed aloud. "Sounds like Tell Twice, or was that your son?"

"Will," she said, her voice sticky sweet now that she wanted something from me. "I'm a little drunk. I'll call you back tomorrow."

"Yes. Call Ambassador Real at this number at noon," and then before she could hang up, I snapped: "Did you really interview old Doc Jones, the Puebla drunk?"

"Yes. I mean," she added quickly, "that I know who you mean. The animal doctor. But he's dead, isn't he?"

"Yes, he is dead," I said. "Goodbye, Helen."

And the old drunk would be. Maybe right now, before Helen Cooper could crawl into bed with some young gigolo not fit to shine Tell's boots.

Bursts of song and loud voices came up the stairwell and into my bedroom.

"Will," Johnny stuck his head into the room. "The girls are downstairs. As you suggested, I did not mention the telephone call."

"Good." It had not been a suggestion, as Johnny well knew.

"Sofía looks so pretty. She is a charming girl."

"She is?" I had always found her timid and tongue-tied. "I will be

278

right down. Please get through to Jorge and tell him to pay the old Doc off. Immediately. Then join us."

"Doc who?"

"Jorge will know. It is important that he be paid. He should have been taken care of years ago."

When I left the bedroom, Johnny was in the study placing a call in the name of Ambassador Real.

Although the house was not in my name and could not be traced to me, I owned it. The famous motion picture director who loaned it to me whenever I had need was never without what he called snow. It was merely a favor in return for the technical aid from the United States of America, which, to ensure a supply of morphine, had sent its top poppy agronomists to teach the simple farmers of Sinaloa the process of changing a beautiful flower to a drug that would make our business with illegal alcohol insignificant. The house that allowed him all of the cocaine that his bulbous nose could sniff would be the warehouse for our new connection.

The living room was full of boisterous and exuberant drunks. More than half of them were middle-aged movie executives. Some had brought their wives. Others had brought someone else's wife. A few had netted attractive, nubile studio whores, commonly called starlets. There was a sprinkling of uniforms, some with ribbons pinned on, which I assumed were some kind of decorations for valor.

Sofía, her face flushed with excitement—for a change—was talking animatedly to one of the uniforms. I scanned the room, but did not see Elena Cooper. Once into the crowd, I was jostled by a fat, balding man, without coat or tie and with a drink in each hand.

I elbowed him in passing. Both of the drinks sloshed over his hands, but the idiot kept on smiling. I detest physical contact, especially with strangers.

"Sofía," I called, thinking she might lead me to the Cooper girl.

"Daddy." She put on a smile. "I want you to meet Guillermo Canela."

He turned around to meet me; he seemed a younger and darker version of Tell Cooper.

"Of course," I said smiling. "You are our Mexican hero, Pancho, the pilot that rams the Japanese right out of the air."

"My name is Guillermo, sir, and ramming that Zero was certainly not my idea."

"I admire your modesty," I said. "But you must know that at the moment you are as well known as any movie star."

"Yes," he said wryly. "I guess so."

"Oh, Daddy," Sofía gushed. "He was being chased up Hollywood Boulevard by a bunch of girls."

"And she saved me," he said. "I felt like the fox with the hounds closing in. They had ripped off my shoulder boards and ribbons and were working on my shirt when the door of that big, black Buick opened up and Sofía yelled, '*Venga acá, paisano.*' I dove right in. And that is how I came to crash your victory party, Mister Riley."

"You are welcome. I am glad you were rescued by a Riley."

"I thank you again," he said, smiling at my simple daughter, who could not seem to stop grinning foolishly back. "Would you like a souvenir?" he said, unpinning his golden wings from the khaki tunic. "They got everything else, even my hat."

"Oh, yes, Memo. I would love to have them."

"Sofía," I said, speaking Spanish, "while I am sure that you understand that Ensign Canela never meant the offer in a romantic sense, it is somewhat like offering a girl a fraternity pin. It might prove to be an embarrassment later."

"Not to me," he said and helped her pin it on just above one of her large breasts, a feature that reminded me of her well-endowed mother.

"If you leave the Navy soon," I said, "you could cash in on all of the free publicity. You are even better known in Mexico than here. One *diputado* even made a speech demanding that you be transferred to the Mexican 201st pursuit group somewhere in the Philippines."

"I would have liked that better than making speeches."

"Acting," I said quickly, "is not at all like making speeches, and it pays better."

"I have a standing offer to fly copilot for Major Cooper. He will probably match my Navy pay."

"Which is?"

"Two hundred and twenty-five dollars."

"I will give you a contract with a five hundred dollar-a-week guarantee for the first year and, if you work out, triple it the second."

"Are you serious?"

"Yes," I said truthfully. "I am."

At that moment, a wave of heavy perfume warned me, so I avoided both hug and kiss. The studio called her Linda Black. She was this year's sex symbol. Big tits, long legs and a pouting look that men found exciting. She wiggled her ass and tits and pouted and talked in a little girl's voice, so every male over twelve got an instant hard-on. I had one, once, myself. Unfortunately she was as incompetent an actress in bed as on the screen; she thought more of her own satisfaction than of mine. I finally sent her away and had a real professional whore brought in.

"Will, introduce me to that beautiful boy in blue." Linda pushed her tits out even further from the inadequate brassiere and ogled the boy.

"War ace Guillermo Canela, better known as Pancho the Rammer," I said, thinking that Linda might be more of an inducement to the boy to be an actor than my money would be. "Meet Virginia Sánchez, better known as Linda Black."

"Hey, *paisano*," she said, taking his offered hand and pulling him to her tightly enough to flatten her breasts. "We fit right in. Let's rassle and get black and blue together, Pancho."

"Call me Memo," he said, stepping back uncertainly.

She moved back, eyed him, then stepped up close again, hooked his arm with hers and called for champagne.

Sofía looked at me with the large hurt eyes of a wounded doe. I shook my head at her in dismay. Did she have to show every feeling that crossed her mind? Then, as quickly as it had come, the look was gone and she was smiling again.

"Elena. You did come. See, Daddy. I told you she would."

"You are as beautiful as your mother," I said, taking an instant dislike to the girl. Actually, she could have passed for Sofía's sister had her eyes been green, not smoky blue.

"I know who you are," she said. Her voice was the surprise. It had more of Tell's gravelly quality than the high-pitched tone of her mother. I took her hand, pressed it once and released it.

"I met you once, when you were a baby," I said. "You were with your father."

"And this is Memo," Sofía said, ignoring Linda.

"After you left, I worked for your father," Memo said. "It is a real pleasure to meet you, Miss Cooper."

"Yeah," Linda said, yanking him back. "Me too."

Sofía set her jaw and for a second I thought she might smash a bottle over the raven tresses of our sexy star, but my daughter disappointed me again.

"You and my Daddy used to be best friends," Elena said.

"We still are. The only problem is that silly thing with the book. When one has as many enemies as I do, one must be very careful."

"Why do you have so many enemies?" Memo asked, seemingly more interested in Elena than either Sofía or Linda. My God, I thought. What a stroke of luck.

"It all goes back to the Revolution. I not only supported the land redistribution policy, but I used the little capital that I possessed to restore the sugar mills themselves. I had the good fortune to provide a good product to a sugar-hungry world. I also made a great deal of money. The combination did nothing to endear me to pseudo-revolutionists or inept entrepreneurs."

Memo nodded as gravely as Tell would have. I knew that he would reflect on what I had said and would not believe any of the wild rumors now circulating about me.

"I talked to your mother today," I said to Elena, "about a book—"

"What book?" an eavesdropper who claimed to be an assistant director asked. "You got a new property, Will?"

"I made a most generous offer to your mother," I said to Elena, ignoring the brash, long-haired man who had called me by my first name. "She is to give me an answer at noon tomorrow. Would you like to talk to her then?"

"I would love to, Mister Riley." She turned to a young man with white hair and an old face. "Would you bring me here again, Tommy?"

"Sure. If I can find a cab."

"No need," I said. "Stay over, both of you. This house has more rooms than a hotel. Separate rooms, of course," I added, seeing some hesitation on the part of the girl.

"I would be pleased to stay. And forgive me, Mister Riley, this is my friend, Major Tommy Wright."

We shook hands, and then the skinny young eavesdropper shook hands with both Elena and Tommy.

"I'm Clyde Dahm," he said, "I'm in the movie business too."

He turned to Linda who did not even look at his outthrust hand.

"Where are we sleeping?" Linda asked me.

"We," Elena said, in Spanish, repeating an old Mexican saying, "are a lot of people." Then she blushed and said. "Sorry, Memo. Just slipped out."

"I'll bet it did, honey," Linda said. "And I'll bet my ass you didn't know my real name is Virginia Sánchez and I grew up speaking Spanish."

"About this property you are about to buy, Will," Clyde almost put a hand on my shoulder until I looked straight into his eyes. Then he put his hand behind him and looked away. "I might be able to do a treatment on it. What's the title?"

And that dirty little bitch, her mother's daughter, stared right at my ear and shouted for all the world to hear, "Riley's Golden Ear."

The room spun. I reached out for support but no one was there. Not one person. The floor crashed into my face brutally. Hands lifted me to my feet; all of the hypocritical little beasts were helping me into a chair. My vision cleared. The first face I saw was that of Sofía, observing me anxiously, the way she had once done as a stubborn child when wondering whether to obey me or not.

"I am sorry, if I caused you harm," Elena said. "I had no idea the book meant that much to you."

"It doesn't," I said. "Just a dizzy spell. Too much cognac."

"About the treatment—"

"Not now, lad," Major Wright said, cutting Clyde off.

"No, Major Wright. I really am all right, now. And I would like to see a treatment, if I come to an agreement with the author."

"You would?" Clyde said, startled. And well he should be. I had him figured for some kind of an errand boy; I was right. He was an assistant director, which is about the same thing. "Of course, I would need some kind of a contract."

"I have never read the manuscript," Elena said, "but I know Mommy keeps the first draft in loose-leaf notebooks. How could you make a two-hour movie out of that?"

"Cecil B. DeMille did it with the Bible," I said.

Everyone laughed. Except Clyde. He was likely wondering how much he might ask. I was right.

"A treatment from a book that long would take some time, Clyde stated. "A real investment of time."

"So far it has taken many . . . many years," I said. "I suppose that I might wait a bit more." I turned to Elena. "Has your father read the manuscript?"

"I don't think so. I mean he read some of the first manuscript, but then I left and Mom stopped, but when she went to New York she wrote a bunch, and she might have finished the book. She is such a careful, good writer."

I nodded my agreement. She was good—too good for this imperfect earth.

"Tell you what," I said. "Let us cast the movie. Memo will take the title role, Elena will play her own mother, the famous and fearless newswoman. The major, Tommy, will play the other major, my old friend Tell Cooper. Clyde can take the part of Jorge Rubio, the one Tell always called the Toad, and Johnny can play himself."

"Jorge Rubio does not look like a toad!" Elena said angrily. Of course, she had been mixed up with Rubio's son briefly.

"Maybe not," I said, "but Clyde certainly looks reptilian. We could change his name to Louis Lizard and make him my second in command."

"What about Sofía?" Elena said. "How about a role for her?"

"Well," I said, pretending to think deeply. "I was thinking of giving the role of Lilly, Mexico's greatest sex star ever, to Linda, but she hardly has the body for it. So, I guess you will have to do it, Sofía! Hell, your tits are bigger than Linda's anyway."

There was a silence so complete that I could hear the hum of the refrigerator at the bar. And then, suddenly, to my horror, I began to giggle and then to laugh uncontrollably. I sprang from my chair. With my hand clapped over my ear, I fled up the stairs to the sanctuary of my bedroom.

Chapter 37

Memo Canela

Sofía's father ran up the stairs, giggling. She waited until he disappeared, then went straight to the bar, tilted up a bottle of brandy and spilled it into a large snifter glass. But she did not just cover the bottom half inch or so of the glass. It was half full when I spoke. She set the bottle down so sharply that brandy sloshed out from the bottle onto the bar.

"Hey, Sofía. How about leaving some for the troops?"

The look of terror vanished. She smiled, and her mood changed instantly. "When the cat is away, the mice will play. Want some mouse brandy?"

"No thanks. I'll stick to the champagne."

"I got something better, Rammer." Linda pulled me down to sit alongside her on a couch. She slipped a gold cigarette case from her purse, then tossed the purse onto the floor. She flipped the case open. Inside were six lumpy, hand-rolled cigarettes. I knew what the green tobacco was instantly. In Mexico marijuana was not the rarity that it was in the States. My mother even kept a bottle of medicine in which macerated marijuana was the principal ingredient.

"No," I joked. "I am not a cockroach that needs marijuana for fuel."

She laughed, sprang to her feet, lifted her skirt until I could see her lacy black underpants, garter belt, and a foot or so of creamy rounded thigh, and she danced as she sang the old revolutionary verse about Pancho Villa's "cucaracha" car that could not run because it had no marijuana to smoke.

Tommy Wright's eyes widened, then he flushed, and wrenched them away to look at Elena. She smiled at him, but the look she shot at Linda would have flamed her, had Elena been flying a fighter plane. Clyde turned his head to talk to me, but he mumbled. His eyes did not swivel with his tiny pointed nose, but stayed focused on Linda's crotch. To be honest, so did mine, mostly. Sofía smiled mischievously while Linda swirled to a curtsy, acknowledging the obligatory applause, and then she slipped quickly into Linda's vacated place on the couch, next to me.

"Viva Zapata and Obregón, and Memo Andrés Canela!" Sofía said, lifting her glass to me.

"¡*Viva Zapata!*" I said, "and viva Sofía Riley!"

We drank again and, after Linda took another bow, she asked, "Why do you say you are Canela? Is Canela not your mother's last name?"

"To the Americans," I said, not wanting to confuse her about my dead father, "a last name is the last name. Ergo, I became Canela."

"Ergo, Pancho," Sofía said. "Well, what I want to ask is a favor." She pronounced her words carefully, but without the harsher accent of her Bostonian father, as a small girl learning to read might. "I have my own room at the head of the stairs, first door. Come and have a drink with me . . . talk with me . . . I mean, after you jazz the *paisana*."

"Of course, I'll talk to you before I leave, but I have a room at the Hollywood Roosevelt. At least I did this morning."

"But Pee Pee won't let you go. She is all ready to shoot you down"—she made airplanes of her hands the way fighter pilots do, so skillfully that I laughed—"and tattoo Navy wings on her ass, or wherever it is that she keeps her score. Pee Pee's ass is ample, but perhaps not ample enough."

"Pee Pee. Who is Pee Pee?" Linda glowered down at Sofía.

"Oh, Linda, darling. All of your fans used to call you Passion Pit, but it was too long, so we shortened it to Pee Pee."

Linda drew back a right and swung. I caught her hand and, getting to my feet, tried to block a kick from Sofía, which I did—on the skinny part of my shin.

"Help, Tommy!" I yelled.

He was quick. He had his arms around Linda in a second, holding her so tightly that her breasts almost popped out completely. I turned and caught Sofía by the wrists, lifting her up off the floor and away.

"Let me, loose," Linda yelled, "I won't hit the skinny little bitch. She can go fuck herself for all I care. That's about all she can hope for anyway."

Tommy released her, reluctantly, I thought, and stepped back quickly, out of harm's way.

Sofia leaned against me, sobbing, hot tears dropping onto my hands and wrists. I released her.

"Well, Pancho the Rammer. You want to go someplace with me and ram, or stay here with these Anglos?"

"Anglos? Elena and Sofía are Mexicans just like me."

"Like shit they are. You may think so, but they don't. Maybe you are a coconut, Pancho." She said Pancho like an epithet, which, at times, it had been to me. "Brown on the outside, but white inside. Well, they are white inside and outside and don't you ever forget it."

"I'll get a cab," I said, telling myself that it would be better for everyone if I took her away. Besides, she was a sex machine, and I was horny.

"No," Sofía said. "Memo has a room here. It is his room and you can stay with him, Linda."

"Ask me pretty please," Linda said.

"Pretty please. I apologize."

"Well, Pancho? Shall we ram?"

Before I could answer, Elena who had not said a word, smiled prettily at Linda and said, conversationally, "Speaking as a real Mexican, *tú, pocha, ¡chinga tu madre!*"

"For Christ's sake, Tommy," I yelled. "Grab Elena!"

"What?" Tommy looked at me blankly.

"She called Linda a *pocha*," Sofía explained, "a border Mexican, neither American nor Mexican. And she told her to go . . . ah . . ."

"Come on, Linda. Off we go." I took her by the arm and yanked. She dug her heels in.

"Easy, Pancho. I'll go. You're lucky. Both those bitches are frigid bitches anyway. Where's your car?"

"We'll grab a cab. Come on."

"On V-J night you are going to get a cab?"

"I brought a car, Linda." Clyde jingled keys at her.

"Good. Give the Rammer the keys."

I glanced back over my shoulder at what reminded me of the end of a scene in a play, when the performers remain motionless as the curtain closes. Sofía was cuddled up on the couch with the brandy glass. Tommy was blinking at me. Elena's eyes glared at me. The others seemed afraid to move lest they be singled out for some unknown but terrible punishment.

"Drive her someplace," I told Clyde. "I can't leave yet."

"Go to hell, you goddamn pansy *maricón*," Linda yelled. She lurched out, Clyde trotting alongside, his reedy voice mixing in counterpoint to her brassy curses. The door had hardly slammed before the other guests hurried out, laughing and chattering about Linda Black and the fag fighter pilot, Pancho.

I felt the need for the shot of medicinal liquor that our flight surgeon, Doc Green, had doled out after each strike. "I'll take that brandy, now, Sofía."

She smiled at me, then went to the bar to pour some of her brandy into another smaller shot glass. She brought it to me and sat down alongside me. I lifted the glass to the room, only four of us now, two women and two men.

"To victory and to those not able to drink to it with us."

Elena burst into tears. I realized it was a stupid, melodramatic thing to say. I wondered how I could possibly tell her that I meant it was only the luck of the draw that placed me in this room and not Tell Dos. What I said was, "I was sorry to hear about Tell Dos. I knew him, you know, briefly."

"You did? When? Where?" She smiled at me.

I released my breath in relief. She was a beautiful girl. I could see why Tommy was in love with her.

"I went to the American school briefly. We almost built model airplanes together."

"Tommy flew with him in the Eagle squadron."

"I thought you were young to be a major," I said looking at Tommy. "You flew Spitfires, then?"

"Yes. And then the Fifty-ones."

"The P-51. What a great airplane. I tried to turn with one, over Guam, but it was no contest."

"Turn inside anything," Tommy said. "And fast. Got a Rolls Royce engine. Of course, if someone sneaks up behind you and pulls the trigger, it's all academic."

"I knew a flyer," I told them, "who lost his power up high and glided down toward the China coast. He came down through a layer of clouds right behind a Zero fighter, shot it down with a long burst and then kept on gliding to a water landing. A few minutes later a submarine picked him up. Maybe the pilot that he killed was the world's best. So what?"

"Happened often. Once to me. But the other way around. I got picked up, of course. Hardly burned at all."

"How many times were you shot down, Tommy?" Sofía asked, wide eyed.

"Only twice. Then I got seven of theirs, so I netted out five to the good."

I laughed. I liked the dry wit of the slight, little man. "Will you stay with flying, now that the war is over?"

288

"I don't know." He looked at Elena as he spoke. "I, too, have an offer to fly with what you called the *Aunty* airline. But, before I move from Seattle to Mexico City, I need to know a bit more."

"What can I tell you?" I asked.

"Nothing, I guess. But Elena might."

"Oh," I said. "I see."

And see I did. I looked at Tommy differently. He was young for a major, but then, likely nearly ten years older than Elena. And she was almost as tall as he. Besides, he knew nothing of Mexico and could not speak our language. No, I decided. He was not the man for Elena.

"What about you, Memo?" Elena asked. "Will you become a film star and work for Sofía's father?"

"I think not. I would like to be rich, but I don't like people yelling at me and grabbing at me. And I don't swear much," I added, thinking of Linda. But it was Elena who blushed.

"How about you, Elena?" I said, savoring the name. "Will you marry or choose a career?"

"I don't know." She turned to Tommy and repeated, "I really don't know."

"How about you, Sofía?" I asked."

"Me? I do not know. I have been finished enough. Daddy thinks I have been too much to school. I suppose that I am a little dumb, and much too cowardly to catch a husband."

"All you would have to do is let all of the eligible bachelors know that you are available," I said.

"I am available?" she said in her little girl voice and looking straight at me. She did not show a trace of a smile.

"No, honey," Elena said quickly. "Say, *I am* available."

"Daddy says I make questions out of everything. I take after the wishy-washy side of the family."

"Which is?" Tommy asked.

"Italian-Mexican. Daddy is Bostonian Irish. If God would have given him the tablets instead of to Moses, Daddy would have corrected them."

Sofía seemed genuinely surprised when we all howled with glee at her description of her father.

"Sofía! Sweetheart. Elenita! Memo!"

I jumped to my feet, confused. The voice was so familiar, yet the small pot-bellied man with the brown eyes was not. But then, after he had kissed and hugged both girls and had been called both Johnny and

Juanito, I knew who he was. He shook hands with Tommy and then hugged me. I had to bend down. I could remember looking up at him not too many years before. He stepped back, and as if reading my thoughts, said, "You have grown and I have shrunk, Memo. Or Pancho, as the newspapers call you. We Mexicans are very proud of you."

"*Don* Juan," I said. "It seems a long time since you got me a job with the major."

"A war has been fought. But I am not so old. When we speak English, call me Johnny. I am still young inside." He moved as gracefully as ever to the bar and poured a shot from an unlabeled bottle. He held the amber colored liquid up to the light and said, "I will drink to another ace of another time. One that I have not seen for a long time. Tell Cooper."

He threw the shot down and grimaced with pain. "We used to chase tequila with beer. I think I will change to Alka-Seltzer."

"Johnny." The querulous voice of Riley drifted down the stairwell. "We are not through yet."

"I must go back up." He shrugged at me, then looked at Elena, sadly, I thought, and said, "Ask your mother to compromise. It means little, in the long run, and could be bad, very bad, in the short."

"Johnny!" There was a touch of anger in Riley's voice.

Johnny flashed a smile, teeth as white and perfect as ever, then trotted obediently up the stairs.

"What's that about? The book?" I asked.

"I don't know," Sofía said. "But it's the only reason I am here and not in boarding school, I think. He never takes me places. He sends me places."

"But what have you to do with it then?"

"Nothing, I think. But I did ask Elena to come here. Daddy thinks she might talk to her mother about the book."

"That's just silly," Elena said. "Nobody tells my Mom what to write."

"The same with my mama," I said. "She is a hundred pounds of dynamite."

"Did you know she dated my Daddy?" Elena asked.

"Sure. He even taught her how to fly."

"And that was before they invented airplanes," Sofía said, giggling.

"Sofía!" Elena threw a pillow at her in mock anger.

"What?" Tommy sat up suddenly, blinking. "I guess it must be my turn, sir."

290

"Your turn?" Elena laughed. "To do what, Tommy?"

"Huh?" Tommy rubbed his eyes. "Sorry. I think I've missed too much sleep lately."

"We'll give you a room, Tommy, now that the Passion Pit has moved on. Tommy will be at the end of the hall across the room from Elena, and Memo will be exactly across the hall from guess who?" Sofía pretended to pant like Goofy Dog in the cartoons. We all laughed, except Elena.

"Don't be such a child, Sofía."

"Sorry, Elena. You know where to sleep."

"Goodnight, Sofía."

They kissed on the cheeks and then, surprising me, Elena turned to me and held her arms out.

"Good night, Memo."

I hugged her and patted her back, but it was not just another Mexican abrazo. We released each other reluctantly.

Tommy was already stumbling up the stairs. Elena glanced back worriedly, said "goodnight," and followed Tommy.

Sofía picked up the bottle of brandy and two glasses, beckoning me with her head to follow. When we reached the head of the stairs, her door was ajar. She turned back to one side, inserting a toe to kick open the door.

"Come on in," she said. There was a small coffee table with two chairs, but her bed loomed portentously no more than two steps away. When I sat down, she kicked the door shut, pushed the doorknob lock with an elbow, then sat the bottle and glasses on the table. She filled two glasses. Hers was gone before I tasted mine.

"Daddy knows something about you. Elena too. He knows something about everybody. Something he can use to make them do what he wants."

"And if they don't?" I said, humoring her. She was obviously at the drunken tell-all stage.

"He has them killed."

"Sure he does, Sofía," I said, smiling.

"He does," she insisted stubbornly. "If people do not do what he tells them to, they die or go to sanatoriums or something. Mama is in one. Maybe I am next."

I knew that Willard Riley was a hard-nosed businessman. Maybe even a crooked one. But a murderer? No.

"I'll talk to you in the morning," I said.

But when I stood up, she jumped up and clung to me. "Do not leave me, Memo. Please. I am scared all of the time. Terrified. Take me with you."

"Easy." I stroked her hair and patted her shoulder. "You don't have to stay here, do you?"

"I am twenty-one years old, but I do not have any money. Not a cent."

"But your father is one of the richest men in Mexico. Maybe the world."

"He never allows me cash. The stores let me sign for my clothes. But I cannot even take the train or a bus to San Francisco. If I stayed here, in Los Angeles, one of Daddy's gangsters would find me and . . ."

"I could lend you a couple of hundred dollars," I said, reluctantly, thinking that would be the last of my poker winnings, "but what would you do afterwards?"

"I have a friend in San Francisco. She has a place for me. Daddy will not know about her. And she said I could get a job. Do you think I could get a job, Memo?"

"Of course you could," I said, wondering what she might be trained for. "You are intelligent and willing."

"I am willing, Memo, all right," she said. She looked up at me and held her arms open.

We moved together. She clasped me around my waist, then levered herself up as high and tightly as she could and said, "Stay here with me, tonight."

I bent my head to meet her outthrust lips. They were hot and her breath was quick and sweet to my nostrils. I felt myself get hard and knew that she felt it too. She stood even higher, thrusting her pelvis into me. The click as someone tried the door was, to my ears, as loud as the clang of bells during general quarters on a Navy ship.

"Good night, Sofía," I said loudly. "I will drop in on you in the morning." I pantomimed someone at the door and then walked to it and opened it widely. There was no one there.

"I promise, Sofía," I whispered. "I'll go to my hotel room and get the money. I will help you get away, if you still want to."

"Stay with me tonight, Memo?"

"No," I said, wishing that we were anywhere else but a flight of stairs away from Willard Riley. "I must go."

"You do not want me either," she said dully, then motioned with her head down the hall. "Elena will let you in her room."

292

"Don't be silly," I said, wondering if it were true. "I'll see you in the morning. And I will take you out somewhere. Even if you don't run away."

She shrugged hopelessly.

"Is it a date?" I insisted.

"Yes. Of course. If I am still alive."

Chapter 38

· · · · · · · · · · · · · · · · · · ✈

Willard Riley

There were obviously many people as important as a Mexican ambassador to Paraguay, so I waited for almost two hours before the telephone rang announcing the long distance call from Helen Cooper.

"Hello. Will Riley? Is Elena all right? Is she there?"

"Is that you? Helen," I said. Her voice was high and shrill, but clear. "I can hardly hear you."

"It's Helen Cooper," she shouted. I smiled and held the receiver away from my good ear. I let her shout for a few seconds before I answered.

"Do not shout. I can hear you."

"Elena! What about Elenita?" She was sober and frightened. Good.

"Elena?" I asked.

"Please, Will, for God's sake. Is Elenita all right?"

"I suppose so. She spent the night here. They all did."

"Elenita is at your house? I called the sorority—"

"Oh, she is here all right. But the house is not mine. It belongs to Jack Blount, the director. You must know Jack, he—"

"Will, please. Let me speak to her."

"Of course. I did assign them individual rooms, but you know how young people are today. Who knows where they really slept. If they did at all. Young Memo Canela, the war ace, never slept a wink, at least not in his own bed."

"Memo Canela. Toña's son?"

"Yes, indeed. Sofía found him and brought him to the party. He is certainly a nice-looking boy. The girls threw themselves at him. You should have seen him and Elena dancing. They make a lovely couple."

"You are a real son of a bitch, Will."

"Then you do not want to speak to Elena after all?"

I heard a strangled "Yes." I clicked the receiver on and off and said, "Hello. Operator. Operator!"

"Will!" she screamed. "I'm here. Will!"

"Oh, yes, Helen. What was it?"

"I would like to speak to my daughter, please." She was begging

294

now.

"Of course," I said. I pressed a button. It would ring in the kitchen. Elena, waiting for the signal, would hear it.

"Do you remember my wedding, Helen?"

"Of course. How is Carmen?"

"She does quite well, now, I understand. She is quite lucid at times. But do you remember that our first child was born seven months after the wedding?"

"I never counted."

Never counted? She likely knew to the minute. "All I wanted to say, my dear, is that girls will get pregnant. The boys get excited and forget their little rubber devices, or the girls, their diaphragms—if they come from enlightened families like yours."

I ignored the timid knock on my bedroom door.

"Are you telling me that Tommy Wright is sleeping with Elena?"

"Tommy? Well, I had not even thought of Tommy." I heard the hiss of inhaled air before I called out loudly, "Come on in, dear. The door is unlocked."

"Here she is," I said, holding the telephone out to the girl.

I left quickly, shutting the study door behind me.

Although it took me no more than a minute to reach the extension and ease the receiver off the hook, Helen had already mentioned Toña's son.

"Of course I like Memo. He is keen. Not at all stuck up. And guess what? He knew Tell Dos at the American School. Did you know that?"

"No, I did not. Honey, are you involved with the Canela boy?"

"Involved? Mom! I just met him last night, and I was with Tommy."

"I know those Hollywood parties. People switch partners."

"I know, Mom. Linda Black was at the party. She had some marijuana cigarettes and she danced with her skirt up around her neck and then she tried to seduce Memo, but he wasn't having any." She giggled.

"You didn't smoke any?"

"Mom!"

"Where did you sleep last night? I know you were not at the sorority."

"I had a room here, to myself." She was angry now.

"Honey," Helen said contritely, "I'm sorry. But Will Riley is a devious, dangerous man. I want you out of that house and out of Los Angeles."

"I could rent a room in a nunnery."

"I want you safe, Elenita."

"There are no rooms now. Not even in the sorority. It's closed for two weeks for remodeling. That's why Sofía invited me."

"I'm coming out there right away."

"You won't be able to get on a train. Not for a week, or more."

"I will fly out if I have to, but I will be there soon."

"Will you bring the manuscript for Mister Riley to see?"

My own breath hissed in, so I turned away from the mouthpiece.

"Maybe. But don't tell him that."

"Sofía says that it will be better if you do. She knows something. It might be something bad about Dad."

"About Tell. Nonsense."

"Then about you," Elena said uncertainly. "Memo got a letter from Daddy last week. Maybe he knows something. He's just downstairs. Do you want to talk to him?"

"No!" Helen said sharply. "Stay close to Tommy and do be careful. I love you. Now let me talk to Will Riley."

I managed to reach the head of the stairs before Elena, calling my name, came out of the bedroom.

"Mom wants to talk to you," she said. I nodded, then went in, shutting both bedroom and study doors behind me.

"Hello, Helen."

"I will be out soon, Will."

"With the manuscript?"

"Maybe I could bring the copy."

"Tell could get you on a flight," I said, knowing that she had not been on an airplane since the death of her son.

"I think I can get a sleeper on the train."

"All right, but you might not be here for the trial."

"Trial? What trial?"

"It may not even come to that. I do have some influence, even here, in the States. The problem is that the cops picked up Linda Black, and that is a big news story, as you well know. She was driving erratically. They found the remains of a marijuana cigarette in the ash tray. She broke down and confessed, but she said that she got the marijuana from some Mexicans she met at my house; that is, Jack Blount's house. My God, she might even implicate me."

"But Elenita doesn't smoke pot."

"They found a cigarette case with the initials E.C. on it," I said.

And it was true as of an hour ago. At the party, Linda had left her marijuana, forgotten, still in her cigarette case. The housecleaner, who was married to the butler, both ex-cons, had turned the cigarette case over to me without a word.

"She would not. I know she would not."

"Do you think that the girl might not do a few things in private that she would not do in front of her mommy?"

"Stop it, Will! You know you can keep the police out of it if you want."

"Maybe. Will you bring the manuscript?"

"Yes. Yes!"

"Original and copy?" I allowed her a shrill "yes" before I added, "and the notes."

"Yes, Will. Just leave my daughter alone and do not thrust the Canela boy at her. I beg you, Will."

"Whatever you say, Helen." I allowed myself a chuckle. "What are old friends for?"

"I will be there in a few days."

"You could be here tomorrow, Helen, if you act promptly."

"How?"

"I have a chartered flight leaving Newark tomorrow. Max Rathje is bringing me some special equipment to take back to Mexico with me."

"All right," she said. "But I am terrified of flying."

"I know," I said. "So am I. I came up here by train."

"But you want me to fly out to see you."

"To see your daughter," I corrected her. "But that is up to you, of course. However, the flight will be leaving tomorrow, early. Do you want to be on it or not? I can keep an eye on Elena for you, while you wait for other transportation."

That did it. "Of course, I'll fly. What should I do?"

"Call the Rathje Transport Service at the Newark Airport and find out the when and where. I will call Max to tell him that he will have a passenger. He will be pleased. He hates to fly alone."

"Okay. Someone will meet me at the airport in Los Angeles?"

"I will send Johnny Ávalos to meet your flight."

"Johnny is there?"

"Yes, but not right now."

"Goodbye, then."

"Goodbye," I said and hung up before I added, "and farewell."

Young Elena, trepidation written on her face as clearly as if she

297

were following the shouted instructions from the megaphone of a director in the old silent-picture days, waited just outside the door.

"Elena," I said, "everything is about to be resolved. Your mother will be on her way, in an airplane, tomorrow. She should be here in time for late dinner tomorrow evening."

She smiled angelically. The director would have already shouted, "Happiness!"

"She asked me to tell you not to be angry with her for being so motherly, whatever that might mean. And," I beamed happily at her, "I am sure that I will publish her book myself, and she will be known as one of the world's best biographers."

She squealed with delight and suddenly, before I could avert my face, kissed me full on the lips. I snatched my handkerchief and held it to my lips as she ran joyously down the stairs to spread the good news. I could only hope that those sweet lips had not been sucking one of the boys' cocks last night. I hurried back into the bathroom to gargle with a strong antiseptic before I made my next call.

"This is George Crawford Senior," I said. "Go ahead with the arrangements with Max Rathje. Be sure to make it plain to him that he is not to parachute from the airplane until he sights the Rocky Mountains. That way they will not find the plane for a year. Maybe never."

My next call was also to a local number. "Tell Sam that he should set that alarm to wake up the pilot well before he reaches the Rockies."

"Sure, Mister Benson," he said. "Remember me to Bugsy."

I hung up and sat on the bed, then leaned back and closed my eyes. Without the slightest wish on my part, I saw Linda Black, nude, kneeling in front of me. My erection was huge as well as unexpected. Maybe she would be better this time. And I had her gold cigarette case, with her marijuana cigarettes in it. Of course she would be better. At least she would try harder. I reached for the telephone again and dialed her unlisted number.

Chapter 39

· · · · · · · · · · · · · · · · · · ✈

Tell Cooper

Western Union telegram dated August 16, 1945:

MOM DEAD IN PLANE CRASH. STOP. I AM
DESOLATE. STOP. COME AT ONCE. STOP.
ELENA.

How could Helen have died in an airplane? She swore after Tell
Dos was killed that she would never fly again. What could have forced
her into an airplane?

That question, like an irritating radio commercial, would not leave
my mind. Not even when we hit rough air over the Mojave desert and
the DC-3 bounced almost enough to cost me a full shot of whiskey. As
we taxied up to the airline terminal, I saw Elenita and some little pot-
bellied man standing alongside the baggage cart. I grabbed my coat and
overnight bag and beat the stewardess to the door.

"Say thanks to the captain and tell him that the right wheel hit a
second before the left," I said.

"Pleasure to have you, Major Cooper," she said. A pleasant and
pretty girl. That was a stewardess's major qualification now that a
nursing certificate was not required.

She unlocked the door for me and stepped aside. I suppose she must
have been told about the crash. I ran down the few steps straight into
the arms of Elenita. We sobbed together. Then, like two crabs locked in
a death struggle, we sidled out of the way of the other passengers.

"Hello, Tell."

"Johnny." I heard him, but could not see him.

"It is me, Tell."

The little man with the bowling-ball belly was Johnny Ávalos. The
brown eyes and the voice had not changed, but he had grown much
older.

"It has been a long time, Tell. I wish it could have been a happier
one. I was fond of Helen."

I released Elenita to hug Johnny. When I stood back to look at him, his eyes were filled with tears. I tried to remember how long ago it was that we had first met. He was older than I.

"I am sixty years old, Tell. Sixty."

"I'm fifty," I said. "Helen is fifty-two. Was. She would have been fifty-two this month."

"Luggage, Daddy?" Elenita asked, eyeing the men hauling suitcases from the opened compartment.

"No. I just have this bag. I'll buy what I need."

We turned and walked through the gate in the three-foot-high fence that separated the airfield from the waiting room, and then went outside to the street.

"Shall I call a cab?" I asked.

"Mister Riley loaned us his car," Elenita said. "He has been very good to me, Daddy. I couldn't have called people or even sent that telegram to you if he had not."

"Did you try to call me, honey?"

"Oh, yes, I did. But there was no service. I could not wait and I wanted to see you so badly."

She was crying again. I put an arm around her. Will Riley was a bad enemy, but he could be a good friend. He was a man, I thought, neither black, white nor gray, but more like a zebra with stripes of black and white that never met.

A large Lincoln drove up. The driver opened the doors and asked for my luggage. When we were all seated, he shut us in carefully. He was a big-shouldered man with gray hair and pale skin, but he had the same eyes as Will's Mexican bodyguard. I wondered where Will found them.

"What airline was it?" I asked. "There was no news on the radio nor in the papers in Mexico."

"It was not an airline, Daddy. It was . . . was . . ." She could not continue.

Johnny took over. "It was a chartered flight. She felt compelled to be with Elenita as soon as possible."

"I could have gotten her on a commercial flight."

"Will suggested that," Johnny said, laying a comforting hand on my arm, "but she would not ask you. And then Will had the flight all ready to leave."

"How many were killed?"

"Just the two, Helen and the pilot."

"There were two people on a plane flying from New York to Los

300

Angeles? What kind of a flight was that?"

"A pilot named Rathje in a Bellanca was bringing Will some special photographic equipment just in from England, I think. Helen was happy when she found out about the flight."

"That's right, Daddy. I heard her talking to Will—Mister Riley—and she thanked him over and over. But, oh my God, I wish she had taken the train."

"Go easy on Will," Johnny said to me. "He blames himself for Helen being on that airplane."

"Good airplane," I said. "I've heard of Max Rathje. Good pilot. So what's left is a bad shake of the dice."

"No," Elena said, her eyes open wide with horror. "That can't be. There must be a reason."

"Sure," I said. "Likely God had a good reason." Of course at the time I didn't know that God had chosen Will Riley to load the dice.

We sat in silence. There was little traffic. Ten minutes later we pulled into a circular drive before a house set high in the hills just above Santa Monica.

"Will does live in style," I said. "What we used to call 'high on the hog.' "

"The house is not really his," Johnny explained. "The owner loans it to Will, who loans him something else. I'm not sure what. Maybe it's that house in Acapulco."

"Then it's not really his house?" Elenita asked.

"Who knows?" Johnny said. "But Will Riley has made fortunes from dealing with properties with clouded titles such that no one seemed to know who owned them."

"Like my Cosa stock," I said.

"No, Tell. You could have the cash in a second if you would just sit in one meeting and ask Will for it."

"Maybe, but who cares? While I am no multimillionaire like Will Riley, neither am I a poor, young, barnstorming pilot. TIA is big business now, Johnny."

He looked at me strangely, glanced at Elenita and touched a finger to his lips. She was in the middle and took longer to get out. Johnny strode to my side of the big car. Looking straight into my eyes, he said, "Get out of the aviation business, Tell. Sell out as soon as you can."

I opened my mouth to ask him to elaborate, but then Will was on the steps leading up to the big front door, and Johnny averted his face.

"Tell. I am so sorry." Of all of us, Will Riley had weathered the best. Johnny was wrinkled and almost bald. I still had my hair, but it was more gray than brown, and my face felt to my fingers like a raised topographical map. Riley's hair was as darkly red as ever. His nose was longer, but his pale skin, except for one thin line almost hidden by his hair, was wrinkle-free.

"I will never forgive myself for allowing Helen to board that airplane." Will came down the stairs, slowly, reluctantly. He was afraid, I thought, remembering that time in Puebla when the drunken soldiers had frightened him so. Both of us. Two young men out to conquer the world. We had even married on the same day.

I met him with my arms open for an *abrazo*. As we pounded each other on the back, I asked, "What day was it, Will?"

He stepped back. "What day?"

"We got married the same day. Remember? I flew you to Puebla in that old de Havilland. Helen and I then flew on to Veracruz to be married. That very same day."

"Daddy, go on up and rest." Elenita turned to Riley. "He has been traveling two days straight without sleep."

"Of course. Show him his room, Elena."

"Thanks," I said, feeling better. I awoke the next morning, sunlight filtering through wispy curtains.

The phone rang. When I picked it up. Elenita said, "Daddy. It's seven o'clock."

"A.M. or P.M.?"

It was good to hear her laugh. How like her mother she was, and how different. The voice was Helen. Her stubbornness, as Helen always claimed, was a Cooper trait.

"It's evening, Daddy."

"But the sun is rising," I squinted out the window.

"It is now setting and if you hurry, you can have a sundowner and watch the ocean boil."

"Right. Be down in a bit."

"Tommy and Memo Canela are downstairs. I thought you would like to see them. Neither one knows what will happen to them now that the war is over."

"Ten minutes in the shower," I said, hung the telephone up and rolled out of bed.

Memo and the blondish boy that had to be Tommy Wright stood up, practically at attention, when they saw me trot down the stairs into the

302

huge sunken living room.

I went to Memo first, hugging and pounding, Mexican style.

"Pancho! Pancho the Rammer?" I laughed. So did he, but I could tell that he disliked the nickname. He would know that I would also know that the whole idea was ridiculous, unless the pilot was a kamikaze or had a death wish.

"And you would be Major Tommy Wright."

"Yes, sir. Guilty."

"Thank you again for your kind letter about my son."

"I was sorry about Whitey—your son—and I am terribly sorry about your wife. This has been a bad time. It is rather as if the war just goes on and on."

"Yes. But now I think that it is over, now. Really over."

"Mom says—said," Elenita's voice cracked. "She said that now is the time to make a world congress work."

"Helen knew what should be done," I said, "because she always knew what was really happening, everywhere."

"Daddy. What will we do? I mean . . ." I stopped her with a Mexican hand signal—thumb and index finger tips nearly in contact— that means "just a second." I knew what she meant all right. They had located what was left of the plane, which was merely twisted, fused metal and ashes. There would be no body to mourn over, no ashes to scatter at sunset over the ocean.

"We could hold our own funeral services," I said. "I think that the ones she loved," I added quickly, for Elenita, "are here. We all have memories. Mine go back to another war, to a bright young reporter who sent the best of the war stories back from Paris and who, at times, would sneak a bottle of wine into someone's hospital room. I remember the young mother who took the kid's temperature in centigrade, then, when she used a formula to convert it into Fahrenheit, it was invariably a third higher, and it was full-speed to the hospital."

"I went twice," Elenita smiled. "Then Tell Dos bought one in Fahrenheit. She was always there when we were sick."

"And she stuck up for Jorge against you, Daddy. That was a brave thing to do." She said that defiantly.

"You are right. And so was Helen." Remembering how I had denigrated Jorge's father, shaming him in front of his own son, I added, "I would apologize to Jorge and his father today."

"Who was Jorge?" Tommy asked, glancing sideways at Elenita.

"I remember a beautiful young reporter in Puebla who had Will running in circles about the sugar mills," Johnny said.

"Damn near caught him too," I said.

"With a voice like a songbird," Johnny said.

"Yes," Tommy said. "When I talked to her in New York, by telephone, I called her Elena. I thought she was Elena. The voices were identical."

"Daddy," Elenita asked, crying again. "Do you ever get used to the past tense? She 'was,' and she 'did,' and she 'said.' "

"Yes, you do. I have. I do, and you will too."

"I know that my grandfather Cooper was killed in Chihuahua, but how did my grandmother die? You never told me how your mother died."

"Typhoid fever. It was a killer back then. She had a burning fever. All they could do was wrap her in wet sheets. I helped sprinkle water on them. I was ten years old. Dad told me to say goodbye, so I did. She knew me, she knew that she was dying and she wanted to go, but she whispered goodbye and I know that she meant to smile."

"Oh, Daddy. I cannot bear it."

"Would someone give me a drink?" I asked. Elenita ran to the bar and sloshed some whiskey into a glass. When she handed it to me, she leaned over and kissed my cheek. Her tears and mine mixed.

"Every single thing that lives has got to die," I said." When our loved ones go, we all die a little. We are all diminished. I would like to drink to my beloved wife, Helen. Goodbye."

Everyone echoed my goodbye and drank a toast with me.

"And now," I said, "Helen was Irish on her grandmother's side and told me many tales about Irish wakes. I think she liked them. At least her stories were always hilarious. I remember her quoting an uncle who defended the Irish wake, saying: 'If the dear one is on the road to heaven, why not celebrate? And if not, commiserate.' Drink up!"

We did. When Riley arrived from one of his mysterious secretive business meetings, we were laughing and talking loudly.

"Do you think it proper to behave as if you were at a cocktail party?" Will asked icily.

"Will, it's a wake. You know Helen was almost Irish. She is likely on her way to heaven right now," I said, holding my glass up high. "On her last flight."

"I had nothing to do with that!" Riley said angrily. "I begged her not to fly unless she felt she had to. I did!"

"Of course you did, Will. I was referring to her last flight the way I

304

would my own."

"Metaphorically," Elena said.

"Yes," I agreed. "We are all of us mortal birds. If in our mortal ambitions we fly too close to the sun, we get our tail feathers burnt."

"Right," Memo said. "With no tail feathers, off you go into a spin."

"I'll drink to that," Tommy said.

"Well, I will not!" Riley snapped.

"Come off it, Will," I said, using my cowboy accent. "Who was it at a party in Puebla sang a bunch of verses to Helen and me about the night that a certain Patrick Murphy died and they had to take the ice right off the corpse and put it on the beer."

"It was most certainly not I!" His mouth clamped into that lipless grimace that meant he could not be talked to, so I just shrugged. He spun around. Stiff-backed, he stomped up the stairs.

"We may not see Will for a while," I said, "unless he decides to throw the lot of us out."

I was wrong. He was back in five minutes, an affable, perfect caring host with a smile fixed on his face. "Sir," I said to him. "I know that you are not Will Riley, but you do one fine job of imitating him."

He touched the corner of his eye with a forefinger to signify my astuteness, then went to get another wine cooler for Elenita.

We decided to also say goodbye to the wars. We sang songs, and Riley joined right in. He had a pleasing tenor voice, singing so true to the melody that we let him carry some of the choruses by himself.

Tommy contributed one he had learned from an Eighth Air Corps bomber pilot.

> *Flack, Flack, Christ but there was Flack*
> *In the Ruhr, In the Ruhr*
> *My eyes are dim I cannot see.*
> *Flack bursts they are blinding me*
> *In the Ruhr. In the Ruhr.*
> *In the valley of the Ruhr.*

Johnny sang a few verses of the lovesick Mexican soldier who would chase the lovely Adelita wherever she might go, even if it meant using an armored train or a battleship. Memo taught us a Navy flyer's song, likely edited, I thought, for Elenita.

> *You can save those Goddamn Zeros*

For all those Goddamn heroes!
For I wanted wings until I got those goddamn things,
Now I don't want them anymore.

We sang a half a dozen verses of Memo's song, then Johnny and I harmonized on the funny, bawdy Mexican song advising the young girl, Marieta, not to be a flirty *coqueta,* until I noticed that Elenita was asleep, head on the armrest of her chair. Tommy sat at her feet, leaning against her legs, sitting upright, but also asleep. Johnny, suddenly looking young, smiled, then yawned. Will Riley lay on a couch, eyes closed, but I knew he was not asleep.

"I guess it is closing time," I said, "but before we go, I would like to recite something, almost a ritual in the old *Lafayette* squadron, a toast and a last drink for a lost pilot. It was melodramatic, but so were we. I think Helen would not mind." I held up my glass high as I recited easily from memory.

We meet 'neath the sounding rafters,
The walls around are bare.
They echo the peals of laughter
It seems the dead are there.
So stand by your glasses steady,
This is a world of lies.
Here's a toast to the dead already
Hurrah for the next that dies.

I drank, then flung my glass into the huge fireplace. The glass rang sweetly against the firebricks, but it did not break.

Chapter 40

· · · · · · · · · · · · · · · · · ✈

Tell Cooper

Toña asked me to see her at her home. It was a strange, cryptic message delivered by Memo just before he left on his first official flight as a copilot for TIA.

"Mama wants you to come and see her tonight at seven. She says it is of concern to both of you and begs you to be there."

"Begs?"

Memo shrugged.

"She must be kidding," I said, "but I'll be there."

"Thanks, major. But she was dead serious."

"Okay, and Memo—"

He stopped at the doorway.

"When you get back from Monterrey tomorrow, stop by. I want to talk to you about Tommy."

"Sure, major, but Tommy doesn't need any help. He is good. Very good. He likes to fly these trucks."

I did not dispute his opinion of our airplanes. It is difficult to switch from saddle to plow horse. The former Spitfire pilot, Tommy Wright, had adjusted better than Memo. He was right, but I did not want to talk to him about Tommy's flying skills. I wanted to find out what was going on between Tommy and Elenita. They had been seeing each other for well over a year now and they were not even formally engaged. A Mexican father would have shot him by now.

But all I said was: "Just see me before you go home. Okay?"

"Roger, wilco and out." He threw me a two-fingered salute and left whistling. First commercial flight and not a twitch in his whole nervous system.

Big Memo, who was half the size of Little Memo, caught me staring after the boy, smiling.

"That *tocayo* of mine, he is some boy, eh?"

"He is."

"He'll be running this company one of these days."

"You think I'm getting too old to run it?" I said, pretending anger to hide a real irritation.

"Not yet, boss. But you don't get any younger. Not like Toña. She looks better every time I see her. *Ay*, what a gal!"

"How did you know I was going to see Toña tonight?" I knew how, all right. He had large ears and excellent hearing, while I was beginning to talk louder just so that I could hear my own voice. "Show some respect, or I'll report you to her."

"If you don't, then I won't tell her you sent her son off to Monterrey so he wouldn't be home tonight."

"Out!" I pointed. He left, a little fat man, who somehow mimed perfectly the lanky walk of his namesake. He even whistled the same tune with the same variations. I broke out in laughter, all of my ire at the aging process dissipated.

I reread the bottom line of the yearly financial statement for TIA. Although our cash flow was a bit weak because of our recent acquisition of aircraft, I had become, on paper, a wealthy man. An engine suddenly revved up inside the hangar. I clapped my hands over my ears, leaned back in my chair and shut my eyes. The noise faded and became a melody of fast water on a rocky streambed. I was twelve years old, riding along a deer trail somewhere in the western Sierra Madre, following a trout stream. My father led; I rode behind him with the three *vaqueros* he had contracted to help us drive cattle back to Texas. They would eat, sleep and work with us until we drove the cows into Texas, crossing the river that the Americans call the Rio Grande, but the Mexicans know as the *Río Bravo*.

Maybe, now that I could afford it, I would buy a small ranch, one that would not be subject to confiscation, up north in the state of Chihuahua or Sonora. A quiet place in the mountains with an ice-cold stream racing through it. A big enough level area to land a small plane on. A place to hunt mule deer or wild turkey. Maybe Little Memo would like to learn to ride, tie a diamond hitch on a pack mule, and dress out a buck. The desk telephone finally penetrated my daydream. It had a harsh ominous sound even when I was happy. Our banker, Samuel Suárez, was on the line.

He began talking so fast that I had trouble following him. "Hold on, Sam. Slow down and tell me again."

"Do not sign any documents of any kind until I get there!"

"What? Why?"

"I will explain it all to you personally. Not on the telephone. I will be there in a half an hour. Leaving now."

"Sam, what in the name of . . ." There was a click. I was talking to a dead line. I laughed and wondered what comma had been misplaced on what document. But when Sam did not show up in a half an hour, I was worried. He was the one Mexican businessman who was always punctual.

Then Johnny Ávalos, usually the most courteous of men, walked past the frantic clucking of my secretary right into my office. His handshake was perfunctory and hurried. There was no abrazo and he waved away the offered brandy decanter impatiently.

"Good to see you too, Johnny," I said, grinning.

"I can save you, Tell, but not the company."

"Save me, Johnny?"

"I told you to sell, to get out."

"What the hell are you talking about?"

"CosaBanco has bought the Suárez Banks."

"Sam would never sell."

"His family would and did. He lost control and Will snapped it up. Now Will wants the airline. He does not want to hurt you. I have a contract that will keep you on as general manager and as minor stockholder—if you sell out to us, at book value, now."

Johnny was sweating. His skin was more gray than white, not a trace of brown. He would not meet my eyes.

"How could you take over TIA? We have a great balance sheet and I personally control fifty-one percent of the stock."

"You have no reserve capital. You cannot pay off the loan, and you are a foreigner."

"I do not need more cash than I have. The loan cannot be called in. I have a contract, and Elena Cooper Anderson, a Mexican citizen, owns more of the stock than I do."

"Tell," Johnny's voice broke, "Will controls a hundred politicians. Laws can be changed. Irregularities in your books will be discovered. Please, Tell. Look at the contract."

I read it. There was no provision for the others, but the terms were generous enough for me that I could have taken care of them out of my share. I thought of the ranch. Involuntarily, I touched the desk pen. "Sign it, Tell," Johnny urged, his eyes meeting mine for the first time.

Why not? I thought. And then Big Memo called from outside the door in one of his hoarse whispers that could be heard above the blast of a 2,000-horsepower radial motor.

"Boss, they killed the Señor Samuel Suárez."

"They?" I said loudly.

"The radio said it was an accident," Big Memo said contemptuously. "He was hit by a taxi when he was getting into his car."

"That is not the Toad's style and it doesn't sound like the Stiletto. Who is doing Will's dirty work now, Johnny?"

He slumped back into a chair, clawing at his shirt, struggling to breathe. In the time it took for me to move around my desk to him, he had managed to snatch a pill from his handkerchief pocket and pop it into his mouth. He sat still for a long minute. Then, breathing easier, said, "Sign it, Tell. Make it easier for me—and safer for you and Toña and Memo."

"Memo . . .?"

"Just sign it, Tell," he said quickly. "Sign the contract."

I threw the contract in his lap. "Give it back to Riley. He can use it to wipe his ass."

"I knew it. I knew it would be like this. I tried to tell him. I really did try."

He pushed himself up out of the chair and with the crumpled contract in one hand walked out. An old man who likely thought that he had lost his last friend; maybe he had.

"What was that all about?" Big Memo asked.

"I don't know, except that Johnny Ávalos says that Riley has threatened me and you and even Toña."

"Yes," I confirmed, feeling as puzzled as he was.

"I still got that old .38-20," he said thoughtfully. "I'll have to buy a new holster. It won't fit inside my belt no more."

"Do that. And stay away from dark corners and lighted windows."

"You too, boss." I nodded agreement.

And so it was that when I pulled up in front of Toña's house, I was carrying the old Frontier Colt my dad had given to me. The holster was stiff with age and the pistol seemed to have grown. I was driving one of the new Chevrolet coupes assembled in Mexico. The steering wheel was too close to my belly, so the holster and pistol scraped on it as I slid out. I wondered how I had ever thought the pistol comfortable.

Toña answered the door. I opened my arms, hoping for an abrazo, but all I got was a quick handshake. I handed her a bottle of Viuda de Clicquot. "Would you have the maid put this on ice?"

"Sure. Thanks, Tell, but the maid tonight is me. I sent Luz away for the night. No distractions. I want to talk to you, man-to-man."

I laughed. One of the sexiest women in the world wanted to talk to me, man-to-man. But Toña did not even smile. Likely she saw nothing to laugh at. She had lived in a man's world for so long that she often talked just like one.

"Okay," I said, still trying for a smile, "but could this half of that conversation have a drink while we talk?"

"Why not? While we wait for the champagne to cool, I will bring you tequila, salt and *limón*. Yes?"

She brought a tray from the kitchen, setting it on a coffee table placed between two chairs. We sucked on a lime, threw down a shot of amber tequila, and each of us touched our tongue to salt stuck on a wet spot between thumb and forefinger. Then we sat back. She spoke first.

"You got my note about Helen?"

"Yes. I didn't answer. I didn't answer any of the notes. What was there to say?"

"There was no need to answer. But Helen is gone, and because of that, I have something to tell you."

"Go ahead."

She looked away and asked, "Have you heard about the banker, Suárez?"

"Yes." I told her about his call to me and about the threat that Johnny Ávalos passed on to me from Riley.

"He said Memo too?"

"Yes. And Memo only has ten shares in the company. Paco has thirty and he didn't even mention his name."

"And he named me?"

"Yes. Now why would he name you?"

"Something else happened today. After twenty-five years they discovered that I am a female, so they fired me. Maybe one of those clerks saw me use the women's bathroom."

"You were never really in the army, were you, Toña? I mean there was never an official Lieutenant Canela, was there?"

"No. But for a while, I thought there was. I believed in the Revolution. Then Obregón got me a man's job in the bureau and for a while we tried. Some of us really tried."

"How did it happen? When I first met you, everyone was out to do away with the old corrupt Mexico. What happened?"

"I don't know, Tell. I wish I did. One day all of the *políticos* began to make the same speeches about working together to build a strong Mexico where no one would ever go hungry again, and all the while they were stealing. Every year they stole more and finally these thieves stole the Revolution away from us."

"Like Riley?"

"He is only one of the bigger thieves. Just one of the shameless ones on top of a pyramid of completely corrupt *políticos*."

"Hold on, Toña, there are some honest—"

"It is true," she interrupted. "They think they deserve a lot, so they steal a lot. But they are exactly no more than greedy thieves!"

She lifted a large manila envelope from the table and shook some photographs out. I picked up one that was a bit yellow at the edges. It was Toña laughing into the camera. She has not changed much, I thought. A streak of white in her hair and a bit thicker in legs and hips. Still a beautiful woman.

"You have not changed," I said, showing her the picture.

"Neither have you, Tell. Look." She drew out one of the old pictures.

"Was I ever that young?" I said, looking at the snapshot of a very young pilot, face burned dark by the sun. She had taken good care of that photograph. It might have been taken a few days ago. Something about the helmet puzzled me.

"Where did I get a yellow cloth helmet? I always wore leather. And earphones? I never flew an open plane with a radio."

"Let me see." She took the photograph.

"Wrong one. Here."

"Yes," I said, studying the old, cracked photograph. "I'm standing in front of that old Meyers. Remember?"

She nodded, but did not speak.

"Let me see that other one," I said. She gave it back to me. I looked at it carefully. I could see part of what appeared to be a gull wing and two blades of what had to be a three-bladed propeller.

"That looks to be a modern fighter plane."

"It is. It is an F6F."

"A Hellcat. The kind that Memo flew in the Pacific?"

"Yes."

"Por Dios," I said. "Imagine that. I thought for a bit that it was me. Of course, now that I look at it carefully, I can see it is Memo. He is a good-looking boy, nothing at all like—"

"Tell." Her eyes glinted like wet obsidian. One single tear followed the curve of her high cheek bone. "He does look like you. So much that Johnny knew. And big Memo knew right away. Even Helen knew."

"Helen knew?" I asked. "Knew what?"

"¡*Idiota!* Memo is your son, Tell. You are his father."

"Memo is my son?" Deep inside I knew, but I could not bring the thought out from the dark into the light. "But why didn't you tell me? I mean, before I married Helen?"

"I was not sure that you were the father. I had other men, the way you did women. Then you married, and it was too late."

What would I have done, I wondered, had I been the woman and found myself pregnant. Might I have been as honest as Toña?

"How did Helen find out?" I asked, numbly.

"She knew, that day at the airport, when I got sick. You thought I was airsick, but Helen knew. Of course, she did not know you were the father until Memo went to the American School. Then she knew right away. Of course, I did, too, then. And that is why I took him out of the school. The real reason. You had a family, two children, and a wife that you loved and she loved you. I did not want to hurt any of you. But now . . ."

"But now," I said, finally able to deal with the new role, "we both have hostages to fate, Elenita and Memo. But Will did not mention Elenita. Why?"

"I think it is because he has no affection for his own girl or the son. His legal son, living in a homosexual community in Chicago, is not even his. He values a male heir, but has none. He places no value on his blood daughter, Sofía. Maybe Elena is safe because he does not place a value on her."

"Then Riley was talking about Little Memo, our son," I said. I felt tears in my eyes instantly as the face of Tell Dos flashed in my mind. I turned my head away. "I'll tell Big Memo to stop packing his gun," I said. "It's Little Memo they threaten."

"Riley might kill our son Memo."

"I'll find a way to stop Will Riley. There must be a way. If Johnny would only stand up to Riley—"

"Johnny cannot. He might have been so different if he had not met Riley," she said sadly.

"I thought that *he* was Memo's father," I said, but then added hastily, "Only when I heard you had the baby. He never looked like Johnny."

"Johnny never sleeps with girls. He doesn't even try any more."

I almost said aloud, but did not: *But he slept with you that night. I saw you go into the house and turn the lights off.* What I said was: "What do you mean, *not with girls?*"

313

"He is a *maricón*, a homosexual. He can't get it up with girls."

My face burned.

"I do not mean to embarrass you, Tell, but I grew up with soldiers, and you know how we talk."

I nodded agreement. I knew all right.

"But about that first night in Mexico City," I said. "I had just got in from Puebla. I was going to stay with you, but I got there just as you drove up with Johnny. He went in with you, and then the lights went out."

"And you never even knocked?"

"No. I never did." I could not bring myself to tell her how I had huddled in agony in the dark, feeding on my own pain.

"Johnny was my friend," Toña said. "He still tries to be. He came then to talk to me about his problems with his lover. He was ashamed for me to see him and put out the light. Poor Johnny was in love with Riley's big movie star, Raúl Camargo."

"Raúl Camargo, the most macho of all the Mexicans!"

"That's the one. He would screw anything, male or female, ducks or goats, but he loved only *Raúl*."

"And Johnny loved him?"

"Yes."

"Camargo was killed in a plane crash, ten years ago?"

"He was. Just after he signed a contract to film with Hollywood Artist's Corporation. Riley was furious."

"You think that Riley had something to do with the crash?"

"Johnny thought so. But then later, he would not even talk about it. God knows what Riley threatened him with."

"Helen died in a plane crash," I said. "In a plane chartered by Riley."

"Camargo's plane belonged to Riley's studio."

"The book! Helen was carrying a manuscript of *Riley's Golden Ear* for him to read. He said that he merely wanted to edit a few minor things. Evidently Helen believed him."

"Why wasn't the book published?"

"She had a publisher. But she was revising the final draft. She would rewrite, changing the original, and copy as she wrote. But Helen always kept a copy. She was terrified that she might one day do as Lawrence had done with *Seven Pillars of Wisdom*: lose the only manuscript of her best work and then have to write it all one more time."

"Maybe," Toña suggested, "Riley wanted to buy both original and copy. Then erase everything."

"Or maybe he just wanted them and Helen on that same doomed airplane."

"If he caused Helen's death, he's a dead man."

"We have no proof, Tell. Besides, if a murder was committed in a foreign country, he would have to be extradited. Riley is an extremely wealthy Mexican citizen. You could never convince a court to deliver him to the gringos."

"All we have to do is to convince one man," I said.

"Who?"

"Me." I poured tequila for both and drank mine.

"Us," Toña said, and she drank hers.

"I had an offer a few days ago that even Riley does not know about yet. From an American company with enough money to fight Riley, and they are wired in to the new president. I think that we will sell the company to them."

"But then what will you do?"

"I'll become a detective. I'll have just the one client, one suspect and one judge. No jury."

"Right," Toña said enthusiastically. "We will give the *cabrón* a quick trial and then shoot him."

"We?"

"Sure. You and me."

We? Why not? Once the airlines were sold he would have no reason to harm our children or us. I would have plenty of money to buy information and hire investigators. We could move up to a ranch in Sonora. Old Rodolfo Hernández still ran the state, politically. He was probably up there right now, roping and branding his own cows. But where would we start? If I only had a copy of Helen's manuscript or even her notes, I could smoke him out. Or could I?

"Goddamn it all to hell anyway!" I yelled, frustrated.

"What is the goddamn for?" Toña said in accented but clear English.

"I will be double-damned. Where did you learn to speak English?"

"When Memo went to the American School, so did I. But I went to the one for adults to learn English. So, why the goddamn?"

"I thought that if I could publish the book it would not only bring Riley running into a trap, but it also might hurt him more than a bullet—not that he won't get that too."

"Let's do it. You know a lot about Riley. So do I."

"Maybe Johnny will still talk to me if I am careful. I am not a writer," I said, "but it is a place to start. Maybe we can hire a good

315

writer."

"Also," she said, peeking at me out of the corners of her eyes, "I am very good at typing, flying and fooking."

She could always make me blush and I obliged her, but I also gathered her into my arms.

Her body flowed willingly against mine. All of the soft yet firm curves were still there. So was that elusive mixture of perfume and Toña that had so aroused me before. My right hand slid down onto her hip, then lower, under her dress and back up along the warm thigh. Our lips tasted of lime. We both, as if by mutual consent, drew back slightly to breathe.

Somehow she managed to wriggle out of her clothes. I threw my coat across the room. My shirt covered the coffee table. I was not sure that my boots would come off one-handed, but I tried. The left boot would not. She giggled. I guess I grinned, sat down on her rickety willow couch and tried both hands. No! I wrenched at the boot savagely.

"Wait a second, Tell." Toña stepped over my extended leg, her round, brown buttocks bouncing in front of me, and wrapped her arms around the boot.

"Okay, cowboy. Remember how? Push!"

And push I did. I placed the toe of my right boot on one delectable quivering buttock, and she took two quick steps forward, my boot in her hands. The other came off easier, but the feel of my barely covered foot against her pumped more blood into my tool. So much that it was painful. I stood up and tried to slide out of my pants. They would not slide.

"You have to unbuckle first, if you want to get your pantaloons down past Mount Popo."

I felt as hot and large, at that second, as the volcano that Mexicans affectionately call Popo. I unbuckled, unbuttoned and threw the offending garment against the far wall. I then picked up that squirming, hot and fragrant body and walked toward the hall.

"Take the first door to the left, cowboy," Toña said, still speaking English.

I meant to tell her how well she spoke, but all that came out was a growl. It might have been an English one.

316

Chapter 41

Memo Canela

"But why Mexico City College? Why not the National University?"

"Because I have decided to write in English. I want to write fact, not fiction, and, in Mexico, that is impossible."

"Difficult, yes. Impossible, no."

"What newspaper or magazine can print a truth critical of an important politician and not lose its import permit for newsprint?"

"There are pamphlets, word of mouth, even bare walls."

"That is all right for, you, Jorge. But I am—want to be—a writer."

"You are a writer. You had a story published in a magazine. That makes you a writer."

"I got paid for a story about a nervous bull that killed a sick old circus lion out at the bull ring in the state of Mexico. That does not make me a writer. But you, Jorge. You are a *político*. Secretary of a governor. One day you will be a governor. Maybe a cabinet minister or even a president. But not an honest one."

"Are you calling me a crook?"

"Don't be so touchy, Jorge. You sound like my mother when she talks about the Revolution."

"And you talk like your gringo father. There is a Mexican-hater."

"Is that why he lives here and married a Mexican?"

"It means nothing. I saw what he did to my own father. I could have killed him then. Did you know that I spared the life of that great gunfighter, Major Cooper?"

"Yes. He told me. He would not do that now."

"Not to me he would not!"

"And you are the Jorge Rubio who wants to pay court to my half-sister, the daughter of the evil major?"

He laughed then. A deep gurgling laugh with not a trace of malice. When he was angry, his eyebrows touched and his thick, curly hair bristled, like that of a German shepherd. But when he was happy, he was a chubby, grinning beagle. "Okay. Point taken. How about Elena?"

"Another beer?" He nodded assent. I waved at Juan, once a distinguished scholar in Spain who now eked out a living from his little restaurant-bar catering to American students. He sent his twelve-year-old son over with two bottles of amber-colored Victoria beer. It was cheap and surprisingly good.

"Why do you drink this bricklayer's beer?"

"You, the great Marxist, ask me, the gringo capitalist, why I drink proletarian beer? I will tell you. It tastes good."

Jorge exploded with laughter. "I'll drink to that," he said, and we clinked bottles.

"About Elena?" Jorge asked again.

"Tommy is moving back to the States. He is a vice president in the new company. But no more flying," I added sadly.

"Good. Then it is really over?"

"I don't fly much any more, either. I can't afford an airplane of my own."

"Is it over, *cabrón?*" he said loudly enough to turn the heads of those who understood the epithet.

"No," I said seriously. "I may go back to flying if I don't get a writing job."

"Memo, you really are a *cabrón,*" he said sadly. "If you knew how I felt about Elena, you would not play games with me."

"I am sorry, Jorge," I said, thinking of the young redhead woman from Indiana who had just joined the college's creative writing seminar. "I know how you feel."

"Like hell you do. Now, when can I see your sister?"

"Depends on the major."

"How on the major?"

"He has to give his okay."

"*¡Me cago en diez!*" It was an awful curse, usually used in its pure form only by an anticlerical Spanish refugee. Jorge, for all of his Marxist philosophy, did not have the nerve to combine scatology and God—so he used the euphemistic *diez* in place of *Dios,* or God.

"Don't give up the ship," I said.

"What ship?"

"An expression I picked up in the Navy. I mean that you still have a chance."

"Me? Jorge Rubio Montejo, Mexican politician?"

"The major likes me. He likes Elena."

"So what? Everyone likes Elena. Everyone loves Elena!"

"Well, I like you. Even Elenita seems to have a small bit of esteem for you. Ergo, the major must also, at least, tolerate you."

318

"Memo, the only time I ever met the major we damn near shot each other."

"The major is giving a Thanksgiving party—a gringo holiday to sell turkeys—for the family and a few close friends. I invite you."

His eyes brightened, then clouded. "No, it will not work. He will either run me off or shoot me."

"He may not talk to you, but he doesn't shoot people any more."

"Neither does my father," he said defensively. "I could never shoot anything. Except maybe in the new revolution. Then, maybe."

"New revolution?" I had not heard that from Jorge before.

"If we cannot change the party inside, we will have to do it outside."

"An interesting thought," I said. "But what about the party? I have the loan of a Tri-Pacer. I'll fly you up and back. It will only be a long weekend."

"I don't know. The governor needs a speech for next Tuesday."

"Elena will be flying up with me," I said. "It is a two-hour trip."

"Two whole hours! Of course I'll go."

The new airport was huge. Flights came in daily from all over the world. All of the longer flights from the States were using the big four-motor Douglas airliners that we called C-54s in the Navy.

The cab dropped us at the new TIA hangar. I begged a ride out to the Tri-Pacer from one of the old mechanics who had stayed on. Elenita was standing there, by the airplane, waiting. Jorge paled, then got out of the car slowly. He waited, watching, while I kissed Elenita on the cheek. Then he only shook hands, and carefully, calling her Señorita Cooper. They both decided to use the formal *usted* with each other, but then with me they had to switch to *tú* and use the corresponding verb form. They switched back and forth, getting all mixed up until they were speaking familiarly to each other, but formally to me—and I howled with laughter.

I was still laughing when we taxied out onto the lateral, but they were both mad at me, refusing to talk to me at all.

I had filed a flight plan showing the airport at Hermosillo as the alternate and nearest to my destination at the ranch. Of course the people at the tower all knew me, so I had to hear all of the old jokes again, even the one about Pancho the Pilot washing his hands of the Zeros.

"Okay," the tower finally cleared me. "Takeoff on runway three two zero." They flashed a green light. I acknowledged, swung out onto the runway, checked both magnetos and pushed the throttle forward. On the climb up to ten thousand feet, I established my drift and the true wind, then set a course to the ranch. I set the radio directional finder on a station in the city of Hermosillo, leveled off, and cut the power back to cruising. The noise level was reduced so dramatically that Elenita's voice rang out like a bell.

"You never ever wrote. Not once!"

"I did. I tell you I did!"

I put my earphones back on. After a while, their lips stopped moving. Elenita, sitting alone in back, looked stonily out of the starboard window.

"Rough weather ahead," I said. "Check your seat belts." Jorge looked at me as if to say, "who cares," but he tightened the straps. I glanced at Elenita; she was strapped in just as tightly.

For the uninitiated, a spin is a violent acrobatic maneuver. A snap roll is nothing more than a horizontal spin. To avoid losing altitude, I snapped us through a two- or three-second roll.

Elena screamed. Jorge's mouth opened as if he wanted to yell, but could not find the necessary air.

I came out exactly on course, and within fifty feet of my altitude.

"Pretty good," I said, "for a man who has not been flying much and is in a borrowed airplane."

"Memo, you are a *cabrón!*" Elenita said. It was the worst swear word she ever used. When I glanced back, my eyebrows arched in pretended shock, she took a swing at me, but the belt held her back, so her little fist was a foot short of my chin.

Her doll face looked more like that poisonous little caterpillar with blue eyes that we call "baby face" than my sweet little sister.

"Señorita Elena," Jorge was aghast. "*Tú*—I mean, *usted*—you said a bad word."

"I said my brother is a *cabrón*, and he is, and *tú*, *Jorgito*, also."

"He is a *ca* ... what you said. But a sweet, lovely girl like you should not use that kind of language."

I laughed loudly, then cowered as she menaced again with her small fist.

"Do not strike the pilot," I said, "for he is fragile and might break and then what would you earth-bound creatures do?"

"I may not be a pilot," Elenita said, "but I can tell the difference between a snap-roll and rough air, and so can *Jorgito*."

"Right, *Elenita*," Jorge said.

320

It hurt me to contain the laughter, but I did. They were both speaking *tú* and using the diminutive, affectionate forms of their names. However, I suppose that my mouth must have twitched, which Elenita observed.

"You are not as terribly clever as you think, Memo." I glanced at Elena. She was glaring, angry again. But then Jorge groaned, and she turned to him, her voice anxious.

"*Jorgito*, what is it?"

His face was as pale as that of Elenita, and his eyes were glazed over. I knew immediately both the problem—and the solution.

"Window!" I yelled. "Open your window. Wide, and stick your head out."

One hand held tightly over his mouth, Jorge opened the window. I put the plane into a skid as cold air rushed in. Within a minute, color washed back into his face. When he took his hand away, he noticed Elenita shivering, so he slid the window almost shut. He rode that way, like a dog in a car, with his nose next to the incoming air, until I spotted the pasture and the tall, peeled pine with a scarlet windsock billowing strongly enough to indicate a twenty-knot wind.

A *vaquero*, dressed northern or Texas style, stood up in the stirrups and waved his hat. He then cleared the field of cows.

I came in, Navy style, in a half-circle approach. If you are too high, widen the circle and take more altitude and time away from your approach. Too low? Tighten the circle, shorten the distance, and, if you must, put a wing down and slip away the extra altitude.

I landed opposite a new structure, a stick-and-adobe hangar by the look of it. When I was able to turn to head for it, the *vaquero* was there, waiting. When I could see him clearly, I opened my window and waved. He was a real Texas cowboy, one leg hooked over his saddle horn, smoking a long, thin cigar—the major himself.

Elenita was out before the propeller stopped turning, running up to the major. He reached down and one-handed lifted her up to sit in front of him as he slid back over the cantle.

I swung the plane around, facing the wind, and cut the motor. I slid out, walking quickly over to squint up against the setting sun. How strong my father is, I thought, then said, "You look to be in good health, major."

"You too, Memo." He held a hand down for me to squeeze.

Jorge stood back by the door, half-hidden by the airplane.

"Come over here," I called, "and say hello to the major."

"You remember Jorge Rubio Montejo?"

"Yes," he said pleasantly. "I do." He looked straight at Jorge and smiled as he said, "I won't shoot if you don't."

Jorge managed a sickly smile and nodded.

"He means he won't shoot," I said.

Jorge walked over, extending his hand.

"My mother will be pleased. She does like firecrackers, but not gunshots."

"Daddy," Elenita said, "why isn't Toña here?"

"She is preparing Thanksgiving dinner."

"I thought we were having that tomorrow," I said.

"It is not a traditional meal. She is busy making the *mole* sauce for the turkey tomorrow. *Pavo con mole poblano*."

"For Thanksgiving!" Elenita wailed. She liked the thick, spicy chocolate sauce, but my sister, I was finding out, was a traditionalist.

"I shot two young turkeys," the major said. "One is for mole and the other for stuffing and cranberries."

"Great," I said. "I'll have both."

A jeep drove up and braked. A tall, dark-complexioned boy who might have been a Tarahumara Indian—he had the cheekbones for it—jumped out and walked quickly over to stand in front of the major. He glanced at the rest of us only from the sides and briefly.

"Shall I load the *equipaje* of the señores, major?"

"Yes, Beto. But first I must introduce you to my daughter, Elena; our friend Jorge; and my son, Pancho."

"Pancho?" I said. He never called me Pancho.

"Jorge Rubio Montejo, at your orders," Jorge said.

"Pardon me," the major said, "This young man is Roberto Hernández Carreto, nephew of my old friend, General Rodolfo Hernández."

Roberto shook hands with the others, but he took my hand and kept it. "You are the famous Mexican fighter pilot, Pancho the Rammer. I read a book about you."

My God, I thought. He had read that awful pack of lies printed as a comic book.

"My name is Guillermo Canela," I said.

"Yes, I know the other name. But everyone around here knows who you are. This is the Rancho Pancho and our brand is RP. You are famous here in the Sierras and also in the lowlands, on the coast."

The major, sensing my embarrassment, sent the boy to tie the plane down and to gather up our luggage.

"Enjoy your fame while you can," he said. "One of these days you will look into the mirror and you will see a face that is only vaguely familiar. It might be that of an uncle or an old friend. But it will not be yours, and there will be no more boys to ask you how you shot down all of those airplanes."

"Is that what happens, major?" I asked, not feeling much older at thirty than I had at twenty-two when the war had ended.

"Yes, Pancho. That is what happens."

"Pancho?" I said, with a touch of distaste.

"Do you mind? Beto has talked of nothing else than meeting his hero, Pancho."

"No," I said, "not really."

On the way to the ranch house, Roberto asked me to call him Beto, but insisted on addressing me as *Don* Pancho. Then, obviously nervous, he tried to talk, using both hands of course. As a result, we were almost wiped out twice, while the major, with Elenita balanced precariously with a leg around the horn and riding sidesaddle, loped by, easily beating us to the house.

Mama came running out of the kitchen, yelling and waving a large, chocolate-covered spoon. I got an *abrazo*, plus a brown stripe on my shirt at the same time. Elenita wisely held her wrist with one hand when they kissed. Only then did Mama extend a hand, reluctantly, it seemed to me, to Jorge.

"I have heard my father speak of you, Señora Cooper," Jorge said. "You are, I believe, *paisanos*."

"We are both from Tabasco, but I left the state behind. Your father still carries Tabasco and that old red shirt with him wherever he goes."

"Why, yes," Jorge said, puzzled. "He still has a red shirt from the Revolution. How did you know?"

"I just knew," she said, taking the major by the arm and steering him into a large room with a high, bare-raftered roof, a huge fireplace and a dozen deerskin-covered *equipal* chairs that looked like half-finished drums.

"Everyone into the big room," Mama ordered. "The men will have time for a drink of tequila before dinner. The women will have time for two."

Jorge caught my arm as we tagged along behind them and whispered hoarsely: "Your mother does not like me. I thought that she would. My mother said that she would."

"What did your mother say?"

"She said that my father and your mother were in the army together in Tabasco and then Puebla and that they were . . . ah, very good friends so she should like his son. Me."

I smiled at that logic from Mexico's most famous and sexiest actress. Lilly might have played the role of a Revolution-era *soldadera* woman a dozen times in Riley's films, but she would never understand that small but iron-willed woman who was my mother.

"Stay calm. She'll like you. You both are fuzzy-thinking rebels."

"Fuzzy-thinking rebels!" Jorge echoed, but using his deep, political "speechy" voice.

"Hey, *Jorgito*," my sister intervened. "Make me a martini. You used to be an expert, remember?"

"I was?" Jorge said, surprised.

"Of course. You were almost eighteen years old. You had to be."

"I prefer tequila or whiskey," the major said. "The only time I ever saw Will Riley so drunk that he admitted any weakness was after he had put away five martinis—about a fifth of his body weight."

"Riley had a weakness?" I asked. "What did he do, forget to foreclose on a crippled widow?"

The major smiled and his eyes softened the way they did when he reminisced. "Once we were at the old International . . . ah . . . bar, and he admitted to the terrible sin of being frightened from looking into the wrong end of a Colt .45-caliber revolver."

"He would not have to be drunk to admit that," Jorge said. "Only an idiot would not be afraid."

"Riley had to be drunk," the major said. "He also told one of the girls—waitresses—that he was the legitimate illegitimate grandson of the Irish Pope."

"So the great Willard Riley is just another bastard," I said, unthinking, and then heard my words echoing painfully in my brain. My mother cocked her head at me, her jaw set in that angry thrust. My father's whole face sagged. I knew that I had likely made what my Psychology I professor called a Freudian slip.

"I could shoot myself," I said, not entirely in jest.

"Not necessary," Jorge said so quickly that I wondered if he also might have been born out of wedlock. It had never bothered me consciously, for my fictional father had been a hero of the Revolution, and my factual one had been a hero to me before I had even known he was my father.

"I will save you the trouble, Memo. I shall prepare you one of my world-famous martinis made with five parts gin, one part dry vermouth, and," Jorge grinned wickedly, "a tot of white tequila, garnished with an olive aged and pickled with the hottest of peppers."

Nervous laughter followed. The major looked worried.

"Who was the Irish Pope?" Elenita asked.

"Will—Riley—said that he was sworn to secrecy, and then he went to sleep," the major said, "so I never found out."

The laughter was easier now. Once the drinks were dealt out like so many cards, we talked easier, although Mama and Jorge used words the way two fencing masters might use the points of their epees to probe each other's defenses.

The major put away two tequilas before I was half through with my martini. He held the third up for a toast.

"To my lovely wife, Toña," he said, bowing, "and to my equally lovely daughter, Elenita, and her friend—who, I hope, will be mine as well—and to my true and legitimate son, Memo Cooper Canela."

"Memo Cooper," I said, startling myself. I had not meant to speak aloud.

"And to his ranch, the Rancho Pancho!"

Elenita made a face. "I told you, Daddy, I cannot stand that name. It sounds like the Rancho Raunchy."

"My ranch?" I turned to Elenita. "What are you talking about?"

"Your ranch, of course. I thought you should have it, but the name stinks."

"Are you trying to tell me that the ranch is mine?"

"Yes. Of course. It is true. You are the legal son and heir, along with your charming sister, to the family fortune, but you are also the sole owner of this rock-covered mountain side."

"*Por Dios*," I said.

"Rancho Raunchy," the major said. "My God, she's right. What would you call it, Memo?"

"The brand is registered, and I assume all of the stock is branded RP?"

"Yes. The whole *remuda* of five horses and the entire cattle herd of three," Mama said.

"Well," I mused for a few seconds, and then, looking at the two of them standing closely, touching, I said, "I will allow the two of you to stay on if you pay the taxes—and if we rename it . . ." I paused as I held my half-filled glass up, ". . . Rancho Paramor."

"Right on, brother," Elenita said, then nudging Jorge with one elbow, added, "That is a cool name. Love Ranch, sounds like a Nevada brothel."

My unflappable Mama let her jaw drop open.

I said, "I do not know, sister, never having been in a Nevada brothel."

Before Elenita could answer, there was a bang on our front door. The wiry nephew of General Hernández, bearing an old, battered green trunk on his back, called out: "*Patrón*, where should I put this?"

"That belongs to the señorita," I said, and then turned to Elenita, "That must weigh a ton. What is in it?"

The major pointed a finger down the hall. Beto followed the finger, moving slowly like a hermit crab whose stolen shell is too tight.

"It was sent by somebody that cleaned out Charley Goldberg's office," Elenita said. Looking at Jorge, she explained: "He was Mama's agent and he died just a few weeks after she did. But first it went to Grandpa's house in New York. The people that live there now found out where I live and sent it on to me. Then it took me weeks to get it out of customs. I finally had to pay the *aduana* agent a hundred pesos."

"What was in it?" Jorge asked, adding, "These days that is either an exorbitant tax or an immoderate bribe."

"Just old manuscripts."

"Then you should not have paid anything. It is an old, used trunk. There is no tariff on manuscripts or even on printed material."

"Then they let you look first?" Mama asked.

"Yes. They let me open it and look through."

"But then," the major asked, "why did you pay?"

She turned to her father. She was dry eyed, but I could hear the tears in her voice.

"I paid a bribe Daddy, because when I found that old notebook full of typed pages with notes scribbled in the margins, names and dates written by her hand, I could not bear to read more, nor haggle with the customs agent."

"But," I said, "you have letters from your mother. Why even bother with all that paper?"

"Because there is a gummed label stuck to the outside of that old canvas-backed notebook. Written on the label are three words: *Riley's Golden Ear*."

326

Chapter 42

· · · · · · · · · · · · · · · · · · ✈

Tell Cooper

I was both stunned and ashamed. Some six years had gone by in a flash while Toña and I had seen Paris and put the ranch together. I had hired private detectives. I still paid one monthly, even as I suspected that he was also on Riley's payroll. Every week or so I would open a large ledger with legal-sized ruled pages in it and write a few lines. Then I would set the ledger aside for another week. Now there is no excuse.

A few minutes ago, I was as happy as a man has a right to be. And now I am miserable. Helen is dead, likely murdered, and the man who must have given the order is alive and well. I am alone in my study. Except for the hissing of the gas lamp, it is quiet. The thick adobe walls keep out all sound and the evening chill. My old revolver hangs from its trigger guard on the wall. I use it sometimes, but not often, for a coyote, the wariest member of the canines.

When I do get a shot at a coyote, I close my eyes and see a black-and-white photograph of Will Riley. Then, superimposed on the photograph is the grinning face of a coyote. Rage wells up inside and blood washes the photograph from my vision. Then I yank the trigger and invariably miss.

I have glanced through the notebook. Helen wrote notes with such verve and style that many writers would have been satisfied with them as finished prose. I set aside the notebook, thick with over five hundred typed pages, and pick out a manila envelope from a shoebox full of odd-sized papers. When I open it, there is a handwritten document with official government stamps attached to it. It is dated September 15, 1945, at Chachalacas, Veracruz. It was a deposition by a Benjamin Jones.

My name is Benjamin Jones. Doctor Benjamin Jones. I am a legal immigrant with the classification of "inmigrado" and am now a resident of this village. I once lived in Puebla in the state of Puebla and it was there in 1920 that I was asked to perform a surgical separation of the left ear of William Willard Riley. It was a while after Carranza had been shot. Riley said that he would pay me five hundred pesos for the surgery, but all I ever got was a hundred pesos and a case of bad rum. I drank all of the rum and almost died. It might have been poisoned. I ran away to Veracruz and I almost died there. One newspaper even reported that a dentist named Jones had died from drink. I called to tell them that I certainly was not a dentist and that I was still alive.

That is why Señor Comonfort, who is a reporter for the newspaper, knew how to find me. I am no longer a drunk. I give people free medical care when the pharmaceutical salesmen will leave me samples, and, if they ask, I also help to resolve their disputes, as I am known as an honest, impartial judge. The village gives me a house and food. I have a good woman and I make my own rum. I am sorry I cut off Riley's ear. I would not do it again. Not even for a case of Kentucky rye whiskey.

It was signed by Jones and witnessed by the reporter, Gerardo Comonfort, and the priest, padre Juan García Del Valle. There were thumbprints by all of the signatures. Comonfort had taken no chances. Riley would play hell suing for defamation of character in the United States. And that is where we would get him. First, make the bastard suffer. Then I might teach him how to fly. Without an airplane.

Of course I remember Doc Jones, the town drunk. I had bought him dozens of drinks at the Tres Gaviotas bar. So had most of the other English-speaking residents of Puebla. He had told Johnny Ávalos that he was a graduate of the University of Texas. But when he heard my accent, he told me that he had received his medical degree from a new advanced medical center in Wyoming. He could talk convincingly about cows and horses. He might have been a veterinarian. I had thought of him as an old man, then, but I was only twenty-five when Will lost his ear. Doc Jones might have been fifty years old. That would make him close to eighty now, if he were still alive. I mean to find out.

I turned the gas valve off. With the document in my right hand, I walked back into the big living room. The sun was just then sinking behind the Sierra Madres, leaving the jagged peaks like black paper ripped from a purple sky. The others were standing by the big window, talking quietly. I joined them, placing my left arm around Toña. "Tell?" she asked, moving away slightly. "Why are you wearing the pistol?"

"I don't know," I said. I had no recollection of buckling on my ranch cartridge belt and holster.

"Look," I said, showing her the deposition. "It was old Doc Jones that did it."

"Did what?" Memo asked.

"Cut off Riley's ear. Helen was right. There never were any bandits. Riley kidnapped himself."

"That document is a forgery," Jorge said, his face contorted with rage. "Let me see it?"

He held his hand out. I hesitated, for it was one of a kind, but just then I saw Elenita look at the boy with such compassion, and then at me, begging me with her eyes, that I could not refuse. I handed him the document. His hands trembled as he read it. Then, with what effort I can only guess at, he gave it back to me.

"It appears genuine," he said, "but I do not think that my father knew of it."

"I am not interested in my old feud with your father. All that Memo and I will ever do, when he writes the book, is to print the truth about your father when it is relevant to Riley."

"But I must see the manuscript first!"

I must credit Jorge that when he realized what he had said, he had the grace to blush and add, "With, of course, your permission."

"What do you mean," my son asked, "when Memo writes the book?"

"You will do it, no? The notebook is really a rough draft with all of the margins full of notes. You could bring it up to date. Maybe Doc Jones is still alive in Chachalacas. You will do it, Memo. Please?"

"Yes, of course. I will try. I have read some of Helen Cooper's Mexican articles. We read two of them in class as examples of excellent factual writing. I will write it to the best of my ability and maintain her style and quality," he shrugged as he added, "if I can."

"I know," I said. "I know that this book will be published. I would like Helen's name on the cover."

"How about: By Helen Cooper and Guillermo Canela?" Elenita said.

"I was thinking of a book titled, *Riley's Golden Ear*, authored by Helen Anderson de Cooper and Guillermo Cooper Canela."

Memo smiled, but the boy is so perceptive that he waited for smiles from both Elenita and his mother before he spoke. Then all he said was,

"It is an honor, major."

"It is all right," Jorge said with just the trace of a smile, "unless you go into politics. No one will vote for a Mexican named Cooper."

Elenita squealed with delight. The hateful chore and, at least for the moment, the memories that it had evoked had been overcome. She bounced away from the window, twirled her skirt like a ballet dancer and, smiling all the while, wailed: "I am a poor and hungry girl. All I have had to eat was a horrid olive that made my lips burn."

I narrowed my eyes at her, patted the butt of my revolver, and said, "Tell the truth now, young lady. How many martinis have you had?"

Her laugh was a living echo of her mother.

"Hundreds. At least I have made hundreds. Mother taught me and she was critical. But," she glanced obliquely at Jorge, her eyes full of mischief—just as they had been many years before when she had handed me my flying gloves, each finger filled with writhing caterpillars—"if this was a martini," she said seriously, "then I have to tell you the truth. I have had only one real martini in my whole life."

"One is enough," Toña said. "Shall we eat?"

Chapter 43

· · · · · · · · · · · · · · · · · · ✈

Tell Cooper

The settlement of some thirty people, no more than a *ranchería*, was a day's ride from the ranch. Rodolfo Hernández, as erect in the saddle as a young man, led. I followed him, trailed by the rest of his *vaqueros*, six hard men all armed with Winchester carbines. It was midsummer, hot and dusty, but the sun would soon be down and the evenings in the high country are always cool. The women were already busily clapping out tortillas for the evening meal. The mixed odor of toasting corn tortillas and wood smoke turned the men's heads like hounds on a fresh trail.

"Be alert!" Rodolfo called out. "We have come here to kill a man, not to eat."

He reined in his sturdy mountain horse in front of a broken-down mud-and-stick hut. The only spot of color to be seen anywhere was a red *Carta Blanca* beer sign that was wired to a gnarled hunk of dead mesquite projecting from the shack. Rodolfo flipped the reins over the horse's head, dismounted and held the reins high for the nearest rider to take. I slid off my horse and tied it to a peeled-pole hitching rack on the other side of the shack. Tied there were two horses, both of them small and skinny.

"Everardo Peón! Come out and talk," Rodolfo said loudly enough to be heard throughout the *ranchería*. Of course they would have seen us filing down the mountainside an hour earlier.

Everyone in the settlement seemed to be standing off to one side, listening.

"We are armed!" A thin, reedy voice from inside the makeshift *cantina* warned.

"Do you want to talk first or just come out shooting?" Rodolfo lowered his voice.

"We will talk," a deep vibrant voice answered.

"Come out then. Without guns in hand."

Two men, one older than the other, but both old men, and a teenage boy stepped out, blinking into the sun, now a hand's width above the mountain spine.

The men carried revolvers in holsters set high on their hips, comfortable for riding, but awkward for a quick draw. The boy carried a small-caliber Smith and Wesson revolver thrust in the waistband of his pants. It was pearl-handled, the kind we used to call a lady's pistol.

"Who is called Everardo Peón?" Rodolfo asked. "The one that rode with Villa."

"I rode with Villa," the older man, frail with deeply wrinkled skin and a large, bone-white moustache, said proudly. "I was a Dorado."

"Every old soldier who has even heard of Villa always says he was a Dorado," Rodolfo said. "How do I know you even rode with Villa?"

Light flared in the old, dark eyes. He yelled, "Because I tell you so, *cabrón*," and went for his gun. So did Rodolfo. But they were much too late. My Colt was pointed at the old man's shirt. He stopped his draw with more than half of the pistol barrel still in the holster.

"Likely you lie," I said, hoping he would agree, and we could all ride back home.

"You say that with a cocked pistol in your hand," he said with no trace of fear.

I slipped my revolver back in its holster.

He squinted and cocked his head to see me better. I wondered if he were partially blind.

"Are you a gringo?" he asked without malice.

"Yes."

"I knew some gringos when I was a Dorado. One of them could make a machine gun sing. His name was Tom. Do you know him?"

"No, I do not."

"Maybe he got killed at Celaya. Do you think so?"

"Maybe. My name is Cooper. Did you ever know my father? His name was also Cooper."

"Sure, I did. Tom Cooper. He could make a machine gun sing!"

"Señores," the other old man said, "my brother is old and he does not remember. It is time that we go to my *jacal* and make ready for his trip back across the sierra to Chihuahua." He took a tentative step, stopped and said, "with your permission, señores." He took another tentative step, but then our silence stopped him, and he could not will himself to take one more step.

"Come on, *abuelo*." The young man spoke to his grandfather softly, but his eyes, fixed on me, were filled with pure hatred. "We do not have to stand here and listen to this crazy gringo."

"Yes, you do, boy," Rodolfo said. "We mean neither you nor your great uncle any harm, but we must hear your grandfather tell the story he told a few nights ago in this very *cantina*."

"You want to hear how we took Chihuahua!" His eyes brightened again. "You rode all the way here to hear about Chihuahua?"

"No. It was about your revolver."

"But it is the same as yours, I think. One of the new ones. The cylinder swings out and it cocks itself."

It would have been new some sixty years ago, I thought. "Would you allow me to inspect it?"

He drew himself up to his full height. When he was a young man he may have been over five feet tall. His age had taken away some of his stature, but none of his pride.

"I do not know about gringos, but a Mexican does not loan his pistol, nor his horse, nor his woman!"

I drew again, no faster than before, but showier. When I heard the hiss of surprise from the spectators, I flipped the pistol, caught the barrel and held it out to the old man, butt first.

"A real Dorado would take my pistol as hostage for the return of his own," I said. His thin chest expanded under the faded white-cotton shirt. He drew the heavy revolver slowly, but competently, spun it on the trigger guard and offered it to me, butt first.

We both flipped out the cylinders to check the loads. His, like mine, held a used cartridge under the hammer. I snapped the cylinder back in, careful to keep the hammer over the empty chamber, and then turned the long-barreled Colt over and saw what I had feared. Stamped into the metal just above the trigger guard were the letters, WTC.

"Read the letters above the trigger guard of my pistol." I pointed at the ones on my borrowed pistol.

"I can read," he said petulantly, but turned the revolver over to look. His mouth dropped open. He looked up at me, puzzled. "The letters are the same. I did not know that there was another one, twin to mine. I did not steal that pistol!"

"Then, how did you get it?"

"In a great battle. In Celaya, when we shot off the arm of General Obregón. Or maybe it was Guadalajara."

"Not Chihuahua?"

"Yes, maybe. I was in a great battle, and I killed a man and took his weapon. All I had before was an old, yellow Winchester with a split stock. After I won the pistol, my General Villa made me a Dorado."

He beamed at me. I was no longer an unmannerly gringo, but a *señor* who knew the mettle of an old Villista soldier.

"Last night," Rodolfo said, "you claimed you shot a tall gringo in Chihuahua and took his revolver. That one that the señor has in his hand. Do you deny what you said?"

"Deny. Of course not. If I said that, it must be true, but I think it was at Celaya."

"You shot the tall gringo at Celaya?"

"No. It was Obregón, I think."

"The gringo?" I prompted.

"No," the old man said, after thinking for a few seconds. "I think that Obregón is a Mexican."

"Was," I said. "He is dead now."

"Maybe. I would have to see for myself. They claim that Villa is dead too, but I think that he is just waiting for the right time to call us all together again, and then we will shoot all of the gringos—the white ones and the black ones and the yellow ones too."

"Look, old man," I said, deciding on the direct approach. "Did you meet a tall gringo driving cows north towards El Paso and shoot him for his pistol?"

"Sure," he said, looking straight at me, but his eyes were focused on something far beyond me. "I'll drive your cows to the border. When do we start?"

"No, Everardo," his brother said. "The señor does not want you to herd cows. He looks for the man who shot his father and took that pistol."

"Oh," Everardo said, sliding my revolver into his holster. "Too bad. It is hard to get a job when you are old."

"He must be the one, Tell," Rodolfo said.

"Sure," his *segundo* said loudly, "*Don* Rodolfo is right. Let's shoot the old *cabrón* and go home."

A couple of the *vaqueros* yelled agreement. Even a couple of the locals seemed in favor of shooting the old man. I supposed any kind of excitement was welcome in that dreary place.

I bent down, the better to peer into his clouded eyes and asked, "Try to remember, Everardo, did you shoot a tall American who looked like me?"

The cloud seemed to lift for a second. "Yes, he was a man as tall as you, and fast. He got a shot off before—"

"Before what?"

"I have talked enough. I am tired and I need some rest before we

334

drive your cows, *patrón*."

Some of our *vaqueros* and some of the local people laughed. They would have laughed at a man tied to an anthill with honey smeared on his eyelids.

"Well?" Rodolfo asked. He did not have to complete the question. By all of the laws of men and particularly so in the savage states of Texas and Sonora, I was duty-bound to shoot the old, senile man.

"Give me the pistol," I ordered, holding my hand out for it.

He took it from the holster again but said, in utter bewilderment: "But then I will have no weapon and any man that wishes may kill me."

I slid my new Winchester rifle from its saddle scabbard, holding it out to him. When he took it by the barrel with one hand, I slipped the revolver from his hand, switched it for the one I had, and then dropped the twin Colt into a saddlebag. I unwound my reins and had one foot in the air and my left hand on the saddle horn when the bullet took me low in the back. I found out later it struck not more than a hand span from the spine.

My horse bolted, and suddenly I was sitting on the ground, staring at the young boy yanking at the trigger of his little pistol. The old man peered at the rifle in his hands, wondering, I thought, how to lever a cartridge into a once-familiar weapon. His brother had thrown his hands high in the air, but it helped him not at all. There was a fusillade. All three men jerked awkwardly and fell. The boy crawled, head down, toward me. I was terrified that he would lift his head and look into my eyes, but then a single shot rang out, blowing the top of his head away. My arms collapsed and my head banged into the ground. I floated gently, painlessly away. I thought, surprised, dying is not so difficult after all.

Chapter 44

Memo Cooper Canela

Only twice before have I felt such exhilaration. My first solo flight, and my first kill as a fighter pilot. On both those occasions my heart was beating to an ethereal rhythm that only I—and perhaps an angel or two—could hear. I hear it again, now: Black and Bell have signed a contract to print *Riley's Golden Ear.*

After some seven years of difficult, at times impossible, research and at least five rewrites, I will finally have a hardcover book published, and by a prestigious New York firm. I smile as I walk along Mexico City's crowded downtown sidewalks. I get a smile back from those Mexicans who have not yet learned to scurry along with their heads down.

True, the contract was signed more than a year before, but I could not believe that one day an editor would tell a printer to set up my words in type, pull proofs for me to check, and then let me make any vital, last-minute changes. After all the rewriting, what would I change? Why? Still, the editor warns me that if I make extensive corrections or additions, they will charge me for the added typesetting.

I finally tracked the major down to a hospital in San Antonio. He seemed to be as elated as both Mama and I. She let out a Mexican yell that must have scared all but the terminally ill right out of their beds. The major told me that they found a small sliver of lead that had worked its way close enough to his spine to cause him a great deal of pain, but now that it was out, he was ready for a big *pachanga.* He would certainly fly to Mexico City for mine.

The party will be at my apartment tonight. I have called and left messages for friends. I have, of course, invited Jorge and Elenita, but I still do not know if Jorge will show up. In writing what I have come to call Helen's book, I have come to admire and respect that lady, and I had no choice but to include the role of Jorge's father in the building of the Riley empire.

I have put off showing the manuscript to Jorge, as he has avoided asking to read it. Both the major and Mama have read it and enthusiastically endorsed both content and style, but not even Mama had realized the extent of the corruption in her once-revered political institution. She was so shocked that she had even talked to that old warhorse, General Rodolfo Hernández, about switching allegiance to the party of the extreme religious right, headquartered in Monterrey, a two-hour drive from the U.S. border. Hernández seems to think that they are no longer merely bigoted Catholics trying to bring back the golden days of Porfirio Díaz, but just anti-Marxists fed up with the shameless corruption of the revolutionary government. The political party founded by Calles in 1929 and now known as the Institutional Revolutionary Party, or PRI, has controlled all Mexican elections.

How the city has changed for the worse! The traffic here makes New York and San Francisco streets look deserted. The *glorietas*, the traffic islands that spun the cars around so efficiently when I was a boy, turned out to be chaos when the city tripled its population. The smog is so bad that the overhead sun is often no more than a white blur dimly seen through a brownish veil. My eyes tear and I cough. Only when it rains is there relief. Then the torrential rains wash the filth out of the air and down into the street drains. It no longer rains every afternoon, as it once did, around three o'clock, but it does so instead whenever the proper amounts of dust and moisture combine to form a drop of water. In the dry season there is a constant shortage of water, and yet the whole Lerma River is pumped up over the eight-thousand-foot rim of the valley of Mexico into Mexico City! To top it all, one of the hopeful candidates to the presidency declares, in opposition to birth control, that Mexico needs more, not less, Mexicans!

I have walked the fifteen blocks home because it is much faster than taking a taxi—if I could have found one. I bound up the three flights to my small apartment and ring the bell. No one answers, so I fish the key from a pocket, tuck the large box of proofs under one arm and open the door.

I drop the proofs on a coffee table, then go to the refrigerator for a beer. Drinking a cold, dark Dos Equis, I eye the box of proofs and wonder if—or perhaps when—I will leave the dying city and live along the Pacific Coast. I guess that the "when" and "where" might depend on a very tall, very beautiful and very black girl named April McKay.

The doorbell rings, but before I can rise, it is unlocked and swings open. In strides April, a woven shopping bag in one hand, her key in the other. María, sent by my mother to be my cook and my conscience, trots after her. April does a quick, deep knee bend to kiss my cheek noisily. Then, chattering a mile a minute, she goes into the kitchen with María.

April speaks Spanish as well as I do, maybe better. Like most people who grow up speaking a language, I get sloppy with both grammar and pronunciation. April does not, except when she forgets and, like a human tape recorder, begins to talk like the people around her. Of course, language is her specialty. She is on a grant doing something she calls linguistic anthropology. It sounds to me much like trailing an animal by its scat, except that the migrating peoples she trails are long gone, and they left words instead of feces. She is a bright girl and has a degree from the University of Washington and a doctorate from Columbia. With the help of the G.I. Bill, I finally managed a belated bachelor of arts in history from Mexico City College, the English-language school in Mexico City. They have since upgraded both name and location, and likely would not admit that I ever attended classes in the rooms just above Tato's bar.

"Memo," April called from the kitchen. She has a voice that throbs like the strings of a cello. "How many drinkers?"

"Maybe a dozen."

"How about *mota*?" April, twenty-five years old and liberated, likes to shock old straight-laced Memo.

"Marijuana? I guess just enough for my mother."

"Memo!" She thinks that I am kidding her. I am not. While I do wait for their first meeting with some trepidation, I am also anxious, as a writer and observer, to witness the meeting between irresistible force and immovable object. I have purposely not told either one much about the other.

The doorbell rang again, and I called out that I would get it. At the door, a vaguely familiar middle-aged woman with stringy blond hair and wild green eyes threw herself into my arms. I clasped her, then instinctively stepped back. "Memo. Oh, Memo! You don't even know me."

I recognized the voice immediately. It belonged to the young girl to whom I had loaned two hundred dollars so that she could run away from Willard Riley.

"Sofía," I said, smiling now. "Did you ever get to San Francisco?"

"You are the one, Memo, that had better go to San Francisco, or Seattle, or maybe, better still, Nome, Alaska."

"You know about the book?" I asked, surprised.

"Daddy knows. You have galleys, which are like printed sheets to correct, and he is furious. He is crazy. He is as crazy as I am."

"You're not crazy, Sofía," I said with more conviction than I felt. "Come on in and sit down."

"Could you give me a quick drink?"

"Sure." I led her into the room. "You might as well stay for the party. It's almost time." She was almost an hour early for the announced time, but no one raised in Mexico would arrive until at least an hour later.

April stuck her head out of the kitchen doorway and called out cheerfully, "Hi. I'm April McKay."

"I'm Sofía," she said as if she were ashamed of something. She turned back to me. "A big shot of straight vodka. Right now?"

"Sofía what?" April asked.

"Riley," she said in her little girl voice so low that I could barely hear her. I gave her a squat, old-fashioned glass half full of vodka. There was some acidic scent mixed with her perfume and body odor that I found disturbing.

"No relation to the book Riley—"

"Yes, April," I interrupted. "Are the *antojitos* about ready? Sofía might like to nibble on something."

"Yes, sir, Admiral, sir! I will get the *antojito* detail cracking, sir!"

I laughed and returned her flamboyant salute.

"She is a lovely girl, Memo. I never met a Negro girl before. Daddy sent me to schools where everyone was washed-out white and named Primrose."

She held her glass out to me. I refilled it with a light touch of vodka and a lot of ice.

"I can't stay for the party. I would love to, Memo. But if Daddy finds out I'm here, he will get angry again. He might even send me back to the Walled City."

"Walled City?"

"It's a place where they dry me out every once in a while. It's kind of like a school, but a lot harder to graduate from." She laughed dutifully and then said, "Mama went there too. She finally got out, feet first."

"I'm sorry, Sofía," I said.

"Don't be. I'm all right, except that I get so tired. Sometimes I would like to just lie down and sleep forever." She closed her eyes and the wrinkles smoothed out, and I could see the young woman hidden there.

"Why don't you lie down on my bed? Take a little siesta and wake up bright-eyed and bushy-tailed for our party?"

"Could I, Memo? Would you tuck me in?"

"Sure, I will. Come on."

I heard a series of snorts from the kitchen and knew that I would have comments from both April and María. Sofía took my arm and I walked her into my bedroom, unusually neat for the party. She kicked her shoes off and held her arms out to me. I held her and then swung her up in the air and onto the bed. She weighed no more than a child. I kissed her and tried to lift my head away, but she clasped her hands behind my neck and held me tightly.

"Just a minute more, Memo. Pretend that you took me away to San Francisco with you, and when Daddy came to get me, you threw him off the Top of the Mark!"

I knelt on one knee and waited no more than a couple of minutes before her breathing smoothed out and her hands relaxed. I covered her with a light blanket and left, closing the door behind me.

The first to arrive, so early that they were only twenty minutes late, were my sister, Elenita, and my brother-in-law, Jorge Rubio Montejo.

"I wondered if you would come," I said.

"He would not have," Elenita said after she kissed me, "except that he was told, officially, not to."

"Yes. Can you imagine the nerve of those *cabrones*? To tell me that I am not to be present at a social function? Even a low-class party like this; if I want to go, I go."

"Well," I said, "it was one way to get you here."

"Memo," Elenita, ever gullible, said. "You didn't?"

Both Jorge and I laughed.

"She still thinks that her big brother can do anything," Jorge said. "Even be president of Mexico."

"Or the United States," Elenita said. "And if he doesn't make it, little *Jorgecito* will."

"He is only three years old and not a citizen of anything," I said.

"No matter. When he grows up, he can decide on his citizenship. Maybe he will be president of both countries."

Jorge and I exchanged shrugs. April came bouncing out of the kitchen, and Jorge turned to meet her, arms spread and standing on tiptoe.

"Wow!" he exclaimed as he always did. "There is enough of this woman to go around twice. How about sharing, Memo?"

"I am not a theoretical nor a practicing Marxist," I said. "I am not any kind of a Marxist."

"Speaking of which," Elenita said to me, while she separated April from Jorge and kissed her cheek, "what do you think of the *destapado?*"

In recent years, the political party that under different names—but all with the catchword "revolution" in the title—has controlled Mexican politics absolutely, holds a convention where their candidate is nominated and elected, unanimously. Actually, the candidate is chosen much earlier by the current president, who may be influenced only by a few very powerful men. Because only these very few know who the candidate and new president will be, and because they keep the secret well, the public always speculates on the *tapado*, or the unknown or hooded candidate. When his identity is finally revealed at the convention, he becomes the *destapado* or unhooded one.

The present candidate is a self-proclaimed Marxist, who if not already a Marxist millionaire, would soon become one. The country was readying itself for a devaluation.

"Before we get into a small fight, Memo, let me read the book. We might as well get into it in earnest, when I finish."

I sat Jorge in a corner, and brought him a cold Victoria that he had once called bricklayer's beer and the large box of proofs.

"You could take them home with you," I offered, and then almost panicked before he smiled and shook his head negatively. "No, thanks. I can find what I want to read before the party gets into high gear."

I shrugged and went to get Elenita her martini. She was sitting on an old wicker couch next to April, whispering, glancing at me, and then giggling. They looked up at me, two round-eyed innocents, when I delivered the drink. April had an ivory cigarette holder containing what she called a joint and Mexicans called a *churro*. She was probably waiting for my parents to arrive before lighting up. In the meantime, she sipped on a beer almost as dark as her skin.

The doorbell rang. I let in a young painter and his lover, a columnist for a weekly newspaper about bullfighting. I heard bongo drums from the stairwell and left the door open. Seconds later three Cubans, two men and a woman, danced into the room. One Cuban is noisy, three are deafening.

I was back mixing rum and juice at my makeshift bar when the bell rang again.

"Come on in," April yelled, and then, as I looked up from the rickety card table, she added sweetly, "You must be Memo's *mamita*."

April stood up. Mama tilted her head back to talk to her and said, "Yes I am, Memo's little Mama, and you, I imagine are one of his Cuban friends."

One of April's real talents is an incredible ear for accents. But, as a result, she often unconsciously mimics the speech of those around her. She had been talking to one of the Cubans, and she was black. In Mama's book that made her Cuban.

The major eased in to the room and smiled over Mama's head at April. "No, love. I'll bet that this is one of his American friends. April, May or June?"

"It's April, sir." She curtsied prettily, batting oversized eyes up at him and added, "You must be the lieutenant, captain or major."

He laughed heartily and held out a hand to lift her up. Mama smiled icily. The major held a bulky, awkwardly tied package in his left hand.

"May I take the package?" April asked.

"No, thanks. It belongs to the famous author over there." He waved it at me.

I waved back and, sidestepping dancers, hugged and kissed Mama, hugged the major and led them to where Jorge, engrossed in reading the proofs, sat.

"Jorge, my parents are here."

"What?" He looked at us blankly for a second, then sprang to his feet. "Forgive me." The galley sheet in his hand got pretty well wrinkled while he got the *abrazos* out of the way.

"I am glad to see you here, Jorge," the major said. "I do not want old fights to come between such good friends."

Jorge would have answered, in that slow deliberate way of his, but Mama spoke too soon.

"How is my little grandson?" She had certainly taken helm of the family, I thought. Elenita's baby is now her grandson.

"You are not feeding him any more of that terrible pure-sugar candy?" Mama added before he could respond to the first question.

"No," Jorge said quickly. "My mother sends us some special candy made out of sesame seeds and honey."

"Lilly is in Mexico?" This time she waited for an answer.

"No. She is in Paris, I think, but she has halvah sent to us from a Jewish delicatessen in the Polanco area here in the city."

"That candy is sweeter than ambrosia," the major said, smiling. "More people are hooked on it than on heroin."

"You are giving my grandson dope?" Mama was not being entirely facetious. Lilly was known for her own predilection for cocaine.

"It is just a bit of candy for Sundays, when we take Jorgecito to the zoo at Chapultepec. No more than a bite."

"Let him get back to the book, Mama," I said. "It is not often that he gets a chance to read real literature."

She smiled at me, nodded assent and headed for Elenita and the young painter, both flailing hands in a heated discussion.

"Come on, major," I said. "Let's sit down with a wall at our backs."

Jorge went back to his reading while we found the couch unoccupied and sat down. It was an old joke. Keep the enemy fighters off your tail. Protect your rear. But that dismal day, the enemy would come straight on.

"This is for you, son." He handed me the package. Son? The words "son" and "father" came reluctantly and with some embarrassment to our lips. I slipped the knot, parted the paper, and saw his holstered, bone-handled .45 Colt revolver.

"But this is your old cowboy pistol."

"It's old, but serviceable, just like me. But it's not mine." He flipped his coat open far enough for me to see his old revolver in its new, fast-draw holster.

"But it looks just like the one you carry, the one your father gave to you."

"It is its mate. One day, maybe, I'll tell you how I came by it."

"Tell me now. You'll forget and I will never know," I said sadly.

"I hereby will you, among other worldly goods, my old journal. I tried to write a few things about my life in Mexico and about Will Riley. I soon found out that I am a considerably better pilot than I am a writer, but the story about the pistol is in the old green ledger in my desk at the ranch. I'll send it to you."

"*Por favor*," I said. "Don't forget—and send it registered."

"All right. Now, take off your coat."

He fitted the holstered revolver to me, changing the hang and the tightness of the straps minutely until he was satisfied.

"You carried a revolver when you flew for the Navy," he said. "Did you learn to shoot it?"

"Fair. If I hammer-cocked the pistol first, I was the best pistol shot in the squadron, but compared to you, major, I was unranked."

"Good. All you need to remember is that when you decide to shoot a man, do so. Do not flinch nor think about his shot. Let him worry about yours."

343

"But major, I have seen you draw and shoot, quick as a flash. I can't do that."

"Maybe not now. But, with practice you will. But that is not so important. The one who lives is usually the one that puts the first bullet in the other. Concentrate on a sure draw and a surer shot."

"Well," I said, grinning, "I guess if I had a few .45 cartridges around, I would be ready for bear."

"Do you think I would give you an unloaded pistol?"

My grin turned into an expression of embarrassment. The major never accepted a firearm without checking its chamber. I knew better.

"The hammer is on an empty chamber," he said, grinning back to let me know that he was not angry with me. "Carry it until you get out of the city."

"Maybe I'll come up to the ranch for a bit."

"Good. I would like Elenita and family there too."

"You think that Riley would harm the family of his *segundo*?"

"Riley has no *segundo*, or maybe he is the number one and everybody else in the world is second."

"I have a hankering for the ocean," I said. "Maybe I'll spend a month in Mazatlán before I join you at the ranch."

"No! The state of Sinaloa is Riley country now more than ever. I am sure that he is bankrolling the heroin operation out of Sinaloa."

"Can you document that, major?"

"No, but I do know, and I can prove, that his little bank in Mazatlán has a cash volume larger than that of his largest bank here in the city."

I took my notebook from my side coat pocket and caught the pencil stub as it fell. I wrote on the first blank page I found:

As this book is being printed, one of the Riley chain of banks, CosaBanco de Sinaloa in the city of Mazatlán, has more cash pass through it than does the huge CosaBanco de México in Mexico City. During the early part of World War II, the Americans taught the Mexican farmers in Sinaloa to grow opium poppies to assure an adequate medical supply of morphine. The demand never materialized, but the market for heroin did. Most of the illegal Mexican processed heroin smuggled into the United States is grown in Sinaloa, where Riley owns that miraculously super-successful little bank, CosaBanco de Sinaloa.

344

"*¡Puta madre!*" the major exclaimed, reading over my shoulder. "Maybe I better buy a ranch in Wyoming."

There was a sudden slackening of the conversational music and the drums stopped.

When I glanced up, I saw from a sideways flick of my eyes that the major was holding a pistol in his left hand. I thrust my suddenly clumsy fingers inside my coat to seek the revolver butt.

The obese, squat figure standing still in the doorway was one of the richest and most powerful men in Mexico, Jorge Rubio. He was also the grandfather of the beloved three-year-old, Jorgecito.

He looked directly at the major and waddled purposefully toward him, shouldering aside one of the Cuban dancers with an air of indifference. Perhaps he had not even seen him.

"Close that door," the major ordered.

The Cuban girl danced over, swung an ample hip and slammed it shut.

Rubio blinked his hooded eyes at the pistol and spoke. I knew why the major called him the Toad. Even his voice was a hoarse croak.

"Put the pistol away," he said. "I did not come here to make war."

"All right," the major said and the pistol disappeared. "What does Riley want? Why did he send you?"

"I think that he wants you and Memo and Toña, and maybe even my grandson."

"He knows about the party and the proofs?" I asked.

"He knows about the book. Maybe not about the party."

"How did you know about it?" the major asked.

"Jorge told me. He said that he would go to see how bad the book was."

"It is pretty bad," his son said, standing up, holding a long galley sheet in one hand. "Did you really try to have the major shot by a firing squad?"

"It was a mistake. An error. I admitted it later."

"And the union leader. You shot him?"

"In self-defense."

"In the back?"

"It was a running gunfight. He shot and ran. Anyway, I don't shoot nobody now." He whipped his coat open. "I don't even carry a gun. See?"

Suddenly, the front door flew open. All of us froze, not even breathing, staring into the gaping muzzles of short-barreled, 12-gauge shotguns, the kind of automatic weapons that riot squads and assassins use. There were three men, no more expression on their faces than what is on lizards. They were not wearing uniforms—unless one could call wide-brimmed gray hats, dark glasses and maroon ties a uniform.

The middle one, as sharp-faced as a ferret, spoke: "Everybody, hands high, where I can see them."

"Pepe," the major said conversationally, but holding his hands up, "are you not too old for this business?"

"Maybe, Major Cooper, but if you drop that left hand another inch, you and your neighbors can split up nine pellets from the first shot."

"Including General Rubio?" the major indicated Rubio with a nod of his head. Rubio turned slowly to face the men.

"Specially General Rubio," said Pepe.

"Señor Riley will be furious when he finds out that you have been rude to me," Rubio said, but it sounded more like a question than a statement.

"Who do you think sent us?" Pepe said, smiling slightly, obviously enjoying himself.

"But he promised . . . he told me he wouldn't . . ." Rubio's voice ended in a whisper.

"You cannot come into a man's home and abuse him and his guests," Jorge, who was still holding the galley sheet in one hand, said loudly. "We are not in some barbaric country in Africa or Asia. This is Mexico. We still have some civil guarantees."

"You do, *muchacho*," he said contemptuously. "Take your old lady and get out. You too, fatso," he indicated Rubio with the barrel of his shotgun. "Get out!" His eyes, as expressionless as black buttons, took in the room full of people at a glance. "Everybody out—except Major Cooper, his wife and son."

Pepe stepped aside and swung the barrel as if to sweep the room clear of the others. The artist and the columnist fled, followed by the wide-eyed and atypically silent Cubans.

The kitchen door swung open and Mama, her eyes glinting angrily, staggered out followed by April and María, her hands clenched in her apron. Behind them, a fourth gunman, a square man—almost as wide as he was tall—prodded them with what looked to be some kind of short-barreled automatic rifle.

"Look what I found trying to go down the outside staircase," he said.

"Rubios, out!" Pepe said.

346

"Go on, Elenita. Quickly, with Jorge," the major said. "See to my grandson. Now!"

"Daddy," Elenita wailed.

"Go." I said. "They want to . . . talk to us about the book. Go, now. Please, Elenita."

Jorge pulled Elenita to her feet. She was crying and shaking. He looked at me, hopelessly, then, leading her out past Pepe, said, "If you hurt my friends, I will find you and hurt you."

Pepe smiled at him as if he were a small boy bragging about an imaginary encounter with a tiger.

"You too," Pepe jerked his head at April and María. "The maid and the black *puta*."

María, who always did whatever anyone in authority told her, scurried out. April straightened up, adding another inch to her six feet and glared down at Pepe. "I am a citizen of the United States of America. If you harm me, my government will track you down and shoot you."

Pepe laughed. The other gunmen joined in. "You speak good Spanish, honey. I apologize for calling you a black whore. You got a lot of *pantalones*."

I agreed with Pepe. She had a lot of guts, or "pants" as the Spanish expression has it. But with a strong tang of fear in my nostrils and barely able to control it, I could do no more than plead with my eyes and say, "Go, April. It is a private matter. We will settle it. Go on out, please."

She turned and walked blindly into one of the men obstructing the doorway. He waited until her breasts flattened against his throat, giggled, and then moved, his head cocked, listening to her heels tap away down the stairs.

"Some tits," he said.

"You can leave now," Pepe said, then added, "Toad."

Rubio looked at the major sadly, then turned and very slowly walked toward the door.

"What will it be, then, Pepe?" the major asked. "You shoot women now?"

"The dark one? Toña? She is yours. But yes, you married her. A little late, maybe, but, better late than never, eh?"

"Yes?" the major said, waiting.

"Maybe," Pepe said, "Mister Riley might forgive your wife and boy if you get down on your knees and beg, major." He jerked his head at

Rubio and added, "Right, General Rubio?"

"You will not harm them?" the major said hoarsely. "Word of honor?"

"Of course. We won't hurt anyone. If you do a good job we might even let you go. Right, boys?"

Even as they all laughed at Pepe's transparent promise, I wanted so desperately to live that I almost believed. I know now that the major never, for a second, believed him.

The major nodded acquiescence and carefully lowered himself to the floor, his right hand on the edge of the coffee table. On his knees, he looked directly at Pepe and said, "I beg Mister Riley's pardon for my transgressions and beg him to spare the life of Tell Cooper and his family."

"You did it." Rubio stopped in front of the man at the kitchen door and half turned to look at the major. "You begged on your knees!"

"Are you going to kill me too, Pepe? Did Daddy tell you to shoot me too, or will he do it when I get home?"

I had not heard the bedroom door open.

"*¡Hijo de la chingada!*" the square man at the kitchen door said, surprised. "Hell, it's the daughter of the *patrón*."

"Get out of here, you little whore!" Pepe yelled.

The events that happened next are recorded in a camera much like the one I used when I was a fighter pilot, except this one is inside my head, not behind the electronic gunsight of an airplane.

Whenever I wish, I can replay that scene. I always watch it in slow motion. The actors move with precision, in sharp focus, and brilliantly lit.

First, Rubio reached out and clasped the square man, locked his legs around him, then fell with him to the floor. There was a thump, and a sound like a skull being fractured.

The major drew and shot Pepe high in the chest. He looked puzzled, then he looked up at the ceiling. As he crumpled, the shotgun went off twice into the ceiling before it fell from his hands.

The other two swung their guns to the major. His second shot took the man with the faster reactions first, low around the belt line, putting him down and out of the fight. But then the last man got his shot off. The impact of double-aught buckshot slammed the major's chin to his knees, doubling him up against the couch.

In that split second, I realized that the old revolver, the one that the major had given to me earlier, was cocked and in my hand. I sighted it

348

carefully at the center of the last man's chest. I could see the panic in his eyes as he tried desperately to swing the short shotgun barrel back to me. He did not. I walked over to where he lay, writhing on the floor, cocked the revolver again, aimed it carefully at his head and shot him once more. I can still see the blood and brains exploding upward. I can feel the impact of spongy tissue on my face, and I can smell the hot blood.

I turned to the man who got caught in the embrace with Rubio, and I dragged him away. But as I leveled the pistol at him, Mama screamed at me to stop. "No, Memo. We must have a witness. Put the gun away and help me get Tell to the hospital."

I tried, but could not tell her that the major was dead. He had taken a blast from a twelve-gauge shotgun at about twenty feet. Still, like a little boy, I said, "Yes, Mama." I turned back to the major. I heard sirens in the background and perhaps Jorge and Elenita yelling, but everything faded quickly away as I bent down over the major. I had expected to see the glaze that obscures the window into the brain seconds after death. His breathing was shallow, but I could see his chest move slightly. I jerked his shirt open, sending buttons flying. I saw red froth bubbling from a pierced lung and bright red blood running from his shirt a few inches higher. Blood ran down his coat sleeve. Blood ran from another hole in his upper arm. Only three of the nine pea-sized lead spheres had struck him. The old gunman had so rattled that professional killer, that he hurried his shot and damn near missed entirely.

"Mama," I yelled. "The major is not dead! My father is not dead!"

Chapter 45

Memo Cooper Canela

The two old antagonists ended up a few feet apart in the same intensive-care unit of the American British Cowdray Hospital. The major lived a half an hour longer than Jorge Rubio did. The major died of trauma occasioned by three lead buckshot. Rubio died of a cardiac arrest brought on by the violent confrontation. The major was cremated, Rubio entombed.

Jorge and Elenita took their child, Jorgecito, with them to the funeral services for Rubio. Jorge's giddy mother, Lilly, wired flowers and her regrets from Paris. Elenita told me that she had to listen to a lot of nonsense about "one of the last of the old revolutionary generals." Rubio had never held rank above that of a colonel until Riley decided to buy him a general's rank along with the title of chief of police. He liked the title and prestige, but not the work, which, in any case, was done by an enthusiastic young thug who had worked his way up through the drug hierarchy.

The major's funeral was a simple party or remembrance, not unlike the one I had attended in California when his first wife had been killed and cremated in what was then thought to have been an accident. We know better now.

We held what the major had referred to as an Irish wake. The idea was to grieve loudly, even drunkenly if necessary, and then cry no more.

We held the wake at my apartment for, otherwise, I could not attend. While I am not under arrest, neither am I free. The assassins that burst into our apartment and attempted to kill us were federal agents. They would have loved to have charged me with shooting the agents, but there was one major problem. My weapon had disappeared, and the major's had been pried from his hand at the hospital and then turned over to the police. Of course the pistols were identical in caliber, but not ballistically, and one man had been shot with a weapon other than my father's revolver. Mama was a witness, but not a suspect. Who would dare accuse the legendary Lieutenant Toña Canela of any crime? Which left me.

The other surviving witness was still under observation at the same hospital, for a suspected concussion, but would not or could not talk.

April had called the next day, but when I heard the odd background noise, I said, "Cool the call. Fuzz!" and hung up.

Jorge handed me a beer, clicked bottles with me, and said, "The old general died pretty well, no?"

"Yes. He did. The major knew that too. I saw him glance at your father just before he went for his pistol."

"Is that true?" Jorge asked suspiciously.

"Of course. I noticed that too," Mama said flatly.

I hate to lie. And maybe it was even true, but now Jorge would not ask me again. No one would contradict Mama.

"Your father, he was some *pistolero*. Three of them and he got them all." Jorge raised his bottle to the room. "Here is to the major."

I had decided to tell no one about the man I had shot and killed. Now that the major was dead, only Mama had seen me, and she would not tell.

"I remember a toast that the major liked," I said. "He quoted it at the ceremony we held for your mother in Santa Monica," I said, speaking to Elenita.

"I remember," she said.

"You were asleep," I reminded her.

"Tommy told me. It was an awful toast."

"The major liked it. He had just sung an old ballad about a pilot who has wiped out his airplane, but asks his buddies, as he lies dying, to take out all of the motor parts from various places in his own body and," I sang the last line, "to rebuild the motor again."

"What was the toast?" Jorge asked.

"To the major," I said and held my bottle high, reciting the last stanza:

> *Here's to the dead already,*
> *Damn their eyes, Damn their eyes,*
> *And hurrah for the next that dies.*

"Elenita is right. It is a bad toast," Jorge said.

"No," Mama disagreed. "It reminds me of what we used to say in the days of the Revolution: 'If they are going to kill me tomorrow, they might as well do it today.' "

"Shakespeare wrote that we all owe God a life and he who pays this year is quits for next," I said.

"That is true," Mama said. "They are all true. Why was my Tell shot down and my Memo not? Why Tell and not me?"

"Only God knows," Elenita said.

"God, and Willard Riley in the case of the major," I said.

"Maybe we will get him this time, Memo," Jorge said earnestly.

"Sure. And we Mexicans will sprout wings and fly to heaven."

"Maybe, yes, Memo. There are a few honest politicians and a lot of others who plain hate his guts."

"Wake up, Jorge. He owns all of the *políticos* that count. He runs the drug trade now, for Christ's sake. How many million dollars a week does he pour into the presidency?"

"Not the president!" Elenita was shocked.

"No?" Mama said. "How could the dealers grow, buy and process all the heroin without the knowledge of the governor of the state of Sinaloa? And how could he stay in office without the approval of the president of the republic?"

"Most of the heroin is imported now, along with cocaine from our trading partners in Colombia," Jorge said.

"Mama. It has become a huge business that destroys countries as well as people."

"You are right," Jorge said bitterly. "Corruption is ruining the country. Literally destroying it. And it is not so much that they steal, but what they do to steal that is the biggest problem. For example, a small town mayor, a year or so before his term is up, buys three large bulldozers. Why three tractors and not ten trucks or a food processing plant? For the excellent reason that he gets a twenty percent kickback from the overpriced tractors, but gets little or nothing if he buys the needed trucks or processing plant. The bulldozers will rust away to nothing during the next administration because there was never any real need for them. That happens in a small town. What happens in a large city, a populous state, or the whole Mexican nation?" His voice rang with sincerity. I could see how be would be an effective vote getter.

"You must stop them, Jorge," Mama said. "Go to the president of the party and tell him."

"It can no longer be done within our party or the government. How can you tell where one leaves off and the other begins? Every *político* on his way up takes and gives. Only the president could stop it, working from the top down. But just as he had to steal and reward to get to the top, so does he owe favors to old and dear friends who are no more guilty than he. Will he disinherit his own? I think not."

"But then, Jorge," Mama said sadly, "what will we do? What will you do?"

"I will switch to the PAN party," he said, looking at Mama nervously. "Maybe we can change the present government by votes. If not, we will have to use guns."

"You are thinking of liberalizing the PAN, negating the Church, giving it a broader base and then beat the PRI at the polls?" I said.

"It is an idea. I am not the first. Others have already gone over. Liberal politicians who cannot stomach the present corrupt government."

"It might work," I agreed. "Begin with a base in the north. Concentrate on one city, then one state. You would have all of the border states, except—"

"Except what?" Jorge asked.

"Except that a governmental entity, which is headed by and staffed exclusively by PRI members and is titled *Gobernación*, supervises the polls and counts the votes."

"But, Jorge," Mama said, "the PAN? I know General Hernández thought of joining them too, but they are the same blood-sucking priests that kept us quiet for Porfirio Díaz's slave drivers. The ones who sold Mexico to the foreigners, and," her husky voice soared to a note of despair, "you want to help them!"

"I think Jorge is right. He has a chance. The major said that political parties change, just like people."

"But he never even voted," Elenita said. "He was a resident of Mexico, but a citizen of the United States."

"The major was always right about politics . . . sometimes," Mama said, without a trace of a smile. "Memo," she turned to me, "would you join the . . . that party?"

"No. I am a writer. I will sit on the sidelines and watch and even applaud Jorge."

"I may be a writer too," Jorge said. "If I can talk my mother into pulling some of our money out of France. Maybe I could publish a newspaper in the North. Maybe in Monterrey."

"Good luck," I said.

"We have to go home," Elenita said, standing. "I do not entirely trust the new *nana* with Jorgecito." She kissed me, blinking away tears, but when she hugged Mama, she broke down and sobbed. Then we all did.

The doorbell rang.

Jorge brought out a Browning .380 from a coat pocket. From her purse, Mama slipped a short-barreled Smith and Wesson revolver that I had never seen before. I almost expected Elenita, who hated firearms, to come up with a Derringer. But she was unarmed, as I was.

"Who is it?" I called out.

"It's just Sofía." I opened the door to a slit, saw that she was alone and then slipped the security chain open.

"Come on in, Sofía." I put a protective arm around her. "I'm glad you came back. No one bothered you on the way in?"

"No. The skinny police captain knows me."

"I never got a chance to thank you. You likely saved our lives, Mama and me, when you popped out of that back bedroom."

"I know they killed your daddy, Memo, and yours too, Jorge. I'm sorry, but my Daddy won't bother you any more. He went some place. I brought your gun back."

Her purse hung from a shoulder. She opened it and with both hands lifted my long-barreled Colt out and handed it to me, barrel pointed at my chest. I flinched, but took it and pointed it away from everyone. There was still a slight odor of cordite, which I thought strange. I flipped the cylinder open and pushed out five empty brass casings. Not one live round. I reran that movie in my mind and watched Memo Cooper fire twice.

"What happened to the three live rounds? The other bullets," I added, seeing a lack of comprehension in her face.

"Oh, those. Yes. The live rounds." Her green eyes seemed larger than usual and her pupils even more so. She smiled at me, a little girl telling an adult a secret.

"Someone took that big pistol and shot someone. It was Daddy he shot. I think it was Major Cooper that did it." No one spoke, nor moved, until I asked the inevitable question.

"Did you shoot your daddy, Sofía, with this big gun?"

"Oh, no. I would never do that. I'm not allowed. But I think that other girl did. The one that takes drugs and gets into trouble."

I handed the old Colt to Mama. "Can you hide this for me? I think it had better disappear."

I sat Sofía down on the couch. Elenita sat with her, not talking, but patting her gently on her shoulder.

"You think Riley is really dead?" Jorge asked.

"I think so. Where is Johnny Ávalos?"

"According to yesterday's newspapers he was seen, simultaneously in Miami, Madrid and Paris. He has picked up his marbles and run."

"Then," I said, "if Riley is really dead—"

Suddenly, sirens sounded, engines roared and brakes squealed. We ran to the window. The street was full of plainclothes federal agents and blue-uniformed city police, some of them waving weapons. I saw one short but powerful-looking agent shove a blue-coated policeman so hard that the uniformed man backpedaled desperately backwards, like a man riding a unicycle, until he crashed into one of his own police cars. He pulled out a pistol as he slid down the side of the car and began firing at the agent. The agent was hit, but managed to get a weapon into action before he fell. Then there was a fusillade of shots. We all went to the floor, except Sofía, who had followed Elenita, dutifully, to the window.

"The blue ones are running away," Sofía said, "I guess they lost."

I reached up a hand and pulled her down alongside me. She giggled and snuggled up. "Will you take me to San Francisco, Memo?"

"Sure," I said. "I surely will try."

To Jorge, I said, "I was about to say that there might be a big fight for control of Riley's official and unofficial empires."

"He must be dead," Jorge said, "and they just found out about it."

We both looked at Sofía. She smiled at us and said, "Oh, yes. He got shot. Like the major and General Rubio," she added proudly like a fourth-grader with the right answer.

There was a very long period of silence. As short as five minutes and as long as ten. I slowly raised my head to window level and then willed myself to peer over the sill. Sofía was right. There were no more blue uniforms. Just groups of agents, laughing and brandishing weapons. Here and there, a small bottle of mescal was being passed around. Some men were smoking tobacco, but a few swirls of telltale smoke along with a faint but familiar odor betrayed an occasional agent who preferred marijuana.

"It looks like the federal agents have won the first skirmish," I said, standing up. Mama popped up beside me.

"I think we might get away, if we leave right now," she said. What she meant, of course, was that Sofía and I could get away. No one else was in peril.

"The Cessna is gassed up and flight-ready," Mama said. "Could we make it to McAllen non-stop?"

"Easily," I said. "But could we take off?"

"I could file a flight plan for a local flight without passengers and then fly north to the border at McAllen."

"Good," I said. "Let's go get little Jorgecito and get the hell out of Mexico."

"No," Jorge said. "No one is after me or my family. I will take them to Monterrey, later, but you . . . and," he flicked his eyes at Sofía to include her, but said, "you and your Mama had better leave quick, quick!"

"Okay," I said. "Mama and I will get out quickly."

And we did. First, Jorge and I switched coats. No one, except a charro or a *pistolero* wears a hat in Mexico City, but the major's fine Stetson was still on a shelf where April had placed it. The broad-rimmed hat fit me perfectly. I wrote a short note to April, giving her both the ranch address and Jorge and Elenita's phone number. Like many telephones in Mexico, it was in someone else's name.

"Memo," Mama called, "we must go quickly before they think about us up here."

"Yes, Mama," I said, and I slipped the note for April into the secret place behind the bookshelves.

I walked out first, with Elenita on one arm and Sofía on the other. Sofía, who clung to my arm desperately, did giggle when an agent with a pistol in one hand and a half-empty bottle in the other called out to Elenita. "Hey, *mamacita*, come have a drink with your daddy. That one," he indicated me carelessly with the pistol, "is too busy for you."

"This is my husband," Elenita said indignantly and, taking a handful of the short hair at the nape of my neck, marched me away. Sofía trotted along, still giggling. Even the agent laughed. Then we turned the corner.

Mama and Jorge caught up with us at the parking lot where Jorge had left his car. We hurried our goodbye *abrazos,* and the three of us left Jorge and Elenita there while we walked swiftly another two blocks before I hailed a taxi.

I asked the driver to let us off at the first Metro station. We entered, but left by the subway's opposite exit and took another cab to the airport. Luckily, we were between the awful and impossible phases of traffic, so we made it to the field in a half an hour.

I ran a pre-flight check on the single-engine, four-passenger plane while Mama filed a flight plan. She was gone so long that I was about to go look for her, but finally she came back, riding alongside a grinning airport worker on one of those little carts that pull luggage. She jumped off, blew the young man a kiss and climbed in beside me.

Sofía was in the back, looking out the window dreamily. Mama handled the radio, got our clearance and takeoff instructions, but I flew the airplane. When I left the pattern, I flew south and east toward the volcanoes. Ten minutes out, I turned north and set a course for the little Texas city across the river from Reynosa, Mexico.

As soon as we crossed the brown strip of dirty water that is the border—known as the Rio Grande or *Rio Bravo*—I called the control tower. I identified the flight and the pilot. I started to explain that our flight plan had been altered when Mama took over.

"This is Antonia Canela de Cooper. We are ten minutes earlier than our ETA, but otherwise the flight plan as filed is correct. Would you advise immigration and customs that this will be our first stop in the United States?"

We received quick approval and landing instructions. As I turned into the traffic pattern and made the landing approach, I asked Mama about the flight plan.

"I have an old friend at the tower in Mexico. He is the one who almost shot Riley, but your father stopped him."

"Big error," I said.

"Yes," her eyes clouded for a second. She continued: "He had two flight plans for us. One, local with no passengers, in case the cops or the feds showed up too soon, and one if they did not."

"What will his boss say to him?"

"He will say, 'Lieutenant Solís, you owed the major, and you paid. Congratulations!' And then he will go buy himself a drink."

"I wish I knew more about parts of the major's life," I said.

"Me too." Then Mama smiled a bit and added, "But not too much. Anyway, you have some things being shipped from the ranch. There is a notebook full of your father's writing."

I made a smooth, easy landing on the tricycle gear, taxied over to immigration and customs, cut the motor, and we waited for the inspectors.

"Sofía," I asked, "do you have a visa for the States?"

"No," she said plaintively, "but I have an American passport."

"I thought you were a Mexican citizen," I said.

"I guess I am. I have one of those passports too."

She handed me both. "No," I yelled, seeing the immigration agent walking towards us. "Hide the Mexican one." In those days the state department claimed that an American citizen could not be a citizen of two countries. So did Mexico. The official was a friendly balding man

357

dressed in khakis.

"How are you all?"

"Happy to be back," I said, matching his accent, syllable for syllable. "I'm an American citizen. So is my girlfriend and my Mama has a visa for travel in the United States."

Back in his office, he stamped Mama's passport, did not even look at ours, and said, "Enjoy yourselves in Texas, hear?" We were home free!

"Where did you learn to talk like that?" Mama asked. "It might have been Tell talking."

"I practiced up at the ranch. I can also do the major's accent and yours too, in Spanish."

"Where's your luggage?" asked a big, beefy and sunburned customs man.

"We do not have any," Mama said.

"We travel lightly," I said. I flipped the top off the box of proofs.

"I could buy some suitcases," Sofía said, "and fill them with clothes and stuff. Then I could show you that."

"I'll just look into your luggage compartment," he said, eyeing us warily.

We walked back out to the plane. From the outside, I opened the compartment back of the rear seat. It was, as I knew, empty. Besides maps and navigational aids, so was the cabin.

"That's it," he said querulously. "You ain't got no more luggage than a couple of purses and a box of paper?"

"That is exactly what we have." Mama was beginning to anger. "Is there a law that we have to bring luggage?" Her voice increased in volume as she spoke. When she banged her purse down on an empty luggage cart, he began walking backwards. Looking to his rear for a path of retreat, he turned and ran. I took a deep breath and felt I had been granted a reprieve, for I had heard the loud thump that a large revolver makes—even when it is in a purse, and if that purse is slammed down on a hard, metal surface.

After I had arranged for a tie-down and secured the airplane, we took a cab to look for a hotel.

"Who has dollars?" I asked.

"I take pesos, rubles or pounds," the driver said in Spanish.

"I think that I have enough pesos to pay our fare halfway into town," I said, also speaking Spanish.

"I only have some small change," Mama said. "The major always

358

carried the gringo money."

"You want me to stop halfway?" the driver asked.

"Sofía," I said. "Wake up and tell us if you have any money."

"No. I never carry money. Daddy won't give me any. But I can buy things. I have cards." From her purse she removed an accordion of major credit cards.

The driver pulled off the road. One side was cactus, the other grapefruit trees. It would be a long walk into town.

"You have board and room taken care of, but what about me?" the cab driver complained.

Mama took her new revolver from her purse.

"No charge," the cabby said, lifting his hands high above the wheel. "Shall I take you into town, now?"

"Do not make yourself more of a *pendejo* than absolutely necessary," Mama said. She flipped the cylinder, ejected the shells expertly, and handed the pistol to him. "How much?"

His color came back rapidly, but he was very polite to all of us, especially to Mama.

"It is an excellent weapon and not too old."

"It is brand new. I have only used it once, to shoot a cab driver in Mexico City."

"I will give you whatever I have and throw in the trip to the hotel."

"Which is?" I asked.

"About thirty dollars."

"Give it to me."

He jerked the ashtray from under the dash of the taxi and passed it back to Mama. She turned it over and shook some bills and silver into her lap. "There is only twenty-eight dollars and fifty *centavos*," she said sternly.

"Sorry, Señorita. I must have short-changed myself."

"It is okay, *muchacho*. You can take my son, the author, to the post office so that he can send the *galeras* of his new book to the publishers." When he said nothing, she added grandly: "In New York!"

"It will be a *gran honor*," he said, speaking English and Spanish.

Speaking to them both, I said: "I wish you would speak one language or the other."

"Why?" Mama asked.

Why indeed?

"Okay," I said, using a universal word to start with. "*Okey*, take me to the *correo* so that I can send the *pruebas* of my book to the

359

publishers in the *ciudad* of *Nueva York*."

"Way to go," the driver said, accelerating onto the highway.

"Memo," Sofía said. "Would you drop me off in San Francisco? You promised."

"I did and I will." It was a promise I had made, and like my mother, the little black-eyed woman from Tabasco, and my father, the fair, slow-talking Texan, I kept my promises.

Epilogue

. . . . ✈

Despite excellent reviews, *Riley's Golden Ear* was not an immediate hit. Sales were slow, for it was a thick and expensive book. Then, Riley's empire, like a dying octopus flailing wildly, gave the book more publicity than what a live Riley would have paid for a squad of assassins.

Alacrán Torres, a squat heavy-shouldered man, did not resemble a scorpion physically. It was the short-barreled .22-caliber magnum rifle, set to fire fully automatic, that was his trademark—and the reason for his nickname.

A reporter, Joyce Kaplan, heard a rumor that the confessed murderer of multimillionaire Willard Riley was extremely unhappy. In the chaotic power struggle that followed the murder, he had been forgotten. He had been forced to live in an ordinary cell and to eat the ordinary and disgusting prison fare, and during the weekly conjugal visits, he was forced to sleep with his own wife. He was furious. He was also a resident of what Mexicans called the most expensive hotel in Mexico City: Lecumberri Prison. He was big and tough. But there were others, bigger and tougher, and he was without his .22-caliber stinger. Its equivalent, a supply of ready money, was not forthcoming.

Kaplan bribed her way into the prison cell, where the *Alacrán* talked and talked. He told the red-headed gringa with the funny accent how he had been in the shoot-out with that tough old gunfighter, Major Cooper. They had taken him to the English hospital along with Cooper and Rubio. The other gunmen had died, but not the *Alacrán*. He said he was still in the hospital with a concussion when Riley was shot and killed. Then two men paid his medical bill, and assured him he would be well treated in the "Grand" hotel and be out within a year—with ten million pesos waiting in a bank account in Spain. Then he heard that his contact had been killed in the first week of the drug war. It appeared that no one else remembered the *Alacrán*.

Kaplan promised him help, left him fifty dollars for walking around money, and raced over to the American British Cowdray Hospital. Not one of the investigative police officers or Riley's enforcers had thought to requisition the records. Claiming to represent the *Alacrán*, which in a sense she did, Kaplan asked for copies of the medical bills documenting his arrival and length of stay at the hospital.

Then she checked with both city and federal police. The weapon that had killed Riley was a .45-caliber handgun. The caliber matched the Colt that *Alacrán* Torres had described as the weapon that Cooper had used to kill his assailants, but the weapon that killed Riley had disappeared.

Kaplan wrote the story and airmailed it to New York. She showed a copy to the editor of the Mexico City English-language newspaper, *The News*. To her astonishment, the editor asked for a rewrite of the story and published it in its entirety in the next edition. The New York paper held up the story waiting further documentation, but when the *Alacrán* was killed inside the prison two days later, and later the editor of *The News* was badly beaten, they updated and printed the story.

Kaplan packed an overnight bag and, afraid to use public transportation, hitched a ride to the border with some American tourists. She kept right on north until she reached New York, where she wrote follow-up stories on the Riley murder for the New York papers.

Within a week *Riley's Golden Ear* was on *The New York Times* bestseller list, and there it stayed, climbing steadily until for six weeks it was the best-selling non-fiction book in the United States. Except for one review in *The News* in Mexico City, the book was ignored by the Mexican national press. Only in the radical north did the local, independent newspapers review the book. They also quoted long passages critical of the government.

The old administration changed, and a new one, loudly proclaiming an open and honest regime, began its six-year term. Jorge persuaded a publisher in Monterrey to print the book by guaranteeing all costs. Within weeks the cheap paperback edition was sold out. The publisher hastily ran off twenty thousand, double the original printing. It, too, was sold out in less than a week. The publisher then ordered the printers to print and bind fifty thousand copies, unprecedented in Mexican publishing history.

Local politicians, acting on their own, began to raid bookstores, confiscating copies of *Riley's Golden Ear*, often beating the booksellers as well.

Surprisingly, the new president intervened in favor of a free press and chastised the offending politicians. Now that policy had been set, the national media discovered the book, making it a cause célèbre and making its author famous.

In essence, Guillermo Cooper, a great Mexican investigative reporter, had written a brilliant exposé of the heinous deeds committed by Willard Riley, a cunning, depraved gringo. It was observed that Cooper, born and raised in Mexico, had been a citizen of the United States of America after being commissioned an officer in the U.S. Navy in 1944, while Riley, born and raised in Boston, Massachusetts, had been a Mexican citizen since he bought his first sugar mill in the state of Puebla in Mexico in 1920.

The lovely black girl, April McKay, had come back to the apartment a few days after the shooting to retrieve her few possessions and pick up the note that Memo would most certainly have left for her. The apartment had been stripped. Anything of value was gone, including the bookshelves with the secret niche where Memo had indeed placed a note for her.

The police could or would not give her a clue as to Memo's whereabouts and suggested that she consult her embassy. She did, and they tried to send her back to the police. Then an event took place that turned April from being a complete *Mexophile* to a fanatical *Mexophobe*. Her temporary roommate, a summer school student at the national university, imprudently dated a young Mexican who was working unofficially—a common practice—as an unpaid apprentice federal agent. Thinking the girl wealthy, the naive apprentice handed her a lit marijuana cigarette while in a bar. His boss stepped up, identified himself and arrested her. When he discovered that she really could not come up with five thousand dollars, he slugged his helper and told him to find another line of work. Still, he arrested the girl—he occasionally actually made arrests when little money was involved—and she was sent to prison, where she would spend the next five years.

April, terrified, packed her bags, left her furniture in the rented apartment, and took a cab to the airport. After she checked each one of the major airlines, she took the first available flight to the United States. Her seat companion, a tight-end for the Cowboys football team who was as tall and as intelligent as she was, got off at Dallas, and so did April. Three years later *Riley's Golden Ear* was issued in paperback. She bought a copy when she spotted the book while waiting in a checkout line at the supermarket. The publishers sent her letter to Memo's agent, who sent it on to the author. Memo answered her letter immediately and congratulated her on both husband and baby daughter. They send each other Christmas cards.

Sofía, Riley's only living heir, received a fraction of the estate, not quite ten million dollars. She was in and out of all sorts of detoxification programs for years. The last time, when she was freshly out and full of energy and hope, she called Memo to tell him about her new program, Infinite Art. She had set it up to provide no-strings financial support for promising artists. It was the one thing she never seemed to be confused about. Memo was never completely sure that she really had killed her father. She told him that she was giving a lawn party on the top of a sixteen-story building overlooking the Golden Gate Bridge. She had resolved her problem with drugs and would no longer need them. He told her about his ranch and the redheaded girl he loved. She wished him well and hung up.

A young painter seeking a grant was the last one to talk to Sofía. He asked her to stake him to room and board in one of her cabins with a good view of California's rugged Mendocino coast. She had smiled sweetly, taken the young man by the hand, and led him to the northern, waist-high wall of her penthouse balcony.

"Of course" she said. "I'll take you there. It's just past the bridge and over the mountains. Come on."

Something warned him and he drew back.

She waved an admonishing finger at him and vaulted lightly up onto the wall. She pointed to the myriad of tiny lights streaming across the bridge, then said: "Come on along. Don't be a fraidy cat. It's just a hop, skip and a jump." And then she stepped off into the void.

The major's will was finally probated and his investments evaluated just as Mexico was struck by the worst devaluation in its history.

Memo and Toña joined Elenita in the purchase of a chain of newspapers. Toña finally agreed to take on the job as publisher of the chain after Jorge convinced her that it was not an act of charity or nepotism, for anyone else, himself included, would almost certainly be murdered.

Jorge had not as yet received one peso from his father's estate. General Rubio had died without a will. As a result, the estate was being sued by several women and their children.

Memo bought a small ranch in the mountains overlooking that sea of shimmering white gypsum granules in New Mexico, aptly named

White Sands. Toña arrives each spring for her two-week vacation. For years she brought a guest, a nice Mexican woman, for his inspection. This spring Memo called to tell her that he now has a roommate. That same redhead that was in his writing seminar at college, that same Joyce Kaplan who broke the story about Riley's hired killer, *Alacrán* Torres, has moved in to his house and into his life. As feisty and unpredictable as Toña herself, Joyce does more of the legwork, and Memo, the writing. They are working on a new book about the Mexican drug empire that has come to be more powerful than either the party or the government itself. The working title is *Riley's Golden Legacy.*

Memo works in a room looking out over the vast white desert. The space is a simple workroom with one long table. His old Olivetti with its bilingual keyboard has been replaced with a computer and a word-processing program that has taken most of the drudgery out of rewriting. On one bookshelf, next to the major's old green ledger, are boxed medals from two wars and three nations. There are floor-to-ceiling bookcases and a lectern with an opened dictionary on it. Three framed photographs are hung on the one bare wall. Each is of a young man, goggles pushed back high on his head, smiling sad-eyed into the camera. They are Tell Cooper, Tell Dos and Memo Cooper Canela.

Underneath the pictures are two weapons, both within easy reach. One is a long-barreled Colt with bone grips. The other is a fully automatic Uzi. Both are loaded.

Rancho Paramor, New Mexico, July 14, 1986

The End

365

Historical Context

· · · · · · · · · · · · · · · · · · ✈

Following are summaries of the major events in Mexico from 1907 through the Mexican Revolution that began in 1910 and to the beginning of the novel in 1920.

1907

Three years before the Mexican national presidential elections, President Porfirio Díaz in an interview with an American journalist states that after twenty-seven years of his benevolent stewardship, the Mexican people will be ready to decide their own political future, and that he will not run for the presidency in the 1910 election. The interview is published in 1908.

1909

Thirty-four-year-old Francisco Madero writes and publishes a book quoting the president's statement that he would not run for president in the forthcoming elections, pointing out that Díaz had been first elected president on the one-term-only slogan of *No Reelección*. Since that election, he had not only been reelected several times, but had lengthened the term of office from four years to six. Madero's book was quickly sold out. He sent a copy to President Díaz, then went on a speaking tour where he organized political groups, proclaiming "No Re-election."

Madero met with Díaz, but he was convinced that Díaz would not give up the presidency, suggesting that "force must be met with force."

1910, June

Díaz moves quickly but cautiously against Madero, placing him under arrest in the city of San Luis Potosí, where the family has many friends. Madero, riding a fast horse, races from his poorly mounted guards to a nearby town, where a sympathizer smuggles him aboard a north-bound train. He reaches San Antonio, Texas, where he is in contact with family and followers.

1910, December

Díaz, eighty years old, is sworn in as president.

1911, February

After an abortive attempt to ignite a revolution, Madero attacks Casas Grandes, where he is wounded slightly. Here he joyfully learns of other movements and supporters, including Venustiano Carranza, Pascual Orozco, the budding warrior Pancho Villa in the north, and Emiliano Zapata in the south.

1911, April 1

Díaz attempts to take over the Madero movement by proclaiming that he supports the revolutionary goals of Madero.

Madero answers by demanding the resignation of President Díaz, who counters with an offer to resign, but will not deliver the government to a state of anarchy.

Madero, an ardent spiritualist who consults with various spirits, one of which was the dead liberal President Benito Juárez, takes the city named after the dead hero, Ciudad Juárez, across the river from El Paso, Texas. When both Villa and Orozco order the defending general shot, Madero personally escorts the defeated general to safety.

1911, May 21

Madero ratifies a document in which President Díaz and his vice president will resign, leaving the cabinet minister, Francisco León de la Barra, to assume the interim presidency and call for new elections.

1911, May 31

General Porfirio Díaz leaves the port of Veracruz on a German ship toward exile in Paris.

1911, June

Madero rides into Mexico City as an estimated one hundred thousand spectators cheer. Then, against the advice of his followers, he disbands the revolutionary army. He also agrees to reestablish the liberal constitution of 1857. In July he meets with Zapata, who asks him to replace General Victoriano Huerta, who would one day order the death of Madero. Madero fails to see that Zapata's request is honored by the provisional government, and he loses Zapata's support.

1912, February 12

American Ambassador Henry Lane Wilson is violently opposed to Madero and has told Huerta that he will support anyone who can oust

Madero. Madero seems to court disaster as three separate small rebellions break out. Two of the rebel leaders, including a nephew of ex-President Díaz, are jailed instead of executed. The third, Orozco, defeats one Madero general. Huerta is sent north to defeat him, which he does handily. A grateful Madero promotes Huerta to major general.

1912, February 17

Gustavo Madero, the president's brother, discovers that Huerta is consorting with the imprisoned Felix Díaz. He takes Huerta prisoner at gunpoint and takes him to face brother Francisco. Against all logic, Francisco Madero is convinced that Huerta has a good heart and is loyal, giving him twenty-four hours to disprove the charges.

The next day Huerta, accompanied by General Blanquet, arrests the president. Huerta turns Gustavo over to a mob of soldiers who torture him brutally before murdering him.

President Madero and his vice president, Pino Suárez, are imprisoned.

The following day Huerta asks Henry Lane Wilson if Madero should be exiled or sent to a hospital. Wilson replies that he should do whatever is best for the country. Madero and Pino Suárez are driven out to the extreme end of the isolated penitentiary. Madero is killed with a shot to the head; Pino Suárez is marched to a nearby wall and executed.

1913

The rebels regroup. General Álvaro Obregón raises a company of troops, including Yaqui Indians from Sonora. He soon shows great promise. Carranza, who has taken charge of the Revolution, appoints him commander-in-chief of the Army of the Northwest. Villa forms the Division of the North and using his famous cavalry as shock troops, sends the Huerta troops reeling. Villa, who adored Madero, takes a dislike to Obregón, and comes very close to executing him. Villa has retaken Ciudad Juárez and is pushing Huerta south.

Zapata begins to redistribute lands that had been taken from the original owners.

1914, November

The generals meet to formulate plans for the new Mexican government. Villa and the Zapatistas try to understand the political generals and the complex constitutional amendments proposed. Villa speaks out against Carranza, who has fought against Zapata. Carranza presides over the unconditional withdrawal of American troops in the port city of Veracruz. When Carranza receives a message from the convention asking him to resign, he answers that if certain conditions are met—including the resignation and exile of both Villa and Zapata—he might resign his position as the First Chief of the Revolution.

1914, December 6
Constitutional forces from Aguascalientes move into Mexico City; Villa and Zapata riding alongside each other at the head of their troops.

1915, April 6
Obregón, the best of the self-taught generals, picks a battlefield to go against Villa and his undefeated cavalry. Villa's brilliant general, Felipe Ángeles, attempts to persuade Villa to refuse that battleground as unfit for his lightning cavalry attacks, but Villa insists. He loses one battle and then another over the same terrain just one week later.

1916, May
Carranza calls for a Constitutional Convention to be held in Querétaro. Carranza makes the long, one-day ride by horseback from Mexico City.

1916, December
Carranza and his adherents want a modernized version of the liberal constitution of 1857. What they get is what would be the most radical and socialized document until that of the Russian Revolution.

1917, February 5
The Constitution is ratified. Later the date becomes a national holiday celebrated as the Day of the Constitution. Carranza is elected constitutional president, but has only three years of uneasy rule before losing the support of the key generals.

1920, May 14
Isolated and powerless in the capital, Carranza loads his staff, baggage and the national treasury onto a long train and sets off for his power base in Veracruz. He is betrayed, forced to leave the train, and in the village of Tlaxcalantongo in the mountains of Puebla, he is either assassinated or takes his own life.

85296419R00222

Made in the USA
Middletown, DE
23 August 2018